Southern Sanctuary

To Susan —

Enjoy!

A novel by
Don Pardue

© **Copyright 2007**

Don Pardue

Library of Congress Control Number: 2007904035

ISBN 978-1502359667

Reprinted September 2014

To Barbara,
The wind beneath my wings

Cover design by Victor Pardue

Editing by
Victor Pardue and Donna Pardue Thompson

Acknowledgments

Portions of this book were written in recognition of the military personnel who fought in The Korean War. The conflict began on June 25th, 1950 and continued until July 27th, 1953. Although thousands of U.S. troops willingly served, the continuing war became unpopular among the American civilian population, who often called it a needless war; in fact, the U.N. Forces were never officially declared the victor, for the limited and fluctuating aggression of the war caused it to be unwinnable. As a result, an official permanent peace treaty was never signed.

I also wish to recognize the continuing progress of our Southern states during the last half-century. The Deep South has made great strides in the improvement of race relations, social and intellectual development, and individual opportunity. Although still an imperfect environment, Dixie will always be my home.

Also, I owe a debt of gratitude to my daughter, Donna, who worked many hours in editing this book and also provided continuing encouragement and an inexhaustible supply of creative ideas. In addition, I am indebted to my son, Victor, who not only edited portions of the book and offered helpful advice, but also designed the outstanding cover. And most importantly, as always, to Barbara, my wife of fifty-eight years, whose optimistic and youthful spirit has been my source of inspiration.

Chapter 1

Nicolo Parilli lay motionless in the bottom of the shell crater. The warm, humid night was immersed in a dirty, brownish-gray fog. Except for the occasional muted sounds of distant unintelligible voices, the dismal twilight was eerily quiet. The acrid odor of cordite blended with the misty vapor that saturated the evening air, shrouding the battlefield with the gloomy atmosphere of war. An exploding enemy grenade had damaged the hearing in Nick's right ear; as a result, he turned his head to the right so that his good ear could detect the faint occasional sounds of the obscure voices. He was almost delirious from the lack of sleep and petrified by a pervading fear. Perhaps he had only imagined that he had heard the faint mumbling. Possibly, his exhausted and terrified mind was playing tricks on him. He could be hallucinating. Maybe there were no voices.

Wait! There it is again, he realized. He was now certain that he heard muffled voices … the singsong cadence of oriental language, and coming from a position only a few yards to his left. He had been pinned down in the crater by enemy small arms fire shortly before the murky darkness had moved in. Dead soldiers littered the landscape, and except for the wounded army sergeant that Nick had dragged into the crater beside him, there were no soldiers from his company in the area.

After losing scores of men during the blistering assault of machinegun fire, his entire company had retreated. Because he had momentarily suspended his retreat long enough to pull the wounded man into the crater, his remaining comrades had escaped while he had become trapped beside the dying sergeant in the deep depression. The wounded man had quickly died, with his intestines spilling out through the gaping hole in his abdomen. Nicolo knew that the surviving members of his company had retreated to find cover atop a hill about two hundred yards to his rear. He was alone.

Shortly after he had been pinned down, the enemy forces had pulled back, possibly to regroup for a major attack. From experience, he knew that a mixture of Chinese and North Korean soldiers frequently attacked with hundreds of screaming troops in the darkness of the night. He wondered if he stood a chance of survival if he attempted to escape from the crater and rejoin his comrades on the distant hillside. He feared that some of the enemy had not pulled back and had remained in the immediate area. The muted Chinese voices he now heard confirmed his fear. He wondered how close they were to him, and if they knew that he was taking cover in the crater.

With trembling fingers, he picked up his rifle. Summoning his courage, he cautiously raised his head and peeped over the edge of the crater. Looking in the direction of the suspected enemy, he listened intently for the slightest sound of voices. He heard a shout; and then a movement from above captured his attention. Looking upward, he caught a faint glimpse of the incoming deadly grenade, which the thick blanket of fog had rendered barely visible. It landed in the bottom of the crater only three feet from him. Frozen in terror, he was unable to

8

move. His entire body seemed to be paralyzed. He only stared at the grenade in horror as the seconds ticked away ...

His terrified scream echoed through the small, shabby bedroom before he quickly sat up in bed. It was the same recurring dream and it invariably ended in the identical way. His quick awakening before the grenade exploded caused him to wonder what would have happened if the hellish device had detonated before he became fully awake...Would he have died? Maybe even from fright?

His heart was pounding so rapidly and violently that it seemed that it would burst from his chest. Cold perspiration soaked his face and body. Even his shorts and tee shirt were becoming damp. He figured that his excessive sweating was due more to his sudden withdrawal from alcohol than as a result of the sweltering heat of the night, or his terrifying recurrent dream. He picked up a matchbook from the windowsill. In the glow of the match he peered at his wristwatch: *6:15 a.m.*

He pondered the events that had occurred in his life since his medical discharge from the U.S. Army in California only three weeks earlier. Because he had been in a drunken state during most of his train ride back to his previous home in Chicago, he remembered little about the trip. He had only a clouded memory of his drunken departure from the train when it briefly stopped in a small town in Iowa where he had promptly passed out on a passenger bench in the railway station. Only through the benevolent help of a fellow soldier who recognized him as a passenger bound for Chicago was he able to re-board his coach and avoid being left behind by the train.

Whenever he drank heavily he often suffered from blackouts. He had only a hazy memory of his arrival in Chicago, and he was in total bewilderment about how he had ever been able to locate his father's small decrepit apartment on the west side of the city on Adams Street. With nowhere else to go after being discharged from the army, he had returned to Chicago to temporarily stay with his father,

Donato Parilli. Upon first seeing his father, he had been shocked by his emaciated condition. In order to care for his dad, who was drunk most of the time, Nick vowed to himself that he would stop drinking.

The heat in the small bedroom on this July night was stifling. He lay in bed soaked in cold sweat, realizing how badly he needed a drink. Although he had been without alcohol for two days, his hangover was even more dreadful than it had been yesterday. His head ached, his nerves were on edge, and his stomach was a sour pit. The mere thought of food made him feel like vomiting.

But he was determined to get off the booze. He had made that decision shortly after burying his dad a week ago. A neighbor had found his father dead where he had passed out earlier that evening on a stairwell in an abandoned building on West Madison Street. He had been lying in the hallway for several hours before his body was discovered.

Immediately following his father's death, he had again drowned his sorrow with alcohol for several days; however, fearing that he was nearing the point of no return with his drinking, he became determined to end his lengthy binge. He felt confident that he could remain sober, for prior to the war he had never been a drinker.

In order to take the pressure off his right knee where the piece of shrapnel had been removed, he turned over to lie on his left side. The surgeon had been unable to remove the small bullet fragment from his back that was lodged against his spine, fearing that the procedure might cause paralysis. *He would have to learn to live with it,* the doctors had told him; but it was difficult to live with the numbness and cramps that frequently invaded his legs. In addition, an exploding grenade had almost robbed him of his hearing in his right ear.

He was exhausted but too depressed and nervous to sleep. The mere idea of sleep terrified him; for when he slept, he dreamed, and dreams brought the war back to him. His abrupt withdrawal from alcohol had brought his mind to the brink of hallucination. His mind bordered on delirium, especially when he tried to sleep. He always dreaded the approaching darkness, for delirium is a disease of the night.

From the advice of heavy drinkers, he knew that sudden abstinence from alcohol after excessive drinking was dangerous. He knew that withdrawal would be easier and safer if he tapered off; but Nick Parilli had never been a man of moderation. He had always experienced difficulty in accomplishing any task in gradual increments.

The thousand tiny pricks in his calves and feet told him that the numbness in his legs was returning. Sweat trickled down his chest as he rose in bed and began to briskly massage his lower extremities. He began to violently shiver. *God I need a drink!* he thought.

Realizing that sleep was impossible for him, he switched on the bedside lamp, threw back the covers and rose to a standing position. The dizziness that he experienced when he stood caused him to briefly return to his seat on the bed. He picked up his pack of Chesterfields from the windowsill and lit a cigarette. He deeply inhaled and gagged at the brassy taste of the smoke.

He continued to sit for a while, immobile, puffing his cigarette, contemplating the day that lay ahead of him. His mind was a mélange of confusion and worry. He knew that he would leave the city today; that was the one decision he had made with complete clarity of mind. There was nothing left for him in Chicago. He now had no relatives and few friends in his hometown. His mother's death when Nick was attending college before his enlistment in the army had killed his father's spirit. Now his dad had just died and had been buried as a pauper; also, most of his male friends were either fighting in the Korean War or had moved away. Chicago now seemed an empty place for him. Since his father's recent deterioration into an alcoholic man of the streets before his death, Nick no longer felt any affection for the city.

Although he had no long-range plans for the future, he had decided to leave Chicago behind forever; in fact, he no longer had a desire to live in any large city. Maybe he could find a small town where he could get a fresh start and discover a sense of purpose, a haven where he might find sanctuary from his horrible memories of the war and the terrible way that his father had lived…and died.

Nicolo was apathetic about his future; for he felt neither ambition nor sense of purpose for his existence. The negative events that had taken place in his life in recent years and his war experience had changed him, instilling in him a deep cynicism.

By nature, Nick was an idealist, and, as a younger man, because of his idealism, he had held a simplistic expectancy that most people would be fair and honest. Although he had always hated physical violence, when he was a child in grade school he sometimes had fights with bullies when defending their potential victims. He detested pretentiousness and dishonesty. Because he had always harbored a deep feeling of outrage about the injustice and inequities of the world, he had begun to develop a deep distrust in people. He felt that life was only a game of chance, an existence in which only the fortunate or powerful survived.

He slowly stood and decided to begin preparations to leave. There would be no need to tell anyone of his departure from Chicago, not even the landlord; for the two-room apartment in which his father had made his home had long ago been abandoned. It was unfit for habitation. Out of pity, his father's former employer who owned several tenement houses had allowed his dad to occupy the empty hovel free of charge.

The limited light from the dim lamp only partially revealed the run-down condition of the shabby room. The dingy, plastered walls displayed dirty handprints and large areas where plaster had fallen away, revealing the gray lathing slats behind it. On the planked, painted floor, years of traffic had worn away much of the paint, exposing the bare wood on the most frequently used areas. The floor was spattered with numerous stains, a result of the vomit that sometimes spewed from the bellies of countless drunks who had inhabited the hovel in the past as they sought refuge from winter nights on the street. The musty odor that saturated the interior made the interior even more depressing. The furniture in the two-room flat consisted of junk that his father had either found in abandoned apartments or someone had donated to him.

Favoring his stiff right knee, he slowly limped to the bathroom and yanked the long pull-chain that lit the small naked bulb on the ceiling. The dim light revealed the now-familiar decrepit condition of the small room. The accommodations were sparse: a rust-stained commode, a tiny shower, and beside it an old-fashioned sink with a dirty mirror hanging over it. A single, thin coat of paint on the walls transparently revealed the floral design that had once garnished the small cubicle. The room contained no toilet tissue or towels.

When he looked into the mirror, he was shocked at his appearance, for the image of the man staring back at him appeared much older than his age of twenty-three. Although his three-day growth of beard contributed to his aged appearance, it was the dull expression in his eyes that really masked his youth. They mirrored the lethargic hopelessness that resided in his spirit; for the eyes are the mirrors of the soul; and in his eyes he saw the dull and lifeless image of despair. They reflected the horror of the war, the guilt that he felt because of some of his deeds during the conflict, and the sadness of his father's death.

In spite of the insufferable heat and stuffiness of the room, he began to violently shiver. He was exhausted, both physically and emotionally, and his nerves seemed to be unraveling. He suddenly felt that he might throw up. Holding his head over the sink, he retched repeatedly; however, it was a fruitless effort, for his stomach was empty. He hadn't eaten for two days.

He shaved and then showered in cold water. Since the bathroom contained no towel, he dried himself with one of his khaki army shirts. Although the cold shower had somewhat rejuvenated him, shaving in cold water had left him with several bloody nicks on his face. To stem the flow of blood, he placed small snippets from an old newspaper on the cuts. When he again peered into the mirror, he decided that since he had shaved he looked much better. Although his nose was rather prominent, Nick was a handsome man, with the typical dark-haired Italian demeanor. His deep-brown eyes harmonized with the bronze hue of his skin. With a well-proportioned muscular physique, he stood six feet tall and weighed 175 pounds.

He walked back into the tiny bedroom and again took a seat on the bed, pondering the worrisome tasks that awaited him.

Although his ability to think rationally had mostly abandoned him, he attempted to establish his plans for the next few days. He knew that his ultimate destination was Buras, Louisiana, a small town south of New Orleans where his Uncle Cataldo lived. In a recent letter, his uncle, a commercial fisherman on the Louisiana Gulf Coast, had invited Nick to come to the coast to live after his discharge from the army. Divorced and with no children, Uncle Cataldo was fifty-six years old and the older brother of Nick's Father, Donato. Uncle Cataldo dearly loved his only nephew, Nicolo, as if he were his own son. Although his income from fishing was meager, he wanted his nephew to live with or near him, and find employment on the Gulf Coast.

But before continuing his journey to Louisiana, Nick planned to make a brief stopover in Cedar Valley, Tennessee, the home of Stan Mullins, a former college friend. He and Stan had been roommates in the dorm of a small college in Northern Indiana near Chicago. Nick had been a star running back on the football team at the school prior to his enlistment in the army. After his medical discharge in California before his extended drinking spree had begun he had called his friend. Stan had been delighted to hear from him, and when Nick had told him of his plan to settle in Louisiana, Stan had insisted that Nick visit him for a few days in East Tennessee before resuming his trip to the Gulf. A trip through Tennessee would be slightly off-course in his journey to Louisiana;

however, because of his fondness for his former college roommate, Nick had agreed.

He felt a tinge of optimism as he recalled his former relationship with Stan. Nick had been an only child in the Parilli family, and when he thought of Stan, who also had no siblings, he imagined that their relationship must be like that of brothers. He smiled for the first time in days as he thought of his upcoming visit with his old friend; for the memory of his relationship with Stan was the only positive aspect of his life.

Nick reached to the windowsill for another cigarette, noticing as he lit it that he only had a couple of matches remaining in his matchbook. He had lost his lighter somewhere during his lengthy alcoholic binge.

He slowly stood and decided to get dressed and start packing for his trip. Because most of his army gear had never been removed from his duffel bag, the chore of packing was brief. To lighten his load, he removed about half of the contents from the bag and carelessly tossed the items onto the bed. He would leave them here, he decided, probably to be claimed by some homeless derelict who might later inhabit the wretched apartment. He felt good about ridding himself of anything that might connect him to the army.

Since his discharge he had only bought a few skimpy items of civilian clothing—a couple of short-sleeved shirts and a pair of blue jeans. He carefully inspected them, but after deciding that they were too wrinkled to wear, he stuffed them into the duffel bag with the other garments. Although he disliked the idea, he realized that he would have to wear one of the two uniforms that he had previously hung in the tiny corner closet. He walked to the small closet and removed one of the summer khaki uniforms.

Hanging beside his other uniform in the closet were the ragged clothes that had belonged to his father. Upon seeing them, his sadness almost overpowered him; but he was unable to cry, for since his war experience he had been emotionally numb.

15

When he thought of his father's lonely life, he wondered when he would ever be able to openly express the emotions he felt for his dad. He dressed in one of the uniforms, finished packing, and tossed his duffel bag onto the floor by the door.

Although he wasn't hungry, he realized that he needed nourishment. He limped into the other room, which served as a combination living room and kitchen. The shabby condition of the area was even more depressing than the bedroom and bathroom. A small room measuring about ten by twelve feet, the floor was covered with worn and faded linoleum. The single light bulb on the ceiling provided only enough light to give the area an even gloomier atmosphere. The room contained a small ragged and filthy couch and a small electric range spattered with crusted grease and with only one cooking element. The only remaining appliance was an outdated refrigerator with a burned-out light bulb inside.

The supply of food inside the refrigerator was skimpy, for his father had rarely taken his meals in the apartment and had sometimes stayed away for days. During his stay with his father Nick had only eaten in restaurants. Since he had only rarely seen his dad, he wondered where and when he had ever eaten a meal.

The refrigerator held only a half-quart of spoiled milk, a package of hardened cheese, and a couple of stale doughnuts on a paper plate. Above the electric range on a shelf, he spied a can of pork and beans, a half loaf of stale bread, and a few knives and spoons scattered about. He found a book of matches and placed it in his pocket. Unable to locate a can opener, he used a dull knife to stab open the can of pork and beans and peeled back the top. With the aid of a spoon, he scooped and raked the beans from the tilted can into his mouth, mostly drinking them as he chewed, as if swallowing liquid from a glass. He ate a slice of the stale bread and gagged at the taste, almost throwing up before keeping it down. He began to realize that he was too sick to eat.

He tossed the half-empty can onto the floor and returned to the bedroom. Extracting his wallet, he counted the money that was left of his mustering out pay: *Almost four-hundred dollars*. Certainly not a fortune, but maybe it was enough to reach his destination and pay for his lodging.

He turned and looked at the hovel that his father had called home. It sickened him to realize that his dad had made his home in such a depressing place. He wondered how long his dad had lived this way, and how he had managed to survive in such squalor. He figured that the abandoned apartment had been condemned by the City of Chicago and would probably be razed in the near future. His father's former employer, to whom his dad had given several years of hard work and loyalty, had allowed him to live rent-free in the dilapidated building. It was a structure that was not fit for human habitation. His ex-boss was a wealthy man who owned two businesses and lived in a luxurious home in North Chicago. He knew that Nick's father was grieving and unable to work since the death of his wife and was suffering from the disease of alcoholism. He could have encouraged Nick's father, and since he hadn't yet reached retirement age, he might have even offered him a part-time job. After all, he owned several apartment buildings and could have rewarded his father's many years of hard work and loyalty with a decent small apartment. But he felt that he was doing him a huge favor by allowing him to live in the abandoned, horrid hellhole. After all, it was rent-free, wasn't it? The wealthy man reminded Nick of a glutton who, after being stuffed with food, tosses a discarded chicken bone to a starving dog.

Nick's sad eyes stole a final glance at the interior of the apartment. He then turned his head and momentarily stared at the closet that held his father's pitiful assortment of clothing. He picked up his duffel bag and stepped through the door, gently closing it behind him.

Chapter 2

The whir of the bus engine nearly lulled him to sleep as he reclined in his seat on the left side of the vehicle by the window. The acrid odor of burning diesel fuel filtered into the Greyhound bus as it slowly pulled away from the terminal. The smell reminded him of the heavy equipment used in the war and of other countless journeys by bus that he had made during his years in the military. He was glad that he was leaving both the army and Chicago behind him.

The bus was crowded with people. Scanning the interior, he could see only three or four empty seats, including the aisle seat beside him. Several military men occupied seats: a sailor, a couple of marines, and maybe three or four soldiers. He concluded that one or two of them were going home on furlough. Maybe a few of them were headed back to military bases. Some were probably on their way to the war in Korea. He wondered how many of them would be dead by this time next year - or possibly next month.

A middle aged, obese woman in a satiny blue dress waddled up the aisle toward him, stopping when she reached the aisle seat beside him. She was graying at the temples and wore thick glasses perched on the tip of her nose. She displayed a friendly smile. "Is this seat taken, sir?" Her soft, drawling voice indicated that she was a Southern woman.

"No ma'am," Nick replied. "Have a seat, lady."

"Thank you." Her buttocks were so large they filled the entire bottom of her seat as she wedged into it. She looked at Nick sympathetically and placed her large handbag in her lap. Then she extracted a small, adjustable fan from her bag and began to fan her face with it; for it was hot and stuffy in the cramped quarters of the bus. In order to make room for her beefy, sweaty left arm that nudged his side, Nick scooted toward the window. Taking note of his adjustment, she moved slightly away from him and apologized. "I'm sorry. I hope I'm not crowding you too much. These seats on the bus are so close together and cramped, you know." The soft, slow cadence of her speech projected a melodious, lilting quality.

"That's okay, lady, no problem." Nick smiled at her.

"Are you going home on furlough?" she asked.

"No, ma'am." It was obvious that the lady wanted to talk. Nick had no such desire.

"Well, are you reporting back to your base?"

"No ma'am."

"Oh," she said with a puzzled look. Nick began to feel sorry for her. She seemed like a nice person. Many people had always told him that most Southern people were warm and friendly. Although he wasn't in the mood for conversation, he decided that the nice lady might consider his abbreviated answers rude.

"I was recently discharged from the army," he explained.

"Discharged? But they might draft you back into the army if you're discharged. You might even have to go to Korea."

"I've already been in Korea," he replied, "I was wounded and they gave me a medical discharge. I was in the infantry."

"Oh, you poor boy!" Her eyes reflected sympathy. "Was it bad over there?"

"War is always bad, ma'am." He looked away from her, out the window.

Her expression became sad. "My son, Charles is in the Air Force. He was due to be discharged last year, but because of the war in Korea, President Truman extended all enlistments for a year."

"Where's your son stationed?" Nick asked.

"He's stationed at Chanute Air Force Base here in Illinois. I just left him in Chicago where he was on a three-day pass to visit his brother, Bill. I'm on my way back home to Atlanta. Do you think my son might be sent to Korea?" she asked.

"What does your son think?"

"He says probably not, but I'm terribly scared for him. I'm kinda dumb about what the different branches of service do. I'm afraid he might end up on the front lines in Korea." She continued to nervously fan herself.

"Is your son an officer? Or maybe a pilot?"

"No, he's an airman first class. He works in a legal office."

Nick smiled at her. "Ma'am, I wouldn't worry too much if I were you. They don't send enlisted airmen with office jobs to the war. It's usually only soldiers and marines that end up on the front lines."

"Thank God! Were you wounded bad?"

"No, not very bad." He didn't elaborate.

The bus stopped at a traffic light and he peered out the window at the frenetic activity of the people on the crowded street. Everybody was going somewhere, each of them with a purpose, on a mission, scurrying toward a specific destination. He wished that he were motivated to pursue some goal or could find some purpose for his existence. He envied them.

The lady again turned toward him. "Where are you headed?" She peered over her glasses and continued to fan herself.

"South of New Orleans. A little town on the Gulf called Buras." He didn't elaborate about his planned stopover in Tennessee.

"Well, maybe you and I will be traveling together until I arrive in Atlanta." She smiled at Nick. Without answering, he only returned her smile. He reclined his seat and lay back, pulling the visor of his cap to cover his eyes. He liked this friendly Southern lady, but he wanted to take a nap.

The nice lady took the hint. She became quiet as the whining diesel engine pushed the bus southward. He was as sick as ever, and half-wished that he had surrendered to his misery and downed a couple of shots of booze before he left Chicago. He was again sweating, and his nausea increased as the bus passed through the South Side of Chicago into the putrid stench of the stockyards where his father had worked before taking a job at a bakery on Loomis Street.

Being unable to sleep, his mind drifted back to his father, and the earlier years before his mother died. It was difficult for him to believe that since he had joined the army his father's life had sunk to such depths, for he remembered happier times during his youth when his mother and father had seemed so deeply in love with each other. They had shared laughs together, and as a couple, had gone to watch him play football in high school. He remembered family picnics with his parents on the sandy beach of the western shore of Lake Michigan by Lakeshore Drive.

In material wealth the Parilli family was poor; however, they were rich in the most meaningful aspects of life: family love, loyalty, and spirituality. They were devout Catholics and regularly attended mass. The fact that Nick had no siblings created an even stronger bond between him and his parents. He fondly remembered when he was a small boy the many times that his father had watched him and his friends play hide and seek on West Adams Street, sometimes joining in the game. He also recalled the many quiet times in the early evening after his dad had come home from work, when his parents had relaxed together on the outdoor balcony of their second story low-rent apartment. In their pronounced Italian accent, they would chatter like quarrelsome magpies. They enthusiastically discussed the family, repeated neighborhood gossip, and talked of the Old Country from which they had both emigrated shortly after their marriage when they were both barely out of their teens.

His father had met his mother, Marina, in the city of their youth, Salerno, Italy. They came to America shortly after their marriage to begin a new life in the 'Land of Opportunity.' Unfortunately, with little formal education, his dad's means of livelihood was limited to low-paying, menial jobs, mainly because he had never learned to fluently speak the English language.

But Nick's father was an industrious man, a hard worker who was dedicated to his family. Although the family was never able to accumulate any substantial material wealth and lived in a low-rent apartment, they were highly respected within the Italian community and quite wealthy in the areas of life that really mattered.

But during Nick's college years, his mother had developed cancer, and when she died a year later, it turned out to be his father's undoing. With his son now in Korea fighting the war and his beloved wife no longer with him, he was now completely alone. When Marina died, Donato's spirit was buried with her.

Nick adjusted his seat to an upright position and realigned his cap. He turned to the obese lady beside him. "Do you mind if I smoke?"

"Oh, you're awake. No, I don't mind one bit. Go ahead and smoke. My son smokes whenever he's with me." When Nick lit his cigarette, the lady cleared the smoke from around her face by speeding up the repetitive waves of her fan.

She again looked at him with sympathy. "I know that a lot of soldiers don't like to talk about it, but was it pretty terrible over there? In battle, I mean? But you don't have to talk about it if you'd rather not. Sometimes, though, it helps to talk about it."

"War is hell, Ma'am, and I don't want to return to hell by talking about it." He then looked at her with compassion. "No offense intended, lady."

She again became quiet. Nick snuffed out his half-finished cigarette and again returned to a napping position in his seat.

His mind drifted back to the war. He was filled with bitterness about his war experience. In his nightly dreams, the war was ever-present; but when awake, his conscious mind was aware of it during times whenever he was idle; but when he was busy, even with some meaningless chore, the continuing conflict seemed far-removed from him. It was almost as if he had experienced it in another world, a hellish dream-like episode in a separate life from which he had forever bidden farewell. To protect his psyche from emotional pain, his conscious mind had buried some of the most horrible memories into the deep, protective cocoon of unconscious awareness, mercifully hiding it beneath layers of insignificant data. But in his unconscious mind, the war was forever with him, for it inevitably returned to him in his dreams.

He could see no end to the war. The endless combination of alternating advances and retreats in the conflict indicated that neither side was winning. Nick felt that the war might last for many years. Like most soldiers who were fighting the war, Nick had little understanding of its meaning or cause; for only the leaders—the architects, strategists, and engineers of war who sat importantly behind desks in shrouded conference rooms devising clever plans of destruction understood the logic of war.

His mind was constantly invaded by his belief in the futility of war. He had no answers, only opinions and questions. Immersed in deep thought, he became oblivious to his surroundings. He again analyzed the rationale for war, for he was a meticulous examiner of all moral issues. Festering inside his brain was an internal dialogue, a soliloquy that involved the standard argument offered by the advocates of war and those of his own. The conversation always followed the same pattern and played over and over in his mind:

Why is America fighting North Korea?

Because troops from Communist-ruled North Korea invaded South Korea in violation of the International Peace Treaty.

But how does this affect America?

We have to protect ourselves from the spread of communism, which is like a malignant tumor. If we don't stop its advance, it will ultimately infect the entire world.

But if we want to stop it, why do we wage a limited conflict? The front lines seesaw back and forth. Why not strike the enemy with an all-out fatal blow? Invade Manchuria, or strike the mainland of China?

But that would bring about war. If the enemy mounted a major offensive against us, we would have to declare war.

But aren't we already at war?

No, this is not war...this is only a police action to prevent war. This conflict should not be called 'war.' War is something else. War is hell. This conflict is neither war nor hell.

The hell it isn't! Try telling that to the men in my former regiment! The politicians and generals who are the architects of war play a cruel game of semantics, a clever play on words. In order to prove that they avoided war during their tenures in office, they simply call it something else.

But it is something else. It is a limited police action, which is not as destructive as a real war. If we show too much aggressiveness, the enemy might get really mad and start a war. Millions of people could die.

But thousands of people are already dead, and millions more could die if our 'limited police action' lasts for years. If millions of people are going to die anyway, what's the difference in their dying at a slow, agonizing pace, or killing them quickly and getting it over with? If we're going to wage war on communism, then let's get on with it!

But, you see, we're not waging war. This is only a limited police action to prevent war. Look at the soldiers we would lose in a real war.

24

What about the men who have died in this 'police action?' We lost a large number of men from the 24th Division when the enemy pushed us back to the Pusan Perimeter. Every time we make an advance, the enemy pushes us back.

That's true, but when our lines were forced back, we beefed up our defenses with replacements, the 25th Division, and made another advance.

Yes, but a lot of men were killed in that advance. This war could go on for years. What happens if we run out of able-bodied men to fight the war?

There will always be more men.

Yes, to the makers of wars, there will always be more men to fight them. In their strategic, intricate plans, the war-makers view their war with pride, as an architect or engineer takes pride in a complex building that he has designed and has ordered simpler men to build for him; and when the earth shifts and the building sags, he shores up the drooping side of the structure with timbers; and if those timbers give way under the strain of the increasing weight as the building grows larger and again sags, he replaces the broken beams with larger numbers of timbers; and in his emotionless zeal and pride in his invention of war, living men with flesh and blood become the timbers with which he shores up his hellish creation, because in the war architect's mind, there will always be more timber, for wooden beams, like men, are expendable.

Yes, many men may die, but it is not war. You are badly misinformed, for you don't know what actual war really is.

Only the men involved in the conflict know what it really is: the infantryman whose bloody intestines spill out onto the grassless, cratered soil; the soldier whose legs were blown away by an enemy grenade; the raw recruit who pukes his guts out at the putrid stench of rotting flesh. They all know what to call this mindless insanity: They call it *war.*

These opposing arguments were always playing into the media, discussed by the American people, and smoldering in the depths of his own mind.

The abrupt scream of a crying baby from one of the seats in front of him startled him and brought his mind back to reality. Once again, he had allowed his mind to carry him back to the inherent contradictions of armed conflict. In spite of his loathing of war, Nick realized that it was sometimes inevitable; however, he found it incredulous that the civilized world would sanction war as a means to solve disagreements between nations. Although he saw war as a futile undertaking, he couldn't think of an alternative. *Maybe it's naïve to ever expect people to live in peace,* he thought.

He readjusted his seat to an upright position. Because he had allowed himself to brood over the war, he had been unable to sleep. He considered lighting a cigarette, but because of his continuing headache and nausea, he decided against it. Since he was not in the mood for conversation, he was relieved when he noticed that the Southern lady beside him was asleep. Her head bobbed with each bump and vibration of the bus.

He peered out the window at the level countryside, noticing that it had begun to rain. Listlessly, he gazed at the vapor of steam rising from the heated asphalt highway as the cold rain swept the road. In the distance, the horizon was erased by the misty haze, blending land and sky together into a single nebulous, gray veil.

Glancing at his watch, he figured that the bus might be nearing Indianapolis. His fingers trembled as he groped in his shirt pocket for his cigarettes, but after discovering that he had only two smokes left in the pack he decided to forgo smoking; besides, he was too sick to smoke anyway.

His throbbing headache had returned. *Damn! How much longer is this hangover going to last?* he wondered. He searched in his other shirt pocket for the container of aspirin that he always carried, but realized that he had packed it away in his duffel bag that was stowed in the baggage compartment below.

In an attempt to soothe his headache, he again reclined his seat, closed his eyes, and covered his face with his cap visor.

26

He hoped that his movement hadn't awakened the lady beside him.

The idleness of the bus trip was beginning to get on his nerves. He wished he had brought something to read; for to be idle was to think…and to think was to return to the war. Whenever he had managed to stay busy, even with some meaningless task, he had sometimes managed to avoid reliving his past horrors; but now, with nothing to do but think, his mind again drifted back to the war. He remembered that early in the conflict he had been decorated for bravery, winning the Bronze Star for saving the lives of two fellow soldiers while under heavy enemy fire. The event took place on July 5th, 1950 in Osan, about thirty miles south of Seoul. Soon afterward, he was promoted to staff sergeant, and as the war progressed he was engaged in many battles. The Pusan Perimeter, and Pohang; also, he was a part of the offensive that drove the enemy army back across the 38th parallel into North Korea where the Allies captured Pyongyang. Ultimately, after the Chinese entered the war, he was severely wounded near the Chongjin Reservoir. Ironically, in that battle he was accused of cowardice by his commanding officer, who later had him court-martialed for insubordination.

The incident had occurred during an attack by the Chinese Communists when his squad was pinned down behind a rock wall. The squad of soldiers was commanded by a young, inexperienced second lieutenant. or a 'ninety-day wonder,' as seasoned soldiers often derisively referred to them; for some officers had received their commissions after only ninety days of training at Officers' Candidate School. Heavy enemy machinegun fire raked the area from the top of a nearby ridge as the Allied soldiers hunkered down behind the protective barrier. The young lieutenant in charge of the squad ordered three of his men to advance and destroy the enemy position. Unfortunately, as they stepped into the open area to charge up the hill, the three men were cut to pieces by the relentless enemy fire. The lieutenant re-issued the command, ordering Nick and two other men to eliminate the machinegun.

Nick became paralyzed with fear. He knew that to obey such a foolish order would mean certain death, for to charge up the barren hill with no protection toward a blazing machinegun would be his final act on earth. He felt that the inexperienced lieutenant had issued a stupid order, for he knew that the more sensible tactic would be to order mortar fire to destroy the enemy position. Nick felt that the lieutenant had acted out of panic and inexperience, and that he would continue to dispatch successive groups of men up the hill toward certain death while protecting his own life by cowering behind the wall.

After hearing the order, Nick hesitated. The lieutenant looked at him with anger. "I gave you an order, Sergeant!"

Since none of the soldiers respected the green lieutenant's judgment, neither Nick nor either of the other two men assigned to the mission obeyed.

"I'll have you court-martialed, you damned coward!" the young officer shouted.

Crouching behind the wall beside the officer, Nick glared at him. "Lieutenant Carter, you're just wasting men! It would be suicide! We wouldn't be able to advance ten feet up that hill before we were cut in half by that machinegun fire! You should call for support with mortar fire!"

"I'm ordering you, sergeant! Take Corporal Wiggins and Private Horton and take out that machinegun! Now!"

Nick glared at him. "Screw you, you stupid son of a bitch!"

"What did you say to me?" Lieutenant Carter was furious.

In anger, Nick suddenly spat in the officer's face. Then he reconsidered. His extreme anger replaced his fear as he signaled the other two soldiers to join him. Holding his weapon in front of him, he crawled from behind the wall. Since they respected Nick's judgment and experience, the two soldiers followed him. The three men darted up the hill toward the withering fire of the blazing machinegun, moving in alternating stops and starts. They sometimes took cover behind rocks and dead bodies that littered the area before again moving forward. Nick's two companions were quickly cut down by the relentless barrage of enemy fire, while Nick advanced to within a few yards of the enemy position. He thought he had made it as he prepared to hurl a hand grenade into their bunker.

Ironically, the enemy bullet that struck him saved his life and ended his participation in the war; for although he was severely wounded, he had probably been spared from certain death. Ultimately, mortar fire knocked out the machinegun and reinforcements finally came. The Allied forces continued their advance while Nick and other wounded American soldiers were flown to a military hospital where Nick underwent several hours of surgery. He was later court-martialed when his angry commanding lieutenant charged him with insubordination to an officer. As punishment he was reduced in rank to private and sentenced to three months confinement in the military stockade. Only his wounds and the decoration that he had been previously awarded prevented him from being given a bad conduct discharge. Although he had ultimately obeyed the lieutenant's order, his blatant disrespect of the inexperienced officer was the cause of Nick's conviction. Unfortunately, the lieutenant's version of Nick's initial refusal to obey the suicidal order became common knowledge at military headquarters and among his peers; consequently, the label, 'coward' stayed with him until his discharge.

During his court-martial proceedings one of the presiding judges posed the question: "How could a soldier who has been decorated for bravery in one battle be accused of cowardice in another? How could a man's courage be so inconsistent?" But unlike machines that perform with perfect consistency, man is a creature with countless emotions; sometimes he is brave, but at other given moments he may lose his courage.

Nick felt that war was a demon that infected the soul of man: Emotions have no place in the waging of war. Love, compassion, anger, fear...such feelings are irrelevant. Even cruelty is not the prime motivation or intention of war; for cruelty is only incidental. It is only a by-product of the emotionless efficiency employed in the systematic extermination of men, equipment, and property. The methodical and impersonal aspects of war made it all the more terrifying. Nick had been court-martialed for making the mistake forbidden by the Demon of War: He had shown the emotion of which machines are incapable: the emotion of *fear*...And in doing so, in the eyes of the war architects, he had rendered himself unworthy of being a soldier; for soldiers are supposed to be emotionless machines—only tools used in accomplishing the War Demon's hellish mission: to dispassionately and indiscriminately deal out destruction. The destruction of a hundred men is of no more importance than the annihilation of a bridge, or a building.

Even the innocuous, dehumanizing language of war sickened Nick: Live soldiers who were sent into battle were called 'reinforcements', or 'replacements,' as one might reinforce the sagging underpinning of a house, or replace a broken part of a machine; soldiers who died from hellish wounds were called 'casualties.' Their losses were considered with no more emotion than if a machine had been disabled; to kill enemy soldiers was referred to as 'wasting' them, as a farmer might waste a few seeds when sowing his fields; the incidental killing of thousands of civilians who had nothing to do with the war was known as 'collateral damage.' Their extermination is placed into the same category as the unintentional destruction of an untargeted factory, house, or bridge. The 'killing field' was an area in which enemy soldiers were trapped in a deadly crossfire, as if the killing of human beings was of no more consequence than processing cattle in a slaughter house.

In war, men are supposed to be unfeeling robots— machines that relentlessly march in lockstep without emotion toward death. In Nick's opinion, the Demon of War is a monster over which man has no control. It is a terrible condition in which man has lost all reason.

He thought about his 'heroic' actions in the battle for which he had been awarded the Bronze Star. He decided that his deed was not one of bravery, but rather a moment of madness, an instant in which taking action was less fearful than lying trapped in a foxhole and watching his fellow soldiers die while waiting in trembling fear for his own death.

He slowly raised his seat and sat upright as the speed of the vehicle decreased. Peering out the window, he noted that the bus was now entering the suburbs of Indianapolis. The sidewalks became more crowded and traffic increased as the bus moved closer to the terminal.

Because of his sour stomach, he was not hungry; however, he felt that in order to maintain his strength he should probably eat something when the bus stopped at the terminal. He was depressed and still had the remnants of a hangover that seemed to have no end; however, he was not surprised, for he realized that his alcoholic binge had lasted for several days. *Maybe by tomorrow I'll feel better,* he thought.

Because his stiff knee had begun to throb, he changed the position of his legs. The consequences of the physical injuries he had suffered in the war would probably always be with him, but even more disabling were the wounds that the war had inflicted on his psyche. An unexpected loud noise often terrified him, and stressful events or circumstances frequently initiated panic attacks. Awkward social situations sometimes created such anxiety that his heart would palpitate, causing him to stutter and gasp for breath when he talked.

Damn! I've got to think of something pleasant! he thought. *Maybe things will be different in the South. Friendly people, a slower pace of living that won't be so stressful. I might even settle in a small town where I can find some fairness and justice. It could be that most of the people are nice and friendly, like the lady sitting beside me. It's possible that I can forget the war there. Maybe I can find a sanctuary in the South.*

He heard the repetitious hissing of the airbrakes and the whine of the diesel engine as the bus slowed. The obese lady

31

beside him awoke and was suddenly pressed against him when the clumsy vehicle swung sharply to the right as it pulled into the terminal. After another loud hiss from the brakes, the bus finally came to a stop. The engine continued to idle as the passengers began to leave their seats before the door finally opened.

"Indianapolis!" droned the driver.

Chapter 3

The familiar character of the Indianapolis bus terminal stirred memories in Nick's mind. It typified every station through which he had passed during his travels while in the army. Like people, bus terminals and train stations share a mixture of contrasting moods: anticipation, excitement, grief, loneliness, sorrow—and boredom. Nick witnessed many contrasting activities in the terminal: farmers in overalls moving through the station; businessmen in their flannel suits and Stetson hats, carrying briefcases, scurrying about, trying to make important connections; a middle-age man hugging his soldier son who was returning from the war; a shoeshine boy, popping his rag as he shines the shoes of a traveling salesman, and military men lounging around on benches. The unique blend of odors evoked nostalgia: cologne, perfume, cigar smoke, and the scent of *people.* These elements and the odor of spent diesel fuel combined to deliver the familiar smell of *travel.* The monotonous drone of the loudspeaker announcing the arrival and departure of buses echoed through the cavernous interior of the terminal.

Strangely, more than any other experience, his exposure to bus terminals conjured up memories of his time in the military. He experienced a feeling of melancholia when he remembered his father standing beside him as he boarded the bus to his first military base after joining the army.

Nick was fifth in line to use the pay telephone in the corner of the station. Fearing that he wouldn't have time to make his call before re-boarding the bus, he peered at his watch. Fifteen minutes passed before he dropped a dime into the slot, enabling him to place a collect call to his friend, Stan in Tennessee. After their usual cheerful greetings and a brief conversation, Nick informed him of his planned 6:00 a.m. arrival in Knoxville, where Stan promised to pick him up. After his call, he ate a portion of a sandwich and drank a cup of black coffee. Before returning to the bus, he dropped a quarter into the cigarette machine that delivered a pack of Chesterfields. He bought a newspaper, re-boarded the bus and returned to his former seat. The sandwich that he had partially consumed had left a bitter taste in his mouth and a bad case of heartburn. He removed his service cap and placed it beneath the seat in front of him. His fingers trembled when he fired up a cigarette.

The air inside the bus was hot and muggy. He pulled a handkerchief from his shirt pocket and mopped the sweat from his face.

Although the friendly lady who had traveled beside him was a pleasant person, because of her incessant talking he dreaded sitting beside her all the way to Tennessee. Looking toward the front of the bus, he watched as she re-boarded. Moving awkwardly, she slowly waddled up the aisle toward him, finally stopping beside his seat. She displayed an apologetic smile before she spoke. "I just hate to tell you this, but I won't be riding beside you anymore...I just met this nice lady from Atlanta when I was in the terminal, and she wants me to ride with her. It's not because you weren't good company, though. It's just that she and I have so much in common."

Masking his secret relief, he smiled and said, "That's okay, ma'am."

"By the way. My name is Edna…Edna Williams. I never did get your name." She smiled at him.

Nick grasped her extended hand. "Nick Parilli. I enjoyed riding with you, ma'am."

"Well, good luck to you, Nick."

"Thank you, ma'am. The same to you." He released her hand and returned her smile. She turned and slowly trudged toward the front where she finally took a seat beside her newfound friend. He was mildly amused that the friendly lady had felt the need to apologize for changing seats. He wondered if the woman's presumptuous familiarity with him was typical of Southern people.

He unfolded his newspaper and began to read the front page. His concentration was interrupted by the soft, deep voice that addressed him. "Is this seat taken?"

Nick crushed out his cigarette and glanced upward at the tall army staff sergeant standing in the aisle beside him. He was a large black man who was at least six-feet-six in height and appeared to be about thirty years old. His rugged facial features were contradicted by the curious gentleness reflected in his bulbous eyes. His army uniform bore a patch identifying him as an infantry soldier.

To offer more room for his large body, Nick leaned toward the window. "Help yourself, sergeant." He gestured toward the seat beside him.

The sergeant was carrying a small bag resembling an attaché case, which he placed beneath the seat in front of him as he stooped down to occupy the seat. When he finally sat, his knees pressed against the back of the seat in front of him.

For a long while, Nick and the soldier sat without speaking as the boarding passengers filled the seats of the bus. The bus door finally closed. Then the purring diesel revved up and the vehicle pulled away from the station.

Both men remained quiet for several miles as the bus passed through the suburbs of the city and finally into open country. Nick peered out the window at the flat Indiana landscape, which now carried the hint of the approaching twilight. Scattered, irregular points of light contrasted with the darkness as lights came on when farm people anticipated the coming night.

The soldier beside Nick finally broke the silence. "Where are ya' traveling to, man?" His deep soft-spoken voice was almost a whisper, and resonated with the slow, drawling cadence common to Southern speech.

"I'm going to Knoxville, Tennessee," Nick replied.

"Is that where you live?"

"No, I'm just visiting a friend there. But I may eventually move to some place in the South. Where are you headed?"

"I'm goin' to my home in Augusta, Georgia on a thirty-day furlough. I've been stationed at Ft. Devens, Massachusetts. I've been in Indianapolis visitin' my uncle. After my furlough, I'm bein' sent to Korea."

Nick looked sadly at him. "Damn, that's a tough break for you, Sergeant."

"They say it's pretty bad over there."

"Yeah, it is. I won't lie to you about that." Nick replied.

The sergeant's oversized eyes widened. "You been there?"

"Yeah."

"Reckon you'll have to go back?"

"No. Thank God I'll never have to go back to that hellhole," replied Nick, "I'm out of the army now."

"How did you get out in time of war?" asked the sergeant.

"I got a medical discharge because I was wounded. I was serving a three-year enlistment, but because of my early discharge, I only served a little over two years."

"Were you wounded bad?" The bulbous eyes became larger.

"Yeah, pretty bad. I've still got some shrapnel in my back. They couldn't get it all out. They said it was too dangerous."

"At least it didn't mess you up mentally," said the soldier.

"Well, it screwed up my nerves. I sometimes have panic attacks, especially when I feel stress, like when I meet new people. Talking to a pretty girl would probably make me faint. Also, when it storms, the thunder scares the hell out of me."

There was a lull in the conversation as the Negro sergeant considered Nick's revelation of being wounded. In a soft voice he finally spoke. "Did you like the army?"

"Hell no, I hated it. How about you? Do you like it?"

"Yeah, I really do. I'm a career man. If I survive Korea, I'm gonna re-up again."

Nick smiled at him. "I guess the army is a lot better for you guys, now…Negroes, I mean…since all branches of service have been recently integrated." Nick quickly added, "I didn't mean any offense by what I said—about Negroes, I mean."

"I'm not offended. Hell, I *am* a Negro. Why should I be offended by you callin' me one?"

"Well, what I meant was…I think there should be equality among all men in the army. After all, when our blood is spilled in battle, it's the same red color for everybody, no matter what color our skin is. I just meant that the army is probably more appealing to you since it's integrated."

The sergeant eyed Nick suspiciously. "Hell, man, the army ain't no different than it was before it was integrated. The whites all hang together, and the Negroes all mingle together, just like before. But I guess you could say that it's more integrated than civilian life in the South. Hell, man, I doubt if the South ever integrates."

Nick lit a cigarette. "Well, I kinda know what you mean, I guess. In Chicago, where I'm from, it's integrated in theory, but in reality, it's segregated. Everybody congregates with their own kind. In Chicago, we have black neighborhoods, Puerto Rican neighborhoods, Jewish, Italian…hell, you name it. As the saying goes, 'Birds of a feather flock together.'"

The tall sergeant shifted his weight in the seat and crossed his long legs. "Yeah, but there's a big difference between the

North and South. In Chicago, the segregation is by *choice*, but in the South, you ain't got no choice."

"Then I guess you hate the South," said Nick.

"No, man. I love the South."

"Even though it's not integrated? How can you love it?"

"A Negro can get along fine as long as he knows his place."

"Bullshit!" Nick exclaimed. "Do you mean to tell me you accept that kind of injustice?"

The Negro smiled at him. "Hell, man...there ain't no justice nowhere in the world. A man can't be happy, whether he's black or white, 'til he learns to accept that."

Nick glared at him. He became irritated. Speaking in a louder voice he said, "I could *never* accept that! Why don't you stand up and resist that kind of injustice?"

"And get lynched? Man, you're one of them idealists that wants to change the world. You need to learn to roll with the punches. Us black folks would all be better off if guys like you would learn to accept life just the way it is."

Nick suddenly felt that he had overstepped some invisible boundary. He lowered the volume of his voice. "Hey, man, I'm sorry. I had no cause to start preaching you a sermon. To tell you the truth, I've got a terrible hangover. I've been drinking for days, and my nerves are kinda shot today." He extended his right hand. "By the way, I'm Nick Parilli."

The soldier took his hand and smiled. "My name is Homer Eubanks. My friends call me 'Bo.' Mos' ever'body in Augusta is called either 'Bo,' or 'Bubba.'"

"How about I call you 'Bo,' then?"

"Fine with me, Nick." He grinned. Then he retrieved the satchel from beneath the seat in front of him. He lowered his voice. "I've got a little somethin' here in my bag that'll help them jittery nerves of yours. Care for a little snort of booze?" He extracted a pint bottle of Bourbon from the small satchel.

Nick's mood brightened. "Well, I've been trying to quit. But to be honest, I could sure use a drink right now." When he held up his hand it was shaking. He immediately accepted the bottle from Bo's extended hand. The darkness of the bus interior obscured the furtive activity as Nick scrunched down in his seat and gulped down a generous drink from the bottle. The immediate tingle in his stomach soon filtered into his entire being. He began to feel better.

Nick handed the liquor back to Bo. "Thanks, man. I sure needed that!" He leaned back in his seat in a relaxed position.

"You're welcome. You can have another drink anytime you want it." Bo smiled at him.

It was now completely dark. The men became quiet as the whirring diesel engine pushed the bus into the blackness of the night. Nick peered out the window, noticing that the traffic was sparse. Gazing toward the distant horizon, he observed faint flickers of lightning defining the shapes of the faraway cumulus clouds. The alcohol was beginning to have the desired effect. His nerves began to calm.

Bo took a drink from the bottle. "Say, man, I don't mean to be nosy...but if you were in the army for two years and did a tour of duty in Korea, how come you're only a private? I notice that you don't have any stripes on your sleeves."

"I got busted."

"What for?"

"For insubordination to an officer while in battle. I used to be a staff sergeant."

"Is that why you hate the army?" asked the sergeant.

"That's not the only reason I hate the army. There are lots of reasons. First of all, the Korean War is a bunch of crap that was cooked up by paranoid politicians. The army stinks. I left Chicago for the same reason: corrupt politicians, crooked unions, discrimination against immigrants, like my father. Hell, there's gotta be some justice and fairness somewhere."

"And you think you'll find it in the South?" The Negro sergeant's eyes reflected curiosity.

"I don't know ... will I? You've lived in the South, and I've never been there."

Bo handed the bottle to Nick. "Man, I've lived in both the North and the South. On the surface, they seem to be different but in reality, people are pretty much the same everywhere."

Nick took another swallow of the alcohol, which was beginning to make him more talkative. "Well, maybe. But, you know, there must be a place where a guy can find some fairness and peace. The big cities are full of crooked politicians. Poor people, like my dad was before he died, are cheated and starved out. Also, there's no justice in the army. They discriminate."

"How do you figure that?" Bo displayed a puzzled look.

"Hell, man, look at the way the army exploited Negro soldiers...especially before the government integrated the armed services. The black man is good enough to die for his country, but in most places, he's got few rights and is not good enough to associate with white people, except maybe when fighting a war. It seems to me that you'd be as mad as hell and resent being sent to Korea to fight for a country that won't even accept you!"

For a long while, the Negro remained silent. Other than the relentless whine of the diesel engine, the bus was quiet while many of the passengers slept. Bo's silence caused Nick to wonder if his comments had angered the Negro sergeant.

When he finally spoke, Bo sidestepped Nick's previous comment. "Well, Nick, you were in the thick of battle in Korea. Since you're an experienced veteran and survived the war...do you have any advice for me about how I can stay alive over there?" He took another sip of the booze.

"Not really, pal. Just pray a lot, dig your foxhole deep, and keep your head down." Nick replied.

Bo again offered Nick the bottle. Nick grinned at him, but politely declined. "No thank you, Bo. I've had enough booze for now. But I sure appreciate it. Man, you saved my life!"

The black sergeant put the bottle away and turned to face Nick. His oversized eyes reflected sadness. "Well, man, you gave me some advice, so now I'll give you some. When you arrive at your destination in the South, don't try to *fix it*.

You're a crusader, Nick, and that'll bring you nuthin' but frustration. Things are *what they are*, and people are *who they are*. The South is *what it is*. We didn't create the conditions, and we can't fix 'em, or make 'em right. We just need to adjust to conditions."

Nick frowned. "But if somebody doesn't try to make things better, this world will go to hell in a hand basket!"

With a sad look, Bo hung his head. When he spoke it was only in a whisper. "Then let it go to hell, man. There are two kinds of people in the world: There's the crusaders, or idealists like you, who try to stir up the world and change people's ways. Then, there's the realists, who accept things the way they are. The idealists end up frustrated and unhappy, but the realists adapt to the ways of the world, and are happier because they don't try to solve the world's problems or take life so serious. Learn to roll with it."

Nick was becoming frustrated. "But I no longer want to solve the world's problems. Hell, Bo, I want to find a place where I can *hide* from the world's problems."

The sergeant's face displayed a skeptical expression. "So you intend to drop out? I guess that's okay if you can pull it off. But as angry as you are, I still think you'll be stickin' your nose into things that you can't do nuthin' about."

"Not me, pal. After I visit my friend in Knoxville, I'm going to live with my uncle in Buras, Louisiana. It's a real small town where I'll probably end up living for good. Even if I live somewhere else, I still want to live in a small town. No more crooked big cities for me."

"All towns are filled with the same kinds of people, Nick. Hell, the South is just like every other place."

Nick eyed him curiously. "Are you saying that the South is a bad place to live?"

The Negro smiled. "No, man. The South is a great place to live. I love the South. Some of the best people I know, both Negroes and whites, live in the South. You'll love it, too. Just don't try to change people…Let well enough alone. Just let the South be what it is. It ain't changed in a hundred years, so you

41

ain't gonna change it in your short lifetime. Man, you're huntin' a Utopia. You're chasin' a phantom that don't exist...You can't fix the world—you can only fix yourself. Just let the world be whatever it wants to be."

Nick was becoming frustrated with the lecture. He became nervous and felt that he was on the verge of having a panic attack. He turned his head and peered out the window. Bo took note of Nick's gesture and suddenly became quiet.

The change in scenery told Nick that the bus was entering the suburbs of Louisville. The men remained silent for several miles until the vehicle pulled into the station.

Once inside the terminal Nick and Bo separated, enabling the sergeant to make a phone call while Nick went to the restroom. On his way out Nick bought a newspaper and a box of aspirin. He then re-boarded the bus and returned to his seat.

As the diesel engine idled, Nick reclined in his seat and leafed through the newspaper as the passengers began refilling the seats on the bus. He noticed a Negro couple walking up the aisle. They passed him as they moved toward the rear of the bus. He looked up to see Bo making his way up the aisle toward him. When he reached his former seat, he abruptly stopped beside Nick. He extended his hand. "Nick, ole pal, this is where I leave you."

In total bewilderment, Nick rose from his seat and grasped the Negro sergeant's outstretched hand. "What do you mean? Are you getting back off the bus?"

Bo grinned, exposing his large, widely spaced teeth. He shook Nick's hand. "No, man, I gotta go sit in the back of the bus...Negroes ain't allowed to sit up front with the white folks."

Nick was shocked. "Are you kidding me?"

Bo only smiled. "No, man. We're in the South, now. Sometimes, in Kentucky, a Negro can get away with settin' in the front with the white folks, but they won't allow it when we git into Tennessee. Might as well git on back and claim me a seat before all the black folks that git on the bus take up all the good seats. Take care of yourself, Nick. It's been a pleasure meetin' you, pal ... and don't take life so serious."

Nick released his hand as Bo turned and walked toward the rear of the bus. Nick called after him, "Remember ... when you get to Korea, keep your head down."

Chapter 4

The bus moved southward through the darkness. Other than the monotonous whine of the diesel engine, the interior of the bus was quiet. Nick placed the newspaper in the empty seat beside him and stared out the window at the blackness of the night. He again noticed flickers of lightning in the distant sky.

The soothing effect of the alcohol that he had earlier consumed was beginning to fade; consequently, remnants of his hangover began to return, although to a lesser extent than before. He figured that his nervous system was gradually beginning to stabilize. He opened the box of aspirin and took three of them.

The flashes of lightning grew closer, followed by a delayed roll of thunder that reminded him of the artillery of the war. The bus slightly swayed from the intermittent gusts of wind. Nick became nervous as the storm drew nearer.

Although when in Chicago he had vowed to end his drinking binge, he now regretted his refusal of the last drink that Bo had offered to him. He believed that he probably needed a nap, but the approaching storm had provoked an uneasiness in him that made it unlikely that he would be able to sleep. He wished that he had brought some liquor on board, as Bo had done.

He thought about his long conversation with Bo. Since, by nature, Nick was a private person who seldom shared his feelings with anyone, his participation in the long discussion with the Negro sergeant had left him a bit surprised and embarrassed. But his pent-up emotions had begun to fester inside him. He felt a desperate need to share his feelings with someone. His consumption of alcohol had lowered his inhibitions; also, he felt emotionally safe in sharing intimate thoughts with a total stranger, a man that he would probably never again meet.

He had mixed feelings about the Negro soldier. He was a contradiction: Though obviously uneducated, he appeared to be wise, and Nick sensed that hidden somewhere beneath the veneer of humility, there resided a fierce pride and an unwavering loyalty.

But why had he resigned himself to the acceptance of racial prejudice? Why was he willing to go to war and possibly lose his life for a country that had denied him the simple rights that others had so easily inherited? Bo seemed to be happier, and possess an inner peace that Nick had never attained. Although he felt that Bo had compromised his principles, Nick almost envied his attitude of acceptance that brought such peace to his soul. Here was a man who had been discriminated against for most of his life; yet he was more content than Nick.

When he thought of Bo's assignment to Korea, Nick felt sorry for him; for he realized that even if he survived the war physically unscathed, his psyche would suffer many severe wounds. After Korea, he would never be the same. Would he then retain his stoical attitude? Or would he abandon his attitude of the acceptance of injustice?

He knew in his heart that he could never be like the Negro sergeant. Nick's sense of outrage over unfairness was inherently part of his nature, a necessary component of his psyche that was as much a part of him and as essential to his personality as his heart was necessary to his body.

He noticed a teenager sitting across the aisle a couple of seats toward the front. The lad appeared to be about fourteen years old. He held a trans-radio with an earpiece in his ear. Obviously carefree, he smiled as he bobbed his head to the beat of the music. It stirred memories of Nick's own happy-go-lucky childhood. He envied the young boy.

The bus had now entered the very center of the storm. The vehicle slightly tilted with each violent gust of wind, and the airbrakes hissed as the bus slowed to compensate for the driver's diminishing vision of the road ahead. Sheets of rain drenched the windows in a deafening roar. The flashes of lightning were almost blinding, and the booming thunder vibrated the interior of the bus as Nick's uneasiness escalated to near panic with each clap of thunder.

He felt a gentle tap on his shoulder. Turning his head to the right, he saw the tall figure of the Negro sergeant standing in the aisle beside him. The darkness inside the bus made his features almost indistinguishable. Bo smiled at him. Stooping down, he handed the pint bottle to Nick. He spoke in a whisper. "Here, man…Take it. You need this more than I do. There ain't but a couple of drinks left. Maybe it'll help you weather the storm and git some sleep."

It was almost as if Bo had read his mind, for somehow he had sensed Nick's anxiety and the need for the temporary relief that the liquor would provide.

He returned Bo's smile. "Gee, thanks, Bo. This damned storm's making me a little jumpy. This will really help."

"No problem, pal."

"Sit down with me, Bo. We'll share a drink together."

"Can't do it, man. I don't want to stir up no trouble. Gotta go to the back of the bus with the other colored folks. I'll try to tell you goodbye when you get off in Knoxville. You take care of yourself, man."

Before Nick had a chance to respond, Bo suddenly turned and walked toward the back of the bus.

The intensity of the storm had now diminished. Although the rain was steady, the wind had subsided. The lightning flashes were less frequent, and the thunder rolled from a great distance away. Nick began to feel less fearful.

The dark interior of the bus offered him the opportunity to take a drink from the bottle without being seen by other passengers. He soon began to feel the effects of the alcohol.

He slid the bottle underneath the seat in front of him. Then he reclined his seat and pulled the visor of his cap down over his eyes. The alcohol began to calm his nerves. His eyelids became heavy, and the welcome sensation of weariness relaxed his body. The sound of falling rain on the roof and windows of the bus began to soothe him. For the first time in weeks, he experienced a feeling of peace as his mind drifted into the nebulous brink of unconsciousness.

But his sleep was once again invaded by dreams of the war, and the single event that his conscious mind had been repressing.

During the war he had indirectly helped kill many men; however, in his dream he now remembered that he had *personally* killed three of the enemy with his rifle. Shooting the first two had bothered his conscience; but it was killing the third soldier that made him feel that he had sinned against everything that is holy; for the guilt and shame of his actions were embedded in his soul. As if playing in slow motion, his ghastly dream conjured up the horrible memory in vivid detail: The allied army was rapidly advancing on the Communist troops at Pyongyang, the capitol of North Korea, when Nick recognized an enemy soldier running across the field in full retreat. From a kneeling position, Nick took careful aim with his rifle. He then fired three shots, one of which struck the

47

retreating enemy soldier in the back. Quickly moving ahead, he overtook the wounded soldier, who was lying on his stomach, writhing in agony. With morbid curiosity, Nick flipped the soldier over onto his back in order to get a glimpse of his face. In utter horror, he discovered that the dying soldier was only a boy who appeared to be about fourteen years of age. His youthful, innocent eyes mirrored fear—and the terrible awareness that he was dying. Like a terrified puppy, he began to whimper, as a small boy would cry for his mother. Blood gushed from the gaping hole that Nick's bullet had left as it exited his abdomen. His fearful eyes became locked on those of Nick's before finally becoming glassy and expressionless as his last gasping breath spewed gore from his open mouth. As his life ebbed away, he wet his pants.

Nick felt that he had committed the unpardonable sin, and that his wicked soul was beyond redemption. Instead of assuming a man's responsibility of waging war, the young boy should have been attending school, playing ball with his friends, or frolicking in the woods. He would never grow up to be a man, for Nick's bullet had eliminated that possibility.

After viewing the dying boy, Nick threw aside his weapon. Then he dropped to his knees and vomited.

As usual, he awoke with his heart pounding and his body soaking in cold sweat. Until his terrible dream, he hadn't remembered the event. Ever since he had left the war behind him he had always intuitively known that there was *something else* that his conscious mind had repressed—something that his memory had hidden beneath protective layers of insignificant events…something too horrible for his conscious mind to bear; but since the terrible event had been revealed to him in this dream, he realized that his dreadful deed would now forever be remembered in all of his waking hours. He would somehow have to live with this.

Nick knew that he had always detested the wrongs and cruelty of the world; but with his remembrance of killing the child in battle, he felt like an insincere hypocrite; for he believed that all of the combined hatred, cruelty, and injustice in the world could never equal the transgression of which he was guilty in his own heart.

He wept as he reached under the seat for the bottle of liquor. He lifted the bottle and swallowed the remaining contents.

Again the alcohol began to soothe him. He reclined in his seat, trembling, trying desperately to forget his terrible dream. He lit a cigarette and gazed out the window into the foggy blackness of the night. The rain had now subsided, leaving in its wake only a misty wetness. The distant, occasional rumble of thunder from the retreating storm mimicked the sound of artillery, once again reminding him of the war. He snuffed out his cigarette and again reclined in his seat, soon drifting off into a rare, dreamless sleep.

The braking of the bus awakened him. Peering out the window, he noticed that the vehicle had entered the congested area of downtown Knoxville. The street sign indicated that the bus was moving along Gay Street. After traveling about a mile, the airbrakes sighed as the clumsy vehicle slowed. Then it swung to the left into a narrow alley that led to the terminal. The airbrakes issued another series of hisses, slowing the bus to almost a standstill. After another loud hiss, the vehicle came to a stop. For a short time the driver kept the motor idling. Finally the sound of the whining diesel engine stopped.

"Knoxville!" shouted the driver.

Chapter 5

Twenty-six miles southwest of Knoxville, Cedar Valley, Tennessee hugged the northern bank of the Tennessee River. In the early nineteen-fifties, the small town had a population of about three thousand. Essentially a farming town, it was nestled in the floor of the Tennessee Valley between the foothills of the Smoky and Cumberland Mountain ranges. Located between Knoxville and Chattanooga, it was linked to these larger cities by Highway 11, which served as the main street of Cedar Valley as well as spanning half the country in providing the main route that connected New York to New Orleans.

Travel, as well as shipping to distant destinations was mostly by train; accordingly, the tracks of Southern Railway cut a path through the eastern edge of town, wending its way to faraway cities as well as connecting Cedar Valley to other small towns in the valley. The steam-driven locomotives pulled a mile-long chain of freight or passenger cars. From Cedar Valley, passengers caught the '41' northeastward toward Knoxville and Roanoke, or rode the '42' to Chattanooga and other points in the South.

Cedar Valley, Tennessee was the typical small Southern town. Surrounded by rolling hills of diminishing forests and a patchwork of fertile river-bottom land, the river stretched southwestward to Chattanooga and beyond.

Characteristic of its neighboring towns and villages that sprinkled the valley, the local economy depended on revenue from farming and small businesses that offered little in the way of products and services. For more elaborate purchases it was necessary for the shopper to drive into Knoxville.

All of the small towns in the valley shared common characteristics in their commercial activities, habits, and appearance. On the main street, which consisted of only a few blocks, small businesses were stacked side-by-side into one large complex, spanning the entire city block: a downtown movie theater, where on Saturdays for fifteen cents, children could enjoy double-feature westerns starring Roy Rogers, Gene Autry, or Tex Ritter, as well as a comedy and a cartoon; a couple of drug stores, each with an overhead fan and a soda fountain; a poolroom, two banks, a dry-cleaning business, two or three grocery stores, a high school and an elementary school, churches, and a five and dime store. And none of the towns would be complete without a couple of barbershops, each with a Negro shoeshine boy, where men, regardless of whether or not they needed a haircut, gathered to talk politics, sports, and swap gossip. Because the crime rate was minimal, most of the townspeople left the doors to their homes unlocked at night.

The early fifties was a time of transition for the South. Because of the increasing prosperity, people became more complacent. It was a carefree time for the youth. The Civil War of the previous century had reduced the South to abject poverty; then The Great Depression during the early thirties added to their destitution. However, during the forties, the defense spending of World War II had stimulated the economy. Wages rose and jobs became more plentiful. The

51

house construction boom was in its infancy, but rapidly growing. Since the introduction of the automobile more than fifty years earlier, garages and mechanics had replaced blacksmith shops. However, since small-town Southern people were usually slow in adjusting to change, the evolution had been gradual; for until the early forties, many farmers continued to deliver their produce to the markets in horse-drawn wagons.

As cars became more numerous, the era of drive-ins, both movies and restaurants, became popular throughout the South. Rock and roll music gradually replaced the 'big band' sound of the forties. However, the popularity of country music remained constant. Country artists such as Eddie Arnold, Hank Williams, Ernest Tubb, Roy Acuff, and Homer and Jethro remained popular as radio entertainers in the Southern culture.

The medium of radio survived, but as the main source of family entertainment it was gradually replaced by the modern miracle of television. Radio comedies such as 'Amos and Andy' and the western adventures of 'The Lone Ranger' faded away as TV sets with actual moving images on the screen presented more sophisticated programs. Dick Van Dyke, Jackie Gleason, Lucille Ball in 'I Love Lucy,' James Arness of 'Gunsmoke,' and numerous quiz shows became popular fare for television viewers. The horse and buggy era, although slow in its departure, had gradually faded away in the South.

In spite of the advanced mobility brought on by the increased number of automobiles, Cedar Valley continued to maintain its casual, slow-moving character. Generations of its residents had lived their entire lives, then died and were buried in the isolated environment of the indolent Southern town. Other than the local lock and key factory and a hosiery mill, the town had limited industry. Cedar Valley had experienced little change in the past twenty-five years.

The small town was in the midst of the Bible belt, where most of the simple, common people were devoutly religious; however, many Southerners were suspicious of any lifestyle foreign to their own. Also, they held a distrust of anyone who was 'different.' Although nearly a hundred years had passed since the emancipation of slaves, Southern people were generally prejudiced against Negroes, who had few rights and privileges in the South. While black people were not subject to actual slavery, they were relegated to roles of second-class citizens; for throughout most of the South the only jobs available to black people were chores of menial labor or positions of subservience to white people. Even worse, black children were not allowed to attend white schools. Negroes were prohibited from voting and eating in public restaurants; also, no public restroom provisions were made available to black people. However, the Cedar Valley Greyhound Bus Station had extended a gesture of uncommon benevolence and tolerance to Negro travelers. They had provided three restrooms in the terminal: *Gentlemen, Ladies, and Colored;* however, since the 'colored' sign on the door made no distinction in regard to the gender of the restroom occupant, Negroes were not even granted the dignity of practicing modesty in the restroom that had been provided for them.

Many affluent Southern people prided themselves in being kind and generous to Negroes, often hiring them as cooks, nannies, maids, or groundskeepers for their estates, sometimes boasting that the Negro servant was 'part of the family.' The employers spoke kindly of them, as if they were speaking fondly of a beloved hunting dog or a farm animal; but for a Negro man to express affection or pity toward a white woman, however innocent his intent, could precipitate his death.

But to judge Southern morality solely on its racial discrimination would be to make a gross misjudgment; for, although prejudiced and sometimes opinionated and stubborn, Southern people were generally kind, generous and fair in their dealings with their peers. For the most part, they were hard working, God-fearing people—resolute in their convictions and loyal to their kinfolk and neighbors.

Most Southern whites felt justified in their condescending attitude toward the Negro. Racial discrimination in the South was perpetuated by ignorance and tradition. To the religious white southerner, it was a natural phenomenon ordained by God. In the South, white people saw no moral inconsistency in practicing both racial discrimination and Christianity.

It was in this unpretentious, slow-paced but conflicting culture that the ancestors of the Mullins families had chosen to settle and had lived for several generations.

*   *   *

Stan Mullins sat up in bed. He reached to the nightstand beside him and shut off the annoying ring of the alarm clock. He yawned and vigorously rubbed his eyelids to clear away the remnants of sleep. It was 4:30 a.m., an unusually early hour for him to begin his day. Sleepily, he slowly got up, and without bothering to make up his bed, he strode to the kitchen of his basement apartment and started a pot of coffee. He then walked to the bathroom where he relieved his bladder and proceeded to leisurely shower and shave.

While inspecting his face in the mirror, his bloodshot eyes stared back at him, the penalty for his consumption of a six-pack of beer the preceding night. His short crew cut eliminated the necessity of combing his stubble of blonde hair.

He was pleased with his reflected image, for his face, although not handsome, displayed a pleasant, even-featured ruggedness. His thick neck suggested strength, and his masculine face carried an almost perpetual expression of humor, an appropriate characteristic that matched his personality; for except on rare occasions when he was angry, Stan was usually in a congenial mood. Like Nick, he was twenty-three; also, the two men were almost identical in size.

After leisurely getting dressed, he ate a doughnut and drank a cup of black coffee. He peered at his watch: *5:10 a.m.* He had plenty of time to make his six o'clock appointment to pick up Nick at the Knoxville Bus Terminal.

He left his basement apartment, hoping that his early morning activity hadn't awakened his mother and father in the

54

main part of the house above his living quarters. He knew that his father, Lester Mullins, disliked being awakened before 7:00 a.m.

The faint glow on the eastern horizon indicated that it was too early for the sun to burn away the misty fog that had blanketed the area. He walked across the dew-saturated lawn to his brand new red Ford convertible parked in the driveway. When he started the car, he realized that it would probably awaken his dad. He winced at the loud, resonating growl emitted by the Hollywood muffler that he had recently had installed on the sporty new vehicle. He quickly backed out of the driveway and drove away.

As he drove through the suburbs of the city, he began to reflect on his living arrangement. Residing in the basement apartment of his parents' home was a mixed blessing. The situation had several advantages: His living expenses were minimal, for not only was he living in the apartment rent-free, he also took most of his meals in his parents' house—meals that were prepared by Minnie, the elderly, live-in Negro servant employed by Stan's father. Minnie not only cooked and kept the house clean and tidy, she also did the family's laundry, including Stan's clothes. She made her living quarters in a small attic room in the Mullins' home. An additional advantage was the convenience of using his apartment as an office from which he managed his father's construction business.

But the living arrangement also had some drawbacks: Stan's father was an extremely controlling man who ruled the Mullins' home with an iron hand. Stan felt that his dad's commanding nature had stifled him. Living under the umbrella of his father's domination had cramped his style. Since his graduation from college, Stan had known no other home. Although he dreaded telling his father, he had decided to eventually establish his independence by moving out of his parents' house and renting his own apartment. After all, Stan was financially sound, for his dad had paid him well for managing his construction business.

He swung the vehicle to the right onto Highway 11 toward Knoxville. Since the day was already beginning to heat up, he pulled the vehicle to the shoulder of the road and lowered the top. He chuckled as he wondered what Nick's reaction would be when he saw his old friend drive up in the brand new Ford convertible with the top down. As he pulled back onto the highway, the incoming rush of morning air invigorated him.

Stan was in an exceptionally happy mood. He turned on the radio, repeatedly switching stations in order to find the Southern style of music that appealed to him. *Mona Lisa,* by Nat King Cole, was not country enough; *Nola,* by Les Paul— He liked guitar music, but this high-tech rendition was so electronically doctored-up that it didn't even sound like a guitar...*Candy Kisses,* sung by Eddie Arnold...*Aaah, now that's music!* he thought. Since he was satisfied with his selection, he sang along with the music as he pressed on toward Knoxville.

He began to reminisce about his former relationship with Nick. He realized that they were drastically different in both personality and background. In college, Stan had been outgoing and popular. With a quick wit and a playful nature, he enjoyed playing pranks, and had a predilection for ridiculous humor. Since he was from an affluent family, he was accustomed to always having money. His membership in a fraternity ensured his popularity with the other students, particularly since he seemed to be consistently in a good mood. Except for his adeptness in playing tennis, he was not particularly skilled in athletics; however, he idolized Nick's boxing skills and his heroics on the football team. Further cementing their strong bond was the fact that they had been roommates, and neither of them had siblings.

In contrast, Nick was a loner. He had a reserved, almost brooding personality. Because his father had always held menial jobs, he grew up in a lower-income neighborhood and never knew the pleasure of having money, a fact that his friend, Stan had never fully realized; however, Nick seemed to harbor no jealousy of his friend for his affluence. His opportunity to attend college had been made possible only as a result of his football credentials from high school, which persuaded the college to offer him a partial athletic scholarship. However, because of a knee injury, he was forced to quit football in his junior season. Lack of money became a problem and his grades began to suffer. Also, during this time, his mother had died. Ultimately, Nick had to drop out of school while Stan had graduated. Soon after, Stan became the manager of his father's lucrative construction business in Tennessee.

After he left college, Nick had returned to his home in Chicago for a brief time before enlisting in the army. Although he hadn't seen Stan since they attended college together, they had corresponded regularly after Nick had joined the military.

Stan smiled when he thought of their unlikely friendship and the drastic differences that existed between them. Nick had been reared in a big city and had traveled overseas to fight in the war, while Stan had spent the majority of his life in a small Southern town; and yet, Stan seemed to be the more sophisticated of the two. In fact, Stan felt that Nick's nature sometimes seemed rather naïve, which was uncharacteristic of a man of his experience and background. Accentuating their differences was Stan's burning jealousy of his friend; for Nick possessed the attributes that Stan had been denied: Nick was soft-spoken and handsome, and possessed an unrealistic honesty which bordered on innocence, or even self-righteousness. Stan chuckled when he remembered Nick's criticism of him when he had cheated on a final exam when they attended college together.

However, most of Stan's envy of him was rooted in Nick's athletic skill. He idolized Nick, and often tried to emulate him. Stan considered that maybe the extreme difference in their personalities was the cement that bonded them together. Perhaps each of them sought in the other the attributes lacking in himself.

He was now in downtown Knoxville. He turned the vehicle left onto Gay Street, drove for several blocks, and then turned right into the parking area behind the bus terminal. After parking his car, his excitement mounted as he visually scanned the area in search of his friend. Several travelers were either entering or leaving the station while others were scurrying about in the parking area. Finally, he spotted Nick about twenty yards away with his duffel bag lying on the sidewalk beside him. He was sitting on a bench beside a Negro soldier.

For a moment, he studied his friend as Nick chatted with the black soldier. Then Stan honked his car horn and waved. Nick looked up, and he and the black soldier rose to their feet. Nick grinned and waved back at Stan. He shook hands with the Negro soldier, picked up his duffel bag, and limped in the direction of Stan, who was now trotting toward him. They met near the center of the parking lot in a vigorous, lengthy embrace, with each of them happily laughing.

When they released each other, Stan held him at arm's length and grinned. "Nicky, old buddy! Let me look at you! Man, you look great! I can see that the war left you in one piece!"

Nick returned the grin. "Yeah, and then some! I've even got some extra pieces in me...a piece of shrapnel and a bullet fragment in my back. I also have a piece of steel in my knee!"

"Well, you don't look any worse for wear! You still look great, Nicky!"

Nick smiled. "You look great, too. I can see that you haven't gotten fat from that soft and rich living that you're accustomed to...I can also see that you're still calling me 'Nicky.'"

Stan laughed and slapped him on the back. "I always thought that it had a nice ring to it...sounds kinda poetic...*Nicky Parilli*. It rolls right off your tongue...Don't you think so? Here, let me take your luggage." He took the duffel bag from Nick. They walked to Stan's car and he tossed the bag into the back seat.

"How do you like my car?" asked Stan, as they both slid into the vehicle. "I always wanted to own a ragtop."

"Just another trophy that comes with rich living," quipped Nick, as Stan broke into laughter.

When Stan started the car Nick turned to face him. "Stan, I like to ride in a convertible with the top down, but if I we're gonna talk, you'd better raise the top because I don't hear very well since that hand grenade episode."

"No problem, Nicky." He raised the top. Then he swung the vehicle out of the parking lot and drove away.

Stan spoke in a loud voice, "I noticed you limping as you came to meet me. Is the knee very bad?"

"There's no need to yell at me, Stan. I can hear you. I'm not deaf, at least not yet. To answer your question, the knee's bad, but it's getting better."

Stan lowered his voice to a normal volume. "That's great, Nick. Say, do you reckon you might still be able to box? Or do you think the knee will heal well enough for you to play football again? You know, you could go back to college and play football. If you were to move here, maybe you could go to Carson-Newman, or maybe East Tennessee State."

"No, Stan, my football days are over."

"Oh, man! Too bad! You were really something else on the football field! I remember when the score was tied in that Northampton game and you caught that pass and…"

"Forget it, Stan!" Nick interrupted, "I'm too banged up to ever play football again. Besides, I don't have any passion for it anymore. But I may go back to college if I can get the G.I. Bill."

"Good, Nicky. That's what you should do," Stan replied.

"We'll see. Right now I'm so disoriented I don't know what my long-range plans are."

Stan changed the subject. Laughing, he turned and slapped Nick on the back. "Good old Nicky! I can't believe that we're back together again! I can't wait for you to meet my family! How long can you stay with us?"

"Oh, I don't know … maybe for three or four days. I don't have a hell of a lot of money left. The army doesn't pay the kind of money that you've been making. How long do you *want* me to stay?"

"Hell, man, Stay as long as you can! I'll give you money."

"No need for that, Stan. After I've been here for three or four days, I'll still have enough money to get to my uncle's place in Louisiana."

"Well, if you run short of dough, just let me know." He chuckled. "By the way, pal … who was that nigger soldier you were so chummy with back at the bus station? Was that an old army buddy?"

"No, he's just a soldier I met on the bus. He's a nice guy. He's going home on furlough, and then to Korea … and he's not a 'nigger.'"

Stan only laughed. "Hell, man … the term, 'nigger' is just Southern slang—just an expression. I didn't mean any disrespect by calling him a 'nigger.' I don't really have any grudge against *Negroes*." His last word was saturated with a sarcastic emphasis.

"I hope not, Stan," said Nick, "I saw many Negro soldiers die for their country in Korea."

"Damn, Nicky! I don't see 'em any different than I see white people. We've got a couple of nig … I mean Negroes … working for us at home. Minnie, our maid, is like part of our family, you might say … She even lives with us."

"That's good, Stan. I think Negroes and whites should have the same liberties." Nick lit a cigarette and relaxed in the seat.

Stan again slapped him on the back and broke into raucous laughter. "Still the same old 'Do-Gooder' Nicky! Still the same old creed: *One nation under God, indivisible, with liberty and justice for all!*"

Nick was slightly embarrassed. He laughed and playfully punched Stan on the shoulder. "Go to hell, you arrogant bastard," he said, bluntly. Stan laughed uproariously. Neither of them were lacking in the practice of brutal candor in their relationship.

For a few miles they rode in silence. Finally, with a serious expression, Stan spoke. "Nicky, as you know, because of my perforated eardrum, the draft board said that I wasn't fit for military duty. They ruled me '4F.' I was happy about it then, but now I wish that I had been classified '1A,' so I could have fought with you in Korea."

"I believe that, Stan, but you don't really realize what you're saying. War is hell, man, I mean that literally. It's hell on earth!"

Stan's eyes reflected empathy. "Nicky, from what you said in your letters, I know that the war has kinda beaten you down. I want you to know that I'll always cherish our relationship." The demeanor of his statement was a drastic departure from his usual light-hearted attitude. The solemn tone of his voice reflected a rare sincerity.

Nick flipped his cigarette out the window. "Stan, the war is not the only thing that has beaten me down. After my mother died, my dad, after being cheated by his bosses for years, turned into an alcoholic and died like a bum, without anybody in the world, except my uncle and me, giving a damn. Once when the union called a strike, my dad crossed the picket line just so he could work and feed the family. For that, he was called a 'scab' and got beaten up so bad that he had to go to the hospital. After that, he lost his job. Also, after risking my life for my country and getting blown to hell by an enemy grenade, the army thanks me by court-martialing me. They even put me in prison! The bombs and explosions in the war shook me so bad that every time I hear a loud noise it scares the hell out of me. I'm telling you, Stan—I have these *panic attacks!* And Chicago, the place I come from, is full of crooked politicians, corrupt unions, and crime bosses. *The System* is what's beaten me down. That's why I want to live in a small town somewhere, a place that's far away from either the army or any big city, a place where *The System* has little authority, or effect. Some place that's *real!*"

61

Stan looked into his friend's eyes and saw that he had been to hell and back. He cast a reassuring smile at Nick and placed a hand on his shoulder. "Hey, Nicky...you came to the right place! Cedar Valley is just like *The Garden of Eden,* man! I don't know what it'll be like in Buras, Louisiana, but as long as you're in *this* town you'll never have to be 'beaten down' again, because my dad is the mayor, and my uncle is the sheriff. As long as you're my best buddy, you won't see any hard times around here!" He laughed. "Hell, you could even rob a bank without any hassle as long as you and I are friends!"

"Stan, I don't expect any favoritism, only fairness and an equal chance."

"Damn! Still the same old fair-minded Nicky! Hell, man, in this world you need to accept any kind of help you can get. Everybody else does."

Stan suddenly braked the car; then after a brief stop at the caution light, he turned left off Highway 11 onto Rocky Creek Road. "We're almost home, pal." He grinned at Nick. "After we rest up for a while, we'll spend the day together. I want to show you around town."

"Stan, I don't want to interfere with your routine."

"Don't worry about that. You don't think I'd abandon my best friend, do you?"

"But don't you have to work today?"

"Hell no, man. Today is Saturday, my day off. Anyway, even if today were Monday, I'd still take the day off. I'm my own boss."

"You lucky bastard," replied Nick, smiling.

The backfire from the exhaust of a passing car caused Nick to nervously jump in his seat. He quickly regained his composure.

"Damn, Nicky!" cried Stan, "Why are you so jumpy?"

"Hell, I don't know, Stan. Maybe it's this terrible hangover, or maybe it's because of the war. My nerves are just shot. It's like I was telling you, if I get into stressful situations I have these damned panic attacks!"

Stan turned the car to the right, onto Martin Road. "Listen, Nicky, we're gonna have some fun tonight! We're going to the Fourth of July dance. There'll be some good-looking women there. By the way, how long has it been since you had a woman?"

"Damn, Stan. I'm sorry you had to ask that. It seems like a hundred years."

"Oh, come on Nicky...Didn't you ever bed down any of those cute, slant-eyed South Korean gals?"

"No comment," said Nick. Both men laughed.

"Wait 'til you see some of these sexy Southern Belles," said Stan, "Hell, you'd never even consider dating another snooty Yankee woman. Southern gals know that a man is boss, and they know how to please a man."

"Hell, Stan," said Nick, "I don't even know how to behave around a woman anymore. I haven't even talked to a female in several months."

Stan smiled and replied, "Nicky, I've got a feeling you'll catch up pretty quick, old pal. I still remember the old days when we went to college together. Damn! You had to practically fight the women off of you!"

"I can hardly remember those days, Stan."

"Really? I'll never forget 'em!"

Apologetically, Nick said, "Listen, Stan. I hate to disappoint you, but I can't go to any dance tonight. I don't have anything to wear except my army uniform, and I'm sure as hell not gonna wear that!"

"Hell, don't sweat it, man. You and I are the same size. I can really deck you out nicely, buddy."

"Why are they having a Fourth of July dance tonight? The Fourth isn't until Monday." said Nick.

"Hell, I don't know. Maybe since the Fourth comes on Monday, it screws things up. I suppose that having it on Saturday will enable everybody to get well from their hangovers on Sunday. Some of the guys will be drinking a lot of booze."

"Can you buy liquor in Cedar Valley?" asked Nick.

63

"Not legally. This is a dry county. Most all these small-town Southern counties are dry. But don't worry, I can get all the booze we want."

He swung the vehicle into the wide concrete driveway, drove up the sloping hill, and parked behind a new black Cadillac.

"Here we are … we're home, Nicky."

Chapter 6

Upon his first glance at the Mullins Estate, Nick was amazed at the apparent affluence of the family. The imposing house stood in the middle of the fenced-in, five-acre portion of grassy yard at the front portion of a fifty-acre parcel of land. Centered in the front yard near the street stood a tall flagpole displaying a Confederate flag. At the entrance, by the driveway, a waist-high statuette of a Negro man dressed in jockey's attire mimicked an old fashioned hitching post and served as a support for the large mailbox.

The main house was a large two-story colonial style brick mansion with six white columns adorning the front. The large house stood at least sixty yards from the street halfway up a sloping hill. Its elevation accentuated the majestic appearance of the structure, and reflected the antiquity of the Old South. Directly behind the house were flower gardens and a tennis court. A red barn and a couple of neat outbuildings stood in a field beyond the back yard. The remaining forty-five acres stretched into the distance up the inclining hill where several acres were covered with a heavy growth of forest.

The lush, expansive front lawn was well groomed and immaculate in appearance. On each side of the straight sidewalk that extended from the front porch to the street stood a huge magnolia tree shading the yard. Maple trees, planted in perfectly aligned rows flanked each side of the house, stretching all the way to the street. Directly in front of the large porch was a row of symmetrical, perfectly shaped shrubbery, which was currently being pruned by an elderly, white-haired Negro man. A view of the Mullins property was a study in classical symmetry. The affluence of the Mullins family was obvious.

Although nearly a century had passed since the Civil War, it appeared that Lester Mullins was still enamored with the extinct glory and the ghostly relics of the pre-Civil War Confederacy.

The sweltering heat of the morning sun was beginning to feel uncomfortable. Stan slowly backed the car into the edge of the yard and parked it under the protective shade of a magnolia tree.

He turned to Nick. "Well, what do you think of my humble abode?"

"Wow!" exclaimed Nick. "Damn, Stan. Your family must be rich!"

Stan laughed. "Yeah, my old man is pretty well off, but not me. Hell, compared to my dad, I ain't got a pot to piss in."

"Do you live here, too?"

"Well, yeah, sort of. I live in the basement apartment, but I'm gonna get my own place soon. Come on, get out of the car and I'll show you around the place."

He fetched Nick's duffel bag out of the back seat and they walked up the sidewalk that paralleled the front of the house. The elderly Negro man trimming the shrubbery looked up as they approached him. He was short and scrawny. His blue denim shirt displayed splotches of sweat at his arm pits and in

66

the back between his shoulder blades. He pulled a soiled rag from his pocket and swabbed his sweating face.

"Hey, Rufus!" Stan called out. "This is my friend, Nick Parilli. Remember me telling you all about him?"

"Yessuh, Mistah Stan, I remembuh all right. Howdy-do, Mistah Parilli, suh." His face was again covered with great beads of perspiration. He grasped Nick's extended hand.

"Hello, Rufus," greeted Nick. "Rufus, do you have a last name?"

"Yes suh. My last name's Headrick, suh."

"Nice to meet you, Rufus Headrick," said Nick.

Stan patted Rufus on the shoulder. "Rufus used to live with us when I was a kid. He helped raise me. Ain't that right Rufus?"

Rufus displayed a toothless grin. "Yessuh, Mistah Stan."

"Are my parents up yet, Rufus?" Stan asked.

"No suh, Mistah Stan, I don't think so. But I believe that maybe Minnie is up an aroun'. I believe I saw her face in the kitchen window a little while ago." He continued to smile as he gestured toward the window.

"Come on, Nicky. Let me show you through the house." Stan placed the duffel bag on the porch near the door.

He opened the front door for Nick and followed him into the large foyer. A magnificent chandelier hung from the high ceiling of the spacious, ornate room.

The first images that caught Nick's eye when they stepped into the living room were the high ceiling and spiral staircase that ascended to the upstairs. With the exception of the kitchen, Stan methodically led Nick through the remainder of the downstairs portion of the magnificent house, occasionally commenting on particular pieces of furniture or explaining certain unusual characteristics. The living room and dining room were furnished in American Victorian style. The black walnut pieces of furniture were large and heavily ornamented with the chairs upholstered in velvet. All tables in the two rooms had marble tops. The high walls displayed wide, expensive molding and ornate chandeliers hung from the ceiling.

In spite of the resplendence of the interior, Nick felt that it projected a stiffly formal and rather inhospitable character. The decor of the rooms, the lacy tablecloths, and elaborate flower arrangements reflected a haughty pretentiousness. The overall flavor of the two rooms suggested a feminine influence.

But the den, or study, displayed a character that was a direct contradiction to the décor of the remainder of the house. Comfortable modern furniture surrounded a huge fireplace. Above the mantle was a mounted moose head. The entire wall to the right of the fireplace was comprised of a large bookcase filled with books. The opposite wall boasted a large collection of guns, encased behind the glass door in a cabinet. A desk and comfortable chair occupied the left corner of the room near the fireplace. It was obviously a man's room. The opposing themes reflected by the different areas of the home suggested a tug-of-war between personalities.

Nick had never seen a house of such splendor. The elegance of the interior was in keeping with regal appearance of the exterior of the house. The stately character of the splendid estate reminded Nick of *Tara,* the antebellum house of *Gone with the Wind.*

Apparently, the tour was over, for Stan finally turned toward Nick. "Well, that's about it, except for the upstairs bedrooms. But they're all alike with the same kind of furniture. Later, I'll show you my part of the house downstairs where you and I will be staying, but it's not gonna knock your eyes out with beauty. Let's go into the kitchen and you can meet Minnie. She's probably fixing breakfast for us."

When they walked into the kitchen they were greeted by the toasty, tantalizing aroma of brewing coffee. Minnie was involved in the preparation of a large omelet. On the center table, crisp slices of bacon and an array of sliced tomatoes were neatly arranged on a large platter beside a heaping bowl of hominy grits. Minnie placed a bowl of milk gravy and a pan of steaming hot biscuits beside the other breakfast items.

"Hi, Minnie," greeted Stan. "This man is my best buddy, Nick Parilli. He's the guy that I told you about that's gonna be staying with us for a few days. Nick, this is Minnie. She's like a second mama to me...right Minnie?"

"Yessuh, Mistah Stan, I reckon so." A trace of a smile appeared as she turned to Nick and politely curtsied to him. Nick wasn't accustomed to such politeness and formality.

"I'm pleased to meet you, Mistah Nick." she said.

"Hello, Minnie," answered Nick. Instinctively, he reached to shake her hand, but she only turned away. It suddenly occurred to him that in the South it was not customary for a woman, especially a woman of color, to show such familiarity to a man she had just met...particularly to a white man.

Minnie was a large woman. Tall, and with the bulk of her body bordering on obesity, her large, curious eyes protruded from her rotund face. On her head she wore a white polka-dot red scarf snugly draped over her hair and tied in the back. A large white apron covered the front of her striped housedress. In her demeanor, she seemed more mannerly and to possess more gentility than Rufus, the male Negro grounds-keeper.

Stan grinned. "When's breakfast, Minnie? Nick and I are getting hungry."

"Now Mistah Stan, don't start rushin' me. Mistah and miziz Mullins ain't up yit, an' I still gotta finish cookin' breakfast an' set th' dinin' room table. I ain't got time to dally aroun'. Now go on...Git! An' let me finish breakfast!" She cast a shy smile at Stan. Nick decided that Minnie, because of her relationship of subservience to Stan's parents, would never be so presumptuous as to express herself to them in such a manner.

"Hey Minnie, I'm gonna pour Nick and me a cup of coffee, okay?"

"He'p yo'self, Mistah Stan. You knows where it is."

He poured two cups of coffee and handed one to Nick. "Do you take cream and sugar, Nicky?"

"No, I only drink black coffee," replied Nick.

Then in order to aggravate Minnie, Stan said, "Hurry up with that breakfast, Minnie. Nicky and I don't have all day to dally around!" He grinned. "Come on, Nick, let's go into the study and wait for dad and mom to get up. They should have already been up by now, because it's 7:15."

Carrying their coffee, they walked back to the study and shared a seat on the couch that faced the fireplace. As soon as they were seated, Stan's mother entered the room. An attractive, middle-aged woman of medium height and figure, her facial features bore a close kinship to those of her son. She was well groomed. Exuding the pleasant aroma of perfumed soap, she had showered and applied makeup. Her long tresses of blonde hair were shoulder length, and had been curled and neatly combed. She was wearing house shoes and a terry cloth pale blue robe that was pulled together and tied in the front.

When she entered the room, both Stan and Nick placed their cups on the coffee table. They stood, and walked to meet her.

Stan grinned. "Hi, Mom. Remember me telling you about Nick? Well, this is Nick...Nick Parilli, this is my mother, Mary Jane Mullins."

Stan's mother smiled. She gestured with a slight suggestion of a bow and extended her hand to him.

"Welcome to our home, Nick Parilli." She smiled and then released his hand. "I've been looking forward to meeting you."

"Hello, Mrs. Mullins. I've been looking forward to meeting you, too. Your home is beautiful. I don't believe I've ever seen a lovelier place."

"Why, thank you, Nick. We like it. Has Stan shown you around?"

"Yes ma'am. I'm very impressed."

Stan's father walked into the study. Immediately, his entry introduced a commanding presence to the room. He was a large, middle-aged man. Standing at least six-feet-four in height, his thick neck and broad shoulders suggested strength and power. With the exception of a slight thickness through the waistline, his body was well proportioned and muscular. His shortly cropped brown hair was beginning to thin in the front. Dressed in casual slacks and a short-sleeve shirt, he was clean-shaven and smelled strongly of expensive cologne. His pleasant face bore only a slight resemblance to that of his son.

He stood erectly, smiling. "Well, you must be Nick. Stan told me you'd be paying us a visit. Welcome to our home." His demeanor was dignified and formal.

Nick grasped Lester Mullins' extended hand, noticing his firm masculine, grip. "I'm pleased to meet you sir. I was just telling Mrs. Mullins that I love your splendid house. I don't think I've ever been in a more beautiful home."

"Thank you, son. We're very fortunate to live in a nice home. I understand that you're just returning from the war. Welcome home! We're all very proud of the men who are fighting for our country."

"Thank you, sir. It's good to be home."

Minnie suddenly appeared at the doorway. With a polite curtsy, she announced, "Breakfast is served."

"Thank you, Minnie," replied Mr. Mullins.

Stan spoke up. "Excuse us, Mom, Dad... Nick and I need to wash up a little bit before we eat."

The bathroom mirrored the splendor reflected by the rest of the house. As he washed his hands, Nick noticed the copper faucets, the marble washbasin, and the oversized bathtub.

They joined Stan's parents in the dining room where the food had been placed in the center of the table. Minnie had already prepared four places with dinnerware, cloth napkins and small glasses of tomato juice. A vase containing a mixed variety of flowers had been placed in the center of the table. Stan's parents sat in their customary places at opposite ends of the long table. Nick politely stood, waiting for someone to tell him where to sit. Stan pointed to one of the two remaining place settings. "You can sit there, Nick,"

After Nick was seated, Stan chose his customary seat beside his father, which was across the table from Nick.

Minnie came from the kitchen carrying the sterling silver coffee pot. "Can I serve anybody coffee?" she asked, meekly.

"Sure, Minnie. I guess we all want coffee...as usual. What about you, Nick? Do you drink coffee?" asked Mr. Mullins.

"Yes, sir," replied Nick. He tried to hide his nervousness.

Minnie poured each of them some coffee. "Cream and sugar are in the center of the table," she said, smiling at Nick.

Lester Mullins replied, "We know that, Minnie. Now you may be excused so you can go and have your breakfast."

"Thank you, suh," she set the coffee pot on the table, curtsied and left for the kitchen.

"She seems like a very nice lady," Nick commented.

Mr. Mullins took a sip of coffee. "Yes, Minnie is one of the best darkies in this town. She's been with us for years. Actually, we consider her a member of the family."

"Help yourself, Nick," said Stan. Nick dished a small portion of the omelet, a slice of tomato, and a strip of bacon into his plate. He selected one of the hot biscuits but displayed no interest in the other items of food.

Stan chuckled. "Aren't you gonna try any of Minnie's grits?"

"Is that what you call that food in the bowl?" asked Nick.

"Yeah. Haven't you ever eaten any grits?"

"No. I've never even heard of *grits*. What does it taste like?"

"Try it and see," said Stan.

"No, thanks," Nick replied. Although, to some extent, his appetite had returned, he wasn't hungry enough to experiment with an unfamiliar food that might be an exotic Southern cuisine.

Stan began passing dishes of food around the table to his parents. Having already served himself, Nick was embarrassed. He waited until the others started eating before he began. He decided that it would probably take some time for him to learn the proper manners and etiquette of affluent Southern people.

The food was delicious. After only a couple of bites, Nick realized that his appetite was better than he had earlier thought. He realized that he was feeling much better.

Stan's father eyed Nick. "Stan tells me that you were wounded in the war, Nick. I noticed your slight limp."

"Yes sir. I got out of the service with a medical discharge."

"Well, I'm glad it's over for you. You've done your part. Unfortunately, there are some young men who dodged the draft. Some people don't have any patriotism at all. I've been reading in the paper that a few people are even protesting the war. It's refreshing to see a young man like you who is willing to step up and defend his country."

"Thank you sir," Nick replied.

Stan's mother looked at Nick with sadness. "Was it pretty bad over there? Do you think it left you with any emotional scars?"

Mr. Mullins glared at her. "Mary Jane, you don't ask a soldier a stupid question like that! You should have enough sense to realize that he doesn't want to talk about his emotions!"

Nick felt embarrassed for the lady. Although he didn't want to offend Mr. Mullins, he answered her question anyway.

"Yes ma'am, it was bad in Korea. But I don't think I have any real emotional damage. I'm just a little jumpy sometimes."

Lester Mullins refilled his cup with coffee. He again turned to face Nick. "You're a real man, soldier. I wanted Stan to go into the army … maybe even spend some time in Korea. That might have made a man out of him. But he was ruled 4F. 'Unfit for duty,' they said … on account of a little hole in his eardrum."

Nick didn't answer, for he couldn't think of any response. He recognized that Lester Mullins was an insensitive man who felt the need to control any conversation in which he was involved.

Stan quickly spoke up. "I wanted to go into the army just like Nick. I'm sorry I didn't fight in the Korean War, but they wouldn't take me because of my bad ear." He looked at his dad.

Mr. Mullins' eyes met those of his son. He shook his head sadly. "Stan, looking back on the time they tried to draft you into the army, I don't believe you were *that* sorry they didn't take you. It's probably a good thing they turned you down because you would probably have been killed. Some men, like Nick here, are cut out for combat. But with your non-aggressive nature, I don't believe you would've made a good combat soldier. But your mother and I are proud of you, anyway." He softened the cruelty of his words with a reassuring pat on his son's back. Stan's face reddened with frustration and embarrassment.

Nick felt sorry for him. He stopped eating and looked at Stan's father. "Oh, I don't know about that, Mr. Mullins. Stan might have made a great combat soldier. You can't judge what a man will do in battle by how he behaves in normal society. Nobody's cut out for war. It's not normal for people to kill people they don't even know." His nervousness began to return, causing a slight tremble in his hands.

"Yeah, but some people just don't have the right stuff to fight in war. Let's face it, a lot of men are just plain scared."

"Yeah, I know what you mean…Men like *me*. I can't remember a day of war when I wasn't scared. Every soldier that I ever met was scared in battle." Nick was becoming angry. He felt his heart pounding.

"Nick, you're just trying to be modest. I believe that you were probably plenty *anxious*, but I don't believe you were really *scared*. And even if you were, you still faced war with courage."

There was a lull in the conversation as Minnie brought in a bowl of steaming hot molasses for dessert.

"Excuse my ignorance," said Nick. "That stuff that Minnie brought in looks good, but what is it?"

Stan laughed. "It's molasses. It's like syrup, but much more delicious. We make it from sugar cane. You eat it on a buttered biscuit."

74

"Thank you, Minnie," said Mrs. Mullins. Minnie curtsied, smiled and went back into the kitchen.

Starting with Nick, Stan passed the bowl of molasses around the table. Nick dished out a small portion of the dessert and selected another biscuit from the pan.

Stan's father pushed away his plate. "I'm so full I could pop. That Minnie is gonna kill me yet with her good cooking. Say, Nick ... Stan tells me you used to box in college. He said that you were even better in football. Now those are two activities that take real guts to participate in. I don't know if Stan ever told you, but I used to play football. That's a rugged game."

Mrs. Mullins smiled. "Stan is also a good athlete. In college, he was a great tennis player. He plays tennis with me sometimes, and beats me every time."

"*Tennis?* What kind of a game is *tennis?* It's typical that Stan would play games with his mother because tennis is sure not a man's game. I wanted Stan to play football, but he never had the agility or the stomach for it." said Stan's father.

"But I believe that tennis requires as much agility as football," countered Stan's mother.

"Look, Mary Jane, don't give me a lecture about athletics. What would a woman know about sports, anyway?"

Stan's eyes reflected anger. "Goddammit, mom's right! Tennis probably requires a hell of a lot *more* agility than football!"

"How would you know?" asked Mr. Mullins, "You never had the right stuff to play football...and don't use that kind of language in our home. You're not in a poolroom!"

"Sorry, Dad." Stan hung his head.

Except for Lester Mullins, everyone at the table seemed to be uncomfortable. For a short while they sat without speaking.

Finally, Mr. Mullins placed his hand on the shoulder of his son and smiled at him. "Look, son, I don't mean to be critical of you. All I'm saying is that everybody is different. Some men just have a less competitive nature than others. You're like your mother, here. There's nothing wrong with that. But

75

Nick, here, is one of those competitive men who is inclined toward more masculine things…He boxed, played football, and fought in the war!" He turned to face Nick. "Mr. Parilli, with people like you fighting the war for us, we're sure to win. I'm proud of you."

It was difficult for Nick to believe that a father could be so cruel and condescending to his son. In comparing Stan's manhood to that of a stranger, his father had drawn attention to what he perceived to be his son's deficiencies. It was as if Nick embodied all of the masculine attributes that Lester Mullins had hoped for, but had found lacking, in his own son. A father who would treat his son this way was obviously insecure about his own manhood.

Nick changed the subject. "Mr. Mullins, Stan tells me that you're the mayor of the City of Cedar Valley. That's quite a responsibility."

"Yes, I am. But being mayor in this little town is not that difficult. After all, the population here is only a little above 3,000. Also, my brother is the sheriff and he does a great job of keeping the peace. You won't find much crime in our town."

Lester Mullins took a final sip of coffee, dabbed his mouth with the napkin and slowly stood. "Nick, if you'll excuse Stan and me for just a few minutes, we've got to go into my study and go over some plans for a house we're building. Why don't you get another cup of coffee and wait for Stan in the living room? We won't be but a few minutes. Mrs. Mullins can entertain you until we're through."

"That's fine with me," said Nick. "Take your time."

Lester and Stan Mullins left the room. Stan's mother stood and said, "Nick, I have to go upstairs and finish getting dressed. Minnie will attend to whatever you need. Make yourself comfortable in the living room. Stan will join you very soon."

"Thanks, Mrs. Mullins, for the great breakfast…and for inviting me into your home. I sure appreciate it."

"My pleasure, Nick." She smiled and walked away.

Since Minnie had already removed the coffee pot from the dining table, Nick walked into the kitchen to pour himself another cup of coffee. Minnie was seated on a stool at the kitchen table having her breakfast.

"Hello, Minnie," said Nick, "I just came in here for a little more coffee."

"He'p yo'se'f, suh," she replied, between bites of food. He poured his coffee and chose a stool beside her.

Nick smiled at her. "Minnie, you prepared a great breakfast. I finally got up enough nerve to taste your grits. They're not bad."

Minnie displayed a shy smile. "From what I've heard, people up Nawth don't know what good eatin' is. Say, Mistah Nick, what part of the Nawth do you come from?"

"I'm from Chicago. But I'm moving to the South. I'll probably settle in Louisiana after my visit here."

She took her last bite of the omelet. "How do you like the South so far?"

"I haven't been here long enough to really make up my mind. Do you like the South?"

She stood and began to stack up her dishes and clear away the food from the table. "I like it fine, I guess. Ain't never lived nowhere else. I like livin' with the Mullins. They's been mighty good to me…Treats me like one of the fambly. Why, I hepped raise little Stan. Man, he was a mighty rowdy boy! Always pullin' some kinda prank." She chuckled at the memory.

"Well, if they consider you one of the family, why don't they invite you to sit down and eat with them? After all, there are eight places at that big dining room table."

Ignoring his remark, Minnie turned away from him and began to place the stack of dishes in the sink. A long silence followed as she busied herself with trivialities.

Finally she spoke. "Mistah Nick, I don't mean no disrespec', suh, but you got a lot to l'arn about our ways here in the South. I ain't faultin' you none, 'cause you's from the Nawth an' don't know no better. But I'm tellin' you, right now, that you shouldn't go stickin' yo' nose into other people's business! It'll only bring you trouble. I knows that the Mullins cares for me like fambly. I hope that you'll forgive me for speakin' to you in such a way, but it's for yo' own good, suh."

Nick felt that he had again overstepped some invisible boundary. "I didn't mean to pry into your business, Minnie. I apologize. I had no cause to butt in. Obviously, you seem happy with the way things are."

"Don't know no other way, Mistah Nick. Now if you'll excuse me, I've gotta git back to work."

Carrying his coffee with him, Nick turned and walked back into the dining room. Before he could sit down at the table, Stan walked into the room, displaying an elaborate grin.

"Dad and I got finished with our business for today," said Stan. "Come on, Nicky, we've gotta get moving! I've got a lot to show you today. But first, I've gotta drive out to one of the houses we're building and check on something…after that, we've got the day all to ourselves."

They walked out the front door and Stan picked up Nick's duffel bag. They followed the sidewalk around the corner of the house to the outside stairway to Stan's basement apartment.

Stan had been accurate in his description of his apartment, for the simplicity of the living quarters was a contradiction to the lavish décor of the interior of the house upstairs. Although clean and relatively uncluttered, the apartment was austere in character and contained only the bare necessities for living. The room contained a large, walk-in closet where Stan kept an elaborate stash of clothing. A desk and filing cabinet rested in the corner.

Stan pointed to the unmade bed. "This is my bed, and I don't allow anyone else in it—unless it's a good-looking Southern gal." He laughed and gestured toward the bed beside it. "And this is your bed, Nicky." He tossed Nick's duffel bag onto the bed.

"Stan, I can't stand to wear this uniform for another minute. I have a change of clothes in my bag, but they're wrinkled. Can you loan me something to wear for the day? I'm gonna buy me some clothes as soon as I have a chance."

"Sure, pal. Just pick out something from my closet."

"No, Stan...I'd rather you'd pick something for me."

"Well, okay," Stan replied, "if you're too timid." He took a short-sleeved blue sport shirt and a pair of gray slacks from the closet and tossed them on Nick's bed. "How about socks and shoes?"

"No, I've got plenty of socks, and I can wear my army shoes. They're okay."

Stan draped his arm around Nick's shoulders. "Nicky, old pal, I've got some real classy duds for you to wear tonight. We're really going to deck out for the dance!"

"Stan, I sure appreciate it, man." He quickly got dressed.

They immediately left the apartment and climbed into Stan's vehicle. Stan wheeled the car out of the driveway and sped toward Highway 11, the main road.

"Damn!" Nick exclaimed. "Slow this thing down! I don't want to survive the war only to get killed by a crazy man driving a car like a bat out of hell!"

"Oh, you're just nervous. Probably just suffering from a bad case of combat fatigue." He laughed and delivered a playful punch to Nick's shoulder.

Nick only smiled. "Where are we going, anyway?"

"Got to go check and see if the lumber was delivered to one of the houses we're building. We gotta start putting the roof on the house early Tuesday morning."

"How far we gotta go?"

"Not far, just about five miles."

"Stan, how is the house construction business going, anyway? Is business good?"

"Business is great. We're in the process of building three houses, now. Dad has bought up all the property he can find for a decent price. I do most of the managing of the business. But sometimes it's pretty hard to please Dad."

"I'd say that you pretty well have it made, Stan. I wish I had an opportunity like yours."

Stan slowed the speed of the car. "I don't know, Nicky. Sometimes I wish I was doing something else."

"Why?" Nick asked.

"Can't you see why? Dad doesn't really have any respect for me. Didn't you pick up on that in our conversation at breakfast?"

"Well, he was a little hard on you, I guess. But I'm sure your dad loves you and wants the best for you."

"Yeah, maybe so." Stan turned right onto Wilson Road.

The day was sunny and hot. For a couple of miles, they remained quiet as Nick gazed at the beautiful surrounding farmland. The car passed over a bridge that crossed a broad expanse of Ft. Davis Lake. The crystal clear water was still and unruffled. Like a gigantic mirror, it reflected the azure sky and the fluffy cumulus clouds above. The nearby green foothills gradually rose to blend with the distant, blue hazy ridges of the Smoky Mountains, defining the eastern horizon. He marveled at the beauty of East Tennessee.

Nick eyed the scattered farmhouses as they passed through the countryside. While a few of them were expensive homes, the vast majority of them were modest dwellings in the medium price range. A few were downright shacks, dilapidated structures that were accompanied by rotting, gray barns and outhouses that were nestled in weedy fields behind them. These houses appeared to be almost unfit for habitation. Earlier, when Stan had driven him to the Mullins' home from the bus station, Nick had scarcely noticed the condition of any of the houses in the area. It became obvious to him that the magnificence of the Mullins home was a rarity among the houses in the surrounding area.

Stan pulled the car into a rutted, temporary dirt driveway behind a large flatbed truck full of lumber. In front of the lumber truck were two pickup trucks. To the right of the improvised driveway stood the half-finished shell of a medium-size house. Two men were unloading the lumber

80

from the flatbed truck and placing it in neat stacks beside the house. Upon seeing the arrival of Stan, the workers looked up. Nick and Stan got out of the car and walked toward the house.

One of the workers continued to unload lumber. Having recognized Stan when he drove up, the other man removed his work gloves and stuffed them into his hip pocket. He then walked to meet Stan and shook hands with him.

"Well, I see that the lumber got here," said Stan, "I hated to ask you to come out to the jobsite on the Fourth of July weekend, but I had to get this lumber on the property by today. We've gotta start getting this house under roof by Tuesday afternoon. We were scheduled to start Monday, but it's a holiday."

"No problem," answered the man, "I don't want to get behind any more than you do. Hell, your old man is already breathing down my neck."

"Don't worry about my dad. I'm running this business." Stan seemed to resent the man's allusion to his father.

"Yeah, you may do the runnin,' but your old man does the payin.' When are you gonna get me some more help?"

"Hell, House Cat, I'm working on it. By the way, shake hands with my best pal, Nicky Parilli. Nicky, this is my foreman, Gilbert Jennings…His name's Gilbert, but people in these parts call him 'House Cat.'"

In size, House Cat was about the height and weight of Stan, but more muscular in build. On the back of his head a dirty cap covered a portion of his blonde crew cut hair which stood in stark contrast to his dark, ruddy face, the result of countless hours of exposure to the sun. The skin on his calloused hands appeared to belong to a man twice his age.

House Cat eyed Nick suspiciously as the men shook hands. He spoke with a pronounced Southern drawl. "How ya doin'? You from these parts?"

"I'm doing great," replied Nick. "No, I'm not from around here. I'm from Chicago, originally."

"Yeah, you *sound* like a damned Yankee. By the way, what kind of a friggin' name is 'Nicky?' Sounds like a girl's name." His benign smile softened the sarcastic tone of his remark.

Nick returned his smile. "Well, come to think of it, 'Nicky' does sound like a girl's name. But it's not my name. My name is 'Nick'…'Nicky' is just a disgusting tag that Stan hung on me. By the way, what kind of a name is 'House Cat?' Sounds like an animal's name. How'd you ever get labeled with that?"

House Cat laughed. "That name was handed down to me by my dad. He was also called 'House Cat.' When I was growing up, everybody called me 'Little House Cat.' Now that I'm grown up, I'm just plain ol' 'House Cat.'"

What was your grandfather called?" asked Nick.

" 'House Cat.'" He replied. The three men laughed.

Stan again shook hands with House Cat. "We gotta go. I just came out here to make sure the lumber came in. How about the plywood?"

House Cat pointed toward the house. "We already unloaded it. It's all under that tarp over there." He turned to Nick. "It was good to meet you, *Nicky*, even if you are a damned Yankee."

"Yeah, I was glad to meet you, too, House Cat … *you damned Rebel.*" House Cat only laughed.

Stan backed the car out and pulled away, heading back toward Cedar Valley. "What do you think of House Cat?"

"I like him. Is he good at his job?"

"He's the best. But he's always nagging me for more help."

"I wonder why people call him 'House Cat'?" asked Nick. "And even his dad and granddad are stuck with that nickname."

"Maybe it's because they've always built houses. Hell, I don't know. About half the people in Cedar Valley are stuck with nicknames, and most of those names are passed on to future generations. Some of the nicknames are pretty weird."

Stan drove more slowly on the way back toward town, occasionally pointing out attractive sights and places of interest. Nick was struck by the beauty of East Tennessee: the placid, clear lakes, the plush, green, rolling hills that faded into the distance, and the breathtaking view of the nearby Smoky Mountains. Realizing that he would only be in Tennessee for a few days before pressing further southward, he wondered if Louisiana held the same allure. Having lived most of his life in an overcrowded concrete jungle riddled with crime, corruption, and squalor, he hoped that somewhere in the South he would finally find the home that he had always secretly sought: easy-going, friendly people, a slower pace of living, and magnificent beauty. He realized that no place was perfect, but his brief exposure to the Southern lifestyle convinced him that it was far better than the depressing life that he had left behind. Although he had been in the South for less than a day, he was already strongly drawn to the region.

After they had lunch in downtown Cedar Valley, Stan spent the remainder of the afternoon giving Nick a tour of the small town: the County Court House, the Cedar Valley Museum, the schools, the Memorial Building, Ft. Davis Dam that spanned the Tennessee River, and other places of historical interest. Late in the afternoon, Stan drove them home where they had dinner with Stan's parents. After eating, they retreated to the basement apartment where Nick called his uncle to inform him of his plan to arrive at his home in Buras, Louisiana in three days. Then they began to prepare for their exciting evening at the dance.

Chapter 7

Stan was in a cheerful mood as he drove toward downtown Cedar Valley. He savored the metallic ring of the Hollywood muffler and the clean, fresh smell of the newness in the interior of his car. In the seat beside him, Nick repeatedly switched stations on the radio in search of some music that appealed to him. He finally settled for a song played by the Gordon Jenkins Orchestra, *Again*, sung by Joe Graden. The music of the big band era had always appealed to him.

Stan winced. "Damn, Nicky, can't you find better music than that? It sounds like a funeral dirge!"

He assumed control of the radio and punched the customary middle button that distributed country music. Hank Snow was singing, *I'm Moving On*.

"Now that's good music," said Stan. "Why do you like that stiff, formal stuff that you're always listening to?"

"Stan, you know that I don't like country music. Up North, we call that crap you're listening to 'shit-kickin' music.'"

Stan only laughed. "By the way, Nicky, you look great in those clothes I loaned you. How do they fit?"

"They fit pretty well. I particularly like the color of the shirt and the way it harmonizes with the pants." Since the dance wasn't a formal affair, both men had dressed in casual clothing, sport shirts and slacks. Nick had cast aside his army shoes in favor of a pair of Stan's loafers.

Stan lit a cigarette. "We've got a little time before the dance starts, so what do you want to do?"

"Stan, you know the town. What do you suggest?"

"Want some booze before we go to the dance?"

"Oh, I don't know, Stan. I've been drinking too much lately. But if you want some liquor, go ahead and get it."

"You'd enjoy the dance a lot more if you'd have a couple of drinks. What's a dance without booze?"

"Well, maybe I'll have a couple of small drinks, but that's all. I'm just now getting to feel good after my long binge."

Stan's face bore a mischievous expression. "Have you ever drunk any moonshine?"

"Moonshine? No, I've heard of it, but I've never drunk any. I know that it's booze of some kind. What's it made out of?"

"It's made out of corn, mostly, but sometimes they use potatoes, or whatever else they want to make it out of. Some people around the South call it 'splo'. Hell, man, it's homemade, and it's got a kick like a mule. Come on, Nicky, let's get some splo. But you'll have to go kinda easy on it. It's potent stuff."

"Where do you buy it?"

"At a place out in the country, maybe five or six miles from here. We can get there in ten minutes."

"Well, okay. But you told me that this was a dry county. Does your uncle, the sheriff, know about this place?"

"Hell, I don't know, and I also don't give a damn…and don't start some of your self-righteous crap about always obeying the law." He playfully punched Nick and broke into laughter.

85

Stan turned off into a side road and drove the car in the direction of the bootlegger. He became quiet and appeared to be in deep thought. "Nicky, let me ask you something. When you were living at home with your parents...did your dad respect you?"

"Sure. We had a mutual respect for each other. Why?"

"It just seems that my dad doesn't respect me. No matter what I do, I can never please him. He seems to have a lot of respect for you, though."

"Yeah, well, he probably just doesn't understand you. Maybe he's just obsessed with this heroic stuff that doesn't really define a man—like boxing, football, and fighting in the war."

"No, it's more than that. I don't believe that his admiration for you is based so much on you being a *hero*. I think that he feels that in your life you have always been a part of something that's bigger than you...a cause where your involvement can make a difference. Let's face it, Nicky, you were in the army, where your contribution might have even helped a little in changing the outcome of the war. Hell, even when you were on the football team, you were a part of something that had a cause and a shared purpose." His expression was sad.

"Stan, you *are* a part of something. You're a part of your family, a part of your dad's construction business, and a part of this great community."

"Yeah, that's true, but I'm sure that Dad feels like I didn't *earn* being a part of those things. I was just born into them. I inherited them. I feel useless and undeserving. It seems that I ought to belong to something, to be a part of something bigger, where my participation might make a difference."

Nick groped for the right words. "If you feel that way, maybe you ought to run for public office, join some club, or civic organization. Do you think that maybe your dad made you feel this way?"

Stan became frustrated. "I know damned well he did! He has never been proud of me, no matter what I did. Do you know what I've been thinking about doing? Moving out of the house and getting my own apartment! I might even find me another line of work!" For emphasis, he jabbed the heel of his hand against the steering wheel.

Nick felt sorry for him. "I don't know how smart it would be to quit working for your dad. It's a tough world out there. But finding your own apartment might be a good idea."

Stan slowed the vehicle and turned left into a rutted dirt road that meandered through a small grove of trees and finally into a weedy meadow. He parked the car in front of a dilapidated building in the center of the field. It had been constructed with rough, unpainted lumber that was graying with age, and portions of the front were covered with rusting pieces of corrugated metal. Patches of ragweed and Johnson grass grew between the carcasses of several junked cars that littered the area. On the front of the makeshift building a crude sign read, *Chili's Garage.* Obviously, the 'garage' pretext was only a front for the purpose of their actual business activity: the sale of illegal liquor.

In the gravel parking lot in front of the building, a car backed out from between two other parked vehicles and drove away.

"Well, is this the liquor store?"

"This is it." said Stan.

"Wow!" said Nick, sarcastically. "What an elegant place!"

Stan laughed. "The place may not be pretty, but they sell a lot of moonshine. You can also buy bonded liquor here. I know the guy who runs the place...Chili Barrett. He's a nice guy."

"*Chili?* Is that another nickname?"

"Yeah, I guess so. I never really thought about it. Wait here for me and I'll go buy the booze." He got out of the car and walked into the side door of the building.

Nick switched stations on the radio and idly whiled away the time, waiting for Stan to return with the whiskey. The melancholy voice of Jo Stafford singing, *You Belong to Me* flowed from the radio. He watched as a heavy-set man with a pale complexion and a crop of conspicuous red hair left the building. As he walked toward his car, he briefly studied Nick with an inquisitive gaze; then he got into his car and drove away.

In a short time, Stan returned carrying a paper bag and a soft drink. He returned to his seat behind the wheel of the car and grinned at Nick before removing the pint bottle of booze from the paper bag. "Let's have a little drink, Nicky."

"In a dry county? Right here in front of the place?"

Stan laughed. "Hell yes. Why not? Still the same old cautious Nicky! You don't have to worry. The police won't bother us."

He handed Nick the moonshine and the soft drink. Nick unscrewed the lid of the bottle and sniffed the strong, reeking contents. The homemade liquor was as clear as spring water.

"Does it taste as bad as it smells?" Nick asked.

"This stuff is pretty strong, so you'll have to immediately chase it with a big swallow of that *Coke*." Stan answered.

Nick cautiously took only a small sip and quickly washed it down with a large drink from the *Coke* bottle.

"Whoooeee! Damn, Stan!" he gasped. "My throat is on fire! Whew! Man that stuff is strong! Are you sure it's safe to drink this vile stuff?"

Stan laughed uproariously. "Give that bottle to me, pal! I'll show you how that stuff is supposed to be drunk!" He took a drink from the bottle without bothering with the chaser.

"Aaah, that's good stuff!" Stan displayed a pleasant smile. Nick declined Stan's offer of a second drink.

Twenty minutes later, Stan parked his car in the parking lot beside the Memorial Building where the dance was being held. They swallowed another drink from the bottle. Since alcohol was prohibited at the dance, Stan placed it in the glove compartment.

The sound of the music from the dance grew louder as they walked toward the entrance of the Memorial Building. When they reached the lobby, Stan paid the admission fees for both of them.

A cacophonous blend of music and noisy conversation greeted them as they entered the huge room where the dance was in progress. The interior of the building was actually a gymnasium where Cedar Valley High School played basketball games and held other school activities.

Bleachers rose from the floor on each side of the basketball court; and on the opposite end of the gym was a large elevated stage where high school band concerts and plays were held. An array of colored balloons dangled from the stage and a banner hanging above read, "Welcome to the Annual July 4th Dance."

At least a hundred people were in attendance. Those without dates were seated in the bleachers. Dating couples occupied the seats at tables near the stage.

Many couples were on the gym floor dancing to the music provided by an on-stage stereo system operated by a disc jockey. He had selected a diverse mixture of music styles for the evening entertainment. Because the crowd was composed of people of various ages and tastes in music, the selections alternated between *country* and *popular* music. Sometimes a jitterbug number was included. For the more romantic songs the overhead lights were dimmed. The popular song, *I Can Dream, Can't I?* a Patty Andrews hit of 1949 echoed softly through the large room.

Nick followed Stan as they made their way across the gym floor toward the bleachers. Stan greeted a man. "Hi, Flat Head." They continued to walk toward the bleachers to select a seat.

Nick laughed. "Well, that was obviously a nickname. But how did he ever acquire a name like that?"

"Hell, didn't you get a good look at his head?"

Nick turned for another look at the man. The second glance confirmed that, although insensitive, the nickname was fitting. Stan often spoke to several acquaintances Many of them had nicknames.

Nick and Stan took seats in the bleachers among several acquaintances of Stan's. Some of these people were girls without dates who had come only to observe the event; but most were men who had attended the dance 'stag' who were hoping to become acquainted with one of the unescorted girls. Unfortunately, most of the prettier girls were not in the bleachers; instead, they were either sitting at the tables or on the dance floor with their boyfriends.

Stan greeted several of his friends in the bleachers as he and Nick began to watch the dancing couples on the gym floor and the people seated at the tables. Nick noticed at one of the tables a brunette girl sitting by herself, apparently unescorted. Although she was a considerable distance away, he could see that she was beautiful. She looked around searchingly, as though she were expecting someone to join her.

Nick turned to Stan. "Hey, pal, see that pretty brunette sitting by herself at the center table near the stage? Do you know her?"

Stan spotted the girl. "Sure I know her. She's my cousin."

"Your cousin?"

"She's my first cousin, Lauren, Uncle Larry's daughter."

"Do you mean she's the *sheriff's* daughter?"

"Yep. Why? Are you workin' up an appetite for her? Forget it, Nicky. She's not your type."

"What do you mean, she's not 'my type?' Do you think she's too good for me?"

"No, it's not that. I like her, but she's a little snooty. It's not her fault, though. Her dad has always been very protective of her. Hell, she's the apple of his eye. He doesn't think anyone is good enough for her."

"I wonder why she's alone at a dance?" Nick kept eyeing her.

"I guess she's waiting for Mike." said Stan.

"Mike? Who's Mike?"

"Mike Bronson."

"Well, you said that her dad didn't think anybody was good enough for her. What about this guy, 'Mike Bronson?'"

"Nicky, it's sort of a strange situation. Lauren is twenty-two years old, but her daddy treats her like she's sixteen. He

90

allows Mike to 'date' her to keep other guys away from her. You see, Mike is one of Uncle Larry's deputies. He's more a bodyguard than a date. I don't think Lauren thinks of him as a 'date.' But he claims that he's dating her. Maybe you ought to just forget her."

"Hell, Stan, I was just curious about her. I don't intend to try to date her. But she sure has the good looks. Looking at you, I can't see much family resemblance, as far as having good looks."

Stan only laughed. "Screw you, you ugly bastard!"

Nick chuckled. "What makes you say she's kinda snooty?"

"Maybe she's not so snooty. Maybe it's just her dad that tries to push her into all this 'society' stuff: debutante, beauty contests, finishing school, and all of that pretentious shit. I like her but we really don't have much in common. I can see that you're attracted to her. Would you like for me to introduce you to her? Just remember—if I do, she may just snub you."

"I don't know, Stan. I don't want to tangle with the sheriff. Besides, as you said, she may feel that she's too good for me."

They watched as a stocky, red haired man walked up to Lauren's table. Nick recognized him. It was the man that he had seen at *Chili's Garage*, the place that had sold them the whiskey.

Nick was surprised. He wondered what business the sheriff's deputy had at a bootlegging place. He punched Stan on the shoulder. "Stan…that guy who just sat down with your cousin, Lauren. I saw him earlier at *Chili's*. What could he have been doing there?"

"Oh, Nicky, you must be mistaken. It was probably just somebody who looked like him."

"No, that's him. You were there, too. Didn't you see him?"

"No, but even if it was him, what's the big deal? Maybe he just went there to get something fixed on his car. After all, Chili *does* run a garage, you know. Anyway, this is a small town where everybody knows each other. They may even be kin. Don't jump to so many conclusions."

Nick dropped the subject. He kept eyeing the table where Lauren and the deputy were sitting, while Stan had taken a sudden interest in a pretty, unescorted blonde girl in the bleachers. Soon, Stan was leading the girl toward the dance floor.

He grinned. "Find you a woman and join us! I didn't bring you here to just sit around and lust."

Nick smiled but ignored his suggestion. With fascination, he continued to fix his eyes on Lauren and the deputy, who were now walking together toward the dance floor. The rich, smooth voice of Tony Bennett began crooning the current hit, *Because of you.* As he watched them dance, he noticed that dancing was not the deputy's greatest talent as he clumsily led Lauren around the dance floor. When the song ended, the deputy followed Lauren back to their table. They stood and briefly talked; then he turned and walked toward the door.

Having finished the dance, Stan escorted his dancing partner back to the bleachers where they took a seat beside Nick.

"Nicky, I want you to meet Kathy Martin. Kathy, this is my old college buddy, Nicky Parilli."

"Hi, Nicky." She flashed a friendly grin. Nick decided that when viewed at close range, Kathy was prettier than he had at first believed. Her looks were enhanced by her pleasant smile.

"Nicky, are you just gonna sit here all night?" Stan asked.

"I don't know anybody, Stan. Hell, give me a break!"

"Why don't you find somebody to dance with?"

"I'll tell you what, Stan. I'll ask your cousin to dance if you'll introduce me to her. She's sitting by herself, now. The deputy left a while ago." The thought of meeting her made him nervous.

Stan peered at Lauren's table. "Okay, if that's what you want." He stood and took Kathy by the hand. "Don't be surprised if she snubs you." Trying unsuccessfully to hide his limp, Nick followed them across the dance floor to Lauren's table.

When they neared her table she immediately saw Stan. She smiled, stood and hugged him when they met. Stan introduced Kathy to her, whom she already knew, and then, with an elaborate smile, he introduced Nick. "Lauren, this is my old college pal, Nicky Parilli. And. Nicky, this is Lauren Mullins, my favorite cousin."

She laughed as she took Nick's hand. "Your *only* cousin, you mean! Hello, Nicky. It's a pleasure to meet a friend of *my* favorite cousin." They laughed. Nick felt the soft, smooth texture of her warm hand. He reluctantly released it.

"Do you mind if we join you?" asked Stan.

"Not at all," Lauren replied, "I was beginning to get lonely, sitting here by myself. Mike had to leave. He was unexpectedly called to duty. I may leave shortly myself."

They all took a seat at the table.

"How will you get home?" asked Stan. "Is Mike coming back to get you?"

"No, I drove my own car. Sometimes Mike has to leave with little notice." Nick loved her melodious Southern accent.

In his nearness to her, Nick was nearly spellbound by her radiant beauty. He hadn't been this close to a beautiful girl since he had attended college. In her presence, he felt an awkwardness that he hadn't expected. He became slightly nervous and began to worry that the others might be able to recognize his anxiety.

Kathy said, "Nicky, while we were dancing, Stan told me that you just got back from the war."

"Yeah, but I'm out of the army now."

"Good," she said, "I'm glad it's over for you."

Nick noticed that Lauren's eyes studied him as he talked.

"Nicky has had a terrible time for the last two or three years," said Stan. "He's been through hell. Right Nicky? He also sometimes has panic attacks."

Nick seemed embarrassed. "Aw, Stan, don't spoil the party. They don't want to hear about my neuroses." Nick suddenly jumped as a blast of loud static exploded from the speakers.

93

"See?" Stan exclaimed. "The war has ruined his nerves. He jumps out of his skin every time he hears a loud noise."

Lauren looked at Nick and said, "Well, I suppose anybody's nerves would be jumpy at such a loud noise. I know that it made me jump, too." She seemed protective of Nick.

As Lauren continued to talk to Kathy, her eyes occasionally strayed to those of Nick's. He studied her lovely features. She was a woman of medium height with a stunning figure; but the feature that most captivated Nick was the capricious nature of her expressive blue eyes. They could quickly change from curiosity to sadness, or happiness, mirroring whatever mood she was experiencing at the moment. Her jet black hair flowed to her shoulders, and her bronzed skin contrasted with her white dress and made her perfect teeth appear even whiter when she smiled. She was indeed a beautiful woman. Nick's eyes suddenly captured hers, and for a long while they studied each other as their companions engaged in idle conversation.

"Lauren, what are you doing with yourself these days?" asked Kathy. "Somebody told me you were going back to college. I thought you already had your degree."

"I do have my undergraduate degree from U.T. I'm going back to college to work on my master's degree this fall."

"Are you working anywhere?" Kathy asked.

"I'm working part-time as a receptionist at Dr. Johnston's clinic for the summer. What have you been doing since school?"

"Nothing. I'm resting up from going to school. Right now, I'm just trying to have fun."

Stan grinned. "Speaking of having fun... Kathy? May I have this dance?"

"I thought you'd never ask!" She stood and took his hand and they hurried to the dance floor.

Nick was now left alone with Lauren. Several seconds of silence elapsed. He became more nervous, even speechless. In order to steady the slight tremble in his fingers, he clasped his hands together on the tabletop. He hadn't anticipated his panicky reaction to his first attempt at getting acquainted with a beautiful woman. His war experience was once again gnawing at his nerves. He regretted being introduced to her.

She seemed to sense his anxiety. "Stan has told me a little about you," she said. "You were wounded in the war, weren't you? I'm so sorry all of you soldiers had to be in that awful war." Her demeanor was friendly, but cautious, for she scarcely knew him; however, she seemed somehow attracted to his quiet manner and his obvious loneliness.

When he answered, his voice betrayed him with a slight quiver. He gasped for breath. "I was wounded, but not bad."

"Are you going to be in Cedar Valley for very long?"

"No, I'm...going on to Louisiana in...three or four days."

An awkward silence followed. Nick became almost terrified at the thought of continuing the conversation. His breathing became erratic. The tremble in his hands became obvious as he felt that he was on the verge of having a panic attack. *What's happening to me?* he wondered. His body began to violently shake. He lowered his head in embarrassment, avoiding her eyes.

He felt the warm, tender touch of her hands as they gently clasped his own trembling hands on the tabletop.

"There, now...you don't have to be nervous with me. Relax...Just be yourself, Nicky. You can talk to me..."

He slowly raised his head and saw the compassion in her eyes. When their eyes met, something connected between them. He felt a strange kinship to her. He saw in her eyes the same loneliness, the same yearning that he had always felt within himself. It was as if he were peering intently into a mirror that reflected the feelings within his own soul. He knew in his heart that they were, at least in this moment in time, kindred spirits. He felt that some mysterious message had passed between them. Almost magically, his trembling subsided as his nerves began to calm. In spite of his embarrassment, he smiled at her. Suddenly, she looked away.

"I'm sorry," he said.

95

"You don't have to apologize," she answered.

Stan and Kathy returned to the table, laughing and wheezing for breath. They both took a seat.

"Man, that jitterbug number really tuckered me out!" Stan gasped, "I must be out of shape!"

"Gosh, me too!" Kathy responded.

Stan turned to Lauren. "Well, did you and Nicky get to know each other a little bit?"

"Yes. A little bit," replied Lauren. Nick said nothing.

"Nicky, did you tell Lauren about our good times in college? And how you won a couple of medals during the war?"

"No. Stan, nobody's interested in that."

Stan appeared to be puzzled. "Why haven't you asked her to dance, Nicky? Man, you used to be the best dancer on campus!"

"Stan, why all the questions?" Nick asked.

"No special reason. I just thought we came here to have fun...Same old moody Nicky! Well, *I'm* gonna have fun. Come on, Kathy, let's dance." He eyed Nick curiously when he took Kathy's hand and again led her to the dance floor.

Nick and Lauren quietly watched as Stan and his girlfriend began to dance. Lauren's mood had changed. She again had become more distant and cautious. The conspicuous silence became disquieting to Nick as once again his anxiety began to mount. He became ashamed of the recent breakdown of his nerves. Also, the apparent sudden change in Lauren's mood puzzled him.

He could no longer bear the nerve-wracking silence, which seemed endless. Impulsively, he suddenly blurted out, "Lauren, I'm sorry I behaved the way I did...I don't know what came over me. You see, I sometimes have these nervous spells that come over me. The harder I try to avoid them, the worse they seem to be. It's very embarrassing...Damn it!"

"Hush, Nicky. Dance with me." Her eyes reflected her intuitive understanding of his anxiety. She smiled, reached across the table, and took his hand.

He became apprehensive. "But, Lauren…I can't dance to anything fast. I've got a stiff leg. Maybe we should wait for a slow song."

"Good. They're just starting a slow number, so you don't have an excuse." She gently pulled him up from his chair.

Strains of the romantic Perry Como ballad, *Some Enchanted Evening* echoed through the gymnasium. Once again the lights dimmed as he escorted her to the dance floor and took her in his arms. He held her close, savoring the tantalizing aroma of her raven hair as it brushed against his cheek, teasing him, exciting him. The soothing tempo of the romantic song was slow, enabling Nick to dance without experiencing pain in his knee. They smoothly glided across the dance floor.

She was an excellent dancer, so graceful that she seemed almost weightless, anticipating Nick's every move, responding to his slightest touch. She nestled her head against his chest when he gently pulled her even closer to him. In their coordinated movements, they became as one entity. Her responsiveness to his every lead strengthened his earlier perception of the mysterious kinship that existed between them.

A sense of relief came over him as he began to recognize that he felt more comfortable in her presence; for he realized that he had never before felt this close to a woman. He no longer feared her; in fact, he experienced a sudden urge to share his deepest feelings with her.

For a long while, they danced without speaking, enjoying their closeness. Strangely, at that moment, he *knew* that she intuitively understood the reasons for his anxiety and loneliness. He felt her breath and her lips brushing his neck when she finally whispered, "Is it better now? Are you okay?"

"Yes…I'm much better, now," he answered.

The music stopped and they returned to their table to join Stan and Kathy, who seemed to share an exceptionally happy mood. They all took seats at the table.

Kathy smiled. "I need to go to the ladies' room to powder my nose. Lauren, would you like to go with me?"

"Yes, that's a good idea," Lauren replied. "Would you please excuse us?" Nick and Stan watched as the two ladies disappeared among the crowd of people.

Displaying a happy grin, Stan draped his arm around Nick's shoulders. "Well, I'm happy to see that you and Lauren are finally getting friendly. You looked great on the dance floor!" Then he lowered his voice as if speaking confidentially. "Kathy and I are really hitting it off! Man, she is one hot babe! Listen, Nicky, I need a big favor out of you…Of course, it will probably be a big favor to you, too."

"What kind of favor?" Nick asked.

"Well, I know I brought you here, but I can't take you back home. I'm gonna take Kathy home, if you know what I mean." He winked before he continued. "I need for you to ask Lauren to take you home…She drove her own car, you know."

"Not a chance, pal," Nick replied. "I barely know her. She's a very nice girl. I don't want her to think that you and I cooked up some kind of a 'make out' deal. If you want her to take me home, you'll have to ask her yourself." He laughed. "Of course, I'd much rather ride home with her than with you."

The ladies returned and reclaimed their former seats. Lauren looked at her watch. "I've had a great time, but I promised Daddy I'd be home early. I need to be getting home pretty soon."

"Me too," Kathy replied. She placed her arms around Stan and playfully kissed him.

The lights suddenly dimmed and then quickly regained their intensity. A couple of seconds later a peal of thunder caused Nick to jump as it vibrated the building.

"We'd better go *now*," said Lauren. She quickly stood. "We're going to have a storm. We're liable to get soaked going to our cars."

Stan blurted out, "Lauren, could you do me a big favor? Could you take Nicky to my house for me? Kathy's brother dropped her off at the dance, so she doesn't have a ride home. I promised her I'd take her. I didn't really plan it this way."

Lauren eyed him suspiciously and then turned her eyes to Nick, who only shrugged innocently. She appeared to be indecisive and nervous. Another crack of thunder sent several people scurrying for the exits.

"Okay, Stan, I'll take him home," Lauren responded. "Come on, Nicky, we'd better hurry to my car before the storm really gets here."

They said goodbye to Stan and Kathy and headed for the exit. Nick's limp was obvious when he tried to keep up with Lauren's rapid pace. They walked outside into the first spattering of cold raindrops and quickly scurried to Lauren's vehicle. Another bolt of lightning struck nearby as she pulled out of the parking lot. Nick jerked, but remained fairly calm.

The rain slightly increased in intensity. Nick assumed a relaxed position and tried to ignore his mounting anxiety. Lauren again had changed moods, becoming strangely quiet. The storm had subsided to some extent and remained only moderate for several minutes.

Nick suddenly had the urge to talk to her. Although she had once again become emotionally distant, her former gentle and compassionate attitude had made him feel more comfortable in her presence. Her earlier display of affection had made him less fearful of expressing his feelings to her. He now realized that since his war experience, he had been in a state of emotional numbness. The horrors of the war had caused his conscious mind to repress all emotion. She had reawakened his ability to *feel*—and his sudden rediscovery of the experience of feeling had been more than his emotions could handle.

She seemed preoccupied as she drove slowly through the rainy night with her eyes glued to the highway. Her mysterious silence made Nick uneasy. He broke the silence with trivial conversation. "Did you have fun at the dance?"

Her eyes peered straight ahead. "Yes, it was okay."

"I hope that taking me to Stan's house is not too far out of your way." His tone was apologetic.

Her eyes never left the road in front of her. "Don't worry about it. I don't mind."

It became obvious to Nick that she didn't want to continue the conversation. Apparently, her moods could change as rapidly as the expressions in her eyes. For a while she drove without either of them speaking. He began to worry about the possibility of never seeing her again.

He summoned his courage. "Lauren, are you mad at me about something? Did I say something to offend you?"

"No." Her eyes remained expressionless.

Nick was startled when a simultaneous blast of thunder and lightning exploded very close to them, and the rain suddenly began to fall in torrents. In order to hide the quaking of his hands he clasped them together. His voice began to tremble when he resumed the conversation. "Lauren, forgive me if I'm being too forward, but when we were back at the dance, I thought that I detected something between us—something special that bonded us together…It made me believe that it was okay to *feel* again. Maybe I'm being awkward in the way I'm expressing it, but I sensed that you felt it too."

She didn't answer. Her changeable eyes mirrored sadness as she slowed the car to compensate for the sheets of rain that swept the road. The patter of falling hail joined the deluge of rain in a clamorous roar on the car roof.

"To hell with it!" Nick angrily exploded. "Apparently, I misread the whole situation! My emotions have been so damned screwed up, and I've experienced so much horror in my life I'm not able to handle or understand simple acts of kindness! Don't worry! You won't hear any more friendly shit from me!"

Nick's mounting anger increased his anxiety. His tremble became more obvious. The blinding lightning flashes grew more frequent and violent. Repeated explosions of thunder were almost deafening as hailstones the size of marbles bounced off the roof of the car. The windshield wipers labored uselessly as the violent wind drenched the car and the road with sheets of water. The headlights were unable to penetrate the wall of rain. Since Lauren could no longer see to drive, she pulled the car into the parking area of a closed service station.

The storm worsened. Lightning struck a nearby tree, splitting off a large limb that came crashing down precariously close to the car. Nick's anxiety had now escalated to terror. He shook violently, drew his knees up to his chest into a fetal position, covered his ears, and buried his head in his hands. He began to whimper. The artillery shells were again exploding around him; the grenade was bursting near him, riddling his body with shrapnel; once more he was charging up the hill toward the blazing machinegun; he was once again staring into the terrified eyes of the young boy he had killed.

He felt her arms encircle him as she pulled his trembling body against hers, hugging him tightly. She rocked him gently, as a mother would rock a baby as she repeatedly whispered reassuring words into his ear—sweet words, almost as if she were chanting a simple song. "Now, Now…It's going to be okay. It's just a little storm…it will soon pass. Don't worry…it's just a little storm…just a little storm…"

She continued to hold him for a long while until the storm began to subside. He abandoned his fetal position and sat limply and quietly in his seat until she finally released him. She scooted back to the driver's seat and sat quietly behind the wheel.

He realized that she somehow understood the horrors that resided in his tortured mind. *But how could she? How could anyone who hadn't lived through that terrible hell ever have the slightest understanding of the wretchedness of war?*

His nerves gradually began to calm. "I'm sorry," he said. He hung his head in embarrassment and turned away from her.

The storm was apparently over, but the rain continued to fall steadily in a gentle patter on the car roof. Neither of them spoke for a long while. Tears filled her eyes as she finally turned to face him. "Nicky?" He continued to look away from her. "Nicky, please look at me," she pleaded.

He turned his head toward her and looked into her eyes. She hung her head as she spoke. "Do you remember what you said earlier about your feeling that you and I had somehow bonded? Well…I don't know about that, but I'll admit that I'm attracted to you. I quickly came to my senses because I don't want to lead you on. I don't really know anything about you—we just met. It's impossible for anything to ever develop between us. We have no future together, Nicky."

"Why not?" Nick asked. "I know that I don't have much to offer a girl, and my life is kinda screwed up, but I can change."

"Nicky, you're leaving for Louisiana in three or four days. I don't want to get involved with you for a three-day fling only to see you leave, and then never see you again."

"But maybe I could write to you, and when I get settled in Louisiana, we could…"

"Forget it, Nicky. We're both attracted to each other, but let's face it, we don't really know each other. I'm supposed to go back to college this fall, and, after all, you're just passing through. Neither of us can afford to lose our heads over a little feeling that we think we have for each other. Besides, there are other reasons that a relationship between us would be impossible."

"What other reasons?"

"Nicky, our lives are totally different. Also, I have certain responsibilities…my life is very complicated."

Nick was sad. "Yeah, Lauren, I can't blame you. I really don't have much to offer a proper girl like you. You have class, but I come from a poor family, I'm a college dropout, I'm screwed up because of the war, I'm a drifter without a real home, and I don't even have a job. Hell, I don't even have a purpose. You should run from me, because I…"

Impulsively, she quickly leaned toward him and kissed him. He took her in his arms and they embraced for a long while. She slowly pulled away from him and rested her head on his chest as he held her in his arms. Finally, they released each other. Neither of them spoke.

Again, she finally slid behind the steering wheel. The rain had now diminished to only a small, steady drizzle when she started the car and slowly drove away. She turned left onto Highway 11, and Nick recognized that they were now nearing the Mullins home. He realized that after she left him their brief relationship was probably over—before it had really begun. He knew that if he ever hoped to see her again, he'd better act quickly.

"Lauren, can I call you tomorrow?"

"No, Nicky. Please don't call me. Forget about me."

She wheeled the car into the Mullins' long driveway, drove up to the house and stopped. She kept the motor idling, indicating that she expected him to get out. He reached for her in an attempt to kiss her goodnight, but she only pulled away. "Nicky, please don't try to kiss me." Her eyes expressed sadness.

Without saying a word, he got out of the car. He stood back as she turned the car around, lowered her window, and leaned toward him. "Goodbye, Nicky," she said.

"Yeah, goodbye, Lauren."

She then drove away. He stood motionless and watched as her car disappeared into the wet, misty night.

Chapter 8

Nick awoke early from a near sleepless night. He had spent most of the night thinking of Lauren—dear, sweet *Lauren*. The melodious word rolled off his tongue like a delectable golden drop of nectar. He couldn't get her off his mind. The name stirred ambivalence in him; for her gentle, nurturing nature could unexpectedly change, reflecting a cold, dispassionate disposition.

She appeared to be a contradiction. She had a practical side to her nature in which she seemed determined to conform to her well-laid plans for her future; however, Nick suspected that, hiding beneath her veneer of structured pragmatism was a disposition of spontaneity, a desire to be her own person and to be set free from the constraints of obedience and conformity.

Her unexpected gesture of embracing Nick during his moment of panic and her impetuous kiss during their discussion suggested that, beneath her practical demeanor, she held within her nature a rebellious and untamed spirit.

He had mixed feelings when he thought of Lauren. The fact that he would probably never again see her made him sad; however, the experience of meeting her had also been liberating for him; for she had resurrected a province of his personality that he had repressed for more than two years: the capacity to *dare to feel happy.* In spite of his attraction to Lauren, he began to consider leaving for Louisiana immediately.

A look at his watch told him that it was 10:45 a.m. Although he was still sleepy, he decided to get up. He rose and sat on the bed facing Stan, who was lying on his back in his private bed, snoring. He studied the sleeping figure of Stan, wondering if it would be inconsiderate to awaken him, for he hadn't come home from his date until early morning after Nick had fallen asleep.

Nick looked around the small bedroom, noticing Stan's discarded clothing scattered around the area near his bed. He decided to awaken him; after all, he knew that Stan wouldn't want to sleep away the day.

Nick walked to his bed and shook him. Stan only rolled over onto his side and snorted. After another vigorous shake, he quickly sat up in bed and eyed Nick with a puzzled stare. Gradually, his eyes expressed recognition. With an elaborate yawn, he stretched his arms and grinned at Nick. "Why did you have to wake me up? Hell, I was just having a dream about crawling in bed with Kathy again!"

Nick took a seat on the foot of Stan's bed. He returned Stan's grin. "Damn, Stan, you were with her all night. How much sex can a man handle in one night?"

Stan laughed. "I'm so far behind in that activity it's gonna take me a while to catch up."

Nick stood. "Come on, get up. Let's do something."

"Do what? Hell, this is Sunday!"

"Well, I'm restless. I've got a lot on my mind." Nick began to pace the floor.

"Why are you so restless? Is something worrying you?"

"Stan, I don't want you to take this wrong. You and your family have been great to me. But I was just thinking that maybe I ought to go ahead and leave for Louisiana."

"Why? Don't you like it here?"

"Yes. I love it here, but the mood just hit me to leave."

"Did something happen last night between you and Lauren that got you to thinking this way? Did she do something to piss you off? I noticed when we were sitting at the table at the dance that she kinda snubbed you."

Nick stopped pacing and took a seat on his bed facing Stan.

"No, actually, when she was driving me home, we sort of hit it off. We both felt a closeness toward each other."

"Do you mean that you made out with her?"

"Hell no. Why is it that 'making out' is the only kind of relationship you can imagine between a man and a woman?"

"Do you see something wrong with it? Don't start that sanctimonious shit with me, Nicky! Don't forget, I remember you during our college days."

"I felt something special about Lauren. Listen, buddy, you're my best friend as well as her cousin. My feelings are mixed up. Do you think I'd stand any kind of chance with her?"

Stan frowned. "You're serious, aren't you? I wish I could tell you different, but you're wasting your time even thinking about that! It'd never work!"

"Why? You know her pretty well. Tell me something about her. Why wouldn't it work?"

"Oh man, there are so many reasons I can't even name all of them! First of all, you don't have anything in common. You're like me, just a down-to-earth guy. But she's a spoiled brat. She always got everything she wanted. And another thing is that you're as poor as hell, from a poor family—of course there's nothing wrong with that...but, hell, man, her dad is rich, and he's spoiled her rotten. Also, you're a Yankee, and don't understand Southern ways. Not to mention the fact that you're both as moody as hell. I like Lauren okay, but she looks down on me. She thinks I'm a hick."

"How did her dad get rich? I thought small-town sheriffs didn't make much money. Is he as rich as your dad?"

"He's much more loaded with money than my dad. I don't know how he made his money. Rumor has it that he made some profitable investments."

"Does she get along well with her dad?" Nick asked.

"She worships her dad," said Stan. "But he completely controls everything she does. She thinks he can do no wrong."

"Tell me about her family." Nick began to pace again.

"They have a rather unusual family. Lauren is an only child. Her mom, Bonnie Rose, is handicapped. She's been in a wheelchair since Lauren was about six years old. She practically turned into a recluse. Nobody ever sees her."

"Who raised Lauren?"

"Her dad, Uncle Larry, says he raised her. But most of her upbringing was done by their live-in nanny, a Negro woman by the name of Willie Mae. She's a good looking mulatto about forty-five or maybe fifty years old."

"Is their house as nice as yours?"

"Yeah, but it's a different style house. They live in a rancher about a city-block long, with all the trimmings. Big pool in back, fancy flower gardens… You get the picture. Their house is about five miles from here."

Nick took a seat on the bed. "Back at the dance Lauren mentioned that she's going back to school for a master's degree. What's she majoring in? What does she want to be?"

"She majored in pre-med in undergraduate school. Her dad wants her to be a pediatrician. But Lauren told me that she really wants to be a teacher. So I guess she'll be a pediatrician."

"Well, I guess you're right about us having nothing in common. Actually, she and I live in different worlds."

"Nick, you're my best friend. In fact, you're the brother I never had, so it breaks my heart to tell you this. But as far as dating Lauren, you ain't got the chance of a snowball in hell."

"Thanks for giving me the picture, Stan. You just made up my mind for me. After I call my uncle, I'll leave for Louisiana in the morning."

Stan suddenly stood. "Damn it, man! You're not going to let that stuck-up little bitch run you off, are you? Come on, man! We've got another three or four days we can spend together."

"Sorry, Stan. I've made up my mind."

"Damn! You stubborn bastard!"

Stan walked to the other side of the bed and took a seat with his back to Nick. An awkward silence followed. Nick figured he was pouting.

When Stan unexpectedly turned toward Nick, his face bore an elaborate grin. He stood and walked around the bed to Nick.

"Nicky, I just had a brainstorm! I've got a great idea! Now hear me out before you say anything."

"What's on your mind?" Nick was curious.

"Okay, here's my idea. Do you remember the other day when we went over to the jobsite and House Cat Jennings kept demanding more help? Dad's been trying to hire more help, but most of the able-bodied guys are in the armed services. Dad even wants to start using Rufus. You can forget Louisiana and go to work for me! Then you can stay in Cedar Valley! Hell, you said you liked it here. What do you think?"

"Are you serious?" Nick was surprised at Stan's proposal.

"Damn right! You could go to work Tuesday, right after the holiday."

"Do you have a nice, plush office job for me?" Nick grinned.

"Don't push your luck, pal. I've got the only office job in this company."

"Just kidding, Stan. But what would your dad say? How do you know he'd allow it?"

"Damn it, Nicky! I run the company! But as far as Dad is concerned, he'd be tickled to death. He likes you. Hell, he thinks you hung the moon!"

"But I don't know anything about the construction business. In fact, I don't have any skill at anything, except maybe in boxing or football."

"Well, you know how to carry lumber, don't you? You know how to drive a nail, use a saw, or mix concrete…Hell, Nicky, it doesn't take a brain surgeon."

"What would my official title be?" Nick jokingly asked.

"Title? I guess you could say you'd be a carpenter's helper."

Nick grinned. "Couldn't you come up with a title that sounds a little more impressive? Maybe something a little more dignified… Possibly a title? What about, 'Assistant Home Construction Specialist?'"

"Damn it, Nicky, stop horsing around! Seriously, what do you think of the idea? Come on, pal! It's perfect for you!"

"How much would I get paid? Do I get any special favors because you're my best friend?" Nick again grinned.

"Damn it, you're just trying to make a joke out of my idea. Get serious!" He appeared to be irritated.

"But my uncle is expecting me to come to Louisiana. I'll have to call him and tell him I'm not coming."

"Does that mean that you'll do it?" Stan became excited. "Come on, say yes!"

"Yes."

"Great! Nicky, you won't regret it!" He became energized and began to gather his clothing from the floor. "Come on, get dressed! We've got a lot to do today!"

"What do we have to do that's so important?"

"I want to talk to you about another great idea of mine."

From his closet, Stan selected more clothing for Nick and they quickly got dressed. Nick started to make up his bed.

"Let that go, man," said Stan. "Come on, let's go upstairs and see if we can find some leftovers from Minnie's breakfast."

When they arrived at the kitchen upstairs, Minnie was working in another part of the house; however, warming on the stove she had left the remnants of a lavish breakfast: ham and eggs, hominy grits, biscuits, and hot coffee. Both men took seats at the kitchen table and dug into the breakfast.

"Where are your parents?" Nick asked, sipping his coffee.

"They're at church. They're big church members. Dad's a deacon in the Cedar Valley Baptist Church, and Mom sings in the choir." Stan munched on the ham.

"Don't you ever go to church?" Nick asked.

"No. I got burned out on church when Dad made me go every Sunday when I was growing up. I haven't gone to church in a couple of years, since I turned twenty-one. Hurry up and finish eating. We've got to get moving."

After eating breakfast, they left the house and got into Stan's car. The Hollywood muffler purred smoothly when he quickly pulled out of the driveway and headed toward Cedar Valley.

Stan turned on the radio and adjusted the buttons until he found a station playing country music.

"Where are we going in such a hurry?" Nick asked.

"We're going to find us an apartment, old Pal!"

"An apartment? You've got a pretty good setup where you're living. Why the rush for an apartment?"

"You don't want to keep on living with my parents, do you? Remember, you're officially a resident of Cedar Valley, now!"

"Oh yeah, I keep forgetting that I live here now. If we get an apartment, how do you think your dad will react?"

"I need to break away from Dad and his control. Since you've agreed to stay in Cedar Valley, this is a good time for me to break free."

"He won't be mad at *me* for suddenly leaving, will he? After all, I'm a guest in his house." Nick said.

"No, he'll be so pissed at me that he probably won't even give you a thought."

Nick peered out the window at the passing landscape. Puddles of water deposited by the previous night's storm saturated the low-lying areas. His mind drifted back to his panic attack during the storm, and the tenderness shown by

Lauren during his anxiety. He was unable to stop thinking of her. It saddened him to think that Stan was right when he pointed out the hopelessness of establishing a relationship with her.

"Stan, I know that I'm being stupid, but I can't seem to get Lauren out of my mind."

Stan lowered the volume of the radio. He pondered the remark before commenting. "Nicky, I may have been a little harsh in my assessment of your situation with Lauren. I may have exaggerated a little bit in order to make my point. Although I think it would be a long shot, at best, I don't think it's impossible for the two of you to get together. But I still think it's a mistake. You're too good for her."

"What made you suddenly change your mind? A while ago you seemed certain that it was hopeless."

"Well, by deciding to stay here, you've eliminated one of the biggest obstacles. Let's face it, man, romancing a girl from six-hundred miles away would be kinda difficult." He chuckled at his own remark. "You also got rid of another obstacle by getting a job. That makes two obstacles you've got behind you."

"If I eliminated two obstacles, what do you feel is my *next* biggest obstacle?"

Stan pondered the question. "I'd say the next thing to do is to establish some kind of purpose for your life. Something better than a career as a carpenter's helper, although that's a start."

"How do I do that? I don't know how to do anything, and I don't know what I want to do with my life." Nick seemed to be frustrated.

For a time, Stan remained silent, considering Nick's dilemma as the car entered the suburbs of Cedar Valley. He drove on into town and parked the vehicle by the curb. Finally, he turned to face Nick. "Your biggest obstacle to making it with Lauren is her father, my Uncle Larry—the sheriff. You're not gonna get anywhere with her without his approval."

"Damn! How can I ever overcome that problem?"

111

"Well, Uncle Larry is pretty possessive of her, and he's as stubborn as hell. But he's basically a fair man. If you'd establish a purpose for your life and show that you can make something of yourself, you might be able to sway him."

"Yeah, I can just picture how well I could sway him when I say, 'Sir, I'd like to date your daughter. I understand that she's going to be a pediatrician. Well, I'm also a professional. I just took a job as a carpenter's helper!'"

Stan chuckled. Both men sat quietly and thought about Nick's predicament. Finally, Stan said, "Nicky, I'm still not sure about you hooking up with Lauren, but if you're determined to give it a try, I feel like maybe I ought to help you. I just had another brainstorm."

"Okay, what's the brainstorm?"

"You could go back and finish college. You can get the G.I Bill. You're a veteran now."

"Yeah, I'm a veteran, but I'm also a carpenter's helper."

"But you won't *always* be a carpenter's helper. You can be whatever you want to be if you choose a good major in college. I'll tell you what. If you'll go back to college and get your undergraduate degree, I'll enroll in graduate school for my master's degree and attend school with you."

Nick was astounded. "Do you mean that you'd quit your father's business? Why would you do that? And what would your dad think?"

"I need to break away from my dad. Anyway, it would please him because he always thought that I'd never amount to anything. He knows that he's really just carrying me. That's why he doesn't respect me. I wouldn't even want any financial help from Dad if I went back to school."

"Do you have enough money to go back to college without help from your father?"

"Sure. I've got a pretty good bankroll stashed away. You and I could share an apartment while we attend school. I've even got enough loot to help you financially. Within reason, of course."

"I don't know, Stan. You said that my biggest obstacle to dating Lauren was her father. Even if I do go back to college, that'll help me in the *future*. But I'm concerned about *now!* Right now, Lauren's father will just see me as being a penniless Yankee drifter who is not good enough for his daughter—which is what I am." Nick hung his head in discouragement.

"That's where you've got it wrong, my friend. A poor Yankee drifter is what you were *yesterday;* but today, if you decide to go back to college, you're a hero who served his country fighting in the war, who has decided to make something of himself by going back to college, a man who is ambitious and humble enough to accept a low-paying menial job to help pay his way through school. And a man who has settled in this fine community and wants to help shape the character of this town! What a resume! That's what you tell Lauren and her father."

"Damn! You make it sound pretty good! I didn't realize I had that much on the ball!"

"Well, you have the added endorsement of me, *Lauren's cousin*, being your best friend and character reference."

Nick began to feel better. "You've really given me something to think about. I may just follow your advice."

"There's one more obstacle that I didn't mention." Stan cast a serious look at Nick. "And that's Mike Bronson—the deputy."

"But you said that Lauren didn't care anything about him."

"No. I don't think Lauren cares anything about him, but he thinks he owns her. You'd be smart to keep an eye on him."

"Thanks, I will."

"By the way, Nicky," Stan pointed to a business on the corner. "See that building there, the one with the doctor's name on the window? That's where Lauren works as a receptionist."

Nick eyed the building as Stan got out of the car.

113

"Sit still, Nicky. I'll be back in a minute. I've got to pick up a newspaper so we can look at the want ads. We need to locate an apartment."

In less than five minutes, Stan was back with the newspaper. He walked to Nick's side of the car and sounded excited when he said, "Scoot over behind the wheel. You need to drive so I can find some apartments in the want ads." Stan got into the car and began to scan the advertising section of the paper.

"Here's a possibility," said Stan. "Pull out and drive straight down Broadway and take your first right."

Although they weren't particularly choosy, Stan found a furnished two bedroom apartment with a bathroom on their second attempt; however, because of the necessity of minor repairs to the plumbing, the place wouldn't be available for occupancy for three days.

On the drive home Stan took the wheel. He was exceptionally happy with the way the day had gone. He had taken a giant step toward his independence by finding his own apartment; and in doing so, had made some long-range plans to escape his father's domination. In addition, his best friend was going to work for him. He realized that he had an ulterior motive in offering to help Nick in establishing a relationship with Lauren; for he wanted to create some kind of inducement that would influence Nick to stay in Cedar Valley.

Stan drove slowly toward home. He felt that a great weight had been lifted from his shoulders. Suddenly, he burst into laughter and vigorously slapped Nick on the back. "We did it, Nicky! We got us a place together! Do you know how long I've dreamed of you and I living together, working together? Man, we have a great future ahead of us! Aren't you glad you decided to stay here in Cedar Valley?"

"Yes, I really am, Stan. I feel like I've finally found a home. I like the people here. They're all so open and friendly. I also like your family."

"I'm glad, but sometimes Dad's a pain in the ass. I believe he probably thinks I'm a failure."

"Maybe your going back to school is a good idea. I agree with you about him being a little hard-nosed sometimes."

The blazing mid-afternoon sun had begun to evaporate many of the puddles of water that had been left in the wake of the storm. Nick gazed out the window at the small farm on the right where several Holstein cattle stood in a nearby pond, seeking relief from the heat of the day. The pastoral scene was peaceful, making him feel far-removed from the horrid landscape of war. He was gradually learning to love the serenity of the South.

His reverie was interrupted by the dismal sound of the country song that Stan had chosen on the radio.

"How about a little country music, Nicky?" The voice of Eddie Arnold began to wail the lonesome strains of, *Cattle Call.*

"Damn! More of that shit-kickin' music!" Nick winced.

Stan laughed. "You'll just have to learn to live with it, pal."

"By the way, Stan, do you have a steady girlfriend?" Nick asked.

"I've got plenty of girlfriends, but not a steady. I kinda like Kathy, the girl I took home last night." Stan answered.

"She's really pretty. She has a good personality, too," Nick answered.

"Maybe you and I can work up some double dates. When you start dating Lauren, it's gonna feel strange to be on the same date with my own cousin. I'd have to behave myself."

"But Lauren might not want to date me, Stan," said Nick.

"Why not? I thought you said that you both liked each other."

"I said that I felt that there was some kind of mutual attraction between us, and she said that she felt the same way. But she told me not to call her because she didn't want to get involved with a guy who was going to leave in a couple of days. So she may not even give me a date." Nick explained.

"Yeah, but all that's changed now because you're not leaving in a couple of days. You're going to live here. But she still may not give you a date. I told you she's snooty."

"Hell, Stan, I may not even have the guts to ask her."

"Don't sweat it, Nicky. I can introduce you to dozens of girls. She's not the only fish in the pond."

Stan pulled the vehicle into the Mullins driveway and parked near the house. Nick followed Stan into the basement apartment.

"What are we going to do for the rest of the day?" asked Nick. "It's only a little after four."

"We're going to start getting my clothes together and do a little preliminary packing. You're going to need some decent clothes. Here, help me with these."

Sorting through his closet, Stan removed several outfits of clothing and three pairs of shoes and carelessly tossed them on Nick's bed. "These are yours, pal. Look through my closet and pick out anything else that appeals to you."

"Wow, Stan! No way! I can't do that! This stuff is top-of-the-line. Why, here's a blue serge suit, and these sport coats are really expensive! Hell, there's no way I can accept these!"

"Don't sweat it, man. We're the same size and I've got more clothes than I need. I haven't even worn some of those things, especially the pants. They're like new."

"Damn! Thanks, Stan. I don't know what to say…"

He grinned. "Then don't say anything. By the way, what are you going to be doing tomorrow?"

"What am *I* going to be doing? Don't you mean what are *we* going to be doing?" Nick seemed puzzled by the question.

"I can't be with you for most of the day tomorrow. You know your way around town now," he said, "I didn't tell you this before, but Dad owns a taxi-cab company. The cab driver can't be there on July 4th, so I've gotta drive the cab for him tomorrow."

"Yeah, I guess I can find something to do. Do you have any suggestions?" Nick asked.

"Yeah. The town is having the annual Mimosa Festival at the City Park over by the lake. Why don't you go to that?"

"Aren't you forgetting something? I have no vehicle."

"Oh yeah, I almost forgot." He reached into his pocket and sorted through several sets of keys. "There are two pickup trucks parked in the garage in the back of the house. Take the white Chevy. By the way, you can keep the truck just like it's your own. You can drive it to work, too." He pitched the keys to Nick.

"Stan, are you sure this will be okay with your dad?"

"Damn it Nicky! How many times do I have to tell you that I run this company?"

"Sorry, Stan. Anyway, thanks. But I guess I'll pass on going to the Mimosa Festival. I don't know anybody in this town."

"You know Lauren. Why don't you take her? Or maybe she'll meet you there."

"Oh, I don't know if that's a good idea. If she's planning to go, she'll probably go with that deputy."

"What's the matter, Nicky? Are you afraid of a little competition? She's probably at home. I'll give you some privacy so you can call her. The number's in the book under Laurence Mullins." He walked out of the room.

Nick first made a collect call to his uncle in Louisiana to tell him that he wouldn't be coming, at least for now. His uncle was sad, but seemed to understand. Then he located the Mullins name in the phone book and dialed the number. After several rings, a female answered the phone. Nick recognized the voice.

"Hello?" The melodious sound of her voice excited him.

"Hello, Lauren? This is Nick."

"Who?"

"Nick Parilli…Remember? From the dance last night?"

A long silence followed before she resumed the conversation.

"Nicky, I don't want to hurt you, but I really need to go, now. Anyway, if you'll remember, I asked you not to call."

117

"I know you did, and I really wasn't going to call, but things have changed since we talked."

"What things? What's changed?"

"I'm not leaving. I'm staying here." Nick was becoming nervous. He desperately wanted to control his emotions.

"What do you mean you're 'staying here'? For how long?"

"From now on! I live here now. I rented an apartment."

"Why? Do you have a job somewhere?"

"Yeah. I got a job working for Stan. It's a good job."

"Doing what?"

He studied her tone of voice as she spoke, unable to read her mood. *If only I could* see *her eyes*, he thought. He became more nervous as his breathing became difficult. He began to lose his breath between words. He dreaded telling her his job description. "Well, actually, I'm a... carpenter's helper...but that's only temporary...I'll probably be...promoted...soon..."

"Good for you, Nicky. I'm glad for you."

He was on the verge of panicking. His breathing became irregular, and he began to speak in abbreviated gasps. He thought he had conquered his anxiety when talking to her, but her recent rejection of him had started the whole thing over again. *When am I ever going to be normal again? Why has that hellish war made me so insecure that when I'm under stress I can't even talk to people anymore?* he thought.

"Lauren, I'm getting nervous. Are...you g-going to the...the M-Mimosa Festival tomorrow...at the p-park?"

"The Mimosa Festival? Nicky, are you alright?"

"I gotta go now...can't talk...nervous...please go...to the Mimosa Festival...Oh, to hell with it! Forget it! I...won't ever bother...you...again!"

He hung up the phone and lowered his head.

Chapter 9

The early morning sun bore down on the land and promised another sweltering day. Nick reduced the speed of the Chevy pickup as he entered the outskirts of Cedar Valley. The truck was a 1951 model, only a year old. He enjoyed the clean, fresh smell of new fabric and the spacious interior of the cab. He gripped the steering wheel, noticing the easy handling of the truck. It felt good to once again have a vehicle for his personal use; however, the sign on the cab door served to remind him that the actual owner of the truck was *Mullins Construction Company*.

At 7:00 a.m. when he had awakened, he had noted that Stan was already gone. Nick wasn't hungry and disliked having breakfast in the Mullins home when not in the presence of Stan, so he had requested that Minnie forgo preparing breakfast for him. Instead, he had elected to have coffee in town. He had decided against attending the annual Mimosa

Festival, choosing instead to simply drive around and familiarize himself with the town.

On the west end of town he stopped at a traffic light. Looking to his left, he noticed a white pickup truck that also carried the *Mullins Construction Company* logo on the cab door. It was parked in front of a restaurant. The sign on the front of the building identified the place as *West End Grill.*

His curiosity got the best of him. *Who else would be driving one of the Mullins' company trucks on a holiday?* he wondered. He turned left and parked his truck beside the other pickup.

Once inside, he noticed three men having breakfast at the counter on the left. On the right, five or six people were scattered among the row of booths that lined the wall. Nick recognized the single occupant of the booth nearest the door. The customer was House Cat Jennings, the foreman for *Mullins Construction Company.*

House Cat was just finishing breakfast when he looked up and saw Nick. When he smiled, his eyes and white teeth contrasted sharply with his sunburned face, which appeared even darker in the dim lighting of the café.

"Well, if it ain't my Yankee friend!" He gestured toward the seat across from him. "Sit down and take a load off, Ace."

"Hi, House Cat. I saw that Mullins truck parked outside and thought I'd come in to see who's driving it. Are you working today? On July 4th?" He signaled to the waitress for coffee.

"Hell no! We're so far behind I've been puttin' in about sixty hours a week. There ain't no way I'd work today. I just drive that truck all the time, like it's my own."

Nick took a seat facing him. "I drive a Mullins truck, too. I've got some good news for you. Do you remember telling Stan you needed more help? Well, Stan just hired me yesterday. I go to work for you tomorrow morning."

House Cat was curious. "Are you a carpenter?"

"No, not exactly."

120

"Just exactly what are you then? If you ain't a carpenter, you may not be worth a damn to me, Ace."

"I guess you could call me a carpenter's *helper*. And why in the hell do you keep calling me 'Ace?'"

He laughed. "It just seems like that oughta be your name. Hell, 'Ace' is a lot better name than 'Nicky.'"

"When you call me 'Ace'…is that meant as a compliment, or an insult? By the way, my name is *Nick*, not *Nicky.*"

"Hell, Man! Can't you recognize a compliment when you hear one? You said that you're a carpenter's helper. Well, what I really need is about three good carpenters and a bricklayer. But I guess I could use a carpenter's helper, too. I've had two helpers quit in the last month—Egg Head Joslin and Lamb's Eye Bailey both got drunk and left me without notice. Seems like you can't depend on nobody lately. Shit, now I've only got one carpenter's helper: that nigger handyman, Rufus, the guy that does odd jobs for the Mullins. What kind of helpin' can you do?"

"I can drive nails, saw lumber, carry stuff for you, and mix concrete. Hell, I'm willing to try anything. I'm a fast learner. If you'd rather not give me a try, then I'll just tell Stan I quit."

"Aw, hell! Listen, ol' buddy…I'll take any help I can get. Anyway, I need somebody to shoot the shit with besides Rufus." He laughed. "I think we're gonna get along fine."

The waitress came and brought coffee to Nick. She freshened House Cat's coffee and collected his empty dishes. She smiled at Nick. "May I take your order, sir?"

"No, thank you. This coffee is all I want."

"Put his coffee on my bill, Mary," said House Cat.

"Thanks, man." Nick lit a cigarette. "Care for a smoke?"

"No, I never picked up the habit. Never did drink liquor, either, except for a couple of times when I tried it years ago. Both times, I showed my ass so bad I made up my mind to never try it again. By the way, how did you get hooked up with the Mullins family?"

"I met Stan when we were both going to college about three or four years ago. After I was discharged from the army,

I came here for a visit. Then when Stan offered me a job I decided to stay. I think I'm really going to like the South. How long have you known Stan?"

"Hell, I've known him all my life, I guess. Of course, me an' him didn't run in the same circles. Stan was born with a silver spoon in his mouth. He's a nice guy and a pretty good businessman. He knows how to make a decent profit. But he don't know shit about construction work."

"Well, I didn't know until I got here that Stan's dad is the mayor, and that his uncle is the sheriff." Nick smothered out his cigarette.

House Cat signaled the waitress for more coffee. "Yeah, the Mullins' pretty much control the whole county. They're all as rich as six feet up a bull's ass."

"How did they get so rich? Being mayor or sheriff doesn't pay that kind of money, does it?"

"I don't really know. A lot of people say that they made some good investments. I think they're silent partners in several businesses around town. Are you stayin' at the Lester Mullins mansion?"

"Yes, but only for the next couple of days. Stan and I got a place of our own yesterday, although his dad doesn't know about it yet. We're like a married couple, now." He laughed. "By the way, House Cat, are you married?"

"No, not yet. I may have to go into the army. I wouldn't want to marry some girl and then go to war." He thanked the waitress when she brought more coffee. "Well, if Stan's movin' out, th' shit'll hit th' fan when his dad finds out. But that's what Stan outta do. Hell, his old man tries to control everything he does."

Nick sipped his coffee. "What about the sheriff, Stan's uncle. Is he pretty controlling too?"

"He's worse than Stan's ol' man. That pretty daughter of his, Lauren, is afraid to do anything on account of him. Speakin' of Lauren...man, she's sure a gorgeous little doll! When I went to school with her a few years back, I had a crush on her. Hell, I'd still like to go out with her. But she's way out of my league. There wouldn't be a chance in hell of her dad lettin' her date a construction man—a carpenter!"

"Well, I guess a carpenter's *helper* would stand even less of a chance." Nick commented.

"Are you kiddin' me? Hell, her ol' man would probably have a shit hemorrhage."

Nick lit another smoke. "If you're so far behind in your work, I'm surprised you're not working today."

"Well, I should work today, but I ain't goin' to. Sometime today I've gotta run out to the jobsite to check on some material. But this mornin' I'm just takin' it easy. I might even go to the lake and visit that Mimosa Festival for a while. Want to come along with me?" He stood, tossed a generous tip on the table, and picked up the check.

Nick also stood. "I don't know, House Cat. I didn't really plan on going." He crushed out his unfinished cigarette.

"Oh, come on, Ace. Let's go to the Mimosa Festival. Maybe I can show you around a little bit. You probably don't know the way, so why don't you just follow me in your truck?"

Nick considered his invitation. "Okay, why not? I don't have anything else to do." He wondered if Lauren would be there.

Thanks to House Cat's reckless speed, the trip to the festival location took less than ten minutes. Nick parked his vehicle beside House Cat's truck in a large grassy field by Ft. Davis Lake. There were only a few randomly scattered cars parked in the field, for it was still too early for the festival to begin.

Nick followed House Cat through the maze of vehicles into another large meadow. From the lake, the monotonous drone of a motorboat reflected the mood of the lazy summer day. They strolled onto an asphalt path that generally conformed to the contour of the lake's edge before finally entering into a grove of trees. As they continued walking, the trail became blanketed with alternating splotches of light and shade as the morning sunlight filtered through the leafy arms of the trees.

For such a small town, the festival was an ambitious project. It was obvious that it was a special event to the townspeople. Many workers were busy in the final preparation for the event. Several men were putting the finishing touches on the temporary refreshment stands. Some were distributing wires for the electric equipment that would provide the music. Pairs of the stronger men were carrying large chests filled with ice. Others were setting up small tents as children romped around playing with a mongrel dog and irritating their parents. The womenfolk were carrying baskets of food: meat, buns, jellies, jam, pies, cakes, and other items of food suitable for a summer festival.

By mid-morning, people began to arrive in droves. In order to determine the scope of the event, Nick and House Cat slowly strolled through the entire festival area. Food stands were scattered about the area, offering a variety of refreshments: hot dogs, hamburgers, lemonade, apple cider, sodas, snow cones, and a hodgepodge of other homemade delicacies. The tantalizing smell of cooking food reminded Nick of summer cookouts during his youth.

On the lake, two motorboats towed water skiers between the lazy sailboats; and on the nearby shore was the playground where at least a dozen children were frolicking among the slides, swings, and a large sandbox. They watched as a small boy chased a little girl as he threw sand into her hair.

Preparation was being made for a multitude of recreational activities: square dancing, horseshoe pitching, apple bobbing, three-legged races, cake walks, and the hundred-yard dash. Under the umbrella of a large oak, a string band was warming up; and a barbershop quartet was practicing in a shady clearing near the lake.

For the less energetic or adventurous, several park benches were situated beneath the shade of the mimosa trees near the lakeshore, where parents could take a brief respite from attending to their energetic offspring. From a loudspeaker, strains of country music echoed throughout the park area.

Nick was struck with the closeness of the people, for the overall mood was one of familiarity and fellowship. The people knew and accepted each other. There was an atmosphere of goodwill and kinship that Nick had seldom experienced.

It was obvious that House Cat had established casual friendships with most of the people who had attended the festival. He never introduced any of his friends to Nick, for he was either short on manners or simply had no inclination to initiate superficial or pretentious relationships.

Most of the people he greeted bore nicknames: "Hello, Goat,"—"How ya doin,' Bulldog?"—"Whatta ya say, Marble Head?"—"How's it goin', Snake Eye?"—"See ya later, Egg Head."

Nick had encountered the use of nicknames in northern towns he had visited in the past; however, he had never been in a town where their use was as common and widespread as it was in this small Southern town. He began to recognize that some nicknames were derived from types of animals, and some merely reflected the person's occupation; however, the assignment of a moniker was sometimes intended to describe some kind of deformity, handicap, or misshapen portion of the anatomy: A stoop-shouldered man was called, 'Humpy.' A man with one leg carried the stigma of the insulting name, 'Crip.' A misshapen head evoked the title, 'Flat Head,' 'Anvil Head,' or 'Box Head,' with each specific nickname dependent upon the particular unusual shape of the person's head.

Nick thought it strange that the townspeople practiced such insensitivity in their blatant assignment of such insulting names; but even stranger was the fact that the bearers of the cruelly descriptive nicknames didn't appear to be insulted. In spite of their insensitivity, Nick decided that he liked these friendly Southern people.

House Cat quickly became bored with the festival. He turned to Nick and said, "I've seen all I wanta see, Ace. Hell,

I'd be better off goin' out to the jobsite and piddling around. When you come to work tomorrow, I'll help you all I can. Shit, you seem like a smart guy. I can teach you to be a journeyman carpenter in no time, if you'll just listen to old House Cat. I'll see ya tomorrow, Ace."

"Yeah, see you tomorrow…and thanks, I appreciate your willingness to help me."

"Don't start goin' sentimental on me," he said. Then he walked away, disappearing into the crowd. Nick had immediately taken a liking to him.

He pondered over whether or not he should remain at the festival. Although the people were likable and friendly, they were all strangers to him; however, he didn't know where else he could spend the day, for wherever he went he would only be in the presence of strangers. He realized that Lauren would probably not come to the event—a probability that, at first, made him sad—until he considered the fact that in spite of their mutual attraction, in reality, she also was a stranger to him. He began to regret his recent efforts in trying to establish a relationship with her, for in his initial attempt she had rebuffed him. He decided to abandon any future advances toward her.

He made his way through a rowdy group of teenage boys to a nearby stand to buy a cup of lemonade. The middle-aged man behind the counter smiled at him when he approached his booth.

"Good morning, sir. Isn't it a beautiful day?" Nick greeted, "I'll have a lemonade."

"Well, good mornin' to you, mister!" He eyed Nick curiously as he filled his cup with lemonade. "I can tell by the different way you talk that you're from up North somewhere. Where are you from?"

"Chicago," he answered. "My Yankee accent kinda gave me away, didn't it?" He laughed as he accepted the lemonade.

"It sure did! Here you are, sir. That will be ten cents. Did you move here, or are you just here on a visit?" He accepted the money from Nick.

"I haven't made up my mind, yet. Right now I'm kinda leaning toward staying." Nick was mildly amused at the man's curiosity and presumptuous familiarity with him.

"Where are you stayin'?" asked the man.

"Oh, just with a friend, for now. Why?"

The man impulsively thrust out his hand. "By the way, my name's Billy Joe Davis. And who might you be?"

"I'm Nick Parilli." Nick shook his hand. The man's blunt curiosity caused Nick to wonder if he would unexpectedly ask if he had ever suffered from hemorrhoids.

"I was just going to ask you where you go to church," said Billy Joe. "If you're not attendin' church anywhere, I'd like for you to consider visitin' my church next Sunday."

"Well, thanks for the invitation, Billy Joe, but I'm not ready to settle into a church just now."

"What denomination are you? I'm a Baptist. Most ever'one aroun' here is a Baptist." He seemed proud of his denomination.

"Actually, I'm of the Catholic faith," Nick answered.

"Catholic? Don't know much about that religion. Have you been saved?" He eyed Nick curiously.

"Well, I had my confirmation in the church when I was just a small boy."

"Confirmation? I ain't familiar with that term."

"Well, it's like baptism in your church—the same ritual."

"But have you been *saved?*" His expression was skeptical.

Nick knew that the friendly man meant well, but he was not in the mood to discuss religion with him.

He peered at his watch. "Gosh, Billy Joe, look at the time! I've gotta be going. It was a pleasure meeting you, sir." Nick again shook his hand and quickly walked away.

Billy Joe smiled and called to him, "I'll be prayin' for you, brother."

Nick was beginning to gradually discover more about the Southern personality. He had always heard that people in the South were friendlier than in the North; however, he had never known that they were so inquisitive about personal matters.

At noontime, he ate a hamburger and bought another lemonade. Until early afternoon, he continued to slowly stroll among the various attractions of the festival. He mostly confined himself to the fringe of the activities, seeking the shade, for the advancing day had brought sweltering heat. With his handkerchief, he mopped his forehead and drank the remainder of his lemonade, which had now become lukewarm from the heat of the day. Frolicking children mostly ignored him, but everyone else greeted him.

His lengthy walk in the park had begun to bother his stiff knee. He began to walk with a slight limp. After he decided to rest for a while, he spotted a couple of benches about fifty yards down the hill on the lake shore in the shade of several mimosa trees. He bought a package of cheese crackers to feed the covey of ducks that swarmed the lakeshore and then stepped off the asphalt path onto the grassy field. Moving slowly, he limped down the hill toward the shady haven.

On his left about twenty yards away, he saw row of booths, with each of them displaying a banner bearing the name of a specific candidate running for some political office; however, only a particular name on one of the signs really captured his attention: "Re-elect Laurence Mullins Sheriff."

Then, he saw her. Standing in the window of the booth beside a tall man, she was smiling and distributing some kind of literature to passers-by.

With curiosity, Nick slowed his pace and watched her as she smiled and talked with people who stopped at her booth. Because the crowd of people obscured her view, she hadn't yet seen him. In order to avoid her discovery of him, he quickened his pace and mingled with the gathering of people until he had completed his walk to the bottom of the hill, reaching the row of mimosa trees by the lake. He took a seat facing the lake on one of the benches and lit a cigarette.

His mind was a maze of confusion. He hadn't expected to see her here, especially with the tall man in the booth who was probably her father, the sheriff. Apparently, she was helping him campaign for re-election. Nick knew that Sheriff Mullins would disapprove of Lauren associating with him; consequently, he decided that, after resting for a while he would try to sneak out of this event without being seen by her.

The breeze from the lake became gentler with the retreating afternoon as he watched the lazy sailboats move slowly through the tranquil lake water. He relaxed on the bench and leisurely smoked his cigarette.

His thoughts turned to Lauren. Seeing her again had reawakened his yearning to be with her, but the presence of her father made him, for the first time, realize the hopelessness of it. He was a fool, he concluded, for even entertaining thoughts of having a relationship with her. House Cat had been right: Sheriff Mullins would have a *shit hemorrhage*.

In his previous conversation with Lauren, she had told him that her life was complicated, meaning, of course, that she had neither the time nor inclination to get involved with him. He had blundered badly, he decided, for he had developed an emotional attachment to the first woman who had shown any affection for him since his college experience. He made a silent vow to himself that he would no longer push his presence upon her.

He surveyed the peaceful lake and the countless white ducks that had begun to surround him, begging for bits of food with an unending series of clamorous honks. Carefully keeping his distance from the white domesticated ducks was a colorful wild mallard. Nick tore open the package of crackers and broke them into pieces before tossing small morsels to them, making sure that the mallard also received a portion. He could identify with the isolation experienced by the colorful feathered creature.

He experienced a feeling of accomplishment when he began to make an assessment of his recovery from the horrors of war. Physically, he felt better than he had previously felt in months; and although he still experienced occasional panic attacks, he no longer was dependent on alcohol as an escape from his fear and depression. Even if he never would have a future with Lauren, meeting her had reawakened ambitions and passions in him that he had long ago abandoned. He now had a job and an apartment of his own; also, he had met some congenial people who might even become his friends. Feeling shame from his recent panic attack in the presence of Lauren, he determined that he would no longer cower from his fears. Without flinching, he would meet his demons *head on.*

Since Nick had exhausted his supply of cracker crumbs, the swarm of ducks moved further down the shoreline. With a discordant barrage of quarrelsome squawks, they pestered a young couple lying on a blanket near the shore.

From the southwest, the breezes increased, whipping the shoreline with occasional gusts and forming small whitecaps on the surface of the lake. The wind felt good on his sweating face as he relaxed on the park bench. A glance over his shoulder told him that the crowd had diminished to some extent. He decided to rest for a while longer before leaving the park.

For a long time he sat idly on the bench, enjoying the beauty of the lake and distant mountains, engrossed in deep thought as the day began to wane. The breezes subsided as the afternoon advanced, smoothing the ripples on the surface of the lake. He decided that it was probably time for him to leave the park.

He quickly sensed that someone was behind him. He was startled when he felt the pair of soft, warm hands cover his eyes, blocking his vision.

"Guess who?" Her melodious voice immediately revealed her identity. Nick was unprepared for this turn of events.

Her laugh was spontaneous and playful, like that of a child. She removed her hands from his eyes and hurried from behind the bench, taking a seat beside him.

Nick was surprised. "Lauren! What are you doing here at the festival?" He didn't want her to know that he had already seen her earlier in the company of her father.

She again laughed. "You asked me to come. Remember? But you didn't give me a chance to answer before you hung up on me! What are *you* doing here?"

"I don't know. I guess I came here because I was bored and lonely. I hung up on you because it seemed that you didn't want to come. Also, I was getting panicky again…Damn it!"

She grinned at him. Then she playfully touched the tip of her finger to his nose. "Nicky, what am I going to do about you? You're going to have to get over your fear of me!"

Nick was surprised at her playful mood, which was echoed by her hairstyle and the casual outfit of clothing she was wearing. Her hair had been pulled back into a ponytail, and the brevity of her white shorts revealed the full length of her shapely bronze legs. Her pale blue tee shirt was tucked inside her shorts and mirrored the color of her expressive eyes. She wore no socks with the white sandals that covered her shapely feet. Her casual, girlish demeanor was a vast departure from the dignified, formal lady that he remembered from their last meeting. He began to recognize that there were many facets to Lauren's personality.

Nick was curious. "How did you know I was sitting down here by the lake?"

"I saw you as you walked down the hill. Didn't you see me?"

"No," he lied. "How long have you been here at the festival?"

"Most of the day. I came here with Daddy to help him in his campaign. The Mimosa Festival is a good place for him to reach a lot of people."

"Where is your dad now? Do you have to go back and help him?" Nick feared that her father would discover them together.

"No, he went home for the day. We have the rest of the day to ourselves to do whatever we want!"

"But the day is almost gone, Lauren. Anyway, are you sure you want to do anything with me? Remember, you told me not to call you." He eyed her accusingly.

Her eyes expressed sadness. "Nicky, I really like to be with you. It's just that my life is so complicated…"

Nick hesitated before he spoke. "Look, Lauren, I'm attracted to you, but since your life is so complicated I've decided to back off. I don't want to clutter your life."

Facing him, she laughed and placed her hands on his shoulders. Then she planted a brief, playful kiss on his lips.

"Nicky, why do you always have to be so serious? Why can't you just let things happen? Let's just enjoy each other *now!*"

"But what will happen *tomorrow*, when *now* is gone?"

"We'll worry about it then—*tomorrow*." She smiled at him.

She quickly stood and pulled him to his feet. He followed as she led him up the hill toward the activities.

"Where are we going?" he asked.

"You're going to buy me something to eat… I'm *hungry!* Also, I want to have a little fun before the day is over. Come on, let's have a good time!"

The elderly gray-haired woman behind the counter displayed a friendly smile and spoke to Lauren. "Why hello, Lauren! What can I get for ya'? And who is that nice lookin' young feller you're a-hangin' onto? Is he your new boyfriend? From the way you won't turn him a-loose, I can tell he ain't your kin…unless he's a kissin' cousin!"

Lauren blushed, but continued to grip Nick's hand. "His name is Nicky Parilli…and he's just a good friend. Nicky, this is Jewel Mae Henderson."

"Nice to meet ya, Nicky," she greeted.

"'Good afternoon, ma'am. It's a pleasure to meet you. I always enjoy meeting a friend of Lauren's."

Mrs. Henderson curiously eyed Nick. "Why, he sounds like he's from up North! How did you meet him, Lauren? You say he's just a friend? And are you still a-datin' that deputy?"

Lauren only chuckled. "Don't be so nosy, Mrs. Henderson." She turned to Nick, "What would you like to eat, Nicky?"

"Oh, maybe a hot dog and a lemonade."

"Make it two, and a couple of packs of potato chips." Lauren grinned at her and winked.

The wieners were warming on the grill. The elderly lady slapped two of them in buns and handed the hot dogs to Nick as he gave her the money. She gave Nick his change and again smiled at Lauren. "Didn't mean to offend ya none, honey," she said, "I just wanted to tell you what a pretty couple you make!"

"Why, thank you," replied Lauren, with an elaborate smile.

"Mustard and relish are on the counter. You can pour your own lemonade from that gallon jug that's a-settin' there in the ice. By the way, Lauren, honey, there's a-gonna be a full moon tonight! Don't you two do any huggin' an' kissin'." The old lady giggled.

Lauren laughed and took a big bite of her hot dog while she and Nick walked away. Nick looked back at the elderly lady.

"She seems like a nice lady, but she sure is nosy."

"She is a very nice lady. She doesn't mean any offense by her curiosity. She just likes people. She's helped a lot of people in Cedar Valley. She raised a family of five rowdy sons. Her husband passed away less than a year ago, poor thing!"

"Oh, I'm sorry to hear that," Nick commented.

He didn't realize how hungry he had become until he bit into the hot dog. They strolled as they ate and sipped their lemonade, finally sitting on a park bench beneath a shade tree.

She turned to face him and giggled. "Hold still," she said. "You've got a big glob of mustard on your chin!" She leaned very close to him and with her paper napkin wiped away the smudge.

"Thanks," Nick said. "Did I drip any on my shirt?"

She carefully inspected him. "No, I believe it missed your shirt." She then laughed. "What would you do without me to take care of you, Nicky?"

He chuckled. "I don't know, Lauren. As hungry as I am, it's a wonder I'm not covered with mustard."

When they had finished eating, she impetuously got up from the bench. "Come on, let's have some fun! We've got a lot of things to do!" She tossed the dirty napkins and the refuse from their meal into the trash barrel.

The heat began to subside as the first hints of twilight tinted the atmosphere. Nick noticed that only about half of the initial crowd remained at the festival.

"Lauren, what time does the festival end? It's getting late in the day. A lot of people have left the park."

"Oh, it's not *near* over yet. It's mostly just the old people who have left. It will probably last until midnight." Lauren was excited. Her quickened pace caused Nick's knee to ache as she pulled him along behind her.

"But I thought that people would start taking things down and packing up foods..."

She laughed. "Most of the people have already taken a lot of the food away, but all of the activities are still going full-swing! The City Park Commission will finish cleaning up tomorrow. Nicky, why do you worry about everything? Come on, let's have some fun."

Lauren was beaming with excitement when she locked hands with Nick and hurriedly led him through the park. Like excited teenagers, they enthusiastically competed with others in frivolous activities. They bypassed the dart throwing, archery, and croquet, but joined other couples in horseshoe pitching and shuffle board. When they tired of these playful games, they stood together, laughing and holding hands as they watched children bobbing for apples and competing in the three-legged race. For a while, they joined others in the small section of bleachers as a barbershop quartet performed in front of them.

The lights in the park sprang to life as darkness moved in. Low in the eastern sky, an oversized full moon hovered over the lake. Lauren again clasped Nick's hand and pulled him along behind her. In her enthusiasm, she sometimes skipped, as Nick struggled to keep pace with her. Her haste in moving from one activity to the next amazed Nick. It was almost as if she felt that she was running out of time—that this was the only day—the *last* day that she would ever have to experience this kind of freedom.

She pulled him down the path to the illuminated meadow beside the lake, where the square dance was in progress. Overhead floodlights and colored lamps cast a multicolored blend of light on the level stretch of grass that was surrounded by dozens of square dancers. A fiddle player and a caller stood on the platform at the end of the clearing near the lake. When Lauren and Nick arrived at the ring of people surrounding the dance area, the eager participants were in the process of forming squares. Lauren pulled Nick to the center of the group. The fiddle started screeching out a jumpy tune, and the caller began his monotonous chant: "All join hands, circle to the left—swing your partner, do-se-do—go right and left through, and turn 'em all around."

Lauren threw back her head and happily laughed. "Come on, Nicky, let's join one of these squares!"

"But I've never square danced before! And what about my knee?" He was reluctant.

"Don't worry, it's not hard to do. I'll lead you through it."

At first Nick was clumsy in his effort and made many missteps, but he eventually began to catch on to the basics. Also, the pain in his knee had eased. He looked across the square at Lauren's happy face, and at the jubilant expressions of the other dancers who surrounded him. At that moment, it dawned on him that he was happier than he had been in years. He hoped that his unexpected and newfound joy wasn't fleeting.

He began to learn the basic steps as they danced for more than an hour. Although he was having fun, his knee began to bother him. The group took a break and he gently led Lauren from the dance area. "Lauren, let's sit this one out. My knee needs a rest."

"Okay, Nicky." She smiled, and then peered at her watch. "Oh, no! It's after ten o'clock! The time just got away from me! Nicky, I've got to get home!"

"Do you need to get up early tomorrow? Do you have some special appointment?"

"No, not really. But Daddy will be upset if I don't get home soon."

"How will you get home?"

"I drove my own car." She again nervously looked at her watch as if she couldn't believe the time.

"Well, if you have to go, then I guess it's inevitable," Nick said. "Are you sure you can't take enough time for us to sit and talk for a few minutes? After all, I don't know when we'll get to see each other again."

She again glimpsed her watch, wishing that somehow she could suspend time. "Well, maybe I could stay with you for just a few more minutes, but I'll have to go in a half hour, and that's stretching the limit." She again took his hand and led him down the hill to one of the benches at the lake's edge where they took a seat together facing the lake. A few yards to their right, another couple was seated on a bench, kissing. Soon, they slowly got up and strolled together down the shoreline, holding hands. Lauren watched them walk away. In spite of the sadness in her eyes, she smiled. "Nicky, those young people are *so lucky*."

Darkness had brought cooler air. A soft breeze from the east stirred the surface of the lake, pushing miniature breakers ahead of it, gently caressing the shore. The brilliant moon had risen higher in the sky and cast a luminous, shimmering silver path across the surface of the lake. A stronger breeze ushered in the moist aroma of the lake and the summer night. The romantic atmosphere of the evening in the presence of Lauren stirred a feeling within him that he was falling in love with her.

"Are you cold?" Nick asked.

"Yes, a little bit," she answered.

136

He summoned his courage and placed his arm around her. She reacted favorably, gently placing her head on his shoulder.

He pulled her closer to him. When she raised her head, her expressive eyes reflected a deep yearning. For a brief moment, he gazed into her eyes. Then with tenderness, he kissed her. The kiss was long and passionate. The soft, scented aroma of her raven hair excited him. When he released her, she opened her eyes. Her tears glistened in the soft glow of the moonlight. She then smiled at him.

They continued to cling to each other. She quickly glanced at her watch, but said nothing. He feared that this special night was probably the only one that he would ever spend with her. He wanted to share his renewed optimism with her: his ambitions, his revived spirit, his plans to re-enroll in college, and his recent discovery of a *purpose* in life. She would be leaving him soon. If he wanted to share his dreams with her, he'd better do it now.

"Lauren," he said, "before you leave, I want to discuss some things with you. Remember the other night when you took me to Stan's house after the dance? I told you that I had no job, no purpose, and that I wasn't worthy of you? Well, that's not true anymore. I now have a job. It's not very impressive, but it's a start…and I have my own apartment. Also, I plan to go back to college on the G.I. Bill. Another thing—from now on, I'm going to face my fears…No more running from situations that remind me of the war. I plan to make my home here and make something of myself. For the first time in two years, I'm thinking about the future."

She pulled him to her and playfully kissed him. Then she tenderly embraced him. "Nicky, I'm so proud of you, and I'm glad for you. But just for tonight, let's not think about the future. I've been planning my future since I was a child. Let's just pretend that tonight is all we have, that tonight is *forever*…we'll worry about the future tomorrow."

"But, Lauren, I'd hate to think that tonight is all we have!"

She again nervously glanced at her watch, looked over her shoulder toward the parking area, but said nothing. Pulling him closer, she hugged him. "I'm getting cold, Nicky. Keep me warm."

"Lauren, maybe you should have worn something warmer instead of those shorts." He wrapped his arms tightly around her.

Again, she looked at her watch. "It's getting late, Nicky...It's almost eleven-fifteen. I have to leave you. But you'll have to leave soon, too."

"Why? I might just stay here for a while after you leave."

"Nicky, you can't stay! In fact, you'd better leave now! I almost forgot, they're having a fireworks display at eleven-thirty! You know what that'll do to your nerves. Come on and walk me to my car. We need to get out of here, *now.* I need to go home, anyway." She took his hand to pull him up from the bench.

"No!" he protested, stubbornly. "I told you I'm going to face my fears. I'm going to watch that damned fireworks display! I'll walk you to your car, but I'm coming back!"

She reclaimed her seat beside him. "Okay, if you're staying, then I'm staying here with you!"

"No, Lauren, I need to face this challenge by myself. And what about your father? Won't he be mad at you?"

"Yes. But I'm staying with you, anyway."

Nick was surprised that she would openly defy her father; however, he was more curious about his controlling influence over her. "Lauren, why are you so intimidated by your father? After all, you're an adult with a college degree."

She seemed to be slightly offended. "Nicky, I love my father more than anyone. He's a wonderful man, and I owe him everything. My mother is severely handicapped and Daddy practically raised me by himself. What he wants more than anything is for me to be a medical doctor. That's his dream. And he's spent a fortune in money and time to prepare me for that profession!"

"But what do *you* want more than anything? What's *your* dream?" He realized that he was pressing her.

"Well, I used to think I wanted to be a teacher. But I know that's really only a selfish fantasy of mine. Look, I don't really feel comfortable talking about this." She turned her head and looked away. He dropped the subject.

He again began to consider the futility of attempting to openly date her. *How would her father react to his prestigious daughter dating a carpenter's helper?*

Casually, he asked, "Lauren, are you ashamed of me?"

"*Ashamed* of you? No, Nicky, I'm not *ashamed* of you! Why do you ask me that?" She seemed outraged.

"Okay, let me put it another way. Do you have respect for me? Do you think that you and I could ever have some kind of relationship without hiding it?"

"Nicky, I love to be with you. I would think you should know that by now!"

"Well, it seems to me that we're kinda hiding our relationship at this very moment. Do you intend to keep hiding me from your father? What if I asked you for a date, a regular old fashioned, traditional date, where you and I could be seen together by God and everybody else? What would you say?"

Her silence spoke volumes. "That's what I thought," he said.

He noticed that most of the remaining people at the festival had gradually moved to the lakeside near the mimosa trees and benches in order to be near the display of fireworks. Without warning, a series of small, sputtering explosions followed by whistling hisses burst forth as the first barrage of rockets spewed upward, soaring high into the sky over the surface of the lake. The first explosions were not colorful, but only brilliant flashes followed by several tremendous booms. They vibrated the surrounding area and echoed from the nearby hills with the terrifying simulation of exploding mortar shells.

Nick noticeably flinched before steeling himself against the next barrage. Lauren hugged him tightly but said nothing. The next volley was not as loud as a continuous series of missiles rocketed high over the lake, exploding into beautiful flower-like shapes in a multitude of brilliant yellows, blues and greens. Although Nick trembled, he sat stoically on the bench as Lauren continued to tightly hold him in her arms.

After several minutes of spectacular, evenly spaced episodes, the fireworks display appeared to be over; however it was only a lull in a preparation for the grand finale. Some of the spectators started to wander around the area, while others began to gradually disperse. "Don't leave yet!" cried one of the crowd. "The best part's just now comin' up! In a minute, all hell's gonna break loose!"

A few seconds later, the grand finale began in chaotic fashion. Seemingly with no logical pattern or any planned sequence, a barrage of multicolored rockets of ear-splitting intensity erupted, high over the lake, in a series of cacophonous flashes and booms. The hellish pandemonium of the lengthy event mimicked the sound of an artillery battle.

Lauren continued to cling to Nick. Halfway through the grand finale, Nick slowly pushed her arms away, freeing himself of her protective grasp. "Lauren, please don't hug me right now...I've got to face this alone," he said. With trembling body, he stood and moved closer to the deafening hell toward the edge of the lake. Looking upward toward the terrifying spectacle, he courageously faced his hellish demon. When the display ended, Nick stood facing the smoky aftermath of the fireworks exhibition. The hazy vapor hanging in the air carried the stench of war. He closed his eyes and smiled.

The fireworks display was over. Spectators gradually began to leave the lakeshore until finally, only Nick and Lauren remained in the area. She walked to him and they hugged each other tightly. Without speaking, they stood together until his trembling subsided.

He led her back under the mimosa trees where they both took seats on their former bench, facing the lake. The water was as still as glass, and the moon was now directly overhead. Only the incessant chirping of insects and the sound of an occasional ripple of water intruded upon the silence of the night. For a long while they quietly sat, spellbound by their unplanned intimacy in the soft moonlight. When he again kissed her, he noticed that she was trembling from the chill in the air.

"Lauren, you're getting cold, and it's after midnight. Nearly everybody's gone home. Maybe you'd better be going home, too." Ignoring his suggestion, she continued to cling to him.

"Nicky, I admire you so much! You're conquering your fear of your terrible war memories, and you're making so many improvements in your life. You asked if I was ashamed of you…I'm *proud* of you!" She made no move to start for home.

"Thanks, Lauren." Nick peered at his watch. "Do you think you're going to get in trouble with your father for being out so late? It'll be nearly one o'clock by the time you get home."

She seemed to be ignoring any urgency to start for home. With her head resting on his shoulder, she reclined lazily on the bench. "I wish this night could last forever. Wouldn't it be wonderful if you and I had just met in a place where neither of us knew anybody, and it was just the two of us starting out on a journey?"

Nick was saddened that the evening was drawing to a close. He began to fear that he would never again see her, especially since she had so blatantly violated her father's curfew.

"Lauren, I realize that I told you that I wouldn't pursue you anymore, but would you meet me here again tomorrow night about eight o'clock? Maybe you could slip away for a while…"

The unexpected sound from about twenty yards behind them caught their attention. When they turned to investigate, the beam of a flashlight scanned their faces. She squinted her eyes in an attempt to identify the intruder.

"Oh, God! It's Mike," cried Lauren, "I've got to go!" She hurriedly rose from the bench and tried to straighten her hair.

141

Mike Bronson approached them. "You're out a little late, aren't you, Lauren?" he said. "Your daddy's worried about you. He sent me out to look for you." His flashlight scanned her face.

She tried to remain calm. "Time just got away from me, Mike…and I wanted to stay for the fireworks…"

He switched the beam back to Nick. "Who's this guy? What's your name, mister? Do I know you?"

"No, you don't know me. This is the first time we've met. My name's Nick Parilli."

"You ain't from around here, are you Mr. Parilli? You sound like you might be from up North someplace."

Nick didn't answer. He only stared into the flashlight beam.

"Go get in my car, Lauren." Bronson said.

"Mike, I'm sorry I…" She looked helplessly at Nick.

"I said get in the car, Lauren! *Now!*"

"But I drove my own car, Mike," she said.

"Then I'll take you to your car!" he answered.

She walked around the bench in the direction of the deputy's parked vehicle. As she passed Nick, she said, "I'll try, Nick."

"You'll try *what?*" asked the deputy.

"Never mind," she answered.

"Now you go on, Lauren. Get in my car. I want to have a few words with this *Nick Parilli.*"

She continued to walk up the slope and entered Bronson's car at the top of the hill. The deputy turned to face Nick. "Mr. Parilli, I'm gonna say this only one time to you! I'm warnin' you! Stay away from Lauren. Do you hear me?"

"Yeah, I hear you. You may be a deputy, but you don't control my actions. The last I heard, this is still a free country. And I don't think you have any right to control Lauren's actions, either. After all, she's a grown woman."

The deputy's face flushed. He took a step toward Nick and thrust the flashlight beam directly into his eyes. "Listen, you son of a bitch! I came here trying to be nice to you, and you

142

start mouthing off to me! If I didn't have to get Lauren home, I'd run your ass in, you bastard! I better not ever catch you around her again—do you understand?" With a sneer, he stepped to within inches of Nick, before slowly turning and walking up the hill.

Nick watched the deputy hurry up the slope to his vehicle and drive away. For a long time, he stared at the vehicle until the unmarked police car was out of sight. Then he walked through the deserted park toward his car.

Chapter 10

After having breakfast at the Mullins home, Nick swung his pickup truck onto Highway 11 and followed Stan's truck to the jobsite. Clouds of dust swirled around the vehicles when he parked beside Stan in the grassless yard beside the house. Two other cars and a couple of pickup trucks were parked in the weed-covered field behind the structure.

A twenty-foot ladder leaned against the eaves of the building. Rufus and two other men were on the roof applying rolls of asphalt roofing while a fourth worker was on the ground stacking bundles of shingles to be pulled up to the roof. House Cat Jennings descended the ladder and walked to meet Stan.

Stan was in his usual buoyant mood when House Cat and Nick joined him in front of the unfinished structure.

"Hello, House Cat," Stan greeted, "I brought you a new employee. Remember Nick Parilli, the guy you met the other day? Well, he's gonna be helping you."

"Yeah, I know. Me and him talked about it yesterday. He told me you hired him."

"That's good—I'm glad you had a chance to talk," said Stan. "Nicky, you're now officially an employee of the *Mullins Construction Company.* House Cat will give you some tools. I think he has an extra set. You can put your lunch bag and your jug of water in that big tub of ice, there by the tree, Nicky."

House Cat grinned. "Hello, Ace. I can see that Stan told you to bring a big jug of water. Today's gonna be a scorcher. The plumbers ain't put water in this place yet. I can use your help. We gotta get a roof on this house by quittin' time today. I'll get you started in a minute. Right now, I gotta take a leak." He ignored Nick's offer of a handshake and stepped behind a nearby tree.

"What're you going to do today, Stan?" asked Nick.

"Man, I have a lot of stuff to do today. I probably won't see you until tonight. I've gotta pay some bills, order some materials, and start packing some of my stuff to move into our new place. Also, I gotta tell Dad that we're moving out."

"Good luck with *that,* pal. He's gonna be mad."

"Yeah, I dread telling him. By the way, you'll get along great with House Cat. Sometimes he's a little blunt when he's talking to you, but he's a fair man. Just bear with him and he can teach you the trade."

"Yeah, I noticed that he's not overloaded with tact."

Having completed the task of relieving himself, House Cat was in the process of zipping his pants when he rejoined them.

"Okay, Ace, we might as well get started. By the way, before I forget it, I need for you to take Rufus home after we finish work today. He don't have a ride no more. He used to ride to work with Lamb's Eye Bailey, until the son of a bitch got drunk and never showed up for work anymore. Damn! It's got to where a man can't keep good help."

"No problem," said Nick, "I'll be glad to take him home."

Stan playfully punched Nick's shoulder. "I'll see you tonight, good buddy. Don't work too hard."

145

"Listen, Stan. Since I gotta take Rufus home, I'll be a little late getting back, so tell Minnie not to fix any dinner for me. I'll just eat out."

"*Dinner?* Here in the South, dinner is the *noon* meal…the evening meal is called *supper*." Stan laughed. "See you tonight." He backed out of the dusty yard and drove away.

For the entire day, Nick worked beside Rufus. The men became drenched with perspiration as the heat became stifling with the passing of the day. But Nick was happy; for the sweat that dripped from his face was the by-product of his newly acquired sense of purpose. It felt good to be working again.

For much of the morning, his mind was immersed in thoughts of Lauren and the events of the previous evening. When he had asked her to meet him tonight, before she had a chance to answer, the deputy had unexpectedly intruded. He recalled that as she was leaving, she offered a belated, "I'll try, Nick." He wondered what the odds were that she would be there. He was also thinking about his exchange with the deputy.

House Cat proved to be a good foreman. He moved around over the roof with the agility of a monkey, and because he out-performed the others, he was an inspiration to them, for he led by example. By noontime, the roof of the structure was more than half-covered with shingles. Nick relaxed in the shade of a tree and swallowed large gulps from the gallon jug of water he had brought. Then he dug into the lunch that Minnie had prepared for him. During the brief lunch break, the men scarcely spoke to each other. Although Nick knew Rufus, House Cat hadn't bothered to introduce Nick to the other two workers; however, from their brief conversations while working, he learned that their nicknames were "Goat" and "Snuff Head."

The relentless heat repeatedly drove them to their water jugs; however, the merciless afternoon sun that bore down on the crew of men failed to slow their progress; consequently, by four-thirty, the roof was finished.

House Cat had already gone for the day, and Rufus was experiencing cramps and had become sick from the heat. The two other workers packed away their tools, entered their vehicles, and followed Nick as he drove out of the yard.

"I'm gittin' kinda dizzy, Mistah Nick, I reckon I jus' got too hot," complained Rufus, as Nick drove away from the jobsite.

Nick's truck picked up speed. "Damn, Rufus!" he exclaimed. "Roll down that window! The inside of this cab is hotter than hell! Like an idiot, I left the windows up this morning." With his handkerchief, he wiped the sweat from his face. He looked at Rufus, noticing that he was no longer sweating.

"How come you're not sweating, Rufus? Have you been drinking enough water?"

"No suh, I reckon I ain't. Sometime along about the middle of the afternoon, I spilt my water. It turned over an' it all done run out on the groun' afore I could set it upright."

"Damn, Rufus! Why didn't you ask me or one of the other workers for a drink of water? Hell, you must be dehydrated!" Nick handed him his near-empty water bottle. "Here, drink the rest of this. It's pretty warm, but it will help you 'til we can find some cold water."

"But you ain't got no cup fer me to drink out of, Mistah Nick. I can't drink no water outta your jug without a cup."

"Why in the hell not, Rufus? Is this another mysterious law of the South that I'm not acquainted with?" Nick was frustrated.

"Mistah Nick, I done l'arned a long time ago that a Negro can git into bad trouble if he drinks out of a white man's cup. They ain't no proper white man that'll drink after a black man."

"Rufus, that's bullshit! Now drink that damned water!"

"No, suh…I don' mean no disrespec', but I ain't gonna drink outta that-there jug. Some people says that it's bad luck."

"Bad luck for who? The Negro or the white man?"

"Bad luck fer the Negro, I reckon—'cause he's the one that gets beat up fer drinkin' outta the jug."

"Well, shit! We're almost to the Mullins' house, so I'll stop there before I take you home. You can drink some water in Stan's basement apartment."

"I'd 'preciate it very much, Mistah Nick. I sho' don't wanta bring on no bad luck."

In a short time, Nick pulled into the Mullins driveway. Stan had not yet arrived at his apartment. Once inside, Rufus hurried into the small kitchen and immediately gulped down several glasses of water. After briefly catching his breath, he repeated the process. Then he took a seat on the couch.

"Rufus, just sit there for a while and get over your dizzy spell. Since we're already here, I'm gonna take a quick shower and wash some of this sweat off me before I take you home. I won't be more than a few minutes."

"Okay, Mistah Nick. Jus' take yore time."

In less than fifteen minutes, Nick had showered and dressed in clean clothes. When he walked into the kitchen, Rufus was again drinking water.

"Well, Rufus, are you feeling better now? If you are, I'm ready to go."

"Yessuh, Mistah Nick. I'm much better now. I'm ready, suh."

Nick wheeled the truck down the long driveway toward the street. "Which way do we go, Rufus? Where do you live?"

"I lives down in Bucktown. Jus' turn right an' go all the way through Cedar Valley past the West End Grill. Then ya go 'bout a mile an' turn lef' acrost a little bridge. I'll remind ya when we gets to the bridge."

Nick turned right. "Rufus, please don't call me 'Mister Nick.' It makes me feel old. Just call me 'Nick.'"

"Yessuh, Mistah Nick," Rufus replied.

Nick dropped the subject. He lowered the sun visor and squinted his eyes as he drove toward the setting sun in the direction of town. It was the hottest hour of the day. In front of him, the heated asphalt road shimmered, and the lowered windows allowed the hot blast of air from outside to burnish his face and ripple his hair. He remembered the contrasting coolness of last night when he was with Lauren—by the lake, where the chill of the night had caused her to cling to him for warmth.

He drove through the downtown area and past West End Grill. "Okay Rufus, where do I turn left?"

"Turn lef' after you pass Jack's Drive-In—right there! Then you jus' go a little ways up th' hill an' my house is the corner house on the right. It's a white house."

After crossing the small bridge, Nick drove two blocks and got his first look at Bucktown. The downtown area of the small settlement consisted of only two square blocks of ramshackle buildings that contained a few small businesses: a couple of grocery stores, a hardware business, a barber shop, a tavern, a pool room, a church, and a drug store. The business section was situated in a low-lying area and was surrounded by steep hills that were scattered with a multitude of dilapidated houses. Beyond the hills, the Tennessee River was only a quarter of a mile away.

The population of the small settlement was a mixture, made up of about 90% Negroes, and 10% poor whites. Bucktown was specifically for the Negro—it was *his* town, a habitat that had been assigned to him by his white neighbors—and a place where he was expected to spend his time at the end of each day, for Negroes were not allowed in the town of Cedar Valley after sundown.

When he drove up the hill into the residential area, Nick eyed the row of shabby houses beside the gravel street. A few decent houses were scattered about the community, but most of the others were in disrepair. Some were sagging and unpainted, showing rotten planks that had been bleached gray from their exposure to the elements. Trash that littered the area—old, abandoned cars, worn-out tires, discarded appliances, metal cans mingled with the surrounding patches of ragweed, Johnson grass, and sumac. Behind each house stood an unpainted outdoor toilet. Nick felt that the decrepit

149

little town was the rural counterpart of the Chicago ghetto. It reeked of poverty and hopelessness.

"That's my house, right there," said Rufus.

Nick turned the pickup into the dusty dirt driveway beside the weather-boarded house. Rufus had described the house as being white, but the gray, weathered siding had only been neatly brushed with a transparent coating of whitewash. The tin roof was stained with splotches of rust, and the floor of the front porch displayed patches of plywood that covered the holes where the planks had rotted through in places.

In spite of the run-down condition of the house itself, there was a curious neatness about the arrangement of the surrounding accessories: A neat brick sidewalk linked the front porch to the street, and flanking each side of it was a perfectly aligned row of buttercups; also, the grass in the front yard was lush and neatly mowed. In Rufus' incongruous neatness, Nick detected a profound pride and dignity within his spirit; for it appeared that Rufus was determined to do the best he could with what he had.

"Come on inside fer a little while, Mistah Nick, an' meet my fambly," said Rufus.

Nick checked his watch. "Okay, I guess I have time. I don't have to be anywhere until eight o'clock."

The interior of the house smelled musty but was neat in appearance. The inexpensive furniture was clean, and the tasteful arrangement reflected the same fastidious nature of Rufus. The home was small with only two bedrooms and no indoor bath.

From the kitchen, the pleasant aroma of frying ham drifted into the living room. Nick took a seat on the couch while Rufus walked into the kitchen. When he returned, a middle-aged Negro woman followed him into the room.

Rufus introduced his daughter. "Mistah Nick, this-here's my daughter, Mary Rose, and this feller here is Mistah Nick Parilli."

She performed a polite curtsy and smiled at Nick. "Hello."

Nick returned her smile. "Hello, Mary Rose."

She was a pretty woman, and like her father, small of bone and stature. She had smooth, even facial features, and her white teeth stood out in sharp contrast to her skin, which was very dark. The front of her calico dress was covered with the white apron she wore as she prepared dinner.

"It's so nice to meet you, sir," she said, "I was just preparing supper for us. Would you like to join us? We have plenty." She was obviously more educated than Rufus, for her manners were impeccable; also, her dialect was almost undetectable.

"Well, I hadn't planned on eating with you…"

Rufus grinned. "Oh, come on, Mistah Nick. We don't hardly ever have comp'ny. Besides, it's supper time and you ain't had nuthin to eat yit."

"Well, okay, why not?" He felt that he needed to pass away the time until 8:00 p.m. when he was supposed to meet Lauren. Besides, he liked Rufus.

The front door sprang open and a young Negro boy dashed into the room, instantly stopping in his tracks upon seeing Nick. A scrawny youngster and short of stature, he appeared to be about ten years of age. Like Mary Rose, his complexion was very dark, a characteristic that made his bulbous, surprised eyes whiter by contrast. He stood immobile, frozen in his stance as he stared at Nick in awe.

Rufus laughed. "Ain't no reason to be skeered, Caleb!" he said. Then he looked at Nick. "Caleb's my grandson…Mary Rose's son. He ain't never seen no white man in our house before." He reached to the boy and rubbed his hand through his wooly hair. "Caleb, this here's Mistah Nick. No need to be skeered a-him!"

Nick grinned at the lad. "So your name's Caleb, is it? Well that's a right pretty name. How old are you, Caleb?"

The boy remained quiet and continued to stare at Nick.

"Caleb can't speak," explained Rufus. "Never could speak since the day he was born'd. But he can hear you. He's a smart boy. Jus' can't say nuthin.' He jus' turned twelve years old."

Mary Rose left for the kitchen to prepare the evening meal. The boy kept his eyes glued to Nick.

"Does he know that we're talking about him? Do you think it'll make him feel self-conscious?" Nick was concerned.

"Yessuh, he knows, awright. But it don't bother him none."

"Can't anything be done for him? Can the doctors perform some kind of procedure that will enable him to speak?"

"Don't reckon so. Besides, we ain't got no money..."

Caleb walked closer to Nick and stood directly in front of him. His friendly grin was accompanied by a series of grunts as he attempted to communicate his feelings to Nick.

"Why, I'll be dogged!" exclaimed Rufus, "I do believe he's taken a likin' to you! The on'y other white man I ever knowed him to like is that preacher that lives up the road a-piece."

Nick returned the lad's grin. Rufus walked to the kitchen sink and washed his face and hands.

Mary Rose appeared at the kitchen door. "Supper is served," she smiled and said. With a polite curtsy, she made the announcement with all the aplomb of a hostess seating dignitaries at a banquet.

At the dinner table, Caleb pulled his chair to within inches of Nick. Rufus only grinned. "Le's say a little blessin' before we eat," said Rufus. They bowed their heads. "Lord, thanks fer th' priv'lege of havin' Mistah Nick, here at our table...an' bless this food to th' nursh'ment of our bodies. Amen."

"Amen!" said Nick.

Mary Rose had prepared corn bread, ham, stewed potatoes, poke salad, and iced tea. With the exception of the poke salad, which he had never heard of, Nick ate heartily.

During the meal, Caleb repeatedly left the table in order to fetch one of his toys to show to Nick. Each time he displayed an item, he issued a series of excited grunts. Then he would laugh and leave the room to retrieve another trinket. Finally, he brought in a double-barrel twelve-gauge shotgun and proudly displayed it to Nick.

Nick's eyes widened. "Caleb, you'd better be careful with that weapon! You might be a little young to be playing with a gun." He sadly recalled that the North Korean boy he had killed in the war was perhaps only a couple of years older than Caleb.

"Mistah Nick, Caleb knows how to use that-there shotgun," boasted Rufus, "I trained him good. He goes rabbit huntin' purty reg'lar in th' winter. He's a crack shot with that gun. Right Caleb?"

Caleb grinned and nodded in agreement.

Mary Rose smiled and scolded him. "Caleb, now you quit botherin' Mr. Nick. Let him enjoy his meal. I know you like him, but don't run him off the first time he comes to visit us!"

"Aw, Mary Rose," said Rufus, "he's jes' happy. Let the boy enjoy Mistah Nick bein' here."

The front door partly opened and the head of a small Negro boy appeared. "Hey, miz Luther! Can Caleb come out an' play?"

"Caleb hasn't finished his supper, Leroy," she answered.

"Oh, let him go, Mary Rose," pleaded Rufus. "Th' boy's been cooped up in th' house fer most of the day. He can finish his supper later."

"Oh, alright! But you be back here before dark! Do you hear me, boy?" Before she had uttered the last words, Caleb was already out the door.

"Your son is a special little boy, Mrs.—*Luther*, isn't it?"

"Yes, my husband's name was Elias Luther."

"Was?" asked Nick.

"Yes. I reckon he's dead, but we don't know for sure. The Ku Klux Klan took him out and whipped him one night. He came back home, all bloodied-up, and then before long, he turned up missin'. Maybe he's alive out there somewhere, but I doubt it. He was always high-spirited, especially for a black man."

Nick was surprised. "I've heard about the Klan before, but I didn't know that they were still active. How old was Caleb when this happened?" Nick asked.

"He was about five, I think." She appeared to be sad.

Rufus spoke. "Mistah Nick, Elias was a good man, but he jus' never l'arned to stay in *his place*. He jus' never realized that it's a white man's world."

Having finished the evening meal, Nick and Rufus moved to the shade of the porch while Mary Rose tidied up the kitchen. When she finally joined them, she brought two glasses of lemonade.

The approaching twilight brought cooler air. For a long time they relaxed on the porch, discussing past events of Cedar Valley, the war, and Caleb's inability to speak. They curiously watched the black children playing in the dusty street.

Nick peered at his watch. "Rufus...Mary Rose...I've got to be going. Thank you, Mary Rose, for a most delightful dinner—er, *supper*." He pushed back his chair.

"You're welcome, sir," she replied. "Now, you must come back to visit us again. You're a welcome guest in our home."

"You can count on it, ma'am, I especially want to visit with that fine son of yours again. By the way, Rufus, do you want me to pick you up for work in the morning?"

"Yessuh, if it ain't too much bother."

They walked him to the front steps and continued to watch him as he strolled toward his truck. Turning his head, he waved at them. "See you in the morning, Rufus." He then drove away.

Again checking his watch, he noted that the time was 7:40. He had just enough time to make his proposed 8:00 p.m. rendezvous at the lake with Lauren.

He began to think about the horror story that Mary Rose had told him about her missing husband and his beating by the Klan. She had said that Caleb was only five years old at the time of the event, which would mean that it had been seven years since it had happened. *Maybe activity by the Klan is a thing of the past*, he thought.

At 7:55 he arrived at the city park and pulled his vehicle into the parking area on the hillside overlooking the lake.

Scanning the area, he observed that Lauren's black Buick was not among the few cars that were parked around the area. He left his truck and slowly strolled downhill toward their pre-arranged meeting place—the bench by the lakeside. He took a seat on the bench and viewed the placid panorama of the lake and the distant mountains. The approaching flock of honking ducks made him wish that he had brought some kind of snack for them.

The surface of the lake had calmed as the gentle breeze from the lake had waned with the onset of twilight. He lit a cigarette and became excited with the anticipation of seeing her again. The ducks quickly became bored with him. Apparently realizing that he wasn't going to feed them, they issued a series of disgruntled squawks and waddled away from him, down the shoreline.

He again peered at his watch: *8:00 p.m.* She should be here. A noise from the left drew his attention. Stepping out from a row of shrubbery, Lauren trotted toward him, smiling. As usual, he was impressed with her beauty. She was wearing white shorts that revealed the muscular shape of her tanned legs, and the baseball cap that covered her locks of raven hair gave her the appearance of a teenager. He walked to meet her. Their kiss was long and sensual and happened as naturally for them as breathing.

He slowly released her and looked into her eyes. His heart was racing. "Gee, Lauren, it's great to see you! And you made it at exactly eight o'clock, just as we planned."

He led her to the bench where they sat closely together. She placed both arms around him. "I was afraid that you might not have heard me when I whispered to you that I'd *try* to meet you."

He smiled. "Well, I was afraid you wouldn't be able to come, or maybe you'd be real late in getting here."

She playfully kissed him. "Actually, I made it here earlier than we planned. I've been here for about fifteen minutes."

"Do you mean you got here early? Where have you been? And I didn't see your car anywhere. Where did you park it?"

155

"I hid it. If Mike comes poking around looking for me, he won't see my car. He doesn't know what your vehicle looks like, so it looks like we're safe—that is, if we keep our eyes peeled and we don't let him see us sitting on this bench."

Nick drew away from her. "Do you mean to tell me that we have to hide from that deputy—like cowering criminals?"

She looked offended. "Nicky, can't you be patient with me for a little while? I'm trying to work this thing out!"

"Well, how long do I have to *be patient*? I'm not going to be able to tolerate much more of that deputy!"

"Just try to understand my predicament! By the way, what did he say to you last night after I went to his car?" she asked.

"Let's just say that he wasn't too happy with the situation."

"Oh, it's getting to the point that I can hardly put up with that man!" Her expression displayed anger.

"Then why *do* you put up with him?" To indicate that he wasn't angry, Nick placed his arm around her.

"Nicky, he's not always so mean. In fact, sometimes he's very nice to me. I don't care for him romantically, but I don't want to deliberately hurt him. I told you my life is complicated. Just be patient with me, and don't give up on us. We'll work something out, Nick."

Nick suddenly felt sorry for her. He smiled and cuddled her close to him. "Okay, I'll try to be patient. But I've about *had it* with that deputy. Anyway, let's talk about something more pleasant. Lauren, for the first time in months, I'm getting excited about my life. Do you remember me telling you about the possibility of my going back to college on the G.I. Bill? Well, I think I've decided what I want to do with my life: I want to be a *lawyer!* I can take some political science courses and work part-time. I feel good about the future!"

"Well, that's great. But why a lawyer?"

"Because, for most of my life, I've seen nothing but injustice. I know that I can't change the world, but maybe I can make the world a little better place. I might even get into politics."

"Well, that's great. I'm so proud of you! The practice of law is a very noble profession."

He was now bubbling with enthusiasm. He stood and began to pace in front of her. "That's one reason I have such respect for people like your father. He tries to make the world a better place by enforcing the law and keeping the peace."

"Oh, Nicky! My father will be impressed."

He sat back down beside her. He felt a bit embarrassed about his long-winded speech. "Well, enough about me. What is your dream? The last time we were together you said that your secret desire was to be a teacher, but that your father wants you to be a pediatrician. You said that talking about it made you feel uncomfortable. Maybe that's God's way of telling you that you ought to follow *your own dream.*"

She hung her head. "You know, you could be right. I was a pre-med student in college, but it took me five years to graduate because I also took some education courses. I had some biology courses, and if I just pass a few more subjects, I could take my certification test to be a teacher." Her expressive eyes brightened with her rationale.

"Great, Lauren! Maybe that's what you ought to do with your life." Nick pulled her to him. "You'd make a wonderful teacher."

Her expression again became sad. "Who am I fooling? Do you think I'd disrespect my father's wishes enough to do that? This kind of talk just makes me more frustrated. And as I told you, my life is already complicated enough!"

"I'm sorry to hear you say that. When you were talking about the possibility of becoming a teacher, that's the happiest I've ever seen your eyes."

"Oh, Nicky! The way we're sharing our dreams about what we want to do with our lives! You'd think we're on the verge of getting married!"

"Yeah," he said, with sadness and a bit of sarcasm. "How silly of us! Isn't that a ridiculous assumption?"

For a long time, they sat on the bench, absorbed in the serenity of the evening. The gray veil of twilight crept in, and

157

the rising moon in the east cast a silvery reflection across the surface of the placid lake. In the distance, the pale blue of the distant Smoky Mountains became a misty, luminous gray.

"Are you mad at me, Nicky?" She placed her head on his shoulder. "Oh, Nicky—what am I going to do about you?"

Without answering, he only fixed his eyes on the peaceful lake. A gentle breeze introduced the scent of the cooling night. The mournful wail of a distant train whistle broke the silence of the evening. Suddenly, he felt very lonely.

If only I had the key to unlock her independent spirit—If I could break the chains of her own forging, he thought.

The beam of a flashlight scanned the area. She turned her head to look up the hill toward the parking area. Then, she quickly whispered, "Oh, Nicky! It's him! It's Mike! He's turning around in the parking lot, looking for me!"

Lauren quickly stood and took his hand. She seemed to be in a state of panic as she pulled him up from the bench.

"Come on, Nicky! Hurry, we've got to hide!"

"Hide? Do you expect me to hide from that bastard? You've got to be kidding me!" He was becoming angry.

"Please! Please do it for me! If you don't, it will be all over for us! Just give me just a little bit more time! Oh, please! *I love you, Nicky!*"

Stunned by her profession of love for him, he obediently followed her as she pulled him along the path to the nearby row of shrubbery beside the lake. They crouched silently among the leaves as the deputy walked down the hill and stood near the bench they had vacated. The beam of light scanned the bushes and the surrounding area as Nick and Lauren quietly remained hidden from sight.

Nick was filled with a mixture of rage and shame. He had faced many dangers in the past: fighters in the boxing ring, and in the war he had faced the blazing muzzle of a machinegun. He had even been blown to hell by an enemy grenade without openly displaying fear; yet, here he was, cowering in the bushes from a small-town deputy sheriff. During the war Nick would have killed him as easily as squashing a fly. Although he still carried emotional scars from the war, he had no fear of standing up for either himself or Lauren.

They heard the deputy curse. He extinguished the flashlight beam, trudged back up the hill to his car and drove away.

Lauren followed closely behind as Nick came out of the bushes. He again took a seat on the bench. She continued to stand nervously pacing in front of him, sensing his anger. Avoiding her remorseful eyes, he only stared at the lake. He was consumed with anger and shame. His loathing of the deputy was only surpassed by the anger that he felt toward her, for she had placed him in the impossible position of choosing between his love for her and his manhood.

She sat down beside him and hugged him. He ignored her and continued to stare at the lake.

"Nicky? Nicky, look at me."

He turned his head toward her.

"Please don't be mad at me...I can tell that you're *really* mad at me..."

"What you did is terribly unfair to me. You played on my affection for you. What's even worse, you took my self-respect."

"Oh, Nicky! Please forgive me! I just didn't know what to do. If Mike found us here and then went back and told Daddy..."

He quickly stood. "I was a fool to meet you here tonight! You're not ready for a relationship with me. In fact, you're not ready for a relationship with *anybody*. When we first met, I thought I detected an independent spirit in you. But now I can see that I was wrong. I doubt that you can even go to the bathroom without your father's approval. Unless I can date you openly, then I'll never be with you again because I won't continue to hide from people. Since I know that you don't have the guts to do that, then I'll just end it now! Goodbye, Lauren."

"Wait! Please don't leave me like this...I'm sorry! Nicky, *I love you!*" She tried to restrain him from leaving.

Nick glared at her. "You love me, but you want to *keep it a secret?*" He pulled himself from her grasp and walked up the hill toward his car.

Chapter 11

"Damn, Stan, how could just one man ever manage to accumulate this much junk?" Nick was beginning to sweat from the burdensome task of carrying Stan's belongings into their new living quarters.

Stan laughed. "Well, *you* didn't have much to carry, that's for sure."

The furnished two-bedroom apartment was located on the lower floor of a two-story brick house. The top floor of the large dwelling was occupied by the elderly widowed landlord, and was accessed by a stairway in back.

The structure was old but in excellent repair. In the front yard, two large maple trees shaded the oversized front porch that sheltered the front entrance to the ground floor. Throughout the entire living quarters, an array of outdated but comfortable furniture rested on the hardwood that covered the floors of every room. The off-white walls distributed the clean smell of fresh paint and the interior of every room was immaculately clean and spacious. Nick and Stan were pleased with the apartment, for its location gave them easy access to both the downtown area of Cedar Valley as well as their jobsite; also, at eighty-five dollars a month, the apartment was a bargain.

Nick tossed his armload of Stan's clothing onto the rocking chair and took a seat on the couch. "Whew! I gotta take a break, buddy. Say, I've got an idea. Why don't we determine what each guy pays by the amount of his stuff he brings into the apartment?"

"Hell, at that rate, you'd never pay anything!" said Stan.

"Seriously, Stan, I was only kidding. I want to pay my own way. I don't want you paying all the rent, like you suggested. You've already been too good to me: the job, the clothes, and the generosity of your parents."

"Hell, don't sweat it, Nicky. You can start paying your part when you get on your feet. By the way, House Cat says that you're really catching on fast on your job. You've only been working for him for about a week. You're doing great."

Nick quickly rose from the couch. "We might as well get back to work. We're almost finished."

"Yeah, I think one more load will do it," said Stan.

They trudged out to Stan's car and removed the final two boxes of odds and ends and carried them into the house. Nick placed his portion in one of the bedrooms, while Stan set his box on the living room floor. "Hell, we got it all into the house. Let's rest for a while and have a beer." He flopped heavily on the couch. "Get us a beer out of the refrigerator, will you, Nicky?"

"Don't you want to put things away and straighten up the place first?" Nick was eager to finish.

"Damn it, this is Sunday. We've got all day to finish cleaning up. Take a load off, pal, and drink a beer."

Nick opened two cans of beer and handed one to him. He sat in a chair facing Stan.

Stan smiled. "Tell me something, Nicky. Are you still pouting at Lauren? You haven't seen her in several days, now. What's up with the two of you?"

"Nothing's up. And I'm not pouting at her. I just refuse to slip around and hide in order to be able to date her, that's all. Remember when I told you about the way she pulled me into the bushes in order to hide from Bronson? Well, I would never have hidden from that bastard if she hadn't told me that if he caught us together that it would be the end of our relationship! At first I was mad, but now I'm more worried than mad. She seems to have some kind of fear of him…I wonder why?"

Stan sighed. "Hell, man, I don't know. If you'll remember, I told you that dating her wasn't a good idea. But in a way, I'm kinda sorry you didn't hit it off. Too bad…Maybe you would have been good for each other." He sipped on his beer.

"I thought you told me that we were a misfit for each other. Make up your mind." Nick lit a smoke.

"Well, at first I thought so. But now I'm beginning to see that Lauren needs a guy like you. Maybe you could free her from the strangling clutches of her old man. Damn it, I know how she feels. I've got the same problem. Dad raised holy hell when I told him we were moving to this apartment. I can't wait to start back to college so I can do something else with my life besides working for him. Have you decided what you're going to major in when you enroll in college?"

"Yeah, I decided I want to be a lawyer."

"A lawyer? Damn! You'll have to go to school forever! You'll have to complete college, then get a law degree, and pass your bar exam. Why do you want to be a lawyer?"

"It's kinda hard to explain. Remember when I told you how I hate injustice? Well, by becoming a lawyer maybe I can offer something to the world that will help further the cause of justice. This is a nation of laws. I know I can't change the world, but maybe I can get into politics and help change some laws that are unfair to people."

"Hell, the same old 'fair-minded, goody-two-shoes' Nicky. Sometimes, when laws are stupid, you just have to overlook 'em. C'mon, man, smarten up!"

"But if a law is stupid, we need to work within the boundaries of law to change it." He crushed out his cigarette.

"Oh, really?" Stan's tone was sarcastic. "Well, let me tell you something about the law in the South. We've got our own ways of keeping the peace. Did you ever hear of the unwritten law?"

"The unwritten law? What's that?" Nick seemed puzzled.

"In the South, if a man crawls in bed with another man's wife, it's okay for the husband to shoot him."

"Shoot him? Do you mean that in the South the husband gets away with killing a man for sleeping with his wife?"

"Well, with a tough jury, he might have to serve a year or two, or he might even get a suspended sentence. But in most cases it'd never go to trial. The grand jury would just toss it out."

"But, that's not justice!" Nick stared at him in disbelief.

"The hell it isn't! It's the best kind of justice! If somebody murdered your mother or your father—would you call the police, or just simply kill the murderer?"

"I'd call the police."

"Bullshit! And what if the law didn't convict the son of a bitch? Would you just let him get away with it?"

"Then I'd work to change the law! If we don't have laws, we might as well be living in the jungle! Stan, I didn't know you felt this way. I thought you believed in law and order."

"Hell, man, I do. I'm not a damned savage! I believe in our justice system, but occasionally, we have to help it along a little bit. Sometimes justice is kinda fuzzy. Know what I mean?"

"Yeah, you're right. Sometimes the law makes mistakes, and what we call 'justice' is not always fair. But it's all we've got."

Stan suddenly stood. He laughed uproariously and slapped Nick on the back. "I kinda had you going there, didn't I, pal? Do you still want to become a lawyer?"

"You bastard!" Nick was slightly embarrassed.

Stan placed his hand on Nick's shoulder. His expression became serious. "I'm proud of you, and I'm sure you'll make a damned good lawyer. Say, hadn't you better be checking on how to get that G. I. Bill to pay for your college?"

"Yeah. I'm gonna check on it this week. If it doesn't come through by September, I may have to wait until winter quarter to enroll. I can hardly wait to get started."

"What's the hurry, as long as you enroll? Listen, I know you've suddenly developed a burning ambition to make something out of yourself. But you don't have to do it overnight! Hell, man, you're getting so serious lately I'm beginning to worry about you. Easy does it, my friend! Are you trying to make a good impression on Lauren?"

"Stan, I really care a lot about Lauren. But I'm trying to make something out of myself for *me*. I have no control over what she does. Unfortunately, neither does Lauren. Only her father has control of her thoughts and actions."

"Well, you might say the same about me." Stan seemed sad.

After several more beers, Stan became slightly intoxicated, and by 9:30 he retired for the evening. Nick straightened up the place a bit and also crawled into bed early.

The remainder of the week quickly passed. Each day, Nick took Rufus to and from work, sometimes having dinner at his house in the evening. He quickly bonded with little Caleb and developed a fondness and respect for Rufus and Mary Rose. The rapid development of his job skills drew praise from House Cat, although sometimes his barbed comments were hard to recognize as approval. He even talked of promoting Nick to a full-fledged carpenter.

Stan had a multitude of duties: He kept the books, wrote the payroll checks, ordered supplies, and supervised crews at two other projects. Sometimes, he either performed finish work on one of the houses or filled in as a cab driver for his dad's taxicab business.

Often, Nick thought of Lauren. He missed her terribly, but figured that her father would never permit her to date him.

On Friday at noon, Stan came to the jobsite with the payroll checks. He issued checks to the employees, withholding Nick's check until last. With a furtive gesture, he motioned for Nick to join him beside his vehicle. "Nicky, I need to talk to you."

"What's up?" Nick sensed trouble.

"Well, I don't know what's going on, but Uncle Larry wants to see you at his office."

"Do you mean that the sheriff wants to see me? What about?"

"I don't know. Did you get into a ruckus with Mike Bronson, his deputy? Or did you insult Lauren in some way?"

"No, I didn't insult Lauren. There's not any love lost between that deputy and me, but I haven't broken any kind of law, to my knowledge. Hell, the sheriff doesn't even know me. We've never even met. What could he possibly want with me?"

"I don't know, buddy. But he had a serious look on his face when he told me."

"When does he want to see me? And where?"

"He wants to see you as soon as you can get there, at his office on the lower floor of the county jail."

"But what about my job, here? Hell, man, I'm working."

"Don't worry about your job. I'll clear it with House Cat, and I'll see to it that Rufus gets home. Now get out of here and drive down there."

"Where is his office?"

"At the county seat. It's just a couple of miles west on Highway 11. As soon as you cross the bridge at the river, it's the first building on the left. You can't miss it. Now, get going."

On his drive to the sheriff's office, Nick began to become nervous. He remembered his former panic attacks during

166

stressful situations. Although he had recently made some progress in his emotional recovery, the mystery of the situation had again made him anxious.

In less than ten minutes, he pulled his truck into the parking area in front of the jail. The building was an austere two-story brick edifice with a wooden porch on the front. Vertical steel bars covered the narrow upstairs windows on the front and sides. The ominous structure had been built only a few feet from the edge of the bridge, leaving the impression that its construction probably took place many years before the bridge was built.

Nick ascended the porch steps and entered the front door into a medium-size room that was obviously the sheriff's office. The powerful odor of disinfectant permeated the empty room. To the right was the sheriff's desk, and behind it rested an oversized, comfortable chair. On the wall facing him was a steel door; also, a locked gun rack encasing several handguns and what appeared to be two shotguns. A ten-gallon hat hung on the wall beside the gun rack. The wall on the left had a steel door that obviously led to the upstairs jail; for he could hear the muffled conversation and clamor of the prisoners as they engaged in their daily jailhouse activities. He took a seat in one of the three chairs that were aligned against the left wall.

Nick waited for several minutes. When he pondered this mysterious confrontation with the sheriff, his palms began to sweat; for this wasn't just *any* sheriff—this was *Lauren's father*.

The sheriff entered through the door beside the gun rack. In stature, he was indeed an impressive figure. He was even taller than Stan's father, and his long-heeled western boots exaggerated his actual height of six-feet-six. His facial features bore a strong resemblance to those of his brother; however, he was heavier through his mid-section. He wore a pair of black trousers and a white, long-sleeved shirt with a gold star pinned to his left shirt pocket. Nick figured that the ten-gallon hat hanging by the gun rack was his.

167

Upon entering the room, his stern expression softened when he saw Nick, who immediately stood when the sheriff entered. He smiled and thrust his hand toward Nick. "Well, you must be Nicky Parilli. You look just like my daughter described you. Have a seat there, son. I'd like to have a little conversation with you." He released Nick's hand and reclined in the comfortable chair behind his desk. Nick returned to his former seat, facing the sheriff.

"Well, how can I help you, sir?" asked Nick, politely. He was mildly surprised that he was able to speak without stammering.

The sheriff opened his desk drawer and extracted a box of cigars and placed them on his desk. He then extended the container to Nick. "Son, would you like a cigar?"

"No, thank you, sir," answered Nick.

Sheriff Mullins stuck a cigar in his mouth and lit it. He studied Nick as he leisurely blew out the match. "I always enjoy a good cigar whenever I sit down for a pleasant conversation. Do you mind if I smoke?"

"No, sir. I don't mind."

"Nick, it's a bit difficult for me to know where to start, so I'll just get to the point. What do you think of my daughter, Lauren?"

Nick's hands betrayed him with a slight tremble.

"There's no need to be nervous, son. I may look mean, but I don't bite." The sheriff chuckled.

"I...really like Lauren. I think that she's a special girl." Although puzzled and a bit nervous, Nick was gradually beginning to regain his self-confidence.

"Yes, she *is* a special girl, Nick, and it appears that she seems to think that you are a special young man...In fact, she seems to be quite attracted to you, son."

"Well, you might say that I'm also attracted to her—although I've never pushed myself on her."

"Tell me a little something about yourself, Nick." He smiled as he curiously eyed Nick. "I understand you helped our country by fighting in the war."

"Yes ...I did my best."

"Well, that's all that could be asked of you. I understand that you're working for my brother, Lester, in the construction business. What are your plans for your life? Do you have a career in mind?"

"I'm going back to college on the G. I. Bill. I plan to become a lawyer, eventually."

The sheriff seemed unimpressed. He blew a smoke ring and playfully poked his index finger through the center. He seemed to be in deep thought.

Another police officer walked into the room from the door that accessed the jail. Like the sheriff, he was also wearing western attire, including his boots and hat.

He eyed Nick with suspicion. The sheriff lazily glanced up at him. "Hi, Ernie. I'd like for you to meet Nick Parilli—Nick, this is Deputy Galyon."

"Hello, Mr. Galyon," Nick stood and extended his hand.

Without responding, the surly deputy continued to examine Nick as if he were trying to remember his face from a lineup or his participation in some recent criminal activity.

"Okay, Ernie, you can leave now," said Sheriff Mullins, "I need some privacy with Nick, here."

The deputy said nothing. He continued to eye Nick before turning and ambling out the front door. Nick returned to his seat.

"Some people don't have any manners, you know? Now where were we?" asked Sheriff Mullins. "Oh, yeah, you were saying that you are going *back* to college. What made you quit in the first place?"

"I went into the army, sir."

"That's a good reason, son. Our country needs more men like you. What about your family? Where are your parents?"

"My parents are both dead. My father was a hard-working Italian immigrant, and my mother was a simple housewife. We lived in a modest Italian neighborhood in Chicago. My mother and father were good, Christian people, and I'm proud of both of them."

"Well, you should be proud of them, Nicky. The hard-working immigrants are the people who made this nation strong."

"Thank you, sir."

"Nick, I want to be completely honest with you. Lauren came to me for my approval for the two of you to start dating. I told her I'd think about it, but I wanted to talk to you first. You seem to be a decent, ambitious young man; however, there's just one thing that has me worried."

"What's that, sir?" asked Nick.

"I just hope that you don't turn out to be one of Lauren's *toys*. You know, she's always come to me to get things that she wants. She wants *this,* she wants *that,* and then *something else.* She's a little spoiled, but she's a good girl, so a lot of times I give in and end up giving her what she wants. After all, she has an independent side to her, and I don't want her to rebel on me. The trouble is, whenever I give in and let her have another *toy,* she usually gets tired of it after a while and gets rid of it. Are you willing to take that risk? Would you like my permission to date my daughter?"

"Yes, sir. You know, maybe Lauren gets bored with material things—frivolous things that don't have much meaning. Maybe she wouldn't get tired of the more meaningful things—like relationships, a career she loves, maybe even children, someday."

The sheriff chuckled. "Well, I can see that you're not only a future lawyer, but quite a psychologist as well." His statement carried a hint of sarcasm.

"I'm sorry. I didn't mean to sound arrogant. After all, you know Lauren better than I do."

The sheriff suddenly magnanimously stood.

"I've decided to let you come calling on Lauren. I'll tell her tonight. I believe that you're a man of character."

Nick rose from his chair. Sheriff Mullins extended his hand to Nick as though he had just clinched a business deal. Nick had never before experienced such a transaction. The sheriff's permission to allow Nick to 'come calling' had the archaic ring of the Civil War era. It reminded Nick of the antiquity of the arranged marriages of a bygone age when the potential bride had no choice in the matter.

The sheriff released Nick's hand and both men turned to leave the room. Nick suddenly hesitated and turned toward him.

"Oh, by the way, Mr. Mullins. One of your deputies, Mike Bronson—am I going to have trouble out of him? He really likes Lauren, you know."

"Nicky, don't worry about Deputy Bronson. He'll give you no problem."

Nick drove toward home with a buoyant spirit. *He no longer would have to hide from the world when he was with Lauren.* In addition, he had maintained control of his emotions in the stressful discussion with the sheriff. He was proud of the progress he had made since his return from the war.

Chapter 12

Nick slowly pulled his vehicle into the concrete driveway of Lauren's home. Immediately, he was surprised by the drastic difference in style of the houses in which Lauren and her cousin, Stan had been reared. The long ranch-style brick dwelling was situated in the center of a perfectly level lot and surrounded by large shade trees. Unlike the stately, perfectly aligned trees of the antebellum mansion, the trees in the expansive yard were of a mixed variety and randomly arranged. Beside the winding marble-embellished sidewalk, a green and white hammock stretched between two maple trees near the center of the perfectly groomed yard. In every aspect, the estate suggested a character of casual opulence—a direct contrast to the perfect symmetry and formality of the Lester Mullins home.

Nick rang the front doorbell. A middle-aged Negro woman appeared at the door. Small and pretty, she had the trim figure of a younger woman. Her light-bronze skin, wavy hair, and even features suggested a trace of white blood in her ancestry. She was soft-spoken and courteous. With a polite gesture she invited Nick into the living room.

Displaying an elaborate smile, Lauren immediately came to meet him and quickly introduced him to Willie Mae. As usual, Lauren was radiant. She was casually dressed, wearing white slacks and turquoise shirt. Her raven hair smelled of fresh shampoo. After a brief embrace, she took Nick's hand and led him into the den where her mother was seated in a wheelchair reading a book. "Mother, this is Nicky Parilli, the young man I was telling you about—and Nicky, this is my mother, Bonnie Rose."

She put away her book and smiled. "Good evening, Nicky, it's so nice to meet you. I'm sorry, but Lauren's father isn't home yet. He's still on duty." Nick accepted her extended hand.

Lauren's mother was a small woman with graying hair. Her even features bore a kinship to Lauren's and suggested that she had once been beautiful; however, years of confinement to a wheelchair had shriveled her body and eroded away her former beauty. Her hollow eyes reflected an expression of hopelessness.

The female Negro servant walked into the room. "Miss Lauren, can I fetch you anything? Something to drink maybe, for you and the gentleman? How about you, Mrs. Mullins?"

"No, thank you Willie Mae," said Lauren, "Mother already has a drink, and Nicky and I have to leave right away. We're going to the movies."

"It's been a long time since I saw a movie," said Lauren's mother. "I think the last one I saw was a Mary Pickford movie. Do you like Mary Pickford, Nicky?"

"I don't know, ma'am. She's a little before my time."

"Oh, yes, of course she would be. What was I thinking?"

"Mother, if Nick and I are going to make that movie, we need to hurry. But first, I want to show him through the house."

173

"Lauren, could you please push me out to the patio?" asked her mother.

"Let me do it, Lauren," Nick offered. He pushed Mrs. Mullins out the sliding door onto the patio. "Is this okay?"

"Perfect," she answered, "Thank you."

"Come on, Nicky, I'll show you our house," said Lauren.

Mrs. Mullins smiled. "It was nice meeting you, Nicky."

"Yes, ma'am, I'm pleased to meet you, too." Nick answered.

Lauren quickly led him through the entire house. Like the outside of the dwelling, the interior mirrored the modern theme of casual affluence: colorful, modern furniture, with an abundance of modern lamps and throw-cushions and even a beanbag in the corner of the den. The walls displayed large abstract paintings. Nick figured that the colorful décor had probably been selected by Lauren. Directly behind the house beside the patio was a large swimming pool, and beyond that, a tennis court and a lavish flower garden. It was obvious that Lauren's luxurious upbringing bore little kinship to his.

Nick experienced a renewed sense of freedom in his first sanctioned date with Lauren. He no longer feared the discovery by her father of their clandestine meetings, or that they would be stalked by the deputy. They were in a joyful mood, for it had seemed an eternity since they had been together. During their short drive to the Grand Theater, they behaved like playful teenagers, basking in their sudden, unexpected freedom.

Lauren had chosen a romantic movie: *My Foolish Heart*, a Dana Andrews picture of 1950. Following the movie, they shared a hot dog and drank *Cokes* at the corner *Rexall Drug Store,* which was crowded with boisterous high school teenagers. Nick was swept with a feeling of nostalgia, for it evoked happy memories of his former carefree high school years in Chicago—a time of innocence, before he had been hardened by the war.

Nick selected a meandering route on the return drive to Lauren's house. He parked the pickup truck at the Observation

Point, overlooking the lake at Ft. Davis Dam where they shared intimate feelings beneath the luminous glow of the full moon that hung in the eastern sky.

A passing car caught Lauren's attention. She pulled away from Nick, eyeing the vehicle as it passed. Nick was surprised at her obvious concern. "Nicky, I'm not sure, but that car that just went by looked like Mike's car."

"Oh, I don't think so, Lauren. I don't think he'll bother us anymore." He remembered her father's promise that the deputy wouldn't be a problem. Since he and Lauren no longer had to keep their relationship secret, he was somewhat puzzled by her excessive fear of Bronson.

Their time at the lake was brief, for Nick felt that he should take Lauren home early, particularly on their first official date. On the short drive to her home, Lauren became curious about the recent meeting between Nick and her father. She nestled her head on his shoulder. "Nicky, what did you and Daddy talk about when you met with him?"

"We talked about us—you and me."

"Well, what did he say?"

"He just asked me some questions about my life. It all turned out very well. He seemed to like me. He thinks you're special. I agree with him."

"I'm so glad that he likes you." She hugged him and smiled.

They stood at her front door for several minutes, holding each other, dreading their separation. Finally, he kissed her goodnight and she went inside. He walked to his truck parked in the driveway. As he was opening the door, he again noticed a slow-moving car in the street in front of the house. *Was it the deputy's car? Probably not. After all, there might be several 1950 black Ford sedans in this small town.* He backed out of the driveway and started driving toward his apartment.

He couldn't recall ever being happier. His unraveled life was finally beginning to come together again: He was dating the most beautiful girl in Cedar Valley with the blessing of her father; also, he had a job and an apartment of his own; in addition, he was preparing to enroll in college, and he was finally beginning to overcome his fears that had been brought on by the war.

He stopped at a traffic light and switched on his radio. The melodious voice of Nat King Cole was crooning, *Unforgettable*, an appropriate song for his present mood, for he realized that he would never be able to forget Lauren.

The red traffic light switched to green, and Nick slowly pulled away. He had only driven for a short distance when behind him a pair of bright headlights bore down on him, finally moving to within inches of his back bumper. Suddenly, the car swerved as if to pass him, but instead, pulled alongside him and continued to travel in the oncoming lane. It was the deputy's unmarked car, moving beside him so closely that the vehicle was almost brushing his door. Looking to his left, Nick noticed the man in the passenger's seat. The western hat perched on his head identified him as Deputy Ernie Galyon, the surly officer he had met at the sheriff's office. Two short blasts from his siren caused Nick to slow his vehicle and pull over to the curb. The police car swung in behind him and parked.

Nick sat in his car, realizing Mike Bronson's motive for stopping him, but wondering what he could possibly be charged with that would hold up in court, for he had violated no law.

The two deputies approached, flanking each side of his truck. Without moving, Nick continued to sit in his vehicle as Deputy Bronson explored his face with the bright flashlight beam.

"Get out of the vehicle!" Bronson was obviously angry.

Nick continued to sit in his truck. The other deputy walked around to the driver's side, joining his partner.

"I said for you to get out of the damned vehicle!"

Nick ignored his command. "What did I do wrong?"

"I've been following you for several blocks! You ran a stop sign! You also went through that last red light!"

Nick continued to sit. "Then write me a ticket, and I'll be on my way. Why should I get out?"

Bronson flew into a rage. He violently jerked open Nick's door. "Get a-hold of him, Cowboy, and help me pull him out of there!" They tried to wrestle Nick out of his vehicle as he attempted to brace himself to keep from yielding to their force. Ultimately, they were able to wrest him from the truck. In the melee, Nick suffered several scratches on his neck and arms, and Ernie Galyon's cowboy hat was jostled from his head. They pinned him, face first, against the car and forcefully held him there. "Cuff him, Cowboy!" screamed Bronson. The other deputy snapped the handcuffs on Nick's wrists.

"I didn't do anything wrong! What are you charging me with? I didn't run either a stop sign or a traffic light! But even if I did, you can't take me to jail for it! You could never make that charge stick!"

"I'm charging you with resisting arrest, you son of a bitch! That charge will stick! It's your word against the word of two police officers. Help me put him in the police car, Cowboy!" Nick realized that even Deputy Galyon had a nickname— 'Cowboy.' As usual, the name was appropriate.

Cowboy opened the rear door of the police car. Bronson grasped the handcuffs that bound Nick's hands and jerked him backward toward the police car. In the process, Nick lost his balance, falling on his back to the street.

"So you're still trying to resist arrest, are you? You Yankee bastard!" Reaching into his hip pocket, he pulled out a blackjack. In anger, he delivered several blows to Nick's head.

Nick was now on the verge of unconsciousness. With the help of his partner, Bronson heaved Nick into the back of the police car.

Bronson pulled away from the curb and sped away. He turned to his partner. "Cowboy, call the wrecker service and have his truck towed in. We're takin' this bastard to jail!"

Cowboy inspected his hat, noting that it had become crumpled and dirty during the scuffle. He looked over his shoulder through the crosshatched steel barrier at Nick. "Look what you did to my hat, you son of a bitch!"

Nick slowly began to regain his senses. He became nauseous and stifled an urge to vomit. Blood began to flow freely from the cuts on his scalp, dripping onto the front of his shirt. Although the night was warm, he began to violently shiver. During the struggle, he had somehow wrenched his right knee, causing it to painfully throb.

Nick was angry. "Bronson, you and I both know what's really going on, here! You're going to catch hell from Sheriff Mullins! You arrested me for nothing!"

"Listen, you son of a bitch, don't say another word to me, or I'll stop this car and beat the hell out of you again! You went whinin' to the sheriff an' got him to let you date Lauren! Well, what's he gonna think of you now? Hell, you ain't nothin' but a jailbird, you bastard!"

On the way to the jail, Nick remained quiet, brooding, as the two deputies engaged in idle conversation. At last, they parked the car in front of the county jail.

Without any resistance from Nick, they hustled him up the steps to the front porch and then into the sheriff's office that adjoined the stairway to the upstairs jail. Sheriff Mullins had already gone home for the day. The steel door on the left was solid, with only a small peephole at the top that enabled officers to see inside the corridor that accessed the stairs to the jail. Galyon unlocked the door and Bronson viciously shoved Nick inside.

Nick turned to face him. "Doesn't the law entitle me to make a phone call?"

"Yeah, maybe tomorrow. I think I'll let you cool off a little bit before I let you make a call. Anyway, who would you call? After tonight, you won't have a friend in this town!"

Nick stood in the lonely corridor of the jail as he heard the metallic clang of the massive steel door close behind him.

Chapter 13

Soon after Nick was pushed into the jail corridor, he attempted to climb the steps that led upstairs to the jail complex, but his knee began to ache so severely that he feared that he couldn't make it. He collapsed on one of the steps. Deputies Bronson and Galyon, who had been eyeing him through the peephole in the steel door unlocked the door and entered the corridor.

"Okay, jailbird, you gotta go upstairs with the other losers," said Bronson.

"I've got a bad knee. I don't believe I can make it up those stairs." Nick explained.

"Alright, you damned wimp! If you're too stubborn to walk up the stairs, then we'll carry you up." Each of the deputies grabbed an arm. They half-carried and partially dragged Nick up the flight of steel steps while he cried out in agony with pain from his knee.

"Don't wake up the prisoners, stupid, or you might get the hell beat out of you by one of them. Right now, they're probably the only friends you've got." Bronson laughed.

The deputies left him and went back down the stairs. Nick eyed his surroundings. The dirty walls displayed Graffiti and crude obscene drawings. A former prisoner had autographed one of the walls with the message, "Billy Don was here." Three dim overhead bulbs provided the only light in the jail complex, which was composed of three large cells as well as a 'drunk tank,' and a special cell for women, which had a separate entrance and was hidden behind a veneer of steel plating. The barred doors on the three cells had been left open, allowing the prisoners to mingle with each other, while the door to the drunk tank was locked.

Counting the two people in the drunk tank, twenty-one prisoners occupied the jail. Rasping snores broke the silence of the complex, as many of them were sleeping. A few were sitting on their steel bunks merely passing the time, while a couple of them were reading. Only a few of the bunks had mattresses, most of which were filthy. One man was sitting on his bunk directly beneath a light bulb reading from a small Bible. To enable him to see in the dim light, he squinted his eyes. He wore bifocals and held the book close to his face.

The stench inside the jail was overwhelming. A sickening mixture of stale cigarette smoke, urine, feces, and body odor saturated the air. There were no provisions for keeping clean—no wash basins, mirrors, nor soap. Only a bare faucet over a drain in the concrete floor enabled the prisoners to have drinking water.

In order to relieve his throbbing leg, Nick chose an empty bunk and sat down. Fearing that he might catch lice, he was glad that the bunk had no mattress. He tried to keep from touching anything.

He felt a sudden urge to urinate. In the dim light, several roaches scurried away as he hobbled toward the commode in the corner of the cell. Looking downward prior to relieving himself, he suddenly began to retch, for the sickening sight before him almost made him vomit. The plumbing to the lidless commode was apparently clogged, for a disgusting mixture of feces and urine completely filled the receptacle to the brim, even spilling over onto the floor. He realized that this horrid hellhole was not fit for human habitation. No decent human being would subject his fellowman, regardless of the nature of his crime, to such loathsome conditions. Dungeons in the bowels of the castles in the dark ages could not have been worse. He held his breath when he urinated.

He favored his right knee when he slowly limped back toward his bunk. The man reading the Bible looked up at him and set his book aside. "Good evening, brother. I don't mean to be nosy, but I notice that you've been bleeding pretty badly. Were you in an accident?" His soft voice was almost a whisper.

"No, that red-haired deputy, Mike Bronson beat me up with his blackjack. I'd like to clean myself up a little bit, but I've got no place to do it. They don't even provide soap or a mirror in this place."

"No, this isn't exactly the Conrad Hilton, is it? What terrible crime did you commit to get beaten up so badly?"

"Nothing. He arrested me for nothing."

The man smiled. "Yes, I understand, brother. I found out a long time ago that everyone behind bars is innocent. If you don't believe it, just ask 'em."

"Hell, I don't give a damn whether or not you believe me." Nick said. He took a seat beside the man on the bunk. When the man laughed, his eyes expressed his mood.

"Well, perhaps you are innocent. It's not my place to judge you. Whether or not you're guilty is between you and God." He thrust out his hand. "By the way, brother, my name is Luke Temple."

"Nick Parilli," replied Nick. He shook the man's hand.

Luke leaned closer to him, examining his face in the dim light of the cell. "I'll tell you what," he said. "Come over to that faucet with me and I'll clean up your face a little bit. You can't tell where to wipe it off without a mirror." He pulled a

181

clean handkerchief from his hip pocket. "Don't worry, it's clean. Every man ought to have one thing in his life that's clean."

"How did you ever keep a clean handkerchief in this place?"

"I have a close friend who sometimes brings me some of the bare necessities. Come on, let me wash off some of that blood."

Nick followed Luke to the faucet where he proceeded to clean Nick's face.

They returned to the bunk and sat down together. Nick studied the man's features. Luke was a soft-spoken, middle-aged man with impeccable manners. Like Lauren, his expressive eyes reflected his moods. He was light-skinned, tall and gaunt, with an unhealthy pallor in his complexion. With thinning hair and a pronounced Roman nose, his face carried the look of dignity. In spite of the filthy squalor of the jail, his clothing was clean; for he was an articulate man.

"We need to do something about that bloody shirt," declared Luke. "I'm taller than you, but I believe my shirt will fit you." He dug into a satchel and removed a blue pullover shirt. Although wrinkled, the garment was clean and smelled of soap. He handed the shirt to Nick. "Here, put this on. You'll look a lot better." He pulled a tiny hand mirror out of his bag. "Use this mirror so you can see to comb your hair. Got a comb?"

"Sure. Thanks, Luke. I hate to take the shirt, but I really do need to get out of this bloody rag. How can I thank you?"

"You can thank me by passing it on, my friend." He grinned at Nick.

Nick changed into the clean shirt. Then, while Luke held the mirror for him, he carefully combed around the matted hair that covered the cuts on his scalp.

Their conversation had captured the attention of a prisoner seated on a nearby bunk. He was an obese man, with a massive roll of fat hanging over his belt. Because of his excessive weight he struggled when he stood. In order to better hear them he walked over and sat on the bunk across from Nick and Luke.

Nick again spoke. "I sure appreciate what you've done for me, mister. You don't even know me. Why are you being so good to me?"

The other man interrupted. "I'll tell you why he's so good to you. He's a preacher. At least he tells everybody he's a preacher!" His tone was derisive.

"A preacher? Is that true, Luke?" Nick was surprised.

"Yeah, it's true...I am a preacher. I also happen to be a drunk."

The other man laughed. "Did you ever preach a sermon when you were drunk?"

Nick became angry. "Hey, knock it off, mister! Who asked you to join this conversation, anyway?"

"Hell, I was just kiddin.' I didn't really mean to offend the preacher." The man hung his head.

"No offense taken, Double-Gut. I admit I'm a drunk." The preacher only smiled at him.

"Double-Gut? What kind of a name is that?" asked Nick.

"It's not a very flattering name," said the preacher, "Double-Gut Allison—at least that's the name everybody calls him. I never did know his real name. What is it, anyway, Double-Gut?"

"Clarence," said Double-Gut.

Nick took another look at the man. He decided that the obese man carried the nickname for obvious reasons.

The preacher introduced Nick to him.

"Double-Gut, this guy is Nick Parilli. He and I are just becoming friends."

"I'm glad to meet ya," he said, nervously. He shook Nick's outstretched hand.

Nick felt sorry for the man. "Look, pal, if you don't mind, I think I'll call you 'Clarence.'"

He grinned. "That's okay with me."

"Hey! Pipe down over there! Some of us are trying to sleep!" The angry voice came from a nearby cell.

"Sorry, Bobby Ray," answered the preacher. "We'll try to be a little quieter."

An elderly black man ambled up. He was yawning, and rubbing his sleepy eyes with one hand while vigorously scratching his crotch with the other. A stocky, clumsy man who walked with a slight limp, he breathed heavily when awkwardly choosing a seat beside Clarence. He habitually stroked the gray stubble that covered the lower portion of his face. Displaying a toothless grin, he said, "Do you fellers mind if I join you? For some reason, I jus' can't sleep."

"Join us, Satch," answered the preacher. "But we all need to keep our voices quieter so the others can sleep."

Clarence's face bore an apologetic expression when he looked at Nick. "Hey, mister...Nick is it? Listen, buddy, I didn't mean no harm when I made fun of this-here preacher. Hell, we all like to rib him a little bit. He's a good man. He just likes to get drunk now and then." He lit a cigarette.

Nick only laughed. "Clarence, you should apologize to the preacher...Not me. By the way, I lost my cigarettes. Can I bum a smoke from you?"

Clarence handed Nick a cigarette. "Why was it they arrested you? I heard you tellin' the preacher that they arrested you for nuthin'. Of course he didn't believe you."

The preacher corrected him. "I didn't say I didn't believe him. I just believe that a lot of people who go to jail are guilty of something. Most of the people in here are guilty. I'm guilty."

"Well, I'm not guilty of anything!" said Nick. "That deputy charged me with resisting arrest, but he really arrested me because he's jealous of me dating a girl he likes."

"Who's the girl?" asked Clarence. "I've seen him with the sheriff's daughter. It's not her, is it?"

"Not that it's any of your business—but yes, it is the sheriff's daughter," answered Nick.

"Oh, hell!" said Clarence. "Well, you won't be dating her anymore! That's for damn sure!"

184

"I can tell from your accent that you're from somewhere in the North," said the preacher. "There are a lot of things about these small Southern towns that you need to learn, son."

"Yeah, I'm finding that out. But when the sheriff learns that the deputy arrested me for nothing, he'll probably fire him. I'd like to get my hands on that son of a bitch!"

Satch, the black man spoke up. "You're dreamin,' mister. The sheriff ain't goin' to give a damn when he finds out that you was arrested fer nuthin.' They're all as thick as thieves. They're in it together, son."

"What do you mean, 'in it together?' In *what* together?"

"Heck, I don't even know where to start, man. Why don't you tell him, Preacher?"

"You're doing a pretty good job of it, yourself, Satch. You tell him, and keep you voice down."

Satch spoke in a whisper. "Don't worry. If I'm gonna tell him about how crooked this sheriff's department is, I'll sure keep my voice down. I don't want Little Billy to hear what I'm sayin'." He nervously glanced toward a bunk in a nearby cell at the reclining figure of a small man who appeared to be sleeping.

"Who's Little Billy?" Nick asked, softly.

"Little Billy Sneed," whispered Satch. "He's the jailhouse 'snitch,' or 'stool-pigeon.' He tells everything that's said and reports everything that goes on in this jail to the sheriff."

"Why does he do that?" asked Nick. "Hell, he's in jail too! Why would he want to rat on his cellmates?"

"Hell, he ain't charged with nuthin.' He's in jail because he *likes it* here. This is his home. Th' sheriff lets him live here and eat here. He even furnishes him with liquor in return for snitchin' on people. He goes in and out of jail when he pleases." He again nervously glanced at Little Billy who was still lying motionless on his bunk in the adjoining cell.

Preacher Temple smiled. "Don't worry about Little Billy hearing you. He's sound asleep. Can't you hear him snoring?"

Before continuing, Satch again examined the reclining figure. Apparently satisfied that he was asleep, Satch continued. "Jus' wanted to make sure he ain't listenin'. Don't want the sheriff to git a grudge ag'in me."

Nick was still puzzled. "But what could he snitch to the sheriff that would make any difference? What kind of a crime could any of us commit when we're locked up in jail?"

"You'd be surprised," Satch answered. "People sometimes tell other prisoners about crimes they've either committed or crimes they're plannin'. But it's when Little Billy's outside th' jail—on the street, that he brings in the most information to th' sheriff."

"What kind of information?" Nick again studied the sleeping figure of Little Billy.

"Jus' little bits of information he picks up on th' street. Information like his discovery of independent renegade bootleggers who ain't been makin' payoffs to th' sheriff, an' beer joints where a lot of people are drunk, an' where th' sheriff can round up a bunch of people gamblin'. If th' sheriff makes a big haul, he occasionally slips Little Billy a few dollars. Sometimes Little Billy even reports some real crimes—like somebody plannin' to steal somethin' or has beat somebody up. He jus' sneaks around an' picks up information here an' there."

"I imagine his cellmates hate him," said Nick. "I wonder why he never gets beaten up by one of 'em?"

"Hell, man…There ain't nobody in this jail that's fool enough to lay a hand on Little Billy. He's got th' sheriff's protection an' ever'body knows it."

"Damn! What a contemptible character!" Nick said.

"Hell, that ain't the half of it! Y' know this-here jail's full of rats? Well, Little Billy *loves* th' rats! He's even got one that he feeds! Kinda keeps it fer a pet. Named him *Oscar*. That big rat's almost tame—at least to Little Billy."

"My God!" Nick exclaimed. "How disgusting!" He stared at Little Billy with revulsion. "Are there many rats in this jail?"

"Yeah, man! This jail is infested with 'em!"

186

"Damn!" said Nick. He changed the subject. "You were about to tell me about the sheriff's department being as 'thick as thieves,' and being 'in it together.' What did you mean?"

Satch continued, "Let me put it this way," he said. "Th' sheriff and that brother of his run th' whole county. The Mullins brothers have got rich off the money they stole from people, and from th' illegal activities they're involved in."

"How do they steal money from people? Hell, the sheriff just tries to enforce the law! How is that stealing from people?"

Satch laughed. "Well, for one thing, they're stealing money from *you*. You'll have to pay a fine for resistin' arrest before you can get out of jail. If you're not guilty, that's stealin' ain't it?"

"Well, if they make me pay a fine when I'm not guilty, then technically, I guess it's stealing. But this is really just an isolated incident. How could they get rich from an occasional miscarriage of justice?"

"Well, th' miscarriages of justice ain't occasional. Let me tell you how their little racket works. Look around you at th' people locked up in this jail. Some of 'em are as guilty as sin. Maybe one or two of 'em robbed somebody, beat somebody up, or stole his neighbor's chickens. But a lot of the people that pass through this place and pay fines are as innocent as you are. Can you imagine how many people pass through this place in a year?"

"What do the police arrest them for? What are the people who are arrested charged with?"

"Well, they're usually charged with public drunk'ness. This-here's a dry county, y'know. Beer's legal, but hard liquor ain't. Ever' night, 'specially on Saturday nights, th' deputies, or *'fee-grabbers'* as we call 'em, go out an' ride herd on all th' beer joints, arrestin' as many as they can load up. O'course some of 'em are drunk, but a lot of 'em ain't."

"But beer's legal, isn't it?"

"Yeah, but it's ag'in the law to get drunk, no matter what you're drinkin.' If they say you're drunk, then you're *drunk.* It's your word ag'in theirs."

"But can't a man get a lawyer and fight the charge?"

"Yeah, but it's best just to pay th' fine an' go your way. That way, after four hours, you can get out of jail as soon as you pay your fine. Mos' people ain't got money fer a lawyer, anyways. If you decide to fight th' charge, you have to stay in jail 'til th' judge that tries the cases comes around about once a week, unless you can get somebody to post bond fer ya. Hell, even th' judge, Casey Duff, is crooked. Usually when he tries a case an' imposes a fine, he's as drunk as a pet 'coon. An' on top a'that, he runs a poolroom in town where he allows gamblin'—which is ag'in th' law. When a big gamblin' game is goin' on, he secretly tips off th' cops who arrest th' gamblers an' put 'em in jail. Then, before they can git outta jail, he's th' double-crossin' son of a bitch that lays a fine on 'em! Now ain't that a mockery of justice?"

Clarence said, "Well, I'm gonna get me some shut-eye." He grunted from the exertion of standing and waddled to his bunk.

"Goodnight, Double-Gut," said the preacher.

Nick became even more curious about the accusations that Satch had made. "But I still can't see where the sheriff could get rich from the piddling amount he might make from stealing from a few drunks. Anyway, doesn't the money collected from fines go to the county?"

"Hell, son, I doubt if there's any official record of th' arrest. Th' officers just divvy up th' money. Besides, that's not even th' main source of their thievery. Th' real money comes from th' payoffs that the sheriff gets from th' bootleggers. Do you realize how many bootleggers there are in this-here county?"

"But doesn't the sheriff often raid these bootlegging places?" Nick was still puzzled.

"Sure, they 'raid' 'em…after they call first and warn 'em to get ready fer a raid. Then the mornin' paper has a write-up tellin' how th' sheriff is enforcin' th' law by crackin' down on th' bootleggers. If a bootlegger makes a fuss about the price of th' payoff, then he *really does* get busted for bootleggin.'"

"Is this town the only Southern town that operates this way?"

"No, there are a lot of small towns in th' South that do th' same way. Hell, a couple of years ago, right down th' road in Athens, th' county law rigged th' ballot box an' stole th' election. An' then they kept arrestin' th' veterans from the Second World War for drunkenness. A lot of them weren't guilty of nuthin'. The ex-G.I.'s rebelled. They chased th' crooked police out of th' county. Shit, them guys ran like turkeys! It was like a war, with shootin' and everything!" He paused while he chuckled. "Then they reorganized an' elected their own county guv'ment. Hell, there's even been talk that Sheriff Mullins and his band of thieves stole th' last election in this-here county."

"Couldn't the citizens of this county also chase away the crooked police and have their own election?"

"Nope. After the war, patriotism ran high, so people were sympathetic to th' veterans. But the main reason is, people jus' don't know what's goin' on—and what's worse, the ones that do know are afraid to speak up, or jus' don't care."

Nick seemed puzzled. "But if the sheriff is as bad as you say he is, why don't the citizens vote him out of office?"

Satch only grinned. "Hell, th' so-called 'respectable' people think he's a great sheriff. They don't get arrested. They attend church with him and get favors from him, so they never see th' rotten side of' him. It's only th' poor, common people like you an' me—people that ain't got no political clout or social standin' that he picks on an' steals from."

The preacher placed his bony arm around Nick's shoulders and smiled. "Satch, with all that negative talk, you're going to make our friend, Nick, want to leave the South."

"I ain't told him nuthin' but the truth, Preacher."

Nick mulled over the revelation of Satch. He asked, "You said that there are a lot of bootleggers in the area. How does all the illegal booze get into the county?"

Satch grinned. "That's where th' sheriff's brother, Lester comes into the picture. He controls the bootleggin' here in this county. He has regular drivers that go to Nashville to pick it up. He sells to th' other bootleggers and also sells it to th' general public. Even that cabstand he operates is just a front. People go there to buy their bonded liquor. His cabs don't deliver people anywhere. They just deliver booze. He even sells moonshine to th' few who don't have money for the expensive stuff. Some people say he owns a still. Since he's th' mayor, an' his brother's th' sheriff, they've pretty much got free-reign of the county."

Nick looked at the preacher." Is all of what he's saying true?"

The preacher sighed. "Yes, son. I'm afraid most of it is true."

Satch continued. "See how smooth the operation is? Lester Mullins brings in th' illegal booze and sells it, people buy it, then get arrested for drunk'ness or possessin' illegal booze. The sheriff keeps th' fine, as well as the confiscated booze, which he either drinks hisself, or gives it away to some of his political cronies. And th' 'respectable' people don't know, or care, 'cause what respectable person gives a shit about people in jail? Hell, no tellin' how deep this thing goes, considerin' all the pies that th' Mullins brothers got their finger in. No wonder they're rich!"

"For what shall it profit a man to gain the whole world, but lose his own soul?" quoted the preacher, profoundly.

"How do you know all this, Satch?" asked Nick.

"Because my son, Joe, used to work for 'em. I guess they trusted him because, even if he told on 'em, which he finally did, they figured, *who would ever believe a nigger?*"

"Where is your son now? I'd like to talk to him." Nick asked.

"Ain't no way to do that, son. I ain't seen him in years. Th' Klan gave him a whippin' an' he cleared outta here fer good. Said he'd never come back."

"Is the Klan actually still active around here?"

"Hell, man—it's alive and well. It's one of them groups that nobody talks about an' mos' people don't even believe exists."

Nick became deeply depressed. *Maybe Satch is simply lying, or possibly exaggerating; or perhaps he has some private grudge against the Mullins family. After all, Satch is languishing in jail—not the best of places to establish any credibility.* But the preacher had verified the story; although he was also in jail, Nick sensed an inherent honesty in him that attested to his credibility.

"How about the members of the two Mullins families? Do they know about the crooked activities of Lester and the sheriff? What do you think, Preacher?"

"Well, I know both families pretty well. I used to be their pastor. I used to have their respect when I had a church—before I became a drunk. In Lester's family, I don't think his wife knows. He keeps his business private. But I believe his son, Stan knows all about it. After all, he runs his dad's business affairs. He even operates that cabstand sometimes."

"But what about the *sheriff's* family?" Nick asked. "Do you think they know?"

"I don't think so…or maybe they just *don't want to know.* You know how some people are. They sometimes are in denial. Like an ostrich, they often stick their heads in the sand. You know, *see no evil, speak no evil, hear no evil…*"

Nick changed the subject. "Man, this jail really stinks!"

The preacher said, "You know, son, of all the sins we've mentioned, the condition of this jail is probably the gravest sin. I was on the grand jury one time, and we unanimously voted to condemn this filthy jail. Unfortunately, nothing was ever done about it."

Nick said, "Well, at least the prisoners don't usually have to stay in jail for very long."

191

The preacher looked sadly at Nick. "That's where you're wrong, Nick. Some of these poor devils are in this jail serving eleven months and twenty-nine days. That's a long time to live in this filth with no place to even take a bath."

"Preacher, it really pisses me off that these terrible things exist in our society."

"Nick, I read something once that impressed me. I can't remember where I read it, but it goes something like this: 'Evil men prevail in the world when good men choose to do nothing.'"

Nick was sad. "Isn't there anything good about the law enforcement in this county?"

"Cheer up, son. Nothing's all bad, or all good, either. It's just typical of the sinful nature of man. The *city policemen* do a good job. In fact they're honest, hardworking cops as far as I know. It's the county deputies that are the bad apples, and even they do *some* good. They work the traffic, help people who've had misfortunes, protect the public by locking up dangerous criminals, and generally keep the peace."

"Yeah, they may keep the peace, but they *break the law.*" Nick had become completely disillusioned.

"Nick, it will always be that way, for it's the nature of man."

"Are you saying that we should just accept it because it's man's nature?"

"Certainly not. God expects us to stand up to the ways of Satan. He promises that Goodness will ultimately win out."

The men turned their heads toward the shrieking sounds coming from the women's section of the jail. Female shouts rang out. "You little bitch! I'll claw your eyeballs out!"

"The hell you will! You fat whore! Damn! Get off of me! Get off! Do you hear me?"

"What's going on, Bobby Ray?" the preacher asked one of his cellmates.

"Oh, it's just Little Pea Head Stanifer and Dirty Butt Wilson in a drunken fight. When them two women get drunk together, they never do get along!"

192

It occurred to Nick that even the womenfolk of Cedar Valley were not exempt from the widespread plague of nicknames. In a short time, Nick heard the jailer enter the women's lockup, and the drunken fracas ended.

Satch stood. "Well, gentlemen, I'm going to hit the sack."

"Goodnight, Satch," replied Nick and the preacher.

The cellblock became quiet. With the exception of Nick and the preacher, the other prisoners were all asleep. Some were snoring as they flopped on their filthy mattresses while others reclined on bare, steel bedsprings. The hour was getting late.

"I guess that you and I should try to get a little sleep, Nick. Do you have anybody to post your bond in the morning?"

"Yes, but I sure hate to ask him. If I get out, after I pay my fine, I guess I'll move on. I suppose I'll have to leave Cedar Valley." Nick hung his head in dejection.

"Where will you be going?"

"Maybe to Louisiana. I've got an uncle who lives there."

"So you think the answer is to run away, do you?"

"I don't know what else to do, Preacher."

"Nick, you're going to find a similar situation anywhere you go in the South. It may be a little different, but it all boils down to basically the same thing. As long as there's man, there's gonna be sin."

"But Preacher, the odds are stacked against me!"

"You know, the odds were stacked against David, too. All he had was a little rock in a slingshot when he had to face that giant, Goliath. But he showed the courage to not give in to evil. In my opinion, you ought to stay right here and fight for what you believe!"

"But how can I win?"

"Son, just by not ever giving in and standing up to it, you've already won. It's only when you give in to it that you lose. Well, goodnight, Nick."

"Goodnight, Preacher."

The preacher climbed into the top bunk above the bed claimed by Nick. The entire cellblock became quiet as Nick lay on his back on the steel cross-hatching of the lower bunk. His mind was in turmoil as he wondered how he would explain this unhappy event to Lauren. Suddenly, the dim lights flickered and then died, enveloping the entire jail complex in darkness.

Nick spoke softly, "What happened, Preacher? Is it 'lights-out' time?"

The preacher whispered from the top bunk, "No, Nick. They always leave the lights on at night. It's probably just a power failure. Maybe somebody crashed his car into a power pole somewhere close by. The lights will probably come back on as soon as the utility company fixes it. You'll probably sleep better in the dark anyway. Go to sleep."

In the eerie quiet and utter darkness of the jail interior, Nick experienced a feeling of loneliness and despair. *Maybe this is what hell would be like*, he thought. For a long while he lay on his back, motionless, attempting to calm his mind enough to enable him to go to sleep.

A strange noise broke the silence. In an irregular cadence, a series of "ticking" sounds seemed to be coming from the floor. *Tick...tick...tick...*Nick pondered over the cause of the faint repetitive ticking sounds. *It sounds like raindrops hitting the floor*, thought Nick. *Is it raining outside? Is the roof leaking?*

From the bunk above him, Preacher Temple screamed out, "Damn! Something's crawling all over me!" Nick heard the preacher and several other prisoners slapping themselves and cursing. Nick also brushed away something crawling on his face.

Suddenly the dim lights came back to life. Nick saw several rats and hundreds of roaches crawling on the floor, while an army of roaches inched their way across the ceiling before losing their tenuous grasp and falling like drops of rain to the floor. The brief period of darkness had emboldened the hideous creatures, luring them from their nests; but with the return of the revealing light, both the rats and roaches quickly scurried away, and in a short time disappeared into the

194

crevices at the bottom of the walls. After a brief outburst of complaints and curses from the prisoners, they once again settled into their bunks in an attempt to sleep.

Nick was so repulsed by the recent invasion of the detestable creatures that he made no attempt to sleep. He lay on his back engrossed in his hatred of Deputy Bronson, the man responsible for imprisoning him in this hellish place.

A slight movement from his left captured his attention. Beneath the bunk of Little Billy Sneed was a huge rat that had made no attempt to escape when the lights had returned. Nick figured that the monstrous creature was *Oscar*, Little Billy's pet rat. Nick was amazed at the size of the rodent. It was as large as a small opossum. With his hideous head down, he was munching on a scrap of food that Little Billy had apparently left for him. When Nick sat up in his bunk, his movement caused the rat to look toward him. Like tiny reflectors, his beady eyes mirrored the light from the dim light bulbs in the jail. Cautiously, but without any apparent fear, Oscar curiously eyed Nick.

In an attempt to scare the rat away, but with no desire to awaken the prisoners, Nick gently clapped his hands together. Oscar only slightly jumped and then slowly crawled deeper into the space beneath Little Billy's bunk.

Deciding that he would never be able to sleep with the rat in plain view, Nick picked up his bloody shirt, wadded it into a ball, and hurled it underneath the bed where Oscar was taking refuge. Seemingly in no hurry, the hideous creature emerged from beneath Little Billy's bed. Appearing to be more annoyed than frightened, he ambled away, turned his head, and cast a final glance at Nick before disappearing from sight.

Nick shuddered with revulsion. *Why hasn't someone killed that rat?* he wondered. Then he remembered: Because the sheriff protected Little Billy, all the prisoners were afraid to harm the repulsive pet.

Although the rat was a loathsome creature, Nick began to feel pity for him. He began to identify with Oscar; for, like

Nick, the abhorrent animal was simply trying to exist in a hostile environment. Also, because of Nick's war experience in which life is viewed with such disregard, he had acquired a renewed reverence for all living creatures, regardless of their repugnance.

Nick reclined on the steel bunk for most of the night without sleeping. His head and body ached from the beating, and his mind was in turmoil. In principle, maybe the preacher was right. Maybe he should stay in Cedar Valley and fight for what he wanted; but he feared that it would be impossible for him to endure the close proximity to Lauren without ever being able to be with her. If he settled in Louisiana, away from her, then maybe he could somehow manage to forget her. He wondered how she would react to recent events. *Would she condemn him?* He finally drifted into a fitful sleep.

The clamor of the stirring inmates awakened him. The top of his head was sore from the blackjacking, and he still experienced pain in his right knee. He noticed that the preacher was still sleeping.

A stream of sunlight from the barred window gradually lightened the gloomy darkness of the cell. The pungent odor of cigarette smoke permeated the area, again reminding Nick that somehow during last night's scuffle, he had lost his cigarettes. He bummed a smoke from one of the other prisoners.

At 7:00 a.m. he heard the clang of the downstairs heavy steel door opening. The prisoners quickly gathered in the corridor at the top of the stairs.

"What's going on?" asked Nick.

"Breakfast time," answered one of the prisoners.

A small inmate walked up to him. "Are you hungry this mornin'?"

"No. There's no way I could eat anything in this filthy place. Why do you ask?"

"Well, if you're not hungry, can I have your pan?"

"My pan?" asked Nick.

"Yeah, man, your breakfast. If you ain't gonna eat it, don't let it go to waste."

196

Nick accepted his pan from the jailer and turned to face the inmate. He was surprised that the man was Little Billy Sneed, the jailhouse snitch. His clothes were filthy and he reeked of body odor. Dandruff covered the shoulders of his dirty shirt.

Nick studied the man's features. He was a tiny, elfish, middle-aged man, short in stature and was so frail that he appeared to weigh less than a hundred pounds. The top of his balding head sported a few wispy strands of jet-black hair that thickened to a tangled fluff at the back of his head and extended to his shoulders. A thin patch of silky hair sprouted like tiny wires from his upper lip. He had a large beak-like nose, oversized ears, and yellowing teeth with protruding incisors hanging over his lower lip like fangs. When viewing these combined characteristics, Nick decided that he bore an uncanny resemblance to his pet rat, Oscar.

Little Billy again asked Nick, "Well, man…what about it? Can I have your pan?"

Without answering, Nick glared at Little Billy with contempt. He then turned and handed his pan to another prisoner.

To each of the prisoners, the jailer doled out a metal bread pan half-filled with greasy, white gravy. Tossed carelessly on top of the gravy were two slices of white bread. He then passed around to each inmate a tin cup filled with lukewarm black coffee. The prisoners carried their pans and coffee to their individual bunks and silently consumed their breakfast.

The preacher had now awakened. He entered the cell where Nick was sitting and took a seat on the bunk beside him.

"Good morning, Mr. Parilli," he greeted. "I hope you slept well. As for me, I hardly slept a wink."

"You missed your pan," said Nick.

"Yeah—isn't that a shame? I never eat breakfast here. Sometimes I eat supper in the evening. It's not that good. Corn bread and beans, mostly."

"They don't feed the prisoners very well, do they Preacher?"

197

"No, it's terrible. Sometimes the food is spoiled. The sheriff's department gets an allowance from the county that provides adequate funds for decent meals for the prisoners, but the police just pocket the money and feed slop to the prisoners."

"Are you charged with public drunkenness, Preacher?"

"Of course."

"Are you guilty?"

"Of course."

"When do you get out? Don't you have the money to pay your fine?" Nick was puzzled.

"Yes, I have the money, but I decided to just serve my time. You must either pay a seventeen dollars fine, or serve seventeen days. I decided to just do my time. I only have three more days to serve."

"Hell, Preacher, I'll pay your fine. Don't spend any more time in this hellhole."

"No, thank you. If I get out, I'll only get drunk again, so I'll just stay in jail."

"Where do you live, Preacher?" asked Nick.

"I live in Bucktown. Do you know where that is?"

"Yes, I work with a man who lives there. A black man by the name of Rufus Headrick."

"Yes, I know him. He's a fine man. He lives only two houses from me. Too bad about his grandson being a mute."

"Yeah…it sure is…"

The downstairs metal door clanged opened and a loud voice called out, "Nick Parilli, come down to the office!"

"They're calling for you, Nick," said the preacher. Nick stood and shook the preacher's hand.

"I gotta go. It was a pleasure meeting you, sir." He released the preacher's hand and started down the stairs.

The preacher called to him. "Son, remember what I said. You haven't lost the battle until you give up."

"I'll remember that. Thank you, sir."

Nick slowly limped down the flight of steps where the jailer was holding the door open for him. He stepped into the sheriff's office where he found Sheriff Mullins sitting behind his desk. To the left of him, occupying one of the chairs by the wall sat Stan.

Rather than feeling guilty or sheepish, Nick began to experience a consuming anger. Staring directly into the sheriff's piercing eyes, he remained silent, waiting for the sheriff to say something. He was unsure of the possible reaction of either the sheriff or of Stan.

Switching his gaze to Stan, he was surprised to see his mischievous grin. He looked back at the sheriff; although there was no humor in his expression, neither was there condemnation.

"Sit down," invited the sheriff. Nick took a chair beside Stan. "I can't seem to locate any of your personal items, Nick."

"They didn't take my personal stuff. They just threw me in jail," Nick answered, defiantly.

"Nick, I don't blame you for being angry," said the sheriff, "I warned Deputy Bronson not to start any trouble with you. I hope you can put this incident behind you without any hard feelings toward the department—although I don't expect you to be so forgiving of Deputy Bronson. He's really not such a bad guy. In fact, sometimes he's a rather good police officer. He just used bad judgment because of his bad temper, that's all."

"Well, what happens now? That scumbag said that I resisted arrest. Do I owe some kind of a fine?" Nick was still angry.

"Of course not," answered the sheriff. "You're free to go—with my apologies, I might add. As a matter of fact, Stan came here to take you back to your apartment."

Stan stood, and clasped his hand. "I'm sorry, too, Nicky. You shouldn't have to take that kind of crap. Mike is just jealous and has a bad temper. Like the sheriff said, he's not really a bad guy. Hell, I've even gone huntin' with him."

Nick turned to the sheriff. "Sheriff Mullins, I don't like to intrude in your affairs, but I thought I ought to tell you that one of the commodes in the jail is stopped up. Also, there are a lot of rats and roaches in the jail. I'm not trying to tell you how to run the jail, but I thought you probably weren't aware of these things and that you might appreciate knowing about it."

With a blank stare, the sheriff studied Nick's face. Then he smiled. "Thanks for bringing it to my attention, Nick. I've already taken care of those problems. A plumber is coming this week, and I've also called a pest exterminator."

He stood and shook Nick's hand. "Now go on home and clean yourself up, son."

Stan opened the door for Nick, and they started to leave. Suddenly, Nick turned toward the sheriff, who was still eyeing him. "Sheriff Mullins, I just have one more question. Does this have any bearing on my relationship with Lauren, sir?"

"Of course not, Nick. You didn't do anything wrong. But I'm warning you! I won't put up with some kind of feud going on between you and Deputy Bronson, do you hear? I'll talk to him about this, and I'll tell him the same thing. Now go home!"

On the drive back to the apartment, Nick's mind was filled with frustration. He felt relieved that the sheriff hadn't forbidden him to see Lauren; however, he was unsure of her possible reaction. *How would she feel?* In addition, his mind was still in turmoil about the accusations made against the Mullins families by the prisoner in the jail cell. The sheriff had shown empathy and understanding about the injustice that he had suffered. After all, how much emphasis should be placed on the wild accusations of a man in *jail?* And yet...the preacher, who impressed him as a man of integrity had confirmed the story; however, he also remembered that the preacher was a *drunk.*

"By the way, Stan, where the hell's my truck?" asked Nick. "I heard the deputy call a wrecker service last night to have it towed in."

"Don't worry about it, Nicky, I had the wrecker service take it to our apartment."

"Good…Thanks." said Nick.

Realizing that Nick was not in the best of moods, Stan drove to the apartment in silence and parked his car. The truck that had been driven by Nick sat in the driveway. For a while they sat quietly in the car.

Finally, Stan burst into laughter. "What kind of bird can't fly?" To trivialize the incident he was referring to a 'jailbird.'

"Damn it, it's not funny, Stan!" Nick failed to see the humor.

"Sorry, buddy. But, after all, it's not the end of the world. Come on, man! So you got into a little tussle with Mike Bronson! So what? Nobody's blaming you with it."

"How do you think Lauren will react to this, Stan?"

"Don't worry about that. I've already talked the whole thing over with her. She's mad as hell at Mike Bronson. You know, Nicky, I think you've stolen her heart!"

"Stan, I'm puzzled about something. Why in the hell would a classy girl like Lauren ever date a dumb-ass loser like Bronson? She's way out of his league. That's out of character for her!"

"Well, I told you it's a strange situation. She never actually *dated* him, although he'd give his eye teeth to date her!"

"Then what do you call it? For a guy who's not dating her, he seems to have been with her a lot. Hell, the first time I saw her she was with him at that Fourth of July dance!"

"But she didn't have a *date* with him that night. He just went there and met her. Let me explain it to you, Nicky. Lauren would *never* give a guy like Bronson a date. Like I told you before, her father just has him kinda ride herd on her to keep other guys from dating her. Guys won't ask Lauren for dates as long as Bronson is hanging around, because most of them are afraid of him. Uncle Larry is Bronson's boss, and he knows that he can control his behavior with Lauren. If Bronson ever got fresh with her, he knows that her dad would probably kill him! Or he'd wish he were dead! He sometimes just meets her at dances or ballgames and places like that and watches over her like a hawk. Although Uncle Larry likes for Bronson to keep an eye on her, he wouldn't allow a loser like him to actually *date* her. He's really nothing more than her *bodyguard*—or maybe a *chaperone*. As a matter of fact, Lauren has never really seriously dated *anyone* as far as I know."

"Oh, come on, Stan, don't give me that! She graduated from college! Didn't she date college guys when she lived away from home in the dorm?"

"She never really lived away from home. When she attended college she lived at home and drove back and forth to her classes at U.T. I told you before how her dad doesn't like for her to date. I'm sure that she's had dates before, but if she did I'll bet Uncle Larry sure put a stop to it in a hurry!"

"Damn! Poor girl! Why does her dad smother her like that?"

"I don't know. He just doesn't think anyone's good enough for her. That's why I'm a little surprised that he lets her date *you*—no offense intended, pal."

"Then why do you think he allows her to date me?"

"Well, let's face it…She's twenty-two years old now. I guess he's beginning to realize that he can't keep her from dating forever! She'd eventually rebel against him. Also, I believe that Uncle Larry really likes you…and since you're a close friend of mine he probably trusts you. You know, when Bronson arrested you for nothing it probably helped your cause, because Lauren's dad can see Bronson for what he is—a hotheaded, jealous control freak! Uncle Larry is beginning to see that Bronson thinks he owns her. And her dad will not allow anyone else to own her but himself… Larry Mullins—her father!"

"Why would she allow her father to own her like that?"

"Nicky, she's afraid to cross him. Hell, I'm a good one to talk! Dad controls me the same way. Why do *I* put up with it?"

"Damn! What a weird situation! Listen, Stan, let's go inside. I want to discuss something with you."

Nick followed Stan inside and took a seat on the couch while Stan fetched two cans of beer from the refrigerator. He came into the room, handed Nick his beer and sat in a chair facing Nick.

"Man, I'm dying for a cigarette," said Nick. Stan drew his cigarettes from his pocket and tossed the pack to Nick, who quickly lit up. "Aaah…man, this cigarette really tastes good! I was about to have a nicotine fit!"

Stan studied his face. "Okay, you said you wanted to discuss something with me. Let's have it."

Leaving nothing out, Nick proceeded to relate the previous night's jailhouse discussion of the Mullins' activities.

For a brief period, Stan said nothing as he studied Nick's face. Finally, he spoke. "I'm not going to sit here and try to defend my family's honor to you. Haven't we all been good to you? What about the sheriff? If he's the evil bastard that those jailbirds said he is, do you think he would have been so fair and reasonable with you this morning when he let you out of jail? Come on, man! You've been listening to a bunch of prejudiced crap from a bunch of jailbirds! Naturally they don't like the sheriff!"

Nick considered Stan's comments. "But, Stan—what about those accusations they made about the bootlegging? And about you selling booze out of the taxicab?"

"Listen, *Mr. Goody-Two-Shoes!* I don't want to offend you, because I think of you as my brother. But throw away your halo! Aren't you being a little hypocritical? Hell, Nicky, face it! Liquor's been around since man learned how to ferment the shit! It's in people's nature to want a drink occasionally. You like a drink sometimes, yourself! So I sell a little booze sometimes to make a little extra money! What's the harm? If people don't buy it from me, then they'll just get it somewhere else! Anyway, I don't care what your jailhouse buddies told you, but my dad's got no part in it. It's just my own little private enterprise."

"Look, Stan, I've got nothing against a man taking a drink. But if we're gonna drink it, then we ought to make it legal! That way we won't be breaking the law."

"Oh, you and your obsession with obeying the law! Like I told you before, we've got our own ways here in the South. Damn it, instead of being one of us, you've become an intruder! Things have been the way they are here in the South for a hundred years. If you don't want to feel like an outsider, then stop acting like one!"

"What about the terrible conditions in the jail? The place is so filthy that some prisoner might catch some disease! Why doesn't the sheriff clean up the place?" Nick asked.

"Nicky, some of those people are savages. Every time the sheriff cleans it up, the bastards end up trashing the place."

"But what about the sheriff? Is he aware of all the bootleggers here?"

"Hell, I don't know. But what if he is? Uncle Larry is a realist. He's also a good man. He keeps the peace! You won't find very much crime in our little town! Think about it! Compare the way my people have treated you with the way those jailbirds would treat you. Come on, man, lighten up! Don't let those ignorant bastards cloud your mind with that kind of bullshit!

"Well, what you say makes a lot of sense. Maybe I have been a little 'holier than thou.' I'll have to admit that your family has treated me better than I've been treated since I lived at home with my parents. Damn, I'm beginning to feel like an ingrate."

"Well, I'm glad you see through that prejudiced crap! Hell, if I were you, I'd just forget it. Nicky, you've got too much going for you to worry about petty things like getting arrested by Mike Bronson! Let's just take the day off and drink beer. By the way, Lauren wants you to call her sometime today."

Nick took a sip of his beer. He felt like a traitor for listening to the comments of the inmates.

Chapter 14

After his release from jail, Nick's life returned to a more normal state. For weeks he continued to date Lauren; also, the harassment from Deputy Bronson had stopped. He began to regain his optimistic attitude.

He hadn't yet received approval from the government to attend college on the G. I. Bill; consequently, he figured that his enrollment would have to be postponed until the winter quarter. However, Lauren's September enrollment date was rapidly approaching. Several days before her classes were to begin, Nick and Lauren went to the park for a picnic.

He swung the pickup into the broad parking area and parked in the shade of the large oak tree. It was Saturday morning, and a perfect day for a picnic. The sunlight was brilliant, and the summer morning was unseasonably cool. Lauren was bubbling with excitement when he leaned across the seat and playfully kissed her.

"If you'll carry the picnic basket, I'll carry the blanket," she said, "and don't forget the drinks."

"We need to pick a good spot," Nick said. "Do you want a place in the sun or in the shade?"

"It's kinda cool right now. Let's start out in the sun. We can move to the shade if we get hot."

They strolled through the freshly mown stretch of grass until they reached a sloping hill overlooking the lake.

"How about here?" she asked.

"Perfect! If we get too hot, we can move the blanket under the shade of that tree."

"I'd like to get some sun on my legs." she said. They spread the blanket and placed the basket and drinks under a tree.

"Lauren, you're as brown as an Indian already!" he said.

She slipped off her sandals, and with bare feet, stepped onto the blanket. Once again, Nick was captivated by her loveliness. Disheveled locks of her raven hair carelessly fell over her sunglasses, and in the back, it was tied in a ponytail. Her matched canary yellow halter and shorts offered a stark contrast to the bronzed, smooth skin of her back and shapely legs. When he reclined beside her on the blanket he could smell the subtle aroma of her perfume.

Nick looked at her and smiled. "Do you want to eat now or would you rather wait?" he asked.

"Why don't we just have a soft drink and enjoy the sun before we eat? Oh, isn't it a beautiful day? Look at the lake and the sailboats! Oh, Nicky, it's so lovely here!" She contentedly smiled and reclined on the blanket as Nick lay on the blanket beside her. He opened two drinks and handed one of them to her.

"Nicky, would you mind getting that suntan lotion out of our basket and rubbing some on my back and legs?"

"You're trying to get me all excited before we even have our picnic lunch," he quipped.

She laughed. "Do I excite you that easily?" She rolled over onto her stomach. He removed the lotion from the basket and began to massage her back.

"Mmmm, that feels so good, Nicky, and that warm sun feels wonderful."

"Well, the way that sun is bearing down, it won't be long until we'll be hunting the shade." He moved to her legs and continued to massage.

"Now get the front of my legs." She rolled onto her back.

The steady breeze from the lake grew stronger, causing her to shiver. "I'm cold. Keep me warm."

He set aside the lotion and lay down with her, covering her with a towel. Hugging her tightly, he pulled her to him and whispered, "I love to keep you warm." He gently cradled her face between his hands when he kissed her.

He released her and looked directly into her eyes. "Lauren, be honest with me. That time that Bronson arrested me...what did you think about me getting in jail? Were you ashamed of me?"

"Ashamed of you? How could you even ask me a question like that? I was angry at Mike for picking on you."

"Your father didn't seem to be judgmental of me when he released me from jail, but I wonder how he really felt?"

"He didn't say much about it. But I know that he was mad at Mike." She removed the towel and sat up with her arms behind her, bracing herself.

Nick smiled. "I was afraid your father would make you stop seeing me. I don't think he's that crazy about your dating me."

"Nicky, how can you say that?" She took a sip of her drink.

"Well, he probably thought that you'd be rid of me anyway when you start back to college. Or maybe he thinks that if he gave in and let you go out with me, you'd eventually get bored with me and our relationship wouldn't amount to anything. Maybe he'd rather go along with it than fight with you."

She again pulled him to her and kissed him. After slowly pulling away, she smiled. "Honey, as I told you weeks ago—*I love you!* I could never get bored with you!"

"I hope not, Lauren, because since I met you, I'm beginning to be happy again."

She again reclined on the blanket, and he soon joined her. For several minutes they silently lay on their backs, enjoying the warmth of the sun. The breeze from the lake had subsided, causing the early afternoon sun to heat up the day.

She said. "You were right. It's getting a little too hot. Do you want to move over into the shade?"

"I was just thinking the same thing," he said.

They moved the blanket to a comfortable spot in the shade beneath the large maple tree.

"Are you ready for some lunch?" Nick asked.

"If you are. Are you hungry?"

"Sure. Let's see what Willie Mae prepared for us." He dug into the basket.

"Willie Mae? I'll have you know I prepared that picnic lunch myself! And all especially for you! Aren't you impressed?"

"I don't know yet. It depends on what's in the basket."

"Oh, you'll eat it, no matter what's in it because I made it!"

"Well, I am impressed, and also flattered." He laughed.

They took a seat facing each other, crossing their legs. From the basket, Nick pulled out the usual assortment of paper cups, napkins, and disposable utensils. After placing these items on the towel, he removed a bunch of grapes, a large bag of potato chips, and a plastic bag containing two ham and cheese sandwiches. In the bottom of the basket were two large candy bars and a thermos jug of lemonade.

"This picnic lunch looks great, Lauren. Can I pass you something?"

"You can pass me one of those sandwiches and pour me a cup of lemonade, please."

They munched on their food, enjoying their intimacy as they gazed at the peaceful view of the lake and the distant mountains. When they had finished eating, they reclined together on the blanket in the shade of the tree. They quietly rested for several minutes, lying beside each other on their backs.

Nicky," she finally said, "Can I ask you something?" Her searching eyes explored the branches that hovered above them. "I've told you a couple of times that I love you, but you've never told me how you feel about me."

Nick lay silently beside her, attempting to frame the proper words in his mind. He felt that he was in love with her, but he remembered her words on the first night they had met: *My life is complicated...A lasting relationship between us would be impossible.* Although he was sure that they were now in love with each other, many of the complicating circumstances that she had mentioned hadn't really changed.

"Lauren, I've been hesitant to express my true feelings to you because I'm still trying to figure out how we can make this thing work."

"Why wouldn't it work, Nicky? We can *make it work!*"

"Lauren, you'll be going back to college in less than a month. Do you still plan to attend Vanderbilt?"

"Yes. That's where Daddy wants me to go."

"Are you sure? Is there any way you could attend The University of Tennessee instead?"

"No, I don't think so. Daddy has already arranged everything and even paid my tuition."

"Well, I've been worried about something that you and I have never really discussed. For some reason, we've avoided the subject. Remember when I told you I was going to apply for the G.I. Bill so I could go back to college? I was intending to enroll part-time at the University of Tennessee in September for the fall quarter, but since I haven't been approved yet, it looks like I'll have to wait until winter quarter. It'll be pretty hard for us to maintain a relationship when we're nearly two hundred miles apart."

She said, "But I could come home on weekends. We could be together then."

"Yeah, but on *some* weekends you wouldn't come home. And even when you did come home you'd be loaded with homework. I'm afraid we'd drift apart."

"I've also done some worrying about that. But, Nicky, couldn't you go to Vanderbilt, too? Then we could be together!"

"I don't see how. I'll have to work part-time, and I already have a job with Stan. And I'm settled here with an apartment."

"But couldn't you find a job in Nashville? Nicky, what if you meet another girl at U.T.?" Her eyes reflected worry.

"Well, you'll be meeting a lot of guys at Vanderbilt, too."

"What are we going to do, Nicky?"

"Look, you're a grown woman, now. You don't have to do what your dad says or go to the school that he chooses for you."

"Yes, I do, Nicky. In the first place, Daddy wouldn't pay for it if I decided to go to a school of my own choice. We *have* to figure out something. I don't want to lose you. I'd really like to go to school wherever you're planning to go, but Daddy would never stand for it. Maybe you could talk to him about it. He might listen to you."

"Are you kidding? I'm afraid my credibility was ruined when I got thrown in jail."

"Nicky, why don't you go to church with me and my family tomorrow? I'm sure it would make a good impression on my dad—not to mention me." She smiled at him and winked.

"Lauren, I really shouldn't go to church just to make a good impression on somebody. Besides, I'm a Catholic. But maybe I'll go with you sometime. Look, don't worry about our situation, I'll figure something out. Let's just enjoy our picnic."

She smiled at him. "I know you can come up with a plan."

Time passed as they cuddled together on the blanket. Lauren placed her head on his shoulder, appearing to be asleep. She finally raised her head. "Honey, I'm so sorry that they put you in that nasty old jail."

"Oh, it wasn't that bad. By the way, when I was in jail, I met a man who says he knows your family. He's a preacher—Luke Temple. He seems like a holy man, but he stays drunk a lot of the time. I'm puzzled by him."

"I remember him. Poor man, he used to be our preacher."

"What happened to him?"

"His wife left him. About three years ago, she took off with another man. Preacher Temple hasn't been the same man since it happened."

"That's too bad. He said that he lives in Bucktown. In fact he lives very close to Rufus."

"Is Rufus still helping you on the construction job?"

"Yeah. He's a good worker. He really loves Stan, almost like Stan's his own son. You know, he used to live with the Mullins."

"That's not surprising. He helped raise Stan, you know. I feel the same about Willie Mae. She helped raise me, too."

"I'm so sorry that your mother is confined to a wheelchair. What happened to her?"

"She was injured when she fell down the stairs when we lived in a two-story house. That's why we moved to a house that doesn't have an upper floor, so Mother can get around in the house. I was just a little girl when it happened."

"Does Willie Mae live with you?"

"Yes, Daddy had a big room built for her out by the patio. She is really like one of the family."

They continued to lie on the blanket, lazily whiling away the afternoon. Lauren discussed her family and her mother's disability, her childhood, her friends, and her church. Nick told her of his life in Chicago and his college years.

"Tell me about the war. It must have been awful for you." She looked at him with compassion.

"Yes, it was bad. It messed me up for awhile, but I'm getting better, now." His discussion of the war was a brief and sketchy account in which he didn't elaborate on the terrible details.

211

They continued to lie on the blanket. Looking toward the road, Nick saw Bronson's unmarked police car slowly pass. He figured that it was just as well that Lauren hadn't seen it.

In late afternoon, they left the picnic area and Nick drove her home. When they kissed goodbye at the front door, he again reassured her. "Don't worry, Lauren, We'll make it work, somehow." However, for the moment the solution eluded him.

On Monday morning when he picked up Rufus, his mind still dwelled on Saturday's picnic with Lauren. Since Sunday had been such a lonely day for him, he almost regretted that he hadn't yielded to her invitation to attend church with her.

Rufus displayed a toothless grin. "Man, you musta had an interestin' weekend, Mistah Nick. You ain't said nuthin' since you picked me up."

Nick turned right onto Highway 11 and headed toward Cedar Valley. "Oh, I was just daydreaming. I didn't do much over the weekend. I just took Lauren on a little picnic Saturday. I spent Sunday just lying around the apartment with Stan."

"Speakin' of Mr. Stan, I understan' he's gonna be workin' with us today."

"Yeah, that's what he told me. You're a real versatile man, Rufus. You not only do the yard work for the Mullins family, you also help in the construction business. Do you like working for Stan?"

"Yessuh, I sho' do! Mistah Stan is prob'ly my best friend. Why, I hepped raise that boy! Used to take 'im fishin' with me." He laughed at the memory. "I remember one time I tuck 'im fishin' an' he didn't catch nuthin.' He was real dis'pointed 'cause he wanted his pappy to be proud of him. You know whut I did? I bought a string a-fish from another fisherman close by, an' we tuck 'em home. We tol' his pappy that Mistah Stan done ketched 'em—now whut do ya think a-that?" He laughed uproariously.

"Well, I'd say that you pulled a fast one on Mr. Mullins, Rufus." Nick smiled at him.

"Yessuh, we sho' did, that's fer a fact! An' lawdy, that Mistah Stan was always fulla mischief when he was a lad! Man, I sho' got him outta a lotta trouble with his pappy. We done cooked up enough lies together to send us both to hell!"

"Well, I understand you used to live with the Mullins. And Stan told me that you were like a second father to him."

"Yessuh, I'm sho' glad to be a part of that fambly. I been tryin' to git Mr. Stan to start goin' to church ag'in."

"By the way, speaking of church—that time I was arrested I met a preacher in jail that says he's a friend and neighbor of yours—Luke Temple…Remember him?"

"Lawd, yes! He's a *good* friend! Lives jus' up th' street from me. Me an' him's been friends fer years!"

Nick pulled the truck into the grassless area to the left of the house. At least five other vehicles were parked in the dusty yard. The workers were just getting started. Two men were unloading bricks from a flatbed truck. One laborer delivered a wheelbarrow load of bricks to two bricklayers who were working on the walls. Stan and House Cat came to meet Nick and Rufus when they stepped out of the truck.

"It's about time you guys got here," said House Cat. "Musta been a rough weekend." He chuckled, mischievously.

"Hell, House Cat," Nick answered, "it's still not even eight o'clock yet. What do you want us to start working on?"

"We need to put that hardwood floorin' down. I guess me and you can work on it. Stan, why don't you and Rufus start unloadin' that hardwood, an' me and Ace can start layin' it down. When you get a load of it inside, you an' Rufus can start loadin' up that scrap lumber an' haulin' it off."

Since, technically he was the actual boss of the project, Stan was unaccustomed to taking orders from House Cat, particularly in the presence of others.

Stan pretentiously saluted him. "Yes sir, General House Cat, sir!" He laughed and playfully slapped House Cat on the back.

"Screw you," said House Cat. "Now get to work."

213

Rufus and Stan walked to the truck and began to unload it. The merciless summer sun bore down on the men who worked outside. Their shirts became drenched with sweat, initiating many trips to the recently installed water keg.

"Whew! It sho' is hot!" complained Rufus.

"It sure is, Rufus," replied Stan. "Man, it would be nice to have a good cold glass of iced tea right now! I can just taste it!"

Rufus laughed. "Speakin' of iced tea—remember that time you pulled that trick on yo' pappy? Th' time you filled th' sugar bowl with salt? Man, I thought he was gonna explode when he tasted that tea! He never did find out it was you that done it! I know'd it, but I tol' him it musta been Minnie that done it by mistake. Po' Minnie! She sho' caught it fer that l'il caper you pulled! And then I remember th' time you hid his golf clubs…"

Stan mopped his brow. "Did I ever thank you for all the times you saved my ass?"

"No need fo' no thanks. Heck, you an' me was best buddies!"

Inside the house, Nick and House Cat were working on their knees, making great progress on the hardwood floor. House Cat slowly stood and wiped the sweat from his forehead. "Ace, when you first came to work for me, I didn't think you was gonna be worth a shit at doin' carpenter work. But now I can see you ain't half bad in the carpenter trade. Hell, it ain't gonna be long 'til you can hold down a job as a journeyman carpenter."

"Thanks, House Cat."

"Hell, don't let it go to your head. You ain't quite there, yet!"

By the end of the day, the hardwood floor was almost done. Although the progress of the bricklayers had been slower, House Cat was reasonably satisfied with the day's accomplishments. The workers put away their tools and began to leave for their homes. Nick and Rufus tossed their tools in the back and wearily crawled into their vehicle. Stan waved to them as Nick pulled the truck out of the yard. "I'll see you in a while, Stan," Nick called from the truck, "as soon as I take Rufus home...see you tomorrow, House Cat!"

"Yeah, see ya, Ace."

On the drive home, Nick realized how tired he was. But it was a weariness that felt good to him, a soothing balm for his unsettled nature. He experienced an unspeakable peace when he realized that in applying himself to something useful he had now discovered a purpose for his existence. He no longer felt useless or afraid. He realized that the South was not a Utopia, for he had recently been exposed to the negative side of it; but it was by far the best place he had ever lived. Most of the people were honest, hard-working people who displayed a genuine, unpretentious nature. Perhaps it was even possible for Lauren and him to make it together. Maybe he had finally found a home.

When he pulled into Rufus' driveway, Caleb immediately appeared beside the truck to greet them. He was signing with his hands, and with a series of excited grunts he attempted to convey some kind of message to Nick.

"What's he trying to say, Rufus?" asked Nick, as Caleb pointed toward the house.

"He's tellin' us that Mary Rose has supper ready fer us. It takes a while fer ya to understand whut he's a-sayin.'"

"But Mary Rose shouldn't have gone to the trouble of fixing any supper for me. I hadn't really planned on eating with you tonight."

"Aw, come on, Mistah Nick. We jus' glad to have ya."

Caleb took Nick's hand and led him up the steps of the front porch. With a pronounced limp, Rufus followed closely behind. Taking note of his limp, Nick asked, "Rufus, did you hurt your leg today?"

"No, Suh. Ain't nuthin' wrong with me, except fer bein'an ol' man. Dr. Jenson says it's jus' a spell of rheumatism." He had spent several exhausting days of hard work in the sweltering heat, and Nick felt that it was too much for a man so old and frail.

215

Mary Rose had prepared a sumptuous meal of tasty southern fare: fried chicken, stewed potatoes, turnip greens, and corn bread. The meal was topped off by iced tea and apple pie for dessert. Nick was hungry, so he feasted on the meal. Mary Rose fussed over the decorum, and Caleb kept bringing items of interest to the table, including the skin of a jar-fly and a turtle. Several threats from Mary Rose finally persuaded Caleb to sit at the table long enough to eat a portion of his meal.

After dinner, Nick, Rufus and the boy retired to the front porch while Mary Rose cleaned up after the meal. The men engaged in idle conversation as Caleb chased a frisky dog around the yard.

"Mistah Nick, you said that you met that-there Preacher Temple when you was in jail. How would you like to take a stroll up to his house an' pay 'im a visit?"

"That's okay with me, that is, unless he's in jail again. I'd like to see him." said Nick.

The preacher's house was only about two hundred feet further up the hill. It was in terrible disrepair; the sagging tin roof was almost eaten away by rust, and the sides of the house were covered with a cheap grade of asphalt siding that simulated bricks. Ragweed and dandelion had invaded the yard. In the graveled driveway sat a rusting gray 1941 Chevrolet with a missing right front fender.

The preacher was sitting on the weathered front porch, leaning against the wall in a straight-back chair and reading a small bible. An old-fashioned porch swing hung at the opposite end of the porch.

Nick and Rufus had almost reached the porch when the preacher saw them. He raised his head and squinted through his bifocals in order to identify his visitors.

"Well, bless the Lord!" he exclaimed. "Is that Rufus? And, let's see...I do believe that it's Nick...I forgot your last name!"

"Parilli," Nick said. "It's good to see you again, preacher."

'Hello, Preacher," said Rufus, "I was afraid you might not be home. When we was settin' on my front porch, I never did see your car going up th' road."

The preacher smiled. "I didn't drive up the main road, Rufus. I drove home over the little trail down in the valley behind my house. It's a shortcut when I'm driving home from town. Except for having to cross a narrow bridge, it's an easy drive. When my gasoline is low, I often drive home on that back road."

"I ain't seed you in a 'coon's age, preacher. Mistah Nicky, here, says he knows ya."

"Yes, Mr. Parilli and I have met…under the most uncomfortable circumstances, I might add."

"When did you get out of jail?" asked Nick.

"A couple of days after you did. What happened in your case?"

Nick and Rufus took a seat in the swing. "The sheriff didn't charge me with anything. He let me go. He said that the deputy had no business arresting me. See? I told you I was innocent!"

The preacher only smiled. "None of us are innocent, son."

"In the broadest sense, I guess that's true," Nick agreed.

Rufus said, "Preacher, I notice that ya keep usin' them big words. Ya seem to be highly ejacated. Ain't that so?"

"Well, I suppose so. I graduated from a Baptist Seminary. But that doesn't mean I'm smart, because most of the time I behave like a damned fool."

"Preacher, when are ya gonna git you another church?" asked Rufus.

"I'll probably never have a church *building* to preach in. I'm not virtuous enough to be a pulpit preacher. You see, I find myself in a rather awkward position. I don't have the virtue, but I still feel the calling. So I'll keep on trying to do God's will and spreading His message from the streets, woodlands, hollows, jails, or wherever else I can find an ear to hear me. There are other ways to serve God without standing in a pulpit."

217

"But why don't ya try to git ya a *church house*? Is it because th' people won't let ya? Because ya git drunk?" asked Rufus.

"I'm afraid so. You see, some people take exception to a preacher getting drunk, especially if he tries to preach a sermon while drunk, as I foolishly did, on one occasion."

"Well, whut makes ya git drunk, Preacher? Why don't ya ask God to deliver ya from th' Devil's brew?"

"That's my cross that I have to bear, Rufus. I'm something like the Apostle Paul: If you'll recall, the Apostle Paul was afflicted with a thorn in his flesh. He prayed three times to God that He might remove the thorn. But God refused to remove it. In the words of the Apostle Paul: *For this thing, I besought the Lord thrice, that it might depart from me. And he said unto me, my grace is sufficient for thee; for my strength is made perfect in weakness. Most gladly therefore will I rather glory in my infirmities, that the power of Christ may rest upon me.* Second Corinthians, 12: 8-9. The same is true of little Caleb. He also is afflicted with a thorn in his flesh—a thorn that he must bear for the rest of his life."

"But why is it so?" asked Rufus.

"We will never know. Who knows the ways of the Lord?"

"Preacher," said Nick, "I've been doing some thinking since we had our little talk in the jail. Remember what you and that man, Satch were telling me about the Mullins family? About how they were involved in shady operations?"

"Yes, but if you'll remember, it was *Satch* who did most of the telling. However, I did agree with most of what he said."

"Looking back on our conversation, I guess you're right. Satch did most of the talking. But I'm beginning to doubt some of the things he told me."

"Well, of course that's your privilege. What happened that made you start doubting it?"

"For one thing, the sheriff released me from jail without charging me with anything; also, he still allows me to date his daughter. On top of that, Lester Mullins—Stan's dad, has been very good to me. I almost feel like a traitor for listening to some of Satch's comments. Preacher, I can only judge people by the way they treat *me*."

The preacher nodded. "The Good Book says, 'judge not,' but we all make judgments about our fellow man every day. It's unavoidable. But if we are going to judge people, I think you probably have the right idea. Perhaps we should judge our fellow man solely on the way we are treated by him."

Nick said, "But, Preacher, you agreed with most of the bad things that Satch said. Are the Mullins Brothers bad people? According to Satch, they're dishonest. They're…"

Rufus interrupted. "Mistah Nick, I don't mean no disrespec,' suh, but Lester Mullins is a fine man. An' you can't believe a word that Satch Morton says. He's a liar an' a drunk."

"As a matter of fact, so am I—a drunk, that is," said the preacher. "Perhaps you shouldn't believe either of us."

"Preacher, I don't know what to believe. But I want my judgments based on reality," said Nick.

The preacher put aside his Bible. "What is reality, Nick? Our *perception* of the world is the only reality we have. If you perceive that a man is good, then it must be so, at least as far as your experience with him is concerned. If we are going to judge our fellow man, then that judgment should be based on our experience with him rather than what someone else told us about him."

"Well, my experience with all of the Mullins family tells me that they're good people," Nick answered.

"No man is really good, Nick, for Jesus tells us that 'our righteousness is as filthy rags.' This is why we shouldn't be so quick to judge, for we are all stained by sin."

"Reveren' Temple," said Rufus, "didn' you used to be th' preacher fer both the Mullins famblies?"

"Yes, I was. They were very loyal church members; however, like all of us, they are stained by sin."

"Then, if you thought they was guilty of all this meanness, why didn' ya preach ag'in' 'em? Why didn' ya point out their sins from the pulpit, right there in the church?"

"It's not a preacher's job to preach against people or to publicly point out their sins. We should preach the Gospel, the good news, and hope that the people will apply it to their own lives, see their own sin. We shouldn't preach against men, but against evil principles."

"Reveren' Temple, you knows that I'm yer' frien,' an have respec' fer ya, but th' Mullins is my fambly, suh, an' I really think they's good people. Why, I hepped raise Stan—he's like a son to me."

"I admire your loyalty, Rufus, and that goes for you, too, Nick. We should return goodness for the goodness that we receive. Loyalty is a wonderful trait." said the preacher.

Nick grinned. "Preacher, that's just what I'm going to do—return goodness for goodness."

"Good for you. By the way, I take it that you've decided to take my advice to stay here in Cedar Valley."

"Yes sir. As a matter of fact, I'm going back to college. I'll probably start in the winter quarter."

"Really? Good! And what are you going to study? What have you decided to do with your life?"

"I've decided to become a lawyer, sir."

"That's great! I'm sure you can make a difference."

"I hope so." Nick peered at his watch. "Listen, Preacher, I've enjoyed talking with you again, but I really need to go. I hope we meet again soon."

"Let's just pray that it will be under more favorable circumstances than before, son." They all laughed and said their goodbyes.

Twilight was falling when Nick and Rufus left the preacher's house. Nick thanked Rufus and his family for dinner and told them goodnight. He then drove away from Bucktown and returned to his apartment in Cedar Valley.

Several days passed. Nick resumed his relationship with Lauren, and continued to make progress in his job. When House Cat and Nick started construction on a new house, Nick was promoted to a full-fledged carpenter, an advancement that meant more responsibility as well as more pay. At the end of

220

the workday on a Friday afternoon, House Cat packed away his tools and sat down beside Nick. "Ace," he said, "Congratulations on learning your job so fast. I've enjoyed workin' with you, but as you know, all good things have to come to an end."

Nick was shocked. "What do you mean? Are you quitting? Do you have another job?"

"Yeah, I have a new job with Uncle Sam. I joined the army. I leave next week for basic training."

"The army? Why didn't you join the air force? Or the navy? Why did it have to be the army? Do you realize that you'll probably be sent to Korea? Hell, man, have you lost your mind?" Nick stood and stared at him in disbelief. "Do you have any idea what it's like in Korea?"

"Not really, but I expect it to be kinda bad. Anyway, I know you've been there, but don't tell me what it's like. I'd just as soon find out for myself." House Cat smiled at him.

"Does Stan know you're leaving?"

"Not yet. I'll tell him tonight."

"How long have you known this?"

"Not long. But the mood just hit me a few days ago, so I went down and joined up. I'm gonna recommend to Stan that you take over my job as foreman. By the way, these tools are yours. I got no use for 'em anymore." He pointed to his toolbox.

"Thanks, House Cat, but you ought to let me pay you for them. You're going to need money."

"Hell, I don't need any money, Ace. By the way, how would you like to buy a good car? That's something else I won't be needin.' I'll sell it to you for five-hundred."

"I don't know, House Cat, The car is worth more than that. Anyway, I don't have a lot of money. I'm saving up to go back to college part-time. I can't dig into that money. All the ready cash I have is less than four-hundred."

"Hell, I don't want to take all the ready cash you got. Shit, take it off my hands for three-hundred."

"Well, I don't like taking advantage of you, but if you're sure you want to sell it that cheap, I'll buy it. I really need to give Stan his truck back, anyway. But I don't have the money on me right now. Can I pay you tomorrow?"

"Sure. I wouldn't have any way home today without it. I need to keep the car over the weekend so I can date my girlfriend one more time before I leave. I'll bring it to your apartment Sunday." He thrust out his hand. "See you around, Ace."

Nick shook his hand. "House Cat, I just wanted to tell you how much I've enjoyed working with you, and I consider you a friend..."

"Hell, don't start goin' sentimental on me." He then walked to his car and drove away.

Their relationship had ended just when Nick had begun to develop an understanding of his peculiar nature. In spite of his bluntness, he was likable. He was not a deceptive man, for he had no hidden agenda. When dealing with him, a man always knew where he stood; in addition, his barbs were always couched in humor. House Cat was a *man's man*. Although he had some rough edges that could probably never be smoothed, Nick could see that he was a man of character. He had absolutely no diplomacy or finesse—only a callous honesty that endeared others to him; for his ruthless candor was a part of his charm.

The weekend came and went with little incident. For Nick, most of Saturday morning was spent listening to Stan gripe about House Cat quitting him with no notice; however, Stan was in agreement with House Cat's suggestion that Nick take his place as construction foreman.

On Saturday night, Nick took Lauren skating; and on Sunday morning, Nick experienced his first visit to a Protestant Church—Cedar Valley Baptist Church, where he attended both Sunday school and church services with Lauren and her parents. Nick felt that his church attendance might have helped cement his relationship with the Mullins family.

As promised, on Sunday afternoon House Cat delivered the car that Nick had bought from him. The timing was appropriate, for Stan had recently hired a new employee who needed the pickup truck that Nick had been driving. Because of House Cat's aversion to sentimentality, his final farewell was low-key. His final words to Nick were, "See ya around, Ace." He then climbed into another car driven by his girlfriend and she drove away.

When he retired to bed on Sunday night, Nick felt optimistic about the future; however, a worrisome question plagued his mind: How was he going to avoid being separated from Lauren when college classes began in September? During their picnic Lauren had suggested that Nick talk to her father about her possible transfer to the college that Nick planned to attend—The University of Tennessee. Anxiety slowly crept into his mind as he realized that time was running out. He decided that, in the coming week he would talk to Sheriff Mullins about the problem. With that decision, his anxiety began to subside, and he drifted into a peaceful sleep.

Chapter 15

It was noontime when Stan arrived with Rufus at the jobsite. Instead of following the usual routine of being picked up for work by Nick, Rufus had gone fishing for the morning with Stan.

Nick was seated under an oak tree eating his lunch when the men arrived and walked into the dusty yard. Rufus displayed a toothless grin when he approached Nick to report to work. "Man, I caught a whole string a-fish. Mistah Stan still ain't got the hang of it. He ketched on'y one teeny little fish." He issued a mirthful laugh. "I tol' 'im that if he gonna ketch catfish, he gotta put an extra sinker on his hook. Catfish feeds on the bottom."

Rufus limped to the shade of a large tree where four other workers were eating lunch. He squatted and began to pet a stray hound as it begged for scraps of food from the workers. Nick grinned as Stan walked toward him. "I hope you're better at managing the business than you are at fishing," said Nick.

"Me too," Stan answered. "But I had two big catfish slip off my hook just as I was about to reel 'em in! Damn it!"

"I can see that you're better at telling fabricated fish stories than you are at fishing," said Nick.

"Yeah, rub it in!" he said.

Stan's expression became serious. "Listen, Nicky...the reason I took Rufus fishing was to give him a little break from work. He's getting old, and he's been putting in too many long hours in the hot sun. Haven't you noticed that he's been really tired lately? I want you to let him take it kinda easy today. Tomorrow, I'm gonna let him go back to Dad's house and do something easy—maybe some simple job like pruning the shrubs. I just hired a new man who can take his place here tomorrow. Let's give him a little break."

"Yeah, as a matter of fact I've noticed that the heat's getting to him. I'll just let him clean up around the place, and maybe ride into town with me in a little while. I've gotta go to the hardware and get a few items. He can help me load some of the light stuff."

"Good. I need to leave, because I've gotta drive a taxicab for Dad again this afternoon. I'll meet you at the apartment tonight. Say, when are you and I going to double-date?"

"Anytime you want to. In regard to the taxicab—are you really going to operate a taxi service, or is it just a ruse, so you can sell whiskey?"

"Oh, hell! Stop worryin' about it, okay? I've quit that bootlegging crap since that self-righteous lecture you gave me. I'll see you tonight. And go easy on Rufus, okay?"

"Sure, Stan. We'll get together tonight."

Nick watched as Stan sped out of the yard. As usual, country music flowed from the radio of his truck.

After lunch, Nick spent about an hour in assigning jobs and overseeing the other workers; then he and Rufus left for town in Nick's car.

"When did ya git this-here car, Mistah Nick?"

225

"I bought it from House Cat over the weekend." The car was a dark blue 1947 Ford V-8. Although it thirstily drank oil, it was fairly clean and a bargain at the price Nick had paid.

"Mistah Stan tol' me that Mistah House Cat done quit an' jined th' army. Gonna miss 'im, that's fer shore."

"Yeah, I'll miss him, too, Rufus," said Nick.

He turned the car onto Highway 11, dispensing a plume of blue smoke behind him. Ten minutes later, he pulled his car into a parking space in front of a local hardware store.

"Rufus, I'm just going to pick up about four bags of cement and a few other items. I can load them into the trunk by myself. Why don't you just sit in the car and wait for me?"

"No suh, if ya don't mind, I'd like to he'p."

"Okay, Rufus, come with me. You can carry the light stuff."

Rufus lagged behind when he got out of the car and followed Nick toward the hardware store. Suddenly, from the sidewalk, a small white girl dashed between the parked vehicles. She was a scrawny youngster, appearing to be about ten years of age. Although tired, Rufus was quick to react when he obstructed her dash toward the busy street. An approaching car applied its brakes, barely missing the girl. Rufus scooped her into his arms.

When Nick became aware of the near-mishap, he quickly walked back toward Rufus. A small crowd began to gather as Rufus carried the young girl back to the sidewalk.

He tried to soothe the trembling child. "Po' little thing," he said, "you shouldn' go runnin' into th' street like that, little gal. Where's yo' mammy an' pappy?" The child was terrified. When he attempted to set her down on the sidewalk, she was reluctant to let go of him. With her arms around his neck, she clung to him for a long while as Rufus patted her back and continued to soothe her with reassuring words.

A large, stocky man who hadn't witnessed the incident suddenly appeared. When he stepped toward Rufus and the girl, anger showed in his eyes. "Git yer dirty hands off that white girl, nigger!"

226

"But, mistah, I was jus' tryin' to he'p the little girl! She almos' got hit by a car, suh!"

"I said let go of her, you black bastard!"

Nick quickly stepped up to the man. "Look, you prejudiced asshole! You should be giving him a medal instead of a hard time! He just saved that little girl's life! Get away from here before I beat the hell out of you!"

The man backed away. "You ain't heard the last of this, mister," he threatened. Nick glared at the man. He took the trembling child from Rufus and placed her on the sidewalk.

For most of the morning Rufus worried about repercussions that might result from the incident. "Mistah Nick, I don't wish to offen' ya none, but maybe you shouldn' a'got so mean with that man. No sense in rilin' people up. But I sho' 'preciate ya takin' up fer me."

"Rufus, the world would be better off without people like him. Stop worrying about it. Hell, you were a hero. You ought to be proud. You saved the little girl's life." But Rufus was so shaken by the incident that Nick decided to take him home.

While driving back to the jobsite, Nick reflected on the unfairness of the occurrence. Because of his anger, he had been tempted to attack the man who had insulted Rufus.

Since he felt a sudden urge to see Lauren, he left work a half-hour early. From his apartment he called her, asking if he might pick her up for dinner. Since his request was unexpected, she agreed, but with the stipulation that she was to be taken home early, for it was not their usual dating night.

After a quick shave and shower, he picked her up at 6:30, and they set out to have dinner. She was surprised to see that Nick was driving a car instead of the Mullins truck.

"When did you get this car?" she asked.

"Sunday night. I bought it from House Cat. You knew he joined the army, didn't you?"

"No! Why did he do that?"

"I don't really know. I believe that he is searching for something in his life. I know how he feels because I've been searching for something for most of my life."

227

"Yes, but now you've found it, Nicky." She cuddled up to him and smiled.

"Where do you want to eat?" he asked.

"Nicky, I can't stay out long because Daddy doesn't want me to date every night. Why don't we just go to a drive-in for dinner?"

"How about Al's Restaurant?" he asked.

"That's fine. It doesn't matter where we go as long as we're together." Lauren smiled.

He pulled into a space at Al's Drive-In and parked.

The drive-in was the local hangout for high school and college students. Nick looked around him, observing the usual variety of sporty cars and hot rods. A teenager had raised the hood of his car, proudly showing off his customized engine to a couple of friends. Music from a nearby car radio issued the pulsating rhythm of the popular song, *Sixty Minute Man.*

After Nick placed their order with the curb girl, he and Lauren ordered cheeseburgers and a milkshakes.

Nick cuddled her and smiled. "Lauren, I've made up my mind to talk to your father about the possibility of our attending college together at The University of Tennessee. What do you think he'll say?"

"I don't know what he'll say, but I'm sure glad you're going to ask him. Think positive, Nicky! I'm sure that Daddy likes you, now. And Mother is crazy about you! So is Willie Mae."

"Speaking of Willie Mae, how do most white people treat her?" asked Nick.

"Most of them seem to accept her. Of course there are always some people who are terribly prejudiced," she said.

"Lauren, something happened today that really disturbed me," he said. He related the entire episode of Rufus rescuing the small girl who had almost darted into the traffic, and the threatening insults of the prejudiced white bystander.

"Oh, that's terrible, Nicky! Poor Rufus."

"Yeah, every time I start to love the South, something like this happens."

"I know what you mean, but it's not just in the South. The whole world is full of so many cruel, unfair things. For instance, look what happened to our former pastor, Preacher Temple. Like I told you before, a man came along and stole his wife from him. It ended his marriage and ruined his career. This happens everywhere, not just in the South."

"Who was the man?" asked Nick.

"I forgot his name. He was a pharmacist who just took a job at one of the drug stores in town. After he stole the preacher's wife, they left here like a whirlwind."

The carhop brought their food and they began to eat. Looking into the rearview mirror, Nick recognized the unmarked police car of Mike Bronson pass the drive-in. *He's probably looking for the Mullins pickup truck that I've been driving. Since I'm in a different vehicle he won't recognize me,* thought Nick. He didn't mention the appearance of the deputy to Lauren.

For a time they sat quietly, enjoying their food. Finally Nick said, "Was Reverend Temple a good preacher?"

"Yes, he was a very good pastor. He really cared about the people. It's too bad that there's not some way to put the man who stole his wife in jail. It's strange, you know. If a man steals another man's horse, he goes to jail, but if he steals another man's wife, he gets away with it." She sipped on her milkshake.

"Yeah," said Nick, "I wish the South would pass some law that would put a man in jail for adultery."

"Southern people have their own way of dealing with adultery," Lauren said. "A couple of years ago, a man in this town caught another man in bed with his wife and killed him for it. Maybe that's the answer," said Lauren.

"No, Lauren, that's never the answer. We need to seek justice through the court system. To take the law into our own hands would only lead to anarchy."

"But what if there's no law on the books against the offense?" She took the final sip of her milkshake.

"Then we must pass laws, and enforce them." said Nick.

Nick reflected on the terrible way that Rufus had been verbally abused. "Lauren, the South also needs to pass some kind of law against racial discrimination. Look at the way Rufus was treated today."

"I agree with you, but I'm afraid it will be many years before that ever happens. Look, Nicky...you're right about most of the unfairness in the world, but you're becoming obsessed with it! Sometimes I think you're extreme in your quest for perfect justice! You're not a lawyer yet, you know. Stop being so serious, honey! Let's just enjoy being young!" She handed her napkins and empty cup to him. He placed the discarded cups and wrappers on the tray along with a generous tip and blinked his lights for the carhop.

He again saw Deputy Bronson's car, this time pulling into the drive-in to the right of his car. Before moving on, he stared into Nick's face. Because her back was to Bronson's car Lauren didn't see him. Nick was certain that this time the deputy had recognized him. The curb girl took away the tray and he backed his car out of the parking space and drove away.

"Did you get enough to eat?" asked Nick.

"Yes, honey, I'm stuffed. By the way, Nicky, of course you're right about your belief in the justice system. It's just that sometimes you get so upset about it."

"I've been in a war with unfairness for most of my life. I can't help it. It's just part of my nature, I guess. Where would you like to go? Do we have a few more minutes?"

"Yeah, maybe a half-hour. Let's ride over to the park before you take me home."

He turned the car in the direction of the lake. He drove to their favorite meeting place in the park, where he briefly parked for awhile. They cuddled in the car, gazing at the golden moon that hung in the eastern sky over the lake. They were filled with optimism, as they quietly talked of their plans to attend college together. It was as if they were about to embark on a great joint adventure.

Lauren peered at her watch. "I guess you'd better take me home. I want to stay on Dad's good side, especially since you're going to talk to him about us attending school together."

"Yeah, I guess you're right," he said.

Slowly, he pulled the car away from the curb and drove her to her home. After kissing her goodnight, he wheeled the car onto Highway 11 toward his apartment. On his right, he was approaching, Mussey's Tavern, a local bar in the suburbs of town. As he passed the place he recognized a familiar car. The gray color and missing right front fender identified the vehicle. The car belonged to Preacher Temple. He quickly turned his vehicle around and returned, pulling into the parking lot in front of the tavern.

The interior of the tavern was comprised of one large room and a small kitchenette. Behind the small counter that separated the two rooms stood a tall, gray-haired man that Nick assumed was Mussey. Both the front and back walls were lined with a row of booths. Four beer-drinking men were seated in the front, and in the back corner booth, Nick spotted the preacher.

Nick immediately strode to the preacher and greeted him.

"Hi, Preacher! What are you doing here?" Nick chose the seat across from him.

"I'm drinking beer, my boy! And what are you doing here?" His bleary eyes indicated his state of drunkenness.

"I saw your car when I was on my way home. I just thought I'd stop and say 'hello' to you."

The preacher displayed a foolish grin. "Hello."

"How much beer have you had to drink, Preacher?"

"Well, just this one beer, so far." His grin widened. "However, I've polished off most of this pint of vodka that I purchased from your good friend, Stan Mullins at his cabstand." He removed a pint bottle from his jacket pocket and set it on the table in front of him.

"Damn! Stan told me he had quit bootlegging that stuff out of his dad's cab. His dad will give him hell if he finds out because he doesn't know that Stan's been selling it."

The preacher laughed. "That's strange," he said. "His dad was sitting in the cab right beside him when I purchased it."

"I'll be damned! He lied to me!" Nick pounded his fist on the table and hung his head.

"Nick, my boy, you're a fine young man. You're loyal and trusting. However, I fear that you are also a bit gullible."

"You're right, Preacher. I believed him. I guess the things that Satch told me in jail are all true."

"Son, I'm afraid that you've placed yourself in a most awkward position. While there seems to be a reciprocal love between you and the Mullins family, there also seems to be a vast difference in your principles. The question is, how do you intend to resolve this dilemma?"

"My God, Preacher. For the life of me, I don't know!" Nick looked at the pint bottle of vodka that the preacher had placed on the table. "You better put that booze away, or you'll get arrested for sure if the police were to come in here."

"Are you sure you wouldn't like a small libation before I put the bottle away?" He picked up the bottle and gazed fondly at it.

"No thank you. I hardly ever drink the hard stuff."

"How about a beer, then? Mussey," he yelled, "bring my good friend a *Budweiser!*" The bartender obediently brought the beer and placed it on the table in front of Nick "Put it on my tab, Mussey," said the preacher.

Nick became concerned "Look, I don't really want anything to drink. Let me drive you home before you get arrested. I'm afraid you're not sober enough to drive a car."

"You may be right, son. Maybe I should let you take me home. I'd rather not drive when I'm drunk."

The door swung open and deputies Mike Bronson and Cowboy Galyon entered the room. They stopped in the center of the floor and stared at Nick and the preacher. Nick noticed that Deputy Galyon was wearing a cowboy hat. It was identical to the hat worn by Sheriff Mullins. Even his mannerisms were like those of the sheriff. For the first time, it occurred to Nick that Cowboy was painstakingly trying to emulate his boss.

"Well, look what we got sittin' here," Bronson gloated, "Cowboy, we got two drunks that have 'jail' written all over 'em."

"Wait a minute, Bronson," cautioned Nick, "I haven't had anything to drink tonight."

"Oh, yeah? What's in that bottle that's settin' in front of you?" Bronson's sneer became more pronounced.

"I can attest to the fact that he hasn't drunk anything tonight, officer!" said the preacher. "Now, I, on the other hand…"

"Who'd believe a drunken bum like you?" asked Bronson.

From behind the counter, Mussey spoke up. "He's right, Bronson. This young man hasn't even taken a sip of that beer. I just served it to him. He's as sober as I am."

"Bullshit! I been followin' him in my car. Hell, he's so drunk that he's been wobblin' all over the road."

"There's been a mistake here," said the preacher.

"Yeah, and you made it," Bronson said. "Let's put 'em under arrest, Cowboy!"

The deputies advanced as Nick stood. "Don't put your hands on me, Bronson!" said Nick. Ignoring his warning, both deputies reached for him.

Nick's first blow was quick and vicious. The punch had such force that it propelled Bronson backward. He staggered on his heels across the room where he crashed into the men in the booth of the opposite wall. Nick then delivered a barrage of punches to the face of Cowboy, who immediately stumbled backward and crashed into the bar. Preacher Temple stood and stumbled out of his booth, struggling to maintain his balance. He was shocked. "My God!" he exclaimed.

Only the rasp of Bronson's breathing intruded on the silence that now enveloped the room. The beer-drinking men in the front booths quickly scurried out the front door.

233

Instead of making any attempt to escape, Nick welcomed the upcoming combat, for a terrible anger had long been festering inside him. Like a pugilist in a boxing ring, he squared off, awaiting retaliation from the deputies.

Bronson wiped away the blood that flowed from his mouth and pried himself from the booth. He pulled a blackjack from his hip pocket and cautiously moved forward toward Nick. Cowboy Galyon struggled to regain his balance and drew his revolver from the holster, pointing it at Nick. Together, they slowly advanced to within three feet of him.

With lightning speed, Nick again struck Bronson, this time in the nose. Blood spurted, and as he reeled backward, it began to gush onto the front of his shirt. When Cowboy swung the revolver, the butt of the weapon caught Nick squarely in the side of his head. Almost unconscious, he struggled to maintain his balance. Cowboy repeatedly bludgeoned his head, as Bronson, who had now regained his composure, began to beat Nick across the face with his blackjack. "Hold him, Cowboy, while I finish off the son of a bitch!" Moving to a position behind Nick, Cowboy pinned his arms behind him as Bronson continued to beat him.

The preacher became enraged. "I've never before raised my hand in anger against my fellow man! But there's such a thing as righteous anger! Turn him loose, you servants of the devil!" He swung his fist, hitting Bronson in the face. The pitiful blow only served to further enrage the deputy. With one swift blow, he quickly dispatched the preacher. His limp body fell to the floor like a sack of flour.

Nick was now unconscious. He slumped to the floor where he lay motionless beside the preacher. When the deputies stepped back, Cowboy Galyon was still pointing his weapon at Nick. "We ought to shoot the bastard!" he said.

Deputy Bronson picked up the preacher's vodka bottle from the table. He then poured the remaining contents of the bottle onto Nick's face and upper torso.

Bronson turned toward Mussey. "You witnessed what happened! You saw him assault two police officers!"

234

Mussey said nothing.

Grasping Nick's arms, the deputies dragged him to the police car where they lifted him and heaved him into the back seat. They returned for the preacher who had now partially recovered and was seated in the booth with his head resting on the table. Bronson supported him as he led him toward the car. Over his shoulder, he called to Cowboy, "Bring along that vodka bottle as evidence for possession of whiskey."

*   *   *

A vigorous shake awakened Nick. He stared up into the lethargic eyes of the jailer.

"The sheriff wants to see you," he droned.

Nick peered at his watch for the time, only to discover that it had been shattered during last night's brawl with the deputies.

"What time is it?" he asked, as he rose to his feet.

"Eight-thirty. You slept through breakfast." replied the jailer.

A glance around the cell confirmed to Nick that he was in the drunk tank. Two other men were sitting on the side of their bunks while the preacher, with his mouth open, lay on his back in the floor, snoring. Nick's right eye was swollen shut, his head ached, and his hair was glued to his scalp by clotted blood. His nose, swollen to twice its normal size, was possibly broken. It throbbed with each heartbeat.

Nick turned to the jailer. "I've gotta take a leak before I go down to see the sheriff." The jailer released him from the drunk tank and he limped to the commode in the corner of the jail complex. Crushed cigarette butts littered the floor, and roaches scurried away from him as he walked. Just as on his prior visit to the jail, the receptacle was overflowing with human waste. Nick decided to forgo relieving himself. With disgust, he turned and walked away. Looking to his left, he saw the huge pet rat, Oscar dart underneath Little Billy Sneed's bed. Seated on his filthy bunk, Little Billy glared at

235

him. *So the sheriff hadn't cleaned up the jail as he had promised to do,* thought Nick.

The jailer followed as Nick limped to the stairway that led to the sheriff's office. When he hobbled down the stairs the pain in his right knee was excruciating. The jailer unlocked the door to the sheriff's office and Nick hesitantly walked into the room.

Sheriff Mullins was seated in the comfortable chair behind his desk that openly displayed the preacher's empty vodka bottle. He was leisurely smoking a cigar. He eyed Nick with a vapid stare. "Sit down, Mr.Parilli." Nick was surprised by the sheriff's strict formality.

Nick was nervous. "Mr. Mullins, let me explain to you what happened. I was just…"

The sheriff interrupted him. "I prefer that you would address me as 'Sheriff Mullins'. Mr. Parilli, I'm afraid that you've really done it this time. One thing I won't stand for is for somebody to rough-up one of my deputies. Have you seen Deputy Bronson's face?" Nick recognized a side of the sheriff's nature that he hadn't previously detected. He was too confused to think clearly; consequently, he was unable to defend his actions.

The sheriff continued. "Let's see now, what do we have you charged with? First of all, public drunkenness. Then we can add, resisting arrest, assaulting two police officers, possession of illegal alcohol, and possibly driving under the influence. This combination should carry a penalty of a couple of years in jail—maybe more."

"But, sheriff, I swear to you that I didn't drink a drop of alcohol last night!"

"Bullshit, Parilli! Hell, you smell like a damned distillery right now! And what about this bottle?" he pointed to the empty vodka bottle.

"Sir, that isn't mine, and I can prove it. If you'll just ask Preacher Temple…"

"I'm not going to ask that worthless hypocrite anything!"

"But I was just going to take the preacher home when those two deputies came in and…"

"You always have an excuse, don't you? You know, Parilli, there are some advantages to being a sheriff. We're able to obtain information that others find hard to get. In the last few days, I've done some checking on you with the Department of the Army. What I found out is most interesting. According to the U.S. Army, you were court-martialed and busted for insubordination to your superior officer. As punishment, you spent some time in an army jail. Not only that, but you also had a reputation of being a coward. Also, you spent your final days before your discharge lying drunk in the barracks. You came to me awhile back with what appeared to be good credentials: a clean-cut war hero who was wounded in action—an ambitious young man who was going back to college to make something out of himself…a man who was not too proud to work hard at a lowly labor job to better himself.

The sheriff glared at him and continued. "Well, let me cite your *real* credentials—an updated version: You're an arrogant, disrespectful war coward who almost got kicked out of the army for disobeying orders….a lowly drifter and carpenter's helper who has the gall to try to date a decent girl like my daughter! You come here to the South trying to tell us how to live. You had big plans of becoming a lawyer! Lawyer, hell! You're nothing but a worthless drifter and an intruder here!"

Nick was stunned. The sheriff's verbal assault had reawakened his combative spirit. He recognized that he had no defense against such accusations. Realizing that no purpose would be served by citing their recent friendship or trying to appeal to the sheriff's sense of fairness, he decided to deal with the situation in a cold, matter-of-fact manner. "Okay, Sheriff, What's my next step? Should I get a lawyer?"

"Hell, the best lawyer in the country couldn't get you out of the mess you're in. But I'll tell you what I'm willing to do. I thought that Lauren would get tired of you by now and come to her senses; but, for whatever reason, she thinks she's in love with you. I'm willing to drop all charges if you'll just quietly get out of town. But I'm going to add some conditions to my offer: First of all, you leave town without contacting my daughter; second, you don't ever tell her anything about this conversation."

"Well, even if I accept your offer, it'll take a couple of days to get my things together and tell Stan I'm leaving."

"Well, I anticipated that, Parilli. Forget about getting your things together. You can also forget about talking to Stan." From his desk drawer he drew out an envelope. "In this packet, you'll find five-hundred dollars—enough to get you out of town and to get started somewhere. Listen, Parilli! If you want to save your neck, just take the money and go!"

The sheriff picked up the envelope containing the money and contemptuously tossed it into Nick's lap. "Now, get out!"

Nick looked into the sheriff's eyes. His mind was filled with indecision—not about whether or not to take the money, for he already knew that he could never accept it. If he chose to leave town, he probably had enough of his own money to pay his way to Louisiana. However, he was undecided about what his next move should be. If he refused the sheriff's offer, he would surely go to jail; however, his acceptance of it meant that he would never again see Lauren.

Nick's anger began to escalate. He remembered that shortly after his war experience he had suffered panic attacks when under stress. He was now amazed at his courage and presence of mind in the current stressful situation.

His contemptuous demeanor mimicked that of the sheriff's when he tossed the money back onto the desk. "Sheriff Mullins, you spelled out your demands to me, now I'll tell you what I'm willing to do. I can't take your money for two reasons: First of all, I don't take bribes; second, I don't want to soil my hands with dirty money."

"Why you arrogant bastard! You're not in any position to bargain with me!"

"I believe that I am, Sheriff. I came into this town hoping to find some peace and fairness. Instead, I've been harassed by that deputy, discriminated against, beaten up and abused."

"If you don't like the South, then get the hell out of it!" shouted the sheriff. "Go back to Yankee Land!"

"You've got me wrong, Sheriff. I love the South. Some of the finest people I've ever met live here. It's people like you and your fee-grabbing deputies that give the South a bad name!"

In anger, the sheriff said, "Why, you bastard! What do you intend to do? What's your proposition?"

"Here's what I'll agree to. I'll leave town, as you demanded, because there's nothing left for me here, anyway. But instead of that dirty money you tried to bribe me with, I'll use my own money. Also, I'll take the time to pack up my things, talk to Stan, and make some plans before I leave town. I figure it'll take me three or four days."

"If I agree, will you give me your word of honor that you won't contact Lauren?"

"No. It depends on whether or not she wants to see me. The decision is hers—not yours."

"Then there's no deal. You can just go to jail!" said the sheriff.

"I don't believe you are in a position to either threaten me or bargain with me, sir." Nick smiled at him. "Let me promise you something. Although you've controlled Lauren's life to the point that you've almost ruined it, I know that she and I are in love with each other. I'm willing to guarantee that when I leave here, you'll be rid of me for good. I'll never contact her again after I leave Cedar Valley, provided that I leave on my own terms. But if you don't accept my offer and decide to put me in jail, I know that she will wait for me. I'll swear to Almighty God that when I get out of jail, I'll come back to marry her and settle in Cedar Valley. And I'll haunt you and this town until the day you die!"

"You arrogant son of a bitch!" He rose from his chair and glared at Nick.

"Sheriff, it's time to put up or shut up. If you want to put me in jail, then do it now! I'm going to get up from this chair and walk out of here!"

Nick slowly rose from his chair, and for a brief moment, stared at the sheriff. He stepped out of the office onto the porch and gently closed the door behind him.

He struck out walking toward *Williams Wrecker Service*, the company used by the sheriff's department for towing vehicles of people who had been arrested. After retrieving his car, he immediately drove to the apartment that he shared with Stan. He found Stan at home, brooding over Nick's recent altercation with the deputies.

"What in the hell happened to you last night, Nicky? Damn! Look at your face! You need to see a doctor! I've been up all night worrying about you. What happened? Has the world gone crazy? Everybody is as mad as hell!"

Nick explained the entire episode to him, including his conversation with the sheriff.

"Well, I've got some more bad news for you, Nicky. The sheriff has already called my father. Dad told me to fire you! But since you explained how it really happened, I'll talk to Dad. Maybe he'll change his mind. Also, I'll get Dad to talk to the sheriff. Maybe it's not too late to work something out."

"Don't bother to talk to your dad, Stan. This thing would never work out now. Besides, I gave the sheriff my word that I'd leave town. After I pack my stuff, I want to talk to Lauren, that is, if she'll see me. If she won't, then I'll just get the hell out of here."

"Please don't do that, buddy! I thought you were happy here! If you'll just stay here and tough it out, I'll help you. What about our plans to go to college together?"

"Stan, I love you like a brother, and I don't like to hurt your feelings. But you lied to me, pal. You and your dad are both involved in the bootlegging business. The preacher bought his booze from both of you. I found out that everything I was told about the dishonesty of the Mullins family is correct. God forgive me for saying that."

"Damn it, Nick! You need to learn to mind your own business! What difference does any of that make? Couldn't you have just let well enough alone? Also, I told you that getting involved with Lauren was a mistake! Your relationship with her is what brought this whole disaster on us!"

"You're misplacing the blame, Stan. How could a couple of young people falling in love cause all this discord? I'll stay in Cedar Valley for a couple more days, and then I'll be leaving."

"Listen, Nicky! If you leave here without making plans about what you're going to do with your life, it might be the end of our relationship. I had some big plans for us. Give me a week to clean up my affairs and I'll go to Louisiana with you!"

"That wouldn't work, Stan. You've got a good thing here with your family. Besides, you've made up your mind to attend college here. After I see Lauren, I'm leaving Cedar Valley. Maybe you and I can hook up sometime in the future."

"Nicky, promise me you won't leave here until we have time to talk. Maybe you and I could start our own business here in Cedar Valley. I've had just about enough of working for Dad. Hell, man, give me time to think of something!"

Stan watched helplessly as Nick tossed some toilet articles and clothing into his army duffel bag.

"Where are you going, Nicky? You're not leaving town right now, are you?"

"No, I'm not leaving town right now. I've just got to get away for a while, by myself. I need to think. I don't want Lauren to see me like this. Not 'til I heal up a little bit. Also, this will give Lauren time to think. I promise I'll let you know before I leave town for good."

"Where are you going?"

"I'm not sure, but I'll keep in touch."

"Hell, stay here, Nicky. If you need to be alone to think, then I'll leave you alone."

Nick remembered the countless ways that Stan had always befriended him; however, he now felt betrayed by his best pal.

241

Without responding, Nick's eyes expressed sadness when he looked at his friend for a long while. He then walked to Stan and hugged him. After picking up his duffel bag and limping to the door, he turned to Stan and said, "Goodbye, Pal." He walked out the door and closed it.

Chapter 16

Nick dropped the dime into the slot and dialed the number. "Dr. Johnston's Clinic. May I help you?" The business-like feminine answer sounded strange to him; however, he quickly recognized the sweet, lilting quality of her voice.

"Lauren, this is Nick." For a brief moment there was only silence.

Finally she spoke. "Where are you?"

"At the *Rexall Drug Store.* I'm calling you from their pay phone."

"Nicky, what happened? Daddy told me you got arrested last night! I know that it was that awful Mike Bronson!"

"Did your dad tell you what happened?"

"No, he didn't go into detail. He just said that you got in a fight with Mike Bronson. Did you get hurt, honey?"

"Not bad. Just a few bumps and bruises."

"Well, Daddy also said that you told him you were leaving Cedar Valley. Is that true?"

"Yes, I'm afraid it's true." Nick replied.

"But why? What about our future? I thought you were going to talk to Daddy about us…"

He remembered that one of the conditions demanded by the sheriff before releasing him was that Nick would not reveal any of their conversation to Lauren. Although he hadn't agreed to that stipulation, he felt that it would be better for all concerned to abide by the request. After all, how could he tell her of the bitter exchange of words that had transpired between her father and himself? Nick knew that Lauren idolized her dad. If Nick revealed her father's corrupt character, what would be her reaction? The last thing he wanted to do was to force her to choose between them.

"Lauren, I can't explain it very well to you on the phone. I need to see you, so we can talk, so I can explain it to you. What, *exactly* did your father tell you?"

"He didn't explain anything to me. He just said you got into a fight with Mike and got arrested for it, and that you had decided to leave Cedar Valley. But, Nicky, there's no need for you to do that. I'm sure that Daddy will understand because he knows how Mike's been bugging us. When do you want to see me? Do you want to come by the house tonight?"

"No, I can't see you for a couple of days. I'll have to call you and meet you somewhere."

"Nicky, why are you acting so mysterious? Did something happen that you're not telling me?"

"Lauren, just trust me. I'll call you in a couple of days."

Again, there was silence.

"Nicky, you're acting strange. Why do you have to leave? How could you do that to us? Are you that ashamed that you were arrested?"

"No, Lauren, I'm not ashamed. But if there was a reason that I can't tell you right now, and a reason that I could never come back here. Would you…would you…consider going away with me?" Immediately, he regretted the foolish question; for it would mean the abandonment of her life's dream—or of her *father's* dream.

"Why are you asking me that? What happened to our college plans? Nicky, I could never leave Cedar Valley right now!"

"I know. Of course you couldn't. It was foolish of me to ask. Look, I've gotta go. I'll call you soon. Bye, Lauren." He hung up the phone.

When he left the drugstore, he was saddened by the knowledge that Lauren was in bondage to her father. She was his slave as surely as if she wore shackles that bound her to him, stifling her ambitions, her dreams, and her desires.

Nick drove the car westward toward Bucktown and the preacher's house. He thought of his phone conversation with Lauren. The sheriff hadn't told her that he had *demanded* that Nick leave. Instead, he had decided to play innocent, leaving her completely in the dark in regard to where he stood on the matter. For all she knew, her father still condoned their relationship, suggesting that it was Nick's idea to leave town.

The sheriff is a coward, Nick decided; for he feared that if she knew the details of the confrontation between him and the sheriff, Lauren would find out that it was her father who had destroyed their relationship. The sheriff was desperate to keep the truth from her because if she knew that terrible reality she might rebel against him and abandon him. Nick knew that she assumed that everything was normal, that their relationship was intact. It saddened him to realize that when he was gone, she would always hold the belief that he had simply abandoned her and their dreams with no explanation. More than likely, after Nick was out of her life, the sheriff would attempt to comfort her with his claim that the relationship had been doomed from the start because Nick was a worthless vagrant who had abandoned her for no apparent reason. Nick felt that his relationship with Lauren was over, for she couldn't handle the terrible truth. He recognized that she idolized her father so much that knowing the truth would destroy her. *The sheriff has won,* he concluded.

The presence of the preacher's car in his driveway was proof that he had been released from jail. Nick pulled his car

245

behind the vehicle and parked. He limped up the steps to the front porch and knocked on the door.

"Preacher Temple!" he called through the screen door. "Are you at home?"

The preacher came out onto the front porch. "Well, if it isn't Nick!" He shook Nick's hand. "My, but doesn't your face look terrible! I mean your wounds, not your usual handsome features. Have a seat, son. I'm glad you came to see me. Have you seen a doctor about the injuries to your face?" He examined Nick's injuries before taking a seat in a nearby chair.

Nick sat down in the porch swing. "No, my injuries aren't that bad. At least, my nose isn't broken. The wounds to my emotions are worse. How did you get out of jail so fast?"

"I had a friend to pay my bail, my boy. But they're not through with me, yet. I have to go to trial for assaulting a police officer. After all, I struck that deputy. If I hadn't been drunk, I'm sure that the force of my blow would probably have rendered him unconscious!"

Nick chuckled. "I sure appreciate you for defending me. It's too bad that you got into trouble over it."

"Think nothing of it, Nick. Although the Lord teaches us to turn the other cheek, righteous anger is sometimes necessary. You know, as evil as it might sound, it felt rather good when my fist struck the deputy's face." He displayed a mischievous grin.

"Yeah, I know the feeling, Preacher." Nick lit a cigarette.

"Well, is this a social call, or did you come for some religious counseling? Remember, any holy water that I might pour upon you comes from an unclean vessel."

"I just felt like talking to somebody. You once told me that I should stay in Cedar Valley and fight for what I know is right. But now I have no choice. The sheriff told me to either leave town or he would put me in jail on several charges."

"What do you intend to do?"

"I'm leaving town. What choice do I have?" The rusty chains supporting the swing groaned as he gently swung back and forth.

"I suppose there is no other choice, considering the circumstances," said the preacher. "If we had an honest court system, I'd advise you to stay. But I'm afraid the cards are stacked against you, son."

"I wish that there was some way of fighting it, but I don't have the money to hire a lawyer. Also, I'm not a very good person, myself. I might deserve what's happening to me. Maybe this is punishment for some of the terrible things I did in the war." Nick sat immobile in the porch swing.

"You know, Nick, you and I have a lot in common. We're flawed crusaders. We don't have the purity, but we still have the calling. Our quest for fairness and justice defines who we are. It's almost like an obsession, for we can't separate ourselves from it. Unfortunately, an unrelenting crusade for justice always brings discord and revenge."

"I just can't help it, Preacher. I can't tolerate injustice. The sheriff told me that if I didn't like the South I should go back to where I came from in the North. But I love the South. It's my home, now; and if I can figure a way of doing it, I'll spend my life trying to somehow make it a better place."

"I know how you feel, Nick. In spite of the monkey that rides on my back, I try to make the world better," said the preacher. "By the way, have you eaten today?"

"No. I haven't even thought about food. But I guess I could eat something." He pitched his cigarette butt into the yard.

"Well, I'm getting hungry. I thought about making us some soup for supper. How does that sound?"

"It sounds great. Listen, would you mind if I stayed here at your house for a couple of days? I need to be away from people for a while, so I can think. I feel lost, and I don't even have a job anymore. Also, I want to heal up a bit before I go back into town. My face looks pretty bad."

"Stay as long as you like, Nick. I'll be glad to have you. I get lonely sometimes." He went inside to prepare the soup.

The afternoon quickly passed as Nick and the preacher rested on the porch discussing Nick's dilemma. Shade from the oak trees grew longer, stretching across the weedy yard beyond the gravel road and into the nearby meadow. The veil of twilight softened the golden day, and lights came on in the settlement as darkness moved in. Nick and the preacher ate the soup and again retired to the front porch.

From a few yards down the road, the loud roar of a revved-up car engine caught their attention. They looked in the direction of the commotion. Spinning tires threw a spray of gravel behind the fishtailing car. It pulled a trail of dust behind it when it sped away. The semi-darkness and enormous cloud of boiling dust obscured the make and model of the vehicle. They watched as the trail of dust followed the speeding car, snaking its way down the curvy road and disappearing into the distance.

"Man! I wonder what that was all about, Nick?"

"Beats me, but somebody was sure in a hurry."

Almost immediately, several terrifying screams broke the silence of the evening. Out of the settling cloud of dust a small Negro boy came running. He ran up the hill and into the yard, and then onto the porch. It was Rufus' grandson—Caleb.

His large, frightened eyes stood in sharp contrast to his ebony skin. In agitation, he danced around the porch, signing with his hands and bellowing unintelligible grunts and whines as he pointed in the direction of the dust cloud down the road.

"It's Caleb, Preacher," said Nick. "What's he trying to say?"

The preacher stood. He grasped the boy by the shoulders, squatted down and looked him in the eye. "What is it, son? What's the matter?" Amid the excitement, he had momentarily forgotten that Caleb couldn't speak.

Suddenly, Mary Rose came running into the yard. She was moaning as she repeatedly chanted, "Oh my God, oh my God, oh my God…"

Nick quickly grasped her shoulders and pulled her toward him. "What's wrong, Mary Rose?"

"It's Rufus! They got Rufus!" She again began to moan.

"*Who* got Rufus? Who, Mary Rose? Calm down!"

"The Klan! They just came into the house and got him!"

"The Klan? Did you recognize anyone?" asked Nick.

"No, Mr. Nick! They were wearing those white sheets...Oh God, oh God, oh God!"

When Nick released her, she quickly ran to the boy and they hugged each other, crying.

Nick looked at the preacher. "What are we going to do?"

"Those disciples of the devil!" said the preacher. "Come on! I think I know where we might be able to find them before they have a chance to harm him! We'll take your car. We need to hurry!" He looked at Mary Rose. "You and Caleb stay here at my house, Mary Rose. You'll be safe here. We'll be back as soon as we can!" They hurried to Nick's car and sped away.

"Where are we going?" asked Nick.

"I don't know exactly, and I might even be wrong. But I remember a place not far from here where the Klan whipped a Negro man one night. I just stumbled onto it by accident. Turn right on Highway 11, and step on it!"

Nick sped up. "What if they're not at the place you're thinking of? What do we do then?"

"Listen, Nick. They always burn a cross when they're about to do their cowardly devil's work. We need to keep our eyes peeled in every direction for a glow from their fire somewhere on the horizon. Turn left here!"

The tires squealed and the car careened as Nick whipped the wheel to the left and again increased his speed.

"Look! Up ahead! Isn't that a faint glow up on top that hill? Step on it Nick!"

Nick turned sharply to the right and gunned the car. Ahead of them they saw a faint glow.

"Is that the place ahead of us that you were talking about?"

"Yes, it's just over that hill, straight ahead!"

They cleared the brow of the hill, and looking ahead of them, they saw the fire; however, when they came nearer, they discovered only a couple of men burning trash in a field. Nick braked the car and came to a stop. He looked at the preacher. "What now?"

"Drive to the top of Kingston Hill. It's the highest point in town. We can survey the whole town from there."

Nick burned rubber from his rear tires when he pulled away from the curb. "If we don't get there in time, what do you think they'll do to him?"

"Well, it depends on what kind of offense they're accusing him of. If it's something minor, like maybe beating his daughter, or not supporting his family, maybe they'll just whip him a little bit. But if it's a major offense, like whistling at a white woman, or touching a white kid, they'll really lay it on him!"

"Oh, hell! I'm afraid they'll *really* whip Rufus. Damn! What would they do to a black man that flirted with a white woman?"

"They'd already have his grave dug before they ever kidnapped him!" said the preacher.

They reached the top of Kingston Hill and Nick pulled the car over to the curb. The preacher was right. Specific objects and locations could be seen from miles away.

"Do you see anything, Preacher?" Nick's eyes inspected the valley. While they scanned the horizon and the town below them, Nick explained the incident about Rufus rescuing the little white girl, and the behavior of the white man who had censured him. Then he said, "Preacher, what can we do if we find these Klan people? We don't have a weapon. Maybe we should have brought Caleb's shotgun!"

"That's not the answer, Nick. If we had done that, we'd have to shoot some of them for sure. No, this way is best. It may not work, but about all we can do is reason with them."

"Damn, Preacher! We're running out of time! We need to find him quick!" Nick was almost panicky.

The preacher kept eyeing the town below them. "Nick, these hellions enjoy these events so much they'll take their time in this little ritual. They may not have even lit their cross yet. Maybe that's why we can't spot it. But you're right. As soon as we see what we think is a cross burning, we need to get there fast."

"Look! Look there, Preacher! See that glow? It's getting brighter. It looks like it's coming from near the river!"

"Yeah, I see it. It may be another false alarm, but it's all we've got to go on! Let's get there fast!" said the preacher.

They quickly crawled into the car and sped in the direction of the glow near the river. The old Ford spewed out a trail of blue smoke as Nick sped down the hill across Broadway, through the center of town, over the railroad track, and on toward the river.

"It would be just my luck for that damned deputy to stop me and arrest me for speeding," Nick remarked.

"I wouldn't worry about it. After that job you did on his face, he's probably in the hospital!"

Nick slowed the car as he drove closer to the glowing light. He then turned right and traveled parallel to the river through the thick forest. The road narrowed to a weedy lane that was scarcely more than a wide path along the flat river-bottom land. The glow became brighter, and they began to smell wispy traces of smoke drifting through the open windows. The isolated location gave Nick a spooky feeling.

"Slow down, Nick, we're almost there! I think we've hit the jackpot, son! Slow...slow...There it is! About a hundred yards ahead on the left. See it through the trees? It's a cross, alright! And fire climbing toward the sky, and burning like the eyes of Satan! Park here! We'll have to walk the rest of the way!"

Nick killed the headlights and pulled the car over onto the broad road shoulder. He then slowly drove into the edge of the woods behind a patch of thick bushes, hiding the car from view.

They left the vehicle and stealthily walked toward the burning cross. The night was eerily quiet. Over the river, a full moon hung low in the eastern sky. The fishy odor of the river and the musty smell of damp leaves melded into the cool night air. The chirping of crickets spoke of a peaceful summer night, contradicting the mood of the hellish ritual that awaited Rufus. Nick experienced a deep sense of foreboding.

The narrow lane came to a dead-end at the edge of a large meadow. At one end of the clearing stood the burning cross and at the opposite end about a dozen vehicles were parked. A group of Klan members in white robes and hoods congregated near the center. The cross was perhaps ten feet tall and appeared to be crudely constructed with four-by-four posts. It was now totally engulfed in flames that climbed more than twenty feet into the sky, scorching the overhanging branches of surrounding trees and casting flickering highlights on the leaves that hovered above them. Nick whispered to the preacher, "I have a bad feeling about this."

"Nick, we must go where the Lord leads us. Unless we can reason with them before they start their ritual, we won't be able to stop it."

Crouching low to the ground, they slowly sneaked off the narrow lane into the thick growth of trees directly behind the burning cross. The preacher hid behind the trunk of a large oak tree while Nick continued crawling for a few feet and, moving forward behind a blanket of weeds, crept up a bank that overlooked the meadow. He hid behind a thick growth of honeysuckle. Their positions were only a few feet behind Rufus, who was securely lashed to a slim tree, with his back facing them.

They silently waited, watching, crouching behind the bushes, low to the ground. The preacher was so close to Rufus that he could have spoken to him—and if the Klansmen could be momentarily distracted, even sneak forward to untie his bonds and free him; but all they could do was wait...but wait for what? What would they do when his tormentors began their fiendish ritual? Neither Nick nor the preacher had

252

brought a weapon; and even if they were armed…would they shoot the perpetrators?

The group of men began to assemble into a more orderly formation. As a group, they walked to a position directly in front of Rufus. The head of the assemblage stepped forward and began reciting some kind of archaic liturgy, possibly pronouncing sentence on Rufus. Nick and the preacher felt that it was now too late to stop the hellish procedure.

Rufus spoke, "Please, Mistah, I ain't done nuthin'—at least I ain't had no notions to do no wrong…Spare me, please suh…"

The hooded man in front unfurled a horsewhip as another Klansman came forward and turned Rufus around so that his back was toward the man with the whip. He tied his hands in front of him, and then around the tree. He ripped away his shirt so that his naked back was exposed. The preacher bowed his head and prayed.

In the hope of the later identification of any member of the group, Nick's eyes scanned each member, carefully inspecting every detail of his demeanor: each man's height, approximate weight, his stance, inflection of his voice—any unique aspect that might offer a hint of his identity. But their faces were covered with hoods and their long robes covered their entire torsos. From his vantage point overlooking the meadow he was only a few feet from the front row of the Klansmen. Only their shoes were visible below their robes. He saw only one unique distinction. Although some of them wore western boots, only one of them had a conspicuous imprint of a gold star on the toe of each boot.

The first lash of the whip was brutal and brought a horrifying scream from Rufus. The lash had laid open his back with a deep gash that quickly began to drip with blood. Nick trembled with anger and fear. He wished that he had brought Caleb's shotgun, because he now would have no reluctance to use it.

Before the hooded man could again swing the lash, the preacher suddenly stepped from his hiding place behind the tree. He walked into the clearing, and stood beside Rufus. Nick was stunned. *What's he doing? He's going to get himself killed!* When he considered the preacher's boldness, he felt cowardly hiding in the bushes; however, he saw nothing to be gained by standing unarmed beside the preacher. It would be suicide.

The Klansmen were also amazed at the preacher's sudden courageous appearance. The man wielding the whip was the first to speak, as the preacher faced him. "Where did you come from?" he asked.

"I just happened to be passing by. You fellows don't know what you're doing. This man is innocent of any wrongdoing."

"You're in deep trouble, mister," said the Klansman.

Displaying absolutely no fear, the preacher strode forward and stood directly in front of him. "You hide behind those hoods, afraid to show your faces! You're all cowards! Show your face, you cowardly disciple of the Devil!" He stepped forward and jerked the cone-shaped hood off the Klansman's head. The man that he had unmasked was Deputy Mike Bronson. Nick noticed that his face bore the wounds suffered in their recent fight.

Nick now had no doubt in his mind about the identity of the man with the imprint of the gold stars on the toes of his boots: It had to be Bronson's crony...Cowboy Galyon.

Bronson only smiled at the preacher. "You just sealed your doom, mister."

A nearby Klansman spoke up, "Wait a minute, Mike! Don't do anything foolish, or we'll be up to our necks in deep trouble!"

"What if he shoots off his mouth?" asked Bronson.

"Hell, who'd believe him? He's just that drunken preacher!"

"Yeah, but he's a white man! They'd believe him, alright!"

"Hell, Mike, let's just bribe him and finish whippin' this nigger and get the hell outta here...Hey, Preacher, I'll give you fifty bucks and buy you a pint of moonshine if you'll just go on home and forget what you saw tonight!"

"Get thee behind me, Satan!" he screamed. "So help me, God, when I leave here tonight, I'll tell every authority, every agency, everybody who can prosecute you for this deed you've done tonight! By tomorrow morning, everybody in Cedar Valley will know what happened here. Now cut him loose!"

With no hesitation Bronson stepped forward. From beneath his robe he pulled his service revolver and placed the muzzle against the preacher's forehead. The loud report of the pistol echoed through the nearby trees and faded as it again reverberated across the river. With the back of his head gone the preacher fell limply to the ground.

The deputy then walked to Rufus. "Nigger, that preacher just cost you your life." When he shot Rufus in the head, the force of the blast slammed the elderly Negro's face against the tree.

A small wisp of smoke drifted from the barrel of the revolver. Rufus' frail upper torso fell backward and he hung like a skewered animal from the ropes that bound him to the tree. The smell of spent gunpowder mingled with the pungent scent of the burning cross.

Chapter 17

Nick lay quietly, hugging the ground in the thick tangle of honeysuckle. His heart pounded violently, but his respiration was shallow. He feared that even the sound of his breathing might draw the attention of the Klansmen.

He watched as the excited Klan members quickly began to scurry around. A raucous blend of shouts and curses suddenly erupted. Men gathered around Bronson. Some stared at him in awe. Others cursed him, while one of the Klansman reprimanded him. "Damn it Bronson! Have you completely lost your mind? You just killed two men!"

Bronson seemed unperturbed. "Hell, why are you guys so worried? He was just a nigger!"

"But you also just killed a white man!"

"So what? He wasn't any better than a nigger! There ain't anybody gonna miss either one of these nobodies! All we gotta do is get 'em outta here and bury 'em *tonight*. Nobody will ever find either one of 'em. Remember, every one of you is just as guilty as I am! We're all in this thing together!"

He pulled out a pocketknife and casually walked to the tree that held Rufus. With a single slash of the sharp blade, he cut through the rope. Like a rag doll, the limp body of Rufus fell backward onto the grass.

"Somebody help me lift him!" Bronson ordered. "And a couple of you grab hold of the preacher! Billy Jim, drive your pickup over, so we can load 'em up! Get Movin!'"

"Where do you think that preacher came from, Bronson? How'd he know about this, and where to find us? Reckon he was alone?" asked one of the men.

"Hell, I don't know! Maybe a few of you guys better search around the area and see if anybody else came with him, and is still lurkin' around!"

Billy Jim parked his pickup truck near the burning cross and the bodies of Rufus and the preacher were tossed into the bed.

Nick knew that being discovered meant certain death. He realized that if he hoped to escape he would have to move quickly before the men began searching for him; however; since the activity of loading the bodies was taking place only a few feet in front of him, he had been unable to make the slightest move.

At last, the group of men followed the pickup truck as it was driven away from the burning cross to the center of the meadow.

Someone shouted, "Anybody got a pick and shovel in his car?" Another man asked, "Where are we gonna bury 'em?" The general mood was one of chaotic haste.

While the Klansmen scampered around in the center of the meadow, Nick seized the opportunity to escape. He slowly crawled from beneath the mass of weeds, crept down the slope, and sneaked to the narrow lane that led to his car. Using the hedgerow that bordered the lane as cover, he hurriedly limped toward the secluded nook where he had hidden his car.

The shouts of the Klansmen faded as he moved further away from them and approached his vehicle.

He was certain that at any moment some of the Klan members would be leaving. Since this trail was the only exit, Nick knew that when they left, their cars would be moving down the lane directly toward him. Also, he feared that some of them had spread out into the woods searching for him. With trembling fingers, he fumbled in his pocket for his car keys, almost dropping them in the clump of weeds that surrounded his car. He worried about the possibility that his car wouldn't start. In addition, he knew that the sound of his starting engine would certainly alert them.

He climbed into his car and quietly pulled the door shut. Just as he was preparing to start the vehicle, he hesitated. Peering through the dense foliage, he detected the bobbing beam of a flashlight moving down the lane toward him. Although his car was still hidden from view, he knew that it would be quickly discovered when the man with the flashlight arrived.

Moving quickly, he got out of his car and quietly unlocked the trunk. He groped for several seconds in search of some kind of weapon. Finally, his exploring fingers found a tire-tool.

The flashlight continued to move toward him—then it suddenly stopped. The probing beam explored the tangle of honeysuckle that surrounded his car. Once again it resumed its movement, coming directly toward him until it was focused directly on the trunk of his car. Just as the light beam illuminated his face, Nick stepped forward and swung the tire-tool, aiming for the spot where he imagined the man's face was located. The sickening smack of crunching bone told Nick that the swing of his weapon had been on target.

The man fell forward against the trunk of the car and then rolled into the patch of honeysuckle. Nick heard the revving of car engines, and through the grove of trees he could see headlights come to life. Moving quickly, he knelt down and took the flashlight from his victim's hand. With his free hand he yanked the hood from the Klansman's head and examined his face with the beam of the flashlight. He didn't recall ever seeing the man before. Swinging the beam to the man's feet, Nick examined his footwear in search of the telltale stars; however, instead of boots, the man was wearing shoes. From his kneeling position he quickly frisked his victim for a weapon, but found none. After extinguishing the light and hurriedly getting into his car, he tossed the flashlight and tire-tool into the front passenger seat. He wondered if the Klansman had recognized him, or if he had ever met him.

He started his car and quickly backed out from behind the wall of tangled weeds. The lack of space to turn the car around meant that he would have to back the car all the way out of the narrow lane to the main road. Fearing to take the risk of turning on his headlights, he depended on the light of the full moon to light his way. The V-8 engine groaned as it moved the car backward to the main road. When he reached the road, he put the car in first gear and turned the wheel to the right. Glancing back down the narrow lane, he saw the long row of headlights rapidly moving toward him.

Still driving without his headlights, he heard the scream of his tires on the asphalt and smelled burning rubber when he pushed the accelerator to the floor. Luckily, the road was without traffic as he sped down the barren street toward the downtown area. A glance at the rearview mirror told him that none of the trailing cars had yet turned onto the main road, indicating that they hadn't spotted him. After crossing the railroad track, he slowed the car and switched on his headlights. He then turned off the main street and pulled the vehicle into the narrow alley behind a warehouse. He parked the car and turned off the headlights.

He left his car and crept down the alley to the corner of the building near the main street. From his hiding place behind a large shrub, he heard the clatter of the series of cars crossing the railroad track and watched as they sped by him into the night. For several minutes he stood behind the bush, making sure that all the cars had passed. He then returned to his car and slowly drove toward the preacher's house where he knew that Mary Rose and Caleb were waiting…waiting for some hopeful news about Rufus. *How could he ever give them such ghastly news?*

He turned left on Broadway and drove toward Bucktown. To calm his nerves, he lit a cigarette, as he reflected on the terrible events of the evening. The revelation that Deputy Bronson was a member of the Klan had surprised him, but he had no doubt about the identity of the second man—the man with the stars on his boots—*Cowboy Galyon.*

He wondered if anyone else from the sheriff's department was a member of the Klan. *Could the sheriff himself be involved with the outlaw group?* Nick had carefully scrutinized each Klan member; however, their concealment behind the white sheets had made identification impossible. Only their general physical characteristics, such as body bulk and height offered any type of clue. Nick had noticed that only three or four of the men were tall, however, he was unable to determine whether or not they were as tall as Sheriff Mullins. Anyway, Nick couldn't picture the sheriff playing a subordinate role to Bronson.

When looking back over the events of the evening, Nick was dumfounded by the lack of judgment that he and the preacher had shown. To blindly set out, unarmed, to thwart a mission of the Klan was delusional—it was the logic of insanity. *What had they been thinking?* Because the preacher believed in the inherent goodness of men and in the use of persuasion to quell violence, Nick could excuse the preacher's faulty logic; however, he could only attribute his own misjudgment to ignorance.

Before he had moved to the South, he had occasionally heard of the Ku Klux Klan. But in his mind, he had developed a false impression of its character and purpose. He had held an image of them as being a thrill-seeking gang of would-be vigilantes—an annoying group of hell-raisers reminiscent of Halloween hobgoblins—a secret organization of self-righteous renegades whose principal purpose was creating its own laws, and occasionally throwing a scare into an errant black man. He had previously held the belief that although ignorant and misguided, they were reasonable men.

However, the events of this night had given him a rude awakening. He now realized that this organization of outlaws was even more malignant than the enemy in war; for rather than mounting a straightforward attack, the tactics employed by the Klan were more insidious in nature. In the daily routine of life, it was impossible to recognize this kind of enemy, for he may be a friend, a co-worker, or the neighbor next door. The man sitting in the 'amen corner' in church might be the same man who brutally whipped or murdered a Negro on the previous night.

It was after midnight when he pulled into the preacher's driveway. To hide the car from being seen from the street, he pulled the vehicle around to the back of the house and parked in the back yard. Dreading his confrontation with Mary Rose and the boy, he briefly remained in the car. He noticed only a small glow of light coming from one of the back rooms of the house. The preacher's house had no back entrance, so Nick left his car and wearily trudged around to the front of the house, up the walkway, and onto the porch, which was shrouded in darkness.

It was only after he switched on the dim porch light that he saw them. Sitting in the front porch swing were Mary Rose and Caleb, who was tightly clinging to his mother. Upon seeing the expression on Nick's face, Caleb began to uncontrollably sob. Mary Rose only stoically stared straight ahead.

"He's dead, isn't he?" she asked, with no expression. Apparently, she was in a state of shock, for her questions were asked with no more emotion than if she were taking a routine inventory of merchandise in a stock room.

"Yes," Nick answered, "I'm so sorry, Mary Rose."

When he heard the verifying words, Caleb buried his head in his mother's bosom and began to moan.

She calmly looked up at Nick. "Were you there when it happened?"

"Yes. I was helpless to do anything about it, Mary Rose. I was hiding. They never saw me. The preacher and I were fools to think we could stop it. In fact, Rufus might have gotten by with only a whipping if we hadn't shown up—and if they hadn't seen the preacher when he ripped off the Klansman's hood."

"And the preacher—he's also dead?"

"Yes."

"How did it happen?" She looked straight ahead, as if in a trance.

"Mary Rose, maybe we shouldn't talk about the details in front of the boy."

"He's old enough to know about the cruelty of white men. I want him to hear it. How did it happen?" she repeated.

"A man shot both of them."

"What man?" she asked.

"A man on the county police force, a deputy," said Nick.

"What was his name?"

"Mike Bronson. Do you know him?"

"No. What does he look like?"

"Well, if you ever saw him, you'd remember him. He has flaming red hair."

"I've seen the man," she said.

"Mary Rose, I feel terrible about it. I hid like a coward while he killed both of them." Nick looked away from her.

"I'm not faultin' you any, Mr. Nick. What good would come of you getting killed, too?"

"I guess you're right, but I still don't feel too good about it. What are you and Caleb going to do now?"

"I guess we'll just keep on living the best we know how. What else can we do?" She lowered her head and softly wept.

Caleb continued to cling to his mother. Nick walked to the porch swing and sat beside her, hugging both her and the boy. He spoke softly. "Mary Rose, you and Caleb should try to get some rest. Do you want to sleep here at the preacher's house, or would you rather go home?"

"I won't be able to sleep, Mr. Nick. I guess we'll just stay here. Our house would be too lonesome without Daddy. Could you stay with us for a while? I think Caleb is a little scared."

"Sure, Mary Rose. I can stay for most of the night if you need me. I don't have to see Stan until early in the morning."

For a long while he sat on the porch swing, gently swaying in the swing as he held them. Caleb was finally lulled to sleep, and an hour later she also surrendered to her exhaustion, laying her head gently on his shoulder.

It was now nearly 4:00 a.m. Nick stood and placed a cushion behind her head. He picked up the boy, carried him through the house and gently positioned him on the preacher's bed. He then returned to the porch and lifted Mary Rose. He carried her into the bedroom and placed her beside her son. Then he covered them with a blanket. Glancing at the dresser top, he noticed the preacher's personal items: his house keys, car keys, and a handful of pocket change scattered about. Realizing that he might need the keys to the house and maybe even the car keys, he scooped up both sets of keys and pocketed them.

He returned to the front porch and switched off the porch light. For a long time, he sat in the swing. In the east, the horizon paled as daybreak approached. The waning night brought a chill to the air, and the streetlight from the corner lit the countless tiny beads of dew that clung to the grass.

He gazed at the sprinkling of lights in the dark valley that nestled Bucktown, wondering how many Negro families had endured the oppression and indignity suffered by Mary Rose's family. His thoughts turned to Rufus, a poor black man who had never known any life other than hard work and servitude. Because of Stan's emotional closeness to Rufus, Nick dreaded telling him of his death and the terrible way he had died.

The evening's events had thrown his mind into a tangle of confusion. Because of his recent confrontation with the sheriff, he had already made up his mind to leave Cedar

Valley. But what bearing would the murder of Rufus and the preacher have on his departure? He had just witnessed two murders, meaning that he had both a moral and civic duty to report it to someone. But to whom? He didn't trust the sheriff; in fact, he might even be in someway connected to the crime. Yet, Nick wasn't certain that the sheriff's height matched the physical stature of any of the Klansmen. He doubted the sheriff's connection. Nevertheless, he would have to report the incident to some authority, maybe to some federal agent in another county.

Another aspect of the evening worried him: The man with the flashlight had momentarily gotten a glimpse of his face before Nick hit him with the tire-iron. Had the man recognized him? If he had, it would mean that a couple of dozen Klan members now knew that he had witnessed the crime, while other than Deputy Bronson and possibly Cowboy Galyon, Nick knew none of their identities. If the Klan member had recognized him, then his life was now in danger. Also, Nick wondered how badly he had injured the man. When he remembered how viciously he had swung the tire-iron he feared that the blow might have killed him; however, Nick realized that he would be in less danger if the man had died. His mind was in turmoil. He decided to postpone any decision until he talked to Stan.

He reflected on his life in the South. Although he had experienced a recent negative turn of events, his overall exposure had been positive; for he had discovered that, in general, Southern people were friendly and honest. In spite of the tinge of ignorance and prejudice among their ranks, most were hard-working people who were kind and generous to their neighbors. He considered the good people he had met, many of whom had become close friends: Stan, House Cat, Rufus, Mary Rose—and Caleb. He was particularly going to miss Preacher Temple, the men he had worked with, and most memorable of all, Lauren—beautiful, sweet Lauren. It saddened him to realize that he would soon be leaving Cedar Valley…and Lauren.

In the serenity of the early morning, Nick's emotions began to calm. The unseasonable chill in the air shielded him from sleepiness. He looked across the small village at the tranquil view. In the east, the muted light on the horizon gradually brightened to a brilliant coral, blending with the azure haze of the Smoky Mountains and the atmosphere surrounding Bucktown took on a pinkish tinge. The crow of a nearby rooster was answered across the misty valley, signaling the arrival of dawn.

Nick peered at his watch: *6:18 a.m.* In order to visit Stan before he left for work, he would need to leave soon.

He went inside the house and walked to the bedroom. Mary Rose and little Caleb were still asleep. He found a scrap of paper and a pencil and scribbled a note to her, telling her that he would check on them later in the day. He then left through the front door, walked around the house to his car and drove away.

Fearing that the Klan might be looking for him, he took the back roads to Stan's apartment. After a meandering drive, he pulled into the driveway and parked. The light from the window told him that Stan had awakened and was probably getting dressed. He quickly responded to Nick's rap at the door. When Nick stepped inside, Stan immediately hugged him and spoke with anxiety, "Damn, Nicky, I've been worried about you ever since you left me yesterday. I was afraid that you had left town. Where have you been staying?"

Nick took a seat in the recliner. "Oh, just here and there…any place that I could lay my head. Got any coffee brewing?"

"Sure, buddy. You take it black, right?"

"Right. By the way, you look like hell, pal." said Nick.

Stan smiled. "So do you, Nicky. I've been so worried about you that I haven't had much sleep. You haven't been hittin' the booze, have you?" He poured two coffees, handed a cup to Nick, and took a seat on the sofa facing him.

Stan sipped on his coffee as Nick wearily slumped in his chair. Exhaustion had begun to take its toll. Dreading the task that lay before him, he set his coffee down and looked directly at Stan. "I want you to get a good grip on yourself, Stan. What I'm about to tell you is going to be bad."

Stan's face paled. "It must be pretty bad, Nicky. I knew there was something wrong the minute I saw you walk through that door. What is it?"

Nick was blunt. "Rufus is dead. I saw him get killed. The Klan did it. They killed the preacher, too." He turned his head aside, avoiding Stan's eyes.

The enormous sob from Stan caused Nick to hang his head in sadness. For a long time, Stan continued to cry, as Nick stared at the floor. Finally, he walked to the sofa and took a seat beside Stan. Nick hugged him. "I know it's tough, buddy. You and Rufus were so close."

"How did it happen, Nicky?" He wiped his eyes.

Nick explained the entire tragedy: the abduction of Rufus from his home, the search for the burning cross by Nick and the preacher, the whipping, the murder of both Rufus and the preacher, and finally, the way Nick had made his escape—and the possibility that the man with the flashlight had recognized him before Nick had hit him. "Stan, I'm so sorry to bring you such terrible news."

Stan wiped his eyes with his handkerchief. He suddenly stood and began to pace the floor. When he turned to Nick, his face showed anger. "Mike Bronson! That son of a bitch! Poor old Rufus was such a good man. He never in his life even hurt a fly!"

"Well, I hate to bring it up right now, but this terrible event has put me in an impossible position. The sheriff told me to get out of town, but I'm a witness to two murders. If I report it to the authorities, I'll be asked to stay here and testify. If I stay here, the sheriff will put me in jail for those things he had me charged with. But if I leave, I'm letting a man get away with murder."

Stan again took a seat on the couch and buried his head in his hands. "Oh, God! How did all this ever happen?" He again began to sob. He finally regained his composure. "Nicky, we've gotta give this whole thing some serious thought. You know, if that guy with the flashlight recognized you, your life is in danger!"

"I know that, Stan. And since they all wore hoods, I won't recognize any of them. I won't even know if the guy walking beside me on the street is planning to kill me."

Stan again got up and began to pace. "Let's try to examine a couple of scenarios. Let's say that you turn Bronson in to the sheriff for murder. What do you think the sheriff would do? He might not even believe you. Bronson's going to deny it, of course, and with the bodies buried, it would be your word against his. My uncle doesn't like you, and after all, Bronson is his deputy."

"But what choice do I have, Stan? I can't let the guy get away with murder!"

"If the sheriff doesn't believe you—do you think he'd put you in jail for not leaving town?" Stan curiously eyed him.

"Of course he would. He was pretty emphatic about his threat. And remember, I agreed to leave town if he wouldn't put me in jail."

"If you turn Bronson in for murder, maybe you'd be better off in jail. That's the only place you'd be safe because all the Klan would be gunning for you. They'd all go to jail if Bronson turned state's evidence. Maybe he wouldn't be safe, either."

"Well, what do you suggest I do?" asked Nick.

"Well, let's look at another possibility. Let's suppose you didn't turn him in, and just left town."

"And let Bronson get away with murder?"

"That's where I come in, pal. I'll take care of Bronson!"

Nick's face registered shock. "Do you mean you'd kill him?"

"You don't really think I'd let him get away with killing Rufus, do you?" Stan appeared to be dead serious.

"Stan, I don't want any part of murder!" Nick was stunned.

"But you *wouldn't* have any part in it. And wouldn't you like to see him pay for what he did to Rufus?"

"Yes, but I'd like to see him punished legally—by the law!"

"Now, Nicky, this is a perfect example of what I told you a long time ago. Sometimes justice comes in different packages."

"Stan, I want to see him pay for his crime, but I won't agree to anything except letting the courts prosecute him. If we take the law into our own hands, then we're no better than the Klan."

"Nick, sometimes you're a hard nut to crack! If you turn Bronson in to the sheriff, here's what'll happen: He won't believe you, and he'll throw your ass in jail. You'll probably do a couple of years in the pen, and all the while, Bronson is walking free. Then, maybe ten years from now, somebody will dig up a couple of skeletons. But nobody will even know who they belong to, and even if they do, they won't give a crap!"

"Damn! I don't know what to do. I'm in trouble no matter what I do." Nick threw up his arms in frustration.

Stan slowly crossed the room and returned to his seat on the couch. "Nick, your friendship means more than anything to me. But you know, sometimes you're naïve. You're a stranger in this town, with few friends. You have little money and no connections. You're in real trouble, buddy, and you don't have anybody in town that can help you but me. On the other hand, I do have money and connections. I can get things done. This thing is too big for you to handle."

"But what can I do?" Nick asked with frustration.

"Okay, here's what I suggest. Let me take care of it."

"By 'taking care of it'—do you mean *killing Bronson*?"

"Well, I'd like to kill him, but I'm willing to try it your way. I'll tell you what I'll agree to do. I won't kill him, as much as I'd like to. I'll let the courts handle it. My advice to you is to let me give you some money so you can get out of town. That way you'll be safe from the Klan, and also avoid going to jail. I'll report it to the sheriff because he'll believe me. Then, in a few weeks, I'll join you in Louisiana."

"But Stan, you didn't see it happen. Your testimony won't mean much. If they prosecute Bronson, they'll need me as a witness for the prosecution."

"Then the sheriff can bring you back from Louisiana as a witness. When I report it to my uncle, he'll believe me. He doesn't like Bronson much more than he likes you, so he'll arrest him, and jail him. Then I'll get the sheriff to drop charges on you in return for your eyewitness testimony. He'll go along with me because he's my uncle."

"Damn, I don't know, Stan…That sure is a long-shot."

Stan stood. "Nicky, the choice is yours. But once you're in jail there's not a damned thing you can do about any of it. Maybe you ought to leave town pretty soon. You can trust me to handle it. I want to see justice done even more than you do."

"Do I have your word that you won't take the law into your own hands?" Nick placed his coffee on the table and stood.

"You have my word. But I'll have to admit I'd sure like to kill the bastard. Nicky, if you leave town, I promise you I'll come to Louisiana and join you as soon as I get my affairs in order. We can come back here together when you testify." He counted out several bills to Nick. "Here, take this money. You're probably broke. And don't worry about paying me back."

"Thanks, Stan. I'll see you again before I leave."

"Nicky, I would ask you to stay here with me, but you might not be safe here. Where are you going to be staying before you leave?"

"You're right, I may not be safe here. I'm not sure where I'll be staying, but I'll find a place. After I leave here I'm going to pay a short visit to Mary Rose and Caleb. I promised them I'd check on them before I leave town."

"What are you going to do about Lauren?" asked Stan.

269

"I need to see her one more time before I leave. I may not ever see her again, but I can't leave town without telling her goodbye. I also need to tell her about Rufus."

Stan placed his hands on Nick's shoulders and looked him squarely in the face. "Nicky, I don't think that's a very good idea. It's probably okay to tell Lauren goodbye, but I wouldn't mention what happened to Rufus or the preacher."

"Why not? She liked both of them. After all, she has a right to know."

"Well, the first thing she'd do is blab it to her dad. Then, the sheriff would have you picked up, and you'd have an additional charge added to the others—withholding evidence. Hell, if you're gonna tell Lauren, then you might as well stay here and tell the sheriff yourself."

"You may be right. I didn't think about that. I guess it would be a mistake to tell her. But I'm going to see her and tell her goodbye."

"When do you plan to leave?"

"Tomorrow night after I see Lauren," Nick answered, "I need to come back here sometime tomorrow and pick up my clothes. Could you and I spend some time together tomorrow and talk about this before I leave town?"

"Sure, buddy. I'll take the day off. We may not see each other for a long time after you leave."

"Stan, I really want to see Bronson prosecuted."

"You can count on me, buddy. I won't be able to rest until I see that bastard in prison. Nicky, you'd better lay low today, in case that guy you clobbered recognized you. Remember, they murdered two men! If they even think you witnessed it, you won't live to see the sun set tonight!" For the first time, Nick felt the weight of the whole nightmare.

"Don't worry. I don't intend to be seen by anyone in town." He smiled and hugged Stan. "Old pal, I was sorry to bring you such sad news."

Stan stood in the door and waved to him as he drove away.

To avoid being seen by anyone in the downtown area, Nick again took an alternate route when driving to the preacher's house. As he drove, he relived the terrible events of the prior evening. He remembered his scrutiny of the hooded Klan members in his attempt to recognize any identifying characteristic. Other than the unmasking of Bronson and the stars on the boots of Cowboy Galyon, he remembered only one other telltale clue: *A name.* He recalled Bronson yelling at someone with a double name to load the bodies in his pickup truck. *But what was the name? Was it Billy Joe, or Billy Ray? Billy Bob? Billy something...he couldn't remember.* He decided that, in the South, there were as many double names as nicknames.

When he arrived in Bucktown, he noticed Mary Rose and Caleb sitting on their own front porch, indicating that since he had left them they had returned home. He pulled into the driveway, drove around the house and parked in back, so that his car was hidden from the road.

Mary Rose was seated in a chair while Caleb was lying on the porch floor resting his head on the reclining body of a drooling hound dog. Nick greeted them and took a seat beside Mary Rose. The hound lazily slunk away when Caleb sat up. Nick noticed that Caleb's eyes were swollen from crying.

"Well, did you and Caleb get any sleep?" he asked.

"Yes, we slept some. I didn't think I'd be able to sleep, but I was just so exhausted. Thank you for staying with us last night and putting us to bed. We got your note."

"Yeah, I wanted you to know that I was coming back. Look, Mary Rose, I have to leave town. The reason I'm leaving is a long story, but I'll worry about you and the boy when I'm gone."

"You're leaving Cedar Valley? When?"

"Tomorrow night. I'll stay here tonight if you want me to, if you and Caleb are scared."

"I sure appreciate that Mr. Nick, but maybe you'd better not stay with us. People don't look favorably on a white man sleeping in the same house with a colored woman unless the man of the house is at home, too. We took a big chance last night when you stayed with us. I'm afraid those awful white men might come back if people were to object."

"Whatever you decide, Mary Rose. I'm just here to help. Why don't you quit calling me 'Mr. Nick?' Just call me 'Nick.' Okay?"

"Alright, Nick. I'd take kindly to you if you'd stay at the preacher's house tonight. Since it's nearby, Caleb and I could call on you if anybody tried to cause us any trouble."

"I'll be glad to stay there, Mary Rose. One reason I came back is to see if you and little Caleb need anything. You don't have a car, and since you no longer have Rufus…"

"Nick, we could use a few groceries."

"I'll be glad to go to the store for you, Mary Rose. I'll go to Bucktown, so I won't be seen or recognized by any of the Klan members. Do you want to come with me?"

"No, sir. I'd better just stay here with Caleb. Can I just make you a list and give you some money?"

"Sure, you can make me a list, but I don't want any money."

"No sir, I want to give you some money. In this family, we pay our own way."

He could sense her dignity as she proudly walked into the house to write the grocery list. Caleb sat on the porch floor sucking on a Popsicle. He walked to the front yard and sat beside the hound, occasionally letting the mangy dog lick his Popsicle. Nick decided that it was lucky for him that his mother hadn't witnessed the event. He wondered what would happen to the boy now that Rufus was gone.

Avoiding Cedar Valley, he bought the listed items, as well as a couple of candy bars for Caleb at a small grocery store in the dilapidated business section of Bucktown. After returning with the items, he again hid the car by parking it behind the house. When he gave the groceries to Mary Rose, he made an attempt to return her money, but she politely refused to accept it.

Shyly, she smiled at him. "Nick, when I said it would be best if you didn't spend the night, I didn't mean that you had

272

to leave our house during the daylight hours. You can stay here all day, if you've a mind to."

"Thank you, Mary Rose," he said.

She took a seat beside him in the porch swing. Leaning very close to him, she inspected his injured face and sadly shook her head. "Nick, I couldn't help but notice the cuts and bruises on your face. Obviously, you didn't see a doctor. If you don't mind, I'll try to fix them some. The way your nose is swollen it looks like it might be broken. Those cuts should be cleaned, and you need some medicine on them. Do you mind if I try to make it better?" She gently cupped his face in her hands as she moved closer to him and examined the damage.

"No, I don't mind. But I don't think you can do much to make it any better. My nose isn't broken, but it's awfully sore. Go easy when you're working on me."

"Don't worry, Nick. If I start to hurt you, just tell me."

Mary Rose left the porch swing and went inside. She soon returned with a pan of hot water and a small wicker basket that contained a pair of scissors, a variety of medications, and a broad strip of white flannel material. She began to cut the flannel into narrow strips. "I'm gonna make you a poultice. If you don't mind, lie down in the swing so the poultice won't fall off."

With his legs dangling, he lay on his back in the swing as she placed a cushion behind his head. After using soap and water to carefully cleanse the affected areas, she gently swabbed the wounds with antiseptic. She then folded the strips of flannel and applied a thick layer of salve to the fabric. The acrid odor of camphor brought tears to his eyes when she applied the poultice. Instantly, the throbbing pain in his nose became numbed, and his clogged nasal passages began to clear.

"The poultice will stop the swelling and help you breathe." She tossed the leftover pan of water into the yard, packed up her medical items, and took them back inside.

Returning to the porch, she sat facing him as he continued to recline in the swing with the poultice applied to his face.

"Thank you, Mary Rose. My face feels much better," he said.

"You're welcome, Nick. Now rest there for a while and let that poultice do its work."

He spent most of the day sitting on the porch with her and the boy. In mid-afternoon, Caleb was lured away by a couple of his friends. Nick decided that it was time to call Lauren. He went inside to use Mary Rose's phone.

He smiled when he again heard her voice. "Dr. Johnston's Clinic. May I help you?"

"Hi, Lauren—it's me."

"Well, hello! Where have you been? Nicky, I've been thinking a lot about us, and you've got me going crazy with worry. What's going on? You're acting mysterious! Are you still planning to leave? Honey, we need to talk!"

"Lauren, that's why I called. I can't talk for very long, and I can't explain things over the phone. Can you meet me tomorrow night at our favorite spot at the lake?"

"Why do you want me to *meet you* somewhere? Why don't you just come to the house? It's not like we have to slip around to see each other anymore."

"Listen, Lauren, I told you I can't explain it on the phone. For now, I don't want anyone to know I'm seeing you. I'll explain it to you tomorrow night. Meet me at eight, if you can get away. And don't tell anyone you're meeting me. Just trust me, okay?"

"Nicky, I've got a patient waiting. I have to hang up now."

"Just meet me, okay?"

"Okay, 'bye."

"Goodbye, Lauren."

Before returning to the porch, he glanced out the front window. Cruising slowly past the house was a police car. Nick suspected that the police were probably searching for him. He was glad that he had been inside the house when the car drove past. He returned to the porch. Although exhausted, he continued to keep his eyes fixed on the road while staying with Mary Rose for the remainder of the afternoon. It suddenly dawned on him that his presence at Mary Rose's house was placing her and her son in danger.

Twilight was approaching when she went inside and prepared dinner. Nick feared that another police car might be searching for him; as a result, he remained on the porch with his eyes focused on the street. After dinner they only occasionally talked. Nick sat in the porch swing with Mary Rose while Caleb rested on the porch floor with the hound's head in his lap. The hour was late, and Nick was very tired. He stood and spoke to Mary Rose. "Well, I've got to get some rest. I'm going to the preacher's house and go to bed. I didn't sleep any last night."

She also got up. "Thank you, Nick, for everything. Will we be seeing you again before you leave?"

"No, ma'am, I'm afraid not. I'll be leaving for Stan's apartment in the morning before you get up. Is there anything else I can do for you before I leave?"

"No, sir, I don't reckon so. You've been awfully good to us. We'll never forget you."

Caleb stood and started gesturing with his hands.

"What's he trying to say?" asked Nick.

She sadly smiled. "He wants to know if you'll be coming back—if we'll ever see you again," she said.

"I don't know, Mary Rose. Tell him I don't know. We never know what fate has in store for us."

Nick squatted, and Caleb came running to him. He hugged Caleb tightly, noticing how small the boy felt in his arms.

He released Caleb and turned to Mary Rose. "Look, I hate to leave you and the boy. I wish I could stay so I could help you. But if I hang around here, I'm putting you and Caleb in danger. I'll worry about you when I'm gone."

"Don't worry. When we stop bein' so scared, we'll be okay."

Nick thought about his close relationship with Mary Rose and Caleb. He had grown protective of them, for they had become like family to him. He began to realize that he had been thinking mostly of his own safety, without fully recognizing the peril they could possibly be facing. It suddenly occurred to him that he couldn't just walk out of their lives when they were in such danger, much of which had been brought on by their association with him. He quickly turned to face Mary Rose and looked into her eyes. "Mary Rose, I want you to listen to me. Since these men killed Rufus, I can see that they'll stop at nothing. I witnessed the killing and they're looking for me so they can kill me. They might realize that you and Caleb are my friends and that I've been hiding here. They might think that you know where they can find me. For your own safety, you need to take Caleb and leave here, *soon!* Can you drive? And where are you gonna get a car? I know that Rufus never owned one."

"Yes, I can drive. We've already been planning to leave. But I'll have to buy some kind of an old car before we can go."

"Do you have the money for a car?"

"Well, I've got about two hundred dollars saved up. Do you think I could buy some kind of car for about a hundred dollars? We'd need the other hundred just to get by."

Nick fished in his pocket and pulled out the keys to the preacher's car. "Here, Mary Rose, take these. They're the keys to Preacher Temple's car. I don't know what kind of shape the car is in, but I'm sure it will at least get you out of here. Anyway, it's a better car than you could buy for a hundred dollars. I'll park the preacher's car behind your house early tomorrow morning. Do you have some place in mind where you can go?"

"Yes, I already thought about that. Since they killed Daddy, this place feels empty anyway. As soon as I can get things packed up, Caleb and I are going to move to my brother's house. He doesn't live in Tennessee. He lives in…"

Nick interrupted. "Don't say it! I don't want to know who you're moving in with and I don't want to know *where!* But you need to move *soon!"*

"Well, it'll take a few days for me to get things packed up."

"Do it *now*, Mary Rose!"

"But maybe the boy and I will be safe living here for a few days after you're gone. Why would they want to harm us then?"

"They'll know that I told you who did the killing. They want to keep this thing quiet. You and Caleb will never be safe around here. Please tell me you'll get out of here—*fast!* Just take a few of the most necessary items and hit the road. Will you promise me that you will?"

"Yes, I promise."

"I'll have Stan help you get out of here," said Nick. "He'll be glad to help, because he really loved Rufus

He pulled his wallet from his pocket. From the money that Stan had given him, he removed a one hundred dollar bill. "Mary Rose, I want you to take this, and I don't want any argument out of you. I know you are a proud lady, but if you really want to respect my wishes, you'll take it."

Tears filled her eyes. She tucked the money inside her blouse and smiled. "God bless you, Nick Parilli!" she said. She then hugged him. "Goodbye, Nick. You take care of yourself, do you hear?"

"Goodbye, Mary Rose." He turned and walked down the porch steps and then around the house toward his car.

Chapter 18

Nick awoke from a restless sleep, as dreams of the war had once again invaded his mind. He crawled out of bed and peered between the ragged curtains at the gloomy sky. The gentle rain saturated the tin roof with a relentless, soothing patter. It was a gray morning suited for laziness and conducive to staying in bed.

But this was no time for complacency. As he became more fully awake his anxiety intensified. However, he felt reasonably safe while hiding out at the preacher's house. He was sure that other than Mary Rose and Caleb, no one even knew of his close friendship with the preacher.

He had already dressed and had even managed to scrape together a makeshift breakfast of cereal and coffee from the preacher's paltry pantry.

The rusty tin roof had initiated several leaks that dripped steadily from the ceiling. To catch the water Nick placed pots and a couple of porcelain bowls on the floor beneath the drips.

Since neither he nor the preacher would ever again inhabit the place, the impractical gesture caused Nick to wonder why he had even bothered. He supposed that he had done it because it was what the preacher would have wanted. Out of respect for the memory of him, Nick couldn't bear to ignore the leaks.

He walked to the front porch and viewed the misty wetness of the valley. The cold drizzle caused the heated earth to breathe a blanketing fog, bathing faraway objects in a translucent haze.

Looking down the road toward Rufus' house, he wondered if Mary Rose and Caleb were still in bed. He left the porch and got into the preacher's car. With Preacher Temple's extra set of car keys, he delivered the car to their back yard and parked. He peered at his watch: *10:35.* If they were up and around, he still had time to again tell them goodbye; however, he decided against it, for they were probably still sleeping; besides, he hated second goodbyes. He hoped that before this day was over they would quickly pack a few items and leave their home for a safer place.

He returned to the preacher's house and glanced around the interior for a final time. This dilapidated place had been the preacher's home, a horrid hellhole assigned to him by society for surrendering to the disease of alcoholism. Nick was again reminded of Chicago, and the way that his father had lived after he had become an alcoholic. He picked up his duffel bag containing his skimpy belongings, walked out the front door and gently closed it behind him.

The windshield wipers swabbed away the rain as he slowly drove out of the valley. He felt that each event of today was a moment of finality for him. From this point forward, to the places and people that he left behind him he could bid a silent farewell, for he would probably never again see them. As he moved forward with his life, he could erase them from his existence, but not from his mind; for he would forever remember the people and his experiences in Cedar Valley. He had already left House Cat behind, and Bucktown, including Rufus, Mary Rose, Caleb, and the preacher. By the end of this day, he would be saying goodbye to his best friend, Stan—and finally, Lauren, the love of his life. He wondered if he would ever be able to forget her. By tomorrow night, he would begin a new life in Buras, Louisiana, and Cedar Valley would no longer exist for him—except in his memory.

On his drive toward Stan's apartment, he again chose an alternate route, avoiding the main part of town. Being on the open road again aroused his anxiety. He repeatedly glanced into the rear-view mirror to see if he was being followed. The sky grew darker as the rain began to fall more heavily. He drove cautiously and slowly, for he was in no hurry. Rivulets of water collected on the road as his tires pulled a trail of hazy mist behind his car. After completely bypassing the town, he turned onto Highway 11 and drove onward to the apartment. He turned into the driveway and parked behind the apartment building, noticing that Stan's car was gone. Nick figured that he was probably checking on some routine business matter and would probably soon return.

Carrying his duffel bag, he became soaked with rain when he dashed to the front door. Using his key, he entered the apartment and hurried into the bathroom. He relieved his bladder and then pulled a towel from the rack and swabbed his wet hair. In the kitchen, he noticed that Stan had left a half-full pot of coffee. He poured his coffee and took a seat at the kitchen table when he saw the note from Stan on the tabletop.

The message was brief, expressing his regret for not being able to spend the day with Nick, and stating that he had encountered some unexpected problem that would require his attention for most of the day. He added that he would meet him at the apartment tonight after Nick's final rendezvous with Lauren.

With disappointment, he cast the note aside. He had counted on spending his last day in Cedar Valley with Stan. Since he would not be able to see Lauren until tonight, he wondered how he would spend the remainder of the day. He decided that perhaps he should drive back to Bucktown and visit with Mary Rose and Caleb.

280

After eating a ham and cheese sandwich and finishing his coffee, he entered the bedroom and began packing. In the duffel bag, he placed his toilet articles, shoes, and undergarments. From the closet, he removed several hangers of clothing, most of which had been given to him by Stan. He sat on the bed and thought of his friend, and of the alliance they had developed and nurtured since their reunion. Stan had expressed his desire to rejoin him in Louisiana; however, in his heart, Nick realized that it was only a dream that would never become a reality. Stan would never leave Cedar Valley, for much like his cousin, Lauren, he was chained to his father. Nick wondered if, after tonight, he would ever again see Stan—or Lauren.

He picked up his clothing and stepped out the door, locking it behind him. The rain had stopped, leaving in its wake a rising steam from the surrounding fields and the asphalt road. He drove away, once again in the direction of Bucktown.

He again drove the back roads, moving along slowly, engrossed in thought. When he reflected on his time in Cedar Valley he concluded that he was no worse off than if he hadn't come here. After all, his intended destination had initially been Louisiana. In fact, he was a bit better off than if he hadn't stopped here. He had a little more money, a car, and some decent clothing, although they were a gift from Stan. His stop in this small town had simply been a detour, a roundabout way to arrive at his intended destination. When he thought of Cedar Valley, his mind was filled with ambivalence; for his time in this small town had been an incongruous mixture of extreme joy and abject sorrow. He decided that he would attempt to put the whole experience behind him.

He was now driving through the most desolate stretch of road that linked him to Bucktown. At the bottom of the hill where the route curved to the right, a black vehicle was parked in the broad road shoulder. A man stood in the center of the road. He was a large, stocky man with flaming red hair. His stance was determined and rigid, and clinched between his

281

outstretched hands was a revolver, pointing directly toward Nick's car.

Nick immediately recognized Bronson. At first he considered increasing his speed and simply driving into him; however, he quickly reconsidered, for if he surrendered to his desire, the sheriff would have yet another crime to add to the list of charges against him: *Murder.* Or even worse, Bronson might shoot him.

Nick slowed the car as he approached Bronson, who was now pointing the weapon directly at his face. Gesturing with his pistol, Bronson motioned for Nick to pull over onto the road shoulder beside his car. With the gun pointed directly at him, Nick had no other choice but to comply.

Nick realized that Bronson was stopping him for only one of two possible reasons: *To arrest him because he had not left town quickly enough after the sheriff's ultimatum, or to kill him because he had been recognized by the Klan member on the night when Rufus and the preacher were murdered.* He dreaded the confrontation.

Nick pulled the vehicle onto the road shoulder and shut off the motor. Still aiming the pistol at Nick's head, Bronson walked around the car to the door of the driver's side. Standing about six feet from Nick's car, he displayed a sarcastic grin.

"Okay, Parilli, get out of the car—and easy does it, because I know how foxy you can be."

Reaching with his right hand, Nick groped in the car seat for the tire-tool with which he had struck the Klansman on the night of the murders. When looking at Bronson's leering expression, Nick wanted to kill him. For a moment, he remained in the car.

Bronson stepped closer to the car and leveled his weapon at Nick's eyes. "I said get out of there, and when you step out, do it nice and easy." He reached out and partially opened Nick's door, barely leaving him room to exit the car. "At'ta boy, nice and easy, now," he said. As Nick slowly eased out of the car onto the ground, his fingers were now clenched around the tire-tool.

"I can see that we worked you over pretty good," said Bronson, in reference to Nick's mangled face.

"You don't look so good yourself," replied Nick.

The partially closed door afforded Nick the necessary cover to obscure the tire-tool. He held the weapon low, hidden behind his right leg as he stepped out of the car into full-view.

Bronson grinned. "I think I'll work you over a little more before I kill you." He swung the pistol as he spoke. The weapon struck Nick just above the left eye and almost knocked him unconscious. He staggered, and when Bronson prepared to strike him a second time, Nick swung the tire-iron. The steel shaft caught the deputy on the left side of his head, and the sickening crack confirmed that his jawbone was badly injured and possibly broken. He stumbled and slumped to his knees as he unsteadily attempted to stabilize the revolver as he aimed.

Nick again swung the tire-tool, but the blow only caught the deputy on the shoulder. When Bronson fired his pistol, the shot was wild, shattering the side window of Nick's car. Nick's third swing of the makeshift weapon was on target. It again caught the deputy on his left cheek, completely shattering his jawbone.

Bronson fell facedown onto the ground. Nick stood over him with the tire-iron raised. He considered delivering another blow to the deputy's head, but quickly changed his mind; *after all, Bronson may already be dead,* he thought.

Feeling for a pulse, he determined that Bronson was still alive. He dragged the limp body of the deputy into a patch of weeds, hiding him from view.

Bronson's pistol was lying on the ground where he had dropped it. Nick picked it up and tucked it beneath his belt, with the intention of keeping it for protection from future ambushes. He quickly reconsidered, for he knew that if he kept the weapon, he would surely end up killing someone. He pulled the pistol from beneath his belt and hurled it into a patch of weeds.

He flung the tire-iron into the woods, and with an unsteady gait, staggered back to his car and quickly drove away. In the rearview mirror, he inspected his face. His left eyebrow was badly slashed, and the steady stream of blood almost blinded him. The blood had now begun to soak his shirt and drip onto his pants. He became dizzy and feared that he might faint. He pressed the gas pedal, pushing the old Ford to its limit.

Luck had been on his side, for during the fight with the deputy, not a single car had passed. He realized that it would now be necessary to leave town immediately. There would be no evening rendezvous with Lauren, nor a meeting with Stan, for as soon as the police found Bronson's car, they would be searching for him to arrest him for assault—*or possibly for murder*.

In an attempt to stem the flow of blood from his eyebrow, he pressed his handkerchief against the wound. He again peered into the rearview mirror. His face was a ghastly, grotesque caricature. He knew that he would have to find a place to clean himself up before being seen in public.

Nick was still unsure if the deputy knew that he had witnessed the murders of Rufus and the preacher. Perhaps he was only planning to arrest Nick for not leaving town; and knowing that he would visit Stan at his apartment before leaving, he had been *expecting* Nick, for he was standing in the road waiting; however, before he had struck Nick with the pistol, Bronson had said that he was intending to kill him. Maybe he *did know*.

He was unable to think clearly, particularly in regard to what his next move should be. *Should he go back to the preacher's house and attempt to clean himself up before leaving?*

He couldn't bear the thought of leaving town without seeing Lauren. Under the circumstances, if he left with no explanation and with the police searching for him, she would always view him as a shiftless quitter who ran out on their relationship, a fugitive from justice who was too cowardly to face the consequences of his crimes. He decided that, whatever the risk, he *had to see her* before leaving town. If he could somehow explain it to her...somehow make her understand...

He drove into Cedar Valley. When he spotted a phone booth beside a *Sinclair* service station, he pulled the car over and stopped. He dialed Lauren's work number and recognized her sweet voice. "Lauren, we need to talk!" he stammered.

"Nicky, you sound so strange. Is something wrong?"

"Lauren, I can't talk for very long. You've got to meet me!"

"Nicky, I've already told you I'd meet you at the lake tonight. I'll be there for sure."

"No, Lauren! You've got to meet me *now!*"

"Now? Why now? Nicky, I'm working!"

"You've got to meet me now, or you'll never see me again! Don't ask me why, just do it! Please meet me! I can explain!"

"But, Nicky—I'm working! I can't just walk away from my job! Don't you understand?"

"Lauren, get somebody to cover for you. Meet me on the corner in front of the *Rexall Drug Store.* I'll be there in five minutes."

"But, Nicky, I..."

"I'll be there in five minutes. If you're not there, I'll just drive on. In case you're not there, goodbye—and *I love you!*"

When he double-parked at the *Rexall Pharmacy* he didn't see her anywhere. While his motor idled, he waited for a couple of minutes. Just as he started to pull away, he saw her running across Broadway toward his car. She quickly jumped into the vehicle and he sped away.

When she looked at him, she gasped. "My God, Nicky! What happened to you?"

"It's a long story, honey. I've been keeping a lot of it from you, but now I'm going to tell you what's been going on."

"You just told me you *love me!* For the first time, you told me you *love me!* Nicky, if you do, then you won't leave me! No matter how bad things are, and for whatever reason, you can stay, and I'll help you work things out!" She looked closely at his face. "Oh, Nicky! You need to go to a doctor! Let's go back to the clinic and I'll get Dr. Johnston to help you!"

"I can't go back to the clinic, Lauren, and after I explain it to you, you'll know why. Besides, I don't need a doctor. I just need to clean myself up a little."

The bleeding had now mostly subsided with only a trickle of blood oozing into his left eye. The bloody condition of his clothing made him appear to be more severely injured than he actually was. She scooted closer to him and inspected the laceration over his left eye. "Maybe I can help, Nicky. I can clean your face up and see how bad it really is...I can't really tell, with so much blood. Where are we going? Is there some place we can go?"

"I'm going to a place where I've been staying lately. Have you ever been in Bucktown?"

"No. But why have you been staying in a place like Bucktown? I thought you and Stan had an apartment. Why haven't you been staying with him?"

"You'll understand after I explain it to you." He finally turned the car into the preacher's driveway. He then pulled the vehicle behind the house, hiding it from the view of anyone passing in cars.

After they entered the front door. Lauren was shocked when she saw the dilapidated condition of the house. "Who lives in this terrible place?" she asked. "How could people in this little town live in such filth?"

Nick became irritated. "Lauren, everybody's not rich, like your family! Not everybody has a swimming pool and a tennis court! I came from a poor family myself. You've been so sheltered you know nothing about life!"

"I didn't mean anything by my remark, Nicky."

"What if you and I were to marry, and I couldn't afford an expensive place?"

She hugged him. "I'd be willing to live in a cave as long as you and I were together, Nicky. *I love you!* You know that."

"This is preacher Temple's house. It's all he could afford. I've been staying here with him for a while."

Nick lay down on the couch and propped a cushion under his head. She sat in a chair beside him and began to examine his injuries.

"Nicky, who did this to you?"

"It was Mike Bronson. He pulled a gun on me."

"How did you get away from him?"

"I clobbered him with a tire-tool. The police will be looking for me. I hope they don't find out that we're at the preacher's house."

"And where *is* the preacher?" she asked.

"He's not here at the moment. I want to tell you some things about him later. In fact, I want to talk to you about a lot of things. But I'm a little worried that you may not believe them."

"Nicky, before we have a serious talk I want to try to do something about your injuries." She stood and walked into the kitchen. "I'm going to clean you up with hot water and then we can see how bad you're hurt." She placed a pan of water on the electric range and left it there to boil. She then removed some clean towels from a kitchen drawer and sorted through various medicine bottles in the cabinet. "At least the towels are clean," she said.

"Yeah, in spite of the run-down condition of the place, the preacher is really a clean person," he answered.

He elevated his head with a cushion and reclined on the couch, waiting for her. After she came and sat beside him, she gently cleaned around the laceration above his eye and applied iodine to the wound.

"Damn!" cried Nick. "That burns!"

"Sit still! Nicky, it's not as bad as I thought, but you could still use a couple of stitches."

"Slap a couple of *Band Aids* on it. It'll be okay."

"What happened to your nose? It's swollen and it looks like the blood's drier there. Is that from an earlier fight?"

"Yeah. That was the *first* time I got the hell beat out of me," he said, sarcastically.

She stood. "Well, that's about the best I can do, with nothing better to work with." She smiled. "I believe you're going to live, after all!" She took the items back into the kitchen and began to clean up the mess she had made.

She called from the kitchen, "Nicky, if you have to go away for a while—you'll come back, won't you?"

"I don't know, Lauren. We need to talk about that."

When she again took her seat beside Nick, he was lying on his back, almost asleep. He jumped when she playfully poked him. "Okay, Nicky, finish your story. You said you didn't think I'd believe it. Why do you think that? I want to know what's been going on. I want to know what the big mystery is. You've been acting crazy! I've put up with this talk about you leaving because I thought you'd finally come to your senses and stay here. Are you in some kind of trouble? If you are, I want to know what it is, right now! Look, honey…we love each other! Maybe I can help you. If you love me, why haven't you trusted me enough to tell me?" She sat in the cane-bottom chair and curiously looked at him.

He became dizzy when he rose to a sitting position and looked into her eyes. "Lauren, I want to tell you an interesting story. I don't know exactly where to start. I had made up my mind to never tell you any of this, but I've now decided it's something you need to know."

"But why had you made up your mind not to tell me?"

"Because I was afraid that maybe you couldn't handle it— or maybe you wouldn't even believe it. I'm afraid you'll hate me when you hear me say these things. But I couldn't leave here with you believing I had just run out on you for no good reason. You'll probably hate me now, but someday you'll realize that I told you the truth. And if you don't, it'll just prove that our relationship wouldn't have worked anyway."

"What is it about the story that's so incredible that I may not believe it? And why would I hate you for telling me the truth?"

"Brace yourself, Lauren. A while ago you asked me where the preacher is. Well, he's *dead*, and so is Rufus! I saw both of them get murdered!"

She abruptly stood. Her face paled and her eyes widened as she stared in disbelief. "Murdered? Rufus? And the preacher? Oh, my God! When did it happen?" Her legs became weak and she quickly collapsed in a chair, burying her head in her hands. For several seconds Nick remained quiet as she sobbed and moaned.

Finally he continued. "It happened a couple of nights ago. The Klan did it. I was here visiting the preacher when the Klan came and got Rufus. Like idiots, Preacher Temple and I chased after them, thinking that we could somehow stop it. *Hell, some heroes we were!* We didn't even have any weapons with us. All we accomplished was to get both Rufus and the preacher killed!"

Lauren slowly raised her head. She had partially regained her composure; however, she violently trembled as tears streamed from her eyes. "But what made them kill Rufus? And the preacher? What did *he* do that would make them murder *him*?"

"The man who was whipping Rufus killed the preacher because Preacher Temple yanked the hood off of him and could identify him. Then he had to kill Rufus because he had seen him murder the preacher. I saw it all from my hiding place in the bushes. He pulled out a pistol and shot both of them point blank! They would have killed me if they had spotted me! I feel like a coward for hiding!"

"Nicky, you shouldn't feel that way! What good would come of you also getting killed? You said that the preacher yanked off the killer's hood. Did you recognize the man who killed them?"

"Yes. It was Mike Bronson."

"*Mike Bronson?* Are you sure? You must be mistaken!"

"No, it was him, Lauren! I wasn't even twenty feet away from him when he shot them!"

"I somehow always sensed that there was something evil about him. That's why I was so afraid of him. I was more afraid that he would harm *you*... but I didn't think he was capable of committing murder! Did you recognize anyone else?"

"Well, I'm not sure, but I think that deputy, Cowboy Galyon was one of them."

"Well I'm glad they didn't see you. If they knew you witnessed it your life would be in danger!"

"It's possible that they *did* see me. Before I got away, some Klan member shone a flashlight in my eyes right before I knocked him out with a tire-iron and drove away."

"Oh, no! Nicky! You need police protection! Have you reported any of this to my father yet?"

"No, not yet. I may not report it to him at all. I may wait until I get out of here and report it to some federal authority."

"But why *not* report it to my father? He could protect you and you could stay here. They'll need you for a witness anyway. Honey, don't worry! It's all behind you now!" She leaned forward and hugged him. "My poor darling! No wonder you're so depressed! But things will start getting better for you now. You don't have to leave here."

"But that's not the end of the story, Lauren. That's not the real reason I'm leaving."

He started at the beginning. He related to her the story that the jail inmates had told him about the dishonesty of the Mullins brothers—the bootlegging, the payoffs, the false arrests, the filthy conditions of the jail—which he had seen for himself. He told of the night after he had taken her home when Bronson had accosted him and the preacher at Mussey's Tavern, when he had fought Deputy Bronson; only to be severely beaten into unconsciousness and his body doused with liquor before being thrown into jail. He continued by telling her about the reaction of her father, and how he had banned Nick from any future association with her, threatening him with jail if he even told her of their conversation. He related to her the deal that her father had made with him in order to force him to leave Cedar Valley, and how that deal had placed him in an impossible predicament: If he stayed here to testify, her father would jail him; however, if he left town as her father had demanded in order to escape prison, the Klan would get away with murder.

He had vowed to himself that he would never tell her this story; but if she were to ever break her chains of bondage from her father, *truth* might be the key that would unlock those chains.

She had listened patiently, without speaking, until he had completely finished the story; and now she was only capable of eyeing him with an incredulous stare.

She finally spoke. "Nicky, that's terrible about Rufus and the preacher being murdered. That's so sad. I didn't know the preacher that well, but I've known Rufus for all of my life. Poor Rufus—and poor Stan. You know how close they were. I believe what you told me about the murders, and Mike Bronson's cruelty and his unfairness to you. I also believe that you *think* you're right about my father. But you're staking your belief on what a bunch of jailbirds told you. My father is a wonderful man. You're wrong about him! Nicky, I love both of you. Please don't make me choose between you!"

"Lauren, I'm not wrong about your dad. Do you think I'd ever leave here—leave *you*, unless he had demanded it? Come on Lauren! I don't want to hurt you. I just want you to see the truth! Your father doesn't think I'm good enough for you. He doesn't think I'll ever amount to anything! I know that I've been screwed up for the last couple of years, but I *will* do something with my life! I promise you! Your father wants to break us up. He'll try to convince you that you and I could never make it together. But I think we were meant to be together! You're my first love, and you'll always be my only love! We only go around once in this life, and if we let your father break us up we'll both regret it for the rest of our lives! We won't have a second chance! We may both marry somebody else. But when we grow old without each other, we'll look back over our lives and wonder *what might have been*. Then we'll both say, 'If we had just stayed together we could have made it!' Because of your father I have to leave here, but maybe someday I can come back."

"So you're just going to leave here because you're mad at Daddy! You know, he's not perfect! He has a temper, just like you! It's just a personality clash between the two of you!"

"No, it's more than that. Your dad wants me out of here! Lauren, you're blind when it comes to your father's faults! I know that you love your father, but there's just so much that you don't know! He even told me that the only way I can save my neck is to get the hell out of town."

She became angry. "Oh, you're worried about *saving your neck,* are you?" she asked, sarcastically, "Nicky Parilli—the great lawyer! The great defender of justice! You witness two murders and you show your sense of justice by running! Even if you're right about my father—which I'm sure you aren't, you'd leave here to save your neck instead of standing up like the person I thought you were and being a real man!"

"Lauren, you've got your head in the sand! You just said that you love me and would even be willing to live in a cave with me! What motive could I have to make anything up about your father? Until you're able to break away from your dad's domination, there will never be a chance for you and me!"

Lauren's anger increased. "You're right! There's no chance for us, and there never really was! I don't want to ever see you again! Maybe my father is right about you! I want to get out of here! Take me home!"

Nick suddenly stood. "I can't take you home, Lauren. I can't risk being seen. It's too dangerous. It's rush hour, and there'll be people out everywhere. If you want to go home, I'll call Stan. He can come and get you."

"Oh, yes! I forgot! It's too dangerous! I certainly wouldn't want to place you in any danger! After all, *saving your neck* is more important than principles! And you'd leave here and even throw away our relationship to save your neck! I'm sorry, Nicky, but I thought you were brave! I thought I was in love with a fighter!" Her criticism was biting.

For the first time in weeks Nick felt that he was on the verge of having a panic attack. He threw up his hands in utter frustration. "*Lauren!*" He screamed and fell to his knees. He ran his hands over his mangled face and through his hair as if he were trying to pull it out. He stood and looked her directly in the eyes. "Look at my face! Damn it, look at it!" He took her head in his hands and turned her face toward his. "Does this face look like the face of a *coward?* I took all this battering without even explaining it to you because I love you and wanted to protect you from the horrible truth about the *real world!*"

With his energy spent, he released her. Gradually, his emotions began to calm. He regained his composure, and in a calm voice, said, "You don't know what you're saying. If I go back to Cedar Valley, they'll kill me. If I thought you'd ever see the truth about your father, I might stay here and take the consequences. But as long as he keeps you locked in his chains, our relationship doesn't have a chance."

They sat in silence for a while. In total exhaustion, he walked to the phone and called Stan, who happened to be at home. He agreed to come after her within the hour. Lauren retreated to the front porch while Nick stayed inside. They remained separated until Stan arrived.

Stan joined Lauren on the front porch and she followed him into the house. He immediately walked to Nick and hugged him while Lauren turned her back and pouted.

"Damn, man! What happened to your eye? Did you get into a fight with that bastard again?" He walked over and carefully inspected Nick's eye.

"Yeah, it's a long story and I don't have the energy left in me to tell it. Just take Lauren home for me, okay?"

"Sure, buddy. No problem. I'm sorry I got tied up today. Can you come back to the apartment with me for a while before you leave?"

"No, Stan. As soon as I clean up some, toss my clothes in the car and gas up, I'm on my way to Louisiana," he answered.

"God, Nicky, I hate to see you go! But don't worry. I'll join you in Louisiana as soon as I can."

Lauren said nothing.

"What's wrong with you two lovebirds?" asked Stan. "Have you been arguing? I'll step outside so you two can kiss and make up before you leave." He again hugged Nick. "Bye, pal!"

"Yeah—I'll see ya Stan. I'll write to you!" Stan walked onto the porch and waited for Lauren.

When Lauren turned, her face was flushed and held a shy expression. She took a seat on the sofa and hung her head.

"Nicky, I have to go now. I'm sorry that things turned out the way they did between us. Will I ever see you again?"

"Who knows? Maybe someday we'll meet again. Lauren, forgive me. Maybe I shouldn't have said those things about your father. I know you're mad at me, and disappointed in me. But do me one last favor for old times' sake, okay? Please don't tell your father where I am until I have time to get out of here."

When she got up to leave, she neither kissed nor hugged him goodbye. She only turned and walked away. As she passed through the door, he called to her, "Lauren...I love you."

He stood for a moment until he heard the car doors slam shut and the engine start. He strolled to the porch and watched Stan's car disappear into the distance.

Weariness and depression consumed him. He re-entered the house and took a seat on the couch. Since the scathing attack from Lauren, his dread of leaving was even worse than before. He decided that he would soon have to call his uncle in Louisiana and tell him of his planned trip and his estimated time of arrival. He walked into the bathroom and threw up.

With the awareness that he needed to get moving, he went to his car and retrieved the duffel bag that contained his clothing. After returning to the house, he tossed the bag onto the couch and removed a clean outfit of clothing and placed them on the couch. He then stripped off his bloody clothing and carelessly tossed them into the trash bin.

In the bathroom he made a feeble attempt to shave; however, the soreness of his face hindered the effort. With no hot water, his cold shower caused him to violently shiver; however, it served to revive his energy. Returning to the living room, he dressed in his clean clothes. He tried to protect the wounds on his scalp when he delicately ran a comb through his hair.

He was now ready to leave, to tell Cedar Valley goodbye forever. All that remained was calling his uncle and gassing up his car. He figured the trip to Louisiana would probably take about eighteen hours. Remembering that the old Ford was an oil-burner, he decided to buy a few extra quarts of oil to take with him. He hoped the old car would make the trip.

Nick heard a car speed into the driveway and skid to an abrupt stop. He peered out the window at the police car and saw two deputies hurry from the vehicle. *So Lauren didn't waste any time in telling her father where to find me! I knew she was angry at me, but I really didn't think she would betray me like this!*

Quickly, he ran to the kitchen. He raised the back window, crawled through, and dropped to the ground. He quickly scampered into the woods behind the house and hid among the dense growth of trees. From his hiding place he watched the house. In only a short time, he saw Cowboy Galyon's head framed by the open kitchen window as he surveyed the area in back of the house. Creeping around the corner, the other deputy meticulously examined the interior of Nick's car. He then scoured the back yard area as if searching for some vital clue.

"Hell, Bird Dog, why are you inspecting the damned yard? You can see he ain't here! The bastard hauled ass into the woods. He's to hell and gone by now. Let's go back and tell the sheriff."

295

Nick noticed that the deputy, 'Bird Dog' had replaced Deputy Bronson as Cowboy Galyon's partner. He wondered about the significance. *Had the police not yet found Bronson? Could he possibly be dead?* He remained in his hiding place until he heard the police car drive away.

Cautiously, he made his way toward the house when he heard the loud engine of another vehicle pulling into the driveway. The tortuous whine of the vehicle's lower gear had the sound of a large truck. Nick hurried back into the woods just as the nose of a wrecker rounded the corner as it pulled into the back yard. On the cab doors he read, *Williams Wrecker Service.* From the woods, he observed two men hooking the chain from the large boom to the front of his car. He watched helplessly as the wrecker towed away his vehicle.

Now what am I supposed to do? he wondered. He sat among the damp leaves and considered his predicament. He felt that the situation couldn't possible get any worse. In addition to all of the recent negative events, the police had now taken his car, meaning that his only means of travel was walking. But even more discouraging was Lauren's rejection of him—and the way she had betrayed him.

In utter despair, he sat at the edge of the darkening forest and forlornly gazed into the valley at the cluster of dilapidated houses in Bucktown.

Chapter 19

Lauren drank a full cup of water to wash down the three aspirin tablets. Her throbbing headache was the result of spending a sleepless night brooding about her problems. The waiting room of the clinic was filled with frustrated patients. Some were complaining about the doctor's inattention to their scheduled appointment times, while older patients griped about the frigid temperature of the room. In addition, the multitude of phone calls was driving her crazy.

She had difficulty keeping her mind focused on her work. An angry elderly man had rudely censured her for mistakenly pulling the incorrect file folder regarding his medical record, and she had misplaced a patient's insurance card.

Her mind was consumed with feelings of frustration concerning her father—and Nick. *How dare he attack Daddy's character? How could he believe the accusations of prisoners?* And yet—she had never known Nick to lie to her. *And why would he bother to invent lies that would only break up their relationship and cause pain?*

But to believe Nick was to condemn her father. She remembered her dad as a good father and husband—a churchman who regularly donated money to worthy causes and a tireless worker for civic organizations. In the past, she had heard rumors and vague accusations about her father; but such gossip only came with the territory of being sheriff of a small Southern town where people in public positions were under such critical scrutiny. After all, a police officer has the unpleasant duty of arresting people and is certainly going to make enemies...

But I have never known Nicky to lie to me.

She recalled the time when her father had played Santa Claus for the children at church—and the time he had worked all day delivering baskets to poor people, and when he had mowed the lawn for that sick Mrs. Payne when she had the flu, and the numerous times that he had worked on the visitation committee at church...

And yet, I have never known Nicky to lie to me.

She remembered how good her father had been to her mother after her accident, and how he treated Willie Mae just like one of the family...

On the other hand, Nicky has never lied to me—and I love him—maybe even as much as I love Daddy. And Nicky has also been so sweet to me, and with his hopeful optimism, has refused to allow his terrible past to destroy his dreams. I also remember him telling me that as long as I stay locked in my father's chains our love doesn't stand a chance...and even if he can't have me, he wants nothing but the best for me.

When she thought of Nick, she regretted being so blunt with him. Maybe he wouldn't wish to ever see her again. After all, he had pride. And when she had criticized him for trying to *save his neck*, she hadn't meant to imply that he was a coward. She suddenly realized how much she already missed him.

"Ma'am...Ma'am! Could you please notice that I'm here? I've been trying to give you my insurance card! What's the

298

matter with you? You behave like you're in a trance!" The elderly woman was angry.

"I'm sorry, Ma'am, I just don't feel well this morning." She took the woman's card, made a note of it, and returned it to her. "I'm very sorry, lady," she said. She abruptly turned and signaled to Bobbie Sue, the nurse, who quickly joined Lauren at her desk.

"Bobbie Sue, I'm sorry, but I'm just too upset to work for the rest of the day. Could you please take over for me? If you will, I'll owe you one, okay?"

"Well, it's only a half hour 'til lunch. Could you work 'til then? I can cover for you this afternoon. Are you sick?"

"No, not really, I just didn't sleep much last night. I'm going home and get some sleep. Is it okay with you if I go home at lunchtime?"

"Sure. I hope you begin to feel better."

At noon she left the clinic. During the short drive to her home, she again thought about Nick's assertion that her father had forbidden him to see her; however, her dad had told a drastically different story. He had claimed that after his arrest, Nick had become disillusioned with Cedar Valley and had decided to leave. He further alleged that he had attempted to dissuade him from leaving, but to no avail; for Nick had once again developed wanderlust and was determined to leave for Louisiana. *Was it possible that there had been some kind of miscommunication between Nick and her father?*

She pulled her car into the long driveway and parked near the garage behind her father's police cruiser. *What's Daddy doing at home?* she wondered.

She entered the living room, kicked off her shoes, and carelessly tossed her pocketbook onto the couch. The house seemed to be deserted. She walked down the long hallway and discovered that her mother was napping in the master bedroom. Her wheelchair was beside her bed.

Where's Willie Mae? And where's Daddy? she wondered. *Oh, I'll bet Dad's reading his newspaper on the patio—and Willie Mae is probably taking a nap in her room.*

299

Willie Mae's isolated room was actually attached to the main house and only accessible from the patio. As Lauren walked through the patio door, she noticed that the door to the hallway that led to Willie Mae's room was open—and from the open door she heard strange sounds and muffled conversation. She stepped into the hallway and noticed that the door to Willie Mae's bedroom was slightly ajar. Quietly walking in her bare feet and burning with curiosity, she crept to the door and peered through the opening. She saw the nakedness of her father as he was slowly crawling out of Willie Mae's bed. The maid smiled at him as she continued to lie beneath the covers. Neither of them saw Lauren.

Leisurely, her father started to get dressed. Lauren was utterly shocked. She backed away from the door and stood motionless for several seconds.

Willie Mae chose to be humorous. In an obvious mockery of her race, she spoke in an exaggerated dialect of an ignorant Negro woman. "Master, since ya got ya britches on, would you please fetch me a glass of water? That phys'cal exercise done made me pow'ful thirsty!" She giggled.

"Sure, Honey Chile! I'll be right back!" He laughed as he mimicked her dialect. He slowly moved toward the door that Lauren was standing behind.

Terrified by the thought of being discovered, Lauren opened the nearby door to Willie Mae's hall closet and quickly dashed inside. She quietly closed the door only an instant before her father stepped into the hallway and walked past her toward the kitchen.

No one but Willie Mae usually entered her portion of the house. The extra closet in the hallway had always held a strange secrecy and was usually kept locked. Only the maid and Sheriff Mullins had a key to the room. It was Willie Mae's personal storage space for her clothing, shoes, and other personal belongings and had always been off-limits to anyone other than Willie Mae. When she was a child, the only spanking that Lauren had ever received from her father was for sneaking into the forbidden closet.

She waited in the closet until she heard her father's footsteps in the hallway as he returned to the Negro maid with the glass of water. With her ear to the door, she continued to listen as he walked back down the hall and returned to the living room. At last she heard the front door close as he left the house.

Because of the stuffy heat of the small cubicle, Lauren began to sweat. She stood motionless in the enclosed room for several minutes until she was certain that her father had left the house.

She became curious about the mystery of the closet—the aura of secrecy that had always surrounded the mention of it. Lauren became nosy about its contents. Impulsively, she switched on the small light. She noticed the customary feminine items: dresses, blouses, bathrobes, shoes, and boxes full of miscellany on the floor. She dug deeper into the hanging items, sorting through several hangers in search of whatever mystery existed in the closet. Finally, she looked behind a thick winter overcoat that was encased in a garment bag. Behind the coat in the back of the closet she discovered the mysterious, hidden items. Draped over a hanger hung the white sheet and cone-shaped hood of the Ku Klux Klan.

Lauren was horrified. She felt utterly betrayed by her father. When she finally recovered from her initial shock she gathered the incriminating items, silently crept out into the hall, and carefully closed the closet door behind her. With caution, she peered down the hall to make sure that Willie Mae was still in her room. She then quietly hurried to her bedroom where she quickly gathered a few items of her clothing. In the living room she put on her shoes. Then she crept out the front door to her car.

Deciding that she couldn't spend another night in the same house with her father, she tossed the Klan disguise into the back seat and drove away in her car to a motel in the outskirts of town.

Chapter 20

A red sun was breaking the eastern horizon when Nick awoke. He had spent the near sleepless night in the woods behind the preacher's house. Fearing that the police would return, he was reluctant to sleep inside the living quarters. His suspicion that the police knew that he had previously stayed with Mary Rose and Caleb caused him to stay away from their place as well.

After the deputies had gone and the wrecker had towed away his car, he had returned to the preacher's house long enough to obtain a pillow and a couple of blankets to make a bed in the woods.

It was apparent that the sheriff was desperate to arrest him. Was it for the simple reason that he had remained in Cedar Valley in defiance of the sheriff's order for him to leave? Or was there a more sinister reason? Could it be that the police had found Bronson—or his body? Did it have something to do with the Klan killings? If Sheriff Mullins had wanted so badly for him to leave, why was he now trying so desperately to bring him back to Cedar Valley? Nick was undecided about his course of action.

He stood and brushed the leaves from his hair and clothing. His entire face was a throbbing sore, and his knee was stiff from spending the night on the ground. Also his pants were spotted with mud and grass stains, and he badly needed a shave. He would have to risk a return to the preacher's house long enough to clean up and shave. He shook the leaves from the blankets, rolled them up with the pillow and returned to the house.

Once inside, he hurried to the kitchen and drank a couple of glasses of water before tossing the pillow and blankets on the bed. He made repeated trips to glance out the front window as he brushed his teeth and rinsed his face in cold water. His reflection in the mirror was like that of a homeless derelict.

He began to worry about Mary Rose and little Caleb, for he desperately wanted them to leave Bucktown before they were discovered by the Klan. He assumed that they were probably already gone. From the front porch, he looked toward Rufus' house where Mary Rose and Caleb were staying. When he saw their car still parked behind the house he was filled with anxiety. He decided to forgo cleaning up and shaving; instead, he needed to visit Mary Rose and again urge her to leave.

In spite of his fear of being discovered by the police he left the preacher's former home, crossed the back yard, and entered the woods behind the house, where he knew that he wouldn't be seen from the road. He then walked down the hill to Rufus' house where Mary Rose and Caleb were staying. When he rapped on the back door Mary Rose met him in the doorway. She instantly hugged him before speaking. When she finally pulled away from him, she stared at him in surprise. "Good Lord, Nick! Where have you been staying? You look terrible! Caleb was out in the yard playing and he saw the wrecker tow away your car. Where did you go? Did you leave the preacher's house?"

Nick stepped inside. "The reason I look so bad is because I slept in the woods last night. After they towed my car away I was afraid to sleep in the preacher's house."

Caleb came running and threw his arms around Nick. With a big grin on his face, he uttered several unintelligible grunts. He took Nick by the hand, pulled him into the kitchen, and pointed to a kitchen chair.

Mary Rose smiled. "He wants you to eat something. You must be terribly hungry."

"Yes, I'm pretty hungry. But Mary Rose, I'm not worried about eating right now. I'm concerned because you haven't left here yet! When are you going to leave?"

"I'm going to leave here as soon as I get the car repaired. I packed up a few things and I was ready to leave last night, but the car wouldn't start. Can you fix it?" she asked.

"No, I'm not a very good mechanic. Damn! What rotten luck!" Nick became even more concerned.

"Well, don't worry, Nick. I've found a man who's going to fix the car. I've got a good friend named Josie who lives about a mile from here. Her husband, Willard, is a mechanic. While he is repairing the car, Caleb and I are going to stay in their home. So if anybody comes to this house looking for us, we won't even be here." She smiled at Nick.

He was relieved. "Thank God you'll soon be out of here! You and Caleb will both be safe! When will this mechanic start working on your car? You need to leave here immediately!"

"He's coming here this morning to get the car and take it to his garage in his back yard. Then, after he fixes it, I'll have to come back here just long enough to put a few things in the car that I packed away. I won't be in this house for more than a few minutes! Then I'll be gone from here for good!"

"Thank God!" said Nick.

Mary Rose smiled. "Now sit down at the kitchen table and let me fix you and Caleb something to eat."

Caleb smiled and took a seat beside Nick at the table while Mary Rose cooked breakfast for them. While they were eating she looked out the front window and saw a police car pull into the driveway and park. "Oh, Nick! The police just parked outside in the driveway! They're probably looking for you! You'd better get out of here!"

Nick quickly jumped up and ran out the back door into the woods behind the house. He remained hidden among the trees for several minutes before he heard Mary Rose calling to him.

When he left his hiding place and returned to the house, Mary Rose was worried. "They were looking for you Nick! They even entered the house and looked around! Before they came into the kitchen I hid your breakfast plate so they wouldn't know you were here!"

When Nick glanced up the hill toward the preacher's house, he saw the police car in the driveway. "Damn!" he said, "They're looking for me everywhere! I'll have to stay away from the house again tonight! I'll be sleeping in the woods again!"

Mary Rose again hugged him. "Oh, Nick! What in the world are you going to do? They took your car, you don't have a place to stay, and you don't have anything to eat! Also, the police are looking for you at this house and the preacher's house too!"

"I don't Know, Mary Rose. I'll figure out something."

"Well, let me pack away something for you to eat. We don't have much left, but I'll give you whatever we have." While she placed the food in a basket, Caleb grinned at Nick and hugged him.

Just as she handed the food to him, Nick noticed another vehicle pull into the driveway. A Negro man with oil-stained overalls stepped out of a pickup truck. He was the auto mechanic, Willard, who had come to take Mary Rose's car to his garage. Both Nick and Caleb stepped into in the kitchen while she answered the mechanic's knock at the door.

"I came to fix your car, ma'am. Are ya ready? You'll have to steer the car while I push it down to my garage."

"Yes, I'm ready. Come on in. Just give me a minute, okay?"

When she walked back into the kitchen she was crying. She smiled as she reached out and cradled both Nick and little Caleb in her arms. "Well, Nick, Caleb and I will have to leave here with this mechanic. He doesn't have a chain to pull the car, so I'll have to steer my car to his garage while he pushes it. We'll be safe because we'll be staying there with him and his wife, Josie until the car is repaired. Nick, I'm afraid when we part this time, we'll never see each other again."

Nick smiled at her. "*Never* is a long time, Mary Rose. I have a feeling that we're destined to meet again someday. Goodbye Mary Rose...Goodbye Caleb."

Goodbye Nick," she said between sobs, "Caleb and I will miss you." In his reluctance to leave Nick, Caleb clung to his legs. Finally he joined his mother and left the house with the mechanic.

He peeped out the front window and watched as Mary Rose and Caleb climbed into the preacher's car. The mechanic aligned the vehicles and the truck began to push the car steered by Mary Rose. Nick continued to watch as the vehicles faded into the distance. He again retreated to the woods behind the house and made his way toward the former home of the preacher.

When he reached the house the police car was gone. Nick knew that the authorities were desperate to find him. As a result, he decided not to spend any time at the preacher's house. He only stopped there long enough to get a jug of water, some blankets, and a pillow. He placed the package of food that Mary Rose had given him in the refrigerator and returned to the forest behind the house.

Dawn was breaking when Nick became fully awake. Again, he had only occasionally catnapped. He decided that he would never again spend the night in the woods. After two nights of hiding from the authorities, he had become increasingly angry about his predicament; as a result; he decided to get on with his life and face reality by surrendering

306

to the police. However, he didn't want to be captured, for he wanted to reclaim some control over his destiny. Instead, he wanted to voluntarily turn himself in to the sheriff. He gathered his blankets and pillow and returned to the preacher's house.

Nick was hungry. He was grateful that the preacher had left a few edible items in his refrigerator. He munched on these as he also snacked on the food that Mary Rose had given him. He then brewed a pot of coffee, poured himself a cup, and took a seat on the couch.

He realized that he needed to create a plan. To offer him a view of the road he chose a chair near the front window. While he cautiously eyed the road, he lit a cigarette and began to ponder the problems facing him.

He decided that *logic* should dictate his plans. It was now necessary for him to conform to existing circumstances. Since he had no transportation, leaving for Louisiana was out of the question unless he caught a bus. He had no job, no income, and no place to live. He was even at a loss in regard to how he would survive beyond this very day. He was a stranger in the enemy's camp. He pondered his most logical course of action.

Stan had advised him to leave Cedar Valley; however, Lauren had criticized him for not staying and facing his demons. Perhaps she had revealed his hiding place to her father for that reason. In fact, leaving town after witnessing two murders was difficult for him to accept. He decided to face the sheriff, tell him of the killings and live with the outcome.

A glance at his watch told him that Stan had not yet left for work. He picked up the phone and dialed the number.

"Hello?" said Stan.

"Hello, Stan? This is Nick."

"Hi, Nicky! Where are you? I'll bet you're calling from Louisiana!"

"No, I'm not that far away. I'm calling from the preacher's house."

"The preacher's house? What the hell are you doing there?"

"It's a long story. I just called to tell you that I've changed my mind. I'm not leaving. I'm staying in Cedar Valley."

There was a moment of silence. Stan seemed to be digesting Nick's change of plans. "Well, actually, Nicky, under the circumstances, I think that's what you should do. Things have changed since I advised you to leave here."

"What's changed?"

"The shit hit the fan when I told the sheriff about Rufus and the preacher getting murdered. Also, since you witnessed it, he wants to talk to you."

"Did he take your word for it? You said that he probably wouldn't believe *me*."

"Yeah, he believed me. But he wants to hear *your* account of it. He's really pissed off that you planned to leave here after witnessing two killings."

"Hell, he *ordered* me to leave! Anyway, I'm going to his office this morning to tell him what I saw. Is he going to put me in jail when I get there?"

"No, Nicky. Since these murders took place he's practically forgotten all that petty stuff he had you charged with."

"Well, if you told him all about it, and that Bronson did the killing—has he arrested Bronson?" Nick was still wondering if the blow from the tire-iron had killed the deputy.

"No, he hasn't been arrested. Nobody knows where he is."

Nick was worried. He proceeded to tell Stan of his encounter with the deputy on the highway, the exact location of the incident, and how he feared that he might have killed Bronson.

"No, don't worry about that, you didn't kill him. All the cops have combed the county for him, including the entire span of road where you had the fight with him. He's just vanished."

"If I killed him, they might not see his body because I hid him. But his car would still be there on the road shoulder."

"Nicky, they've searched every inch of this county. His car is not on that road shoulder. He's in it somewhere, hauling ass—the bastard!"

Nick breathed a sigh of relief. "Whew! I wouldn't shed any tears if he were dead, but I'm glad that tire-tool didn't kill him."

"That's where you and I differ, pal. I wish it *had* killed him—providing that they didn't nail you for it."

"What's the sheriff's attitude toward me?"

"It's hard to tell. I realize that there's no love lost between the two of you, but this murder thing has kinda crowded out everything else in his mind. When do you plan to come in to the sheriff's office?"

"When would be the best time to meet him there?"

"He'll be there by nine. That's when he usually starts his day. Nicky, I want to be there when you surrender. Maybe I can help you. The two of you sometimes rub each other the wrong way. Maybe I can act as a go-between." He chuckled.

"I'm glad you're gonna be there. Maybe you can help keep me out of jail."

"I don't think he's gonna put you in jail. And Nicky, I'm glad you decided to stay. Maybe we can still follow some of the plans we made. Do you want me to pick you up?"

"No need for that, Stan. It's too far out of your way. Why don't you call the sheriff and tell him that I'll meet him in his office at nine?"

"I'll do that. See ya, buddy."

"Yeah. Goodbye, Stan."

Nick sighed with relief. Although he still worried about being recognized by the Klan, since he had decided to surrender to the police he no longer feared being arrested. He boldly walked to the porch and sat down in the swing. He fired up another smoke and began to reflect on his recent telephone conversation. Stan had told him that the sheriff no longer had plans to arrest him; but even if he avoided jail, he was at a loss in regard to what his future plans should be. He wouldn't allow himself to hope that he and Lauren might somehow rekindle their former relationship, for the sheriff would still be dead-set against it.

Unless Bronson was found, there would be no trial. Nick wouldn't be required to testify, except to the grand jury in order to obtain an indictment. After his testimony to the grand jury, he would probably be free to go wherever he chose until the actual trial took place—after, or if, they apprehended Bronson. But he still worried about retaliation from the Klan.

In the event of a trial Nick wondered what the odds were that Bronson would be convicted. Possibly, he would get off scot-free, especially if the bodies were never found. Other than Nick's eyewitness testimony, what other evidence would the jury have?

He still worried about retribution from an unknown Klan member, so he decided that he would not yet expose himself by retrieving his impounded car. He could possibly do that later. If members if the Klan were searching for him, they would be looking for *his car*. They would hardly notice a nondescript man walking the highway. If he exposed himself long enough to get his car back he would remain in Cedar Valley only long enough to appear before the grand jury and then leave for Louisiana as previously planned. Even if he never retrieved his impounded car, he knew that he could always catch a bus to Louisiana.

Looking at his watch, he noted that the time was now eight-fifteen. The sheriff's office was in the opposite direction of town; consequently, during the trek he would encounter little traffic. Since it was only two miles from Bucktown, he could walk it easily in forty-five minutes. He could have asked Stan to pick him up, but the long drive would be several miles out of his way. Also, he wanted to be alone to think before confronting the sheriff. Besides, although physically drained from lack of sleep, he was emotionally charged with energy; for the recent hopeless disarray in his life was finally coming to a resolution.

To make it more difficult to recognize him, he donned a floppy hat that had belonged to the preacher. Leaving his belongings at the preacher's house, he struck out walking. When he walked past Mary Rose's house he noticed that her car was still gone. He hoped that the mechanic had already repaired it and Mary Rose had made her escape.

Once again, his thoughts turned to Lauren, and the way she had criticized him for his plan to leave town without reporting the murders. When he considered his former preachy attitude and his insatiable thirst for justice, he felt like a hypocrite. It shamed him to realize that, in his heart, he agreed with her.

He crossed the narrow bridge that led to Broadway, turned left, and walked westward toward the sheriff's office. His thoughts drifted to Sheriff Mullins. Maybe he had been too hard on the sheriff. Nick knew that Mullins had broken the law; however, when compared to the sins of Bronson, most of his misdeeds were almost frivolous. Nick began to see himself as others saw him: self-righteous. He remembered the comments of Bo, the Negro sergeant he had briefly encountered on his bus ride from Chicago: *Just let the South be what it is—don't try to fix it! Don't stick your nose into things that you can't do nuthin' about!* Also, the words of Stan still rang in his ears: *Throw away your halo! Aren't you being a bit hypocritical?* And yet—he remembered the preacher's words: *Evil men prevail in the world when good men choose to do nothing.*

His experiences in Cedar Valley had been a contradicting patchwork of good and bad. Most of the pleasant experiences he could attribute to Stan; for it was Stan who had acquainted Nick with the South, and invited him into his home. He had given Nick a job, a vehicle to drive, clothes, and money—and he had introduced him to Lauren. During Nick's roughest times, Stan had been his staunchest supporter. He was glad that Stan would be present when he confronted the sheriff.

The sun had risen higher in the cloudless sky, causing him to sweat from the exertion of his brisk walk. His breathing became labored as he trudged up Brownstone Hill and subsided at the straightaway at *Billy's Drive-In.* He then moved downhill to the river, and across the bridge.

On the left at the end of the bridge he reached his destination. Nick figured that Stan had already informed the sheriff of his decision to surrender, for the police were no longer searching for him. He noticed two deputies' cars parked beside the jail, one of which contained Cowboy Galyon. As Nick walked by him, the deputy eyed him with a vapid stare. Nick walked up the steps to the porch, opened the door, and entered the office.

Obviously, the sheriff had not yet arrived, for seated in his chair behind the large oaken desk was Stan. Nick was surprised.

"Well, Stan, when did you become sheriff?" He removed the floppy hat and tossed it into a chair.

"Damn! Man, you couldn't give me this job! This just happens to be the most comfortable chair in the joint." He reached across the desk and shook hands with Nick. "Uncle Larry's on his way, Nicky, he just called me about ten minutes ago. I'm sure glad you came in on your own accord!"

Nick smiled at him. "On my own accord? Stan, you make it sound like I'm a wanted criminal!"

"No, I didn't mean it that way. I just meant that the cops have been looking everywhere for you. The sheriff wants your account of what really happened. Hopefully, we can quickly get all this behind us and get on with our lives."

"I hope so because my life has been screwed up lately. Hell, just look at my face!"

"Actually, Nicky, it looks a little better today."

"Yeah, it's not as bad as it was. It's just as sore as hell. Are you sure Sheriff Mullins won't throw me in jail?" Nick took a seat in the chair facing Stan.

"I'm not sure, but I don't think he will. I didn't ask him, but I got the impression that he's willing to let bygones be bygones. I think he just wants to question you about the murders. Listen, pal, when you talk to him, play it cool. Don't

312

start any of that preachy talk about justice. Hell, you're not the only one who wants justice."

"Don't worry. I don't plan to get him riled up. By the way, have the deputies been searching for the bodies?"

"I don't know, Nicky. I think they've been spending most of their time searching for Bronson—and you, of course."

The front door swung open and Sheriff Mullins walked into the room. Following closely behind him were Cowboy Galyon and the deputy that Nick knew only as 'Bird Dog.' The sheriff seemed even taller and more commanding than Nick had remembered.

"Well look who's here!" exclaimed the sheriff. "It's about time you showed a little bit of brains!" His tone was sarcastic.

"Hello, Sheriff Mullins," answered Nick.

"How did you get your face so messed up? Have you been trying to assault another police officer?" The sheriff's dislike for him was obvious. Nick didn't answer.

In an attempt to intimidate Nick, Sheriff Mullins stood towering over him. Cowboy Galyon stood beside him, emulating him as closely as possible. He scowled at Nick as if he had an almost irresistible urge to hit him.

The sheriff ignored Stan, focusing his attention on Nick. Moving closer, he continued to tower over him. He placed his hands on his hips. "Listen, Parilli," he began, "I'm going to ask you some questions, and you'd damned sure better be accurate in your answers. You need to think before you say a damned word, do you understand?"

"Yes, sir," Nick answered.

"First of all, I want to know what happened to Lauren. Where is she? She didn't come home last night!"

Nick was surprised. "She didn't come home? Sheriff, I don't have the slightest idea what happened to her. Because of you, she and I weren't on the best of terms the last time I saw her. Maybe she got sick of you controlling her."

Stan attempted to restrain Nick's hostility. He only shook his head at Nick while the sheriff glared at him. "Parilli, I'm gonna let that little comment pass. I've got more important issues to discuss with you. Stan tells me that you witnessed a couple of killings. He said that you told him you saw Rufus and that hypocrite preacher get shot at a Klan gathering!" His expression expressed doubt.

"Yes, sir, I saw it happen."

"Where did it happen?"

"At a place over by the river. I can take you there. I can show you where they burned a cross."

"Well, did you see who did the killing?"

"Yes, sir. It was Mike Bronson."

"How can you be so sure it was him? Klan members wear hoods over their heads!" He eyed Nick skeptically.

"Well, the preacher yanked the hood off his head. That's why Bronson killed him, because it exposed his identity."

"If the preacher was that stupid, then he was a damned fool! After he yanked off the hood—then what happened?"

"Bronson shot him. Then he shot Rufus."

"Even if he did take off his hood, how can you be so sure it was Bronson? It was dark, wasn't it? You'd accuse a man of murder based on what you saw in the dark from a good distance away?"

"But it wasn't dark. It was bright. The whole area was lit up by that burning cross. And I wasn't a good distance away. I was as close to the killing as I am to that door over there."

Cowboy Galyon turned and examined the door. "Sheriff, he's lyin.' There ain't no way he coulda got that close without bein' seen!"

"Shut up, Galyon. I'm asking the questions here!" It was obvious that the deputy sheriff wanted to be a part of the interrogation.

The sheriff pulled a chair from beside Nick and placed it in front of him. He then sat down, facing Nick. He thrust his head forward to within inches of Nick's sweating face. His stare was unnerving to Nick. "Deputy Galyon made a good point, Parilli. How in the hell could you get that close to a killing without being seen?"

"The preacher and I hid in a patch of honeysuckle. They would never have seen us if the preacher hadn't stepped out into the open."

"Well, damn it! I'll ask you again! How in the hell can you be so sure it was Bronson? He was covered with a white sheet! All you saw was his head!"

"Come on, Sheriff! What kind of question is that? Are you pulling my leg? With Bronson, all you need to see is his head! Hell, anybody would recognize Bronson with that shock of fiery red hair! I could have recognized him from fifty yards away!"

"Don't get sassy with me, damn it!" said the sheriff.

Galyon again spoke. "Sheriff, maybe if we worked him over a little bit, he'd watch his smart mouth!"

"Damn it! Shut up, Galyon!"

Nick glanced at Stan, who was shaking his head, silently cautioning Nick to pull his verbal punches.

"Do you know why it's so hard for me to believe you, Parilli?" asked the sheriff. "It's because you had a personal grudge against Bronson. How do I know that you're not just making this up to get even with him? After all, there's no evidence, other than your so-called eyewitness testimony. Hell, if he killed them, where are their bodies?"

"Hell, sheriff, don't ask me! Finding dead bodies is more like your line of work, wouldn't you say?"

The other deputy, Bird Dog spoke. "Maybe we ought to soften his attitude by lettin' him cool off in jail fer a while, sheriff! He's got a smart mouth!"

"Damn it, shut up, Bird Dog! Go sit down over there—or just go away somewhere!"

From behind the sheriff's desk, Stan again shook his head at Nick in an attempt to curtail his defiance.

"Well, just supposing I did believe your story...You need to remember all the details you can about this so-called murder."

"Yes, I know. I do remember some details."

315

"What kind of details? Hell, what could you tell about a group of men who were all dressed alike in sheets?"

Nick remembered the western boots with the stars on the toes. He wanted to relate his suspicion of Cowboy Galyon, but not in Galyon's presence. He felt that he should disclose this information only to the sheriff.

"Well, as you said, with all of them dressed alike, I didn't have a lot to work with." Nick shrugged.

"Then why did you tell me that you remembered some details? In other words, you come in here with a cock-and-bull story about a murder! You claim to have seen it from a few feet away, but it's strange that out of a whole group of Klansmen, not one of them saw *you!* You say Bronson killed two men, but it was dark and you were looking at the whole thing through a bunch of honeysuckle leaves! And the biggest bunch of bullshit is your claim that the preacher was crazy enough to yank off a Klansman's hood! And in addition to that, there are no bodies. And even if all you're saying is true, you could never prove it, because the Klan would have buried the bodies where they'd never be found! So we'd never convict Bronson, anyway! It'd just be your word against his!"

"If that's true, why are you hunting Bronson?"

"Who says we're hunting him?"

"Well, where is he? And if he didn't do it, why is he hiding?"

"Who says he's hiding?"

"If he's not hiding, then where is he?"

The sheriff ignored the question. Moving closer to Nick, he made an attempt to be more diplomatic. "Son, I don't mean to call you a liar. I'm just saying your story is full of holes. But I'm willing to listen and consider your account of it. Now think hard! Re-live that moment! Is there anything that you can remember that would help us to identify one of those men? Their heights, maybe a voice—a name? If you can't come up with something more, we'll probably have to drop the case. Are you sure you can't identify anyone? I think you're wrong about Bronson!"

"Sheriff, I came in here to tell you the truth. I'm just telling you what I saw. If you don't believe me, then that's your misfortune, because Bronson is going to get away with murder! I took a chance on going to jail to testify to this."

"Well, I'll probably still put you in jail."

"For what? On those same trumped-up charges you had against me? You know damned well that I was framed!"

"Listen you damned punk! You can't talk to me that way!"

Nick became angry. He had tried to be a good citizen by voluntarily surrendering to the sheriff. But once again, he was surrounded by deputies and threatened with jail.

"Listen, Parilli," said Sheriff Mullins, "You don't have anything on anybody. I'd let you go if I thought you'd go your way and forget this pipedream of yours. But you'll keep on stirring up trouble wherever you go. You'd keep going to other agencies until you got some crusading do-gooder to believe you, and bring shame on this town. You know, I knew you were trouble when I first met you!"

Nick glanced at Stan, who only shook his head and helplessly shrugged. Apparently, he was as scared of his uncle as he was of his dad.

The sheriff moved even closer until their noses almost touched. "Parilli, you're going back to jail! With all the charges I have against you, you'll do at least two years! That's enough time for this so-called murder to be forgotten around here! People in this town don't want Yankee meddlers like you!"

"Listen, sheriff, get out of my face, damn it! Your breath smells like a septic tank!"

"Why, you son of a bitch!" The sheriff backhanded him.

Instantly, Nick spat in his face. The sheriff stood and cursed. He threw a hard punch that struck Nick directly on his injured nose, sending him reeling backward in his chair. This time Nick had no doubt that his nose was broken.

Nick struggled to stand, but the deputies quickly closed in and restrained him. Cowboy Galyon brutally twisted his left arm behind him when Nick attempted to escape his grasp.

317

"Stand him up, boys!" ordered the sheriff, "I'm going to teach him a little lesson before I put him in jail to rot!"

The deputies pinned Nick's arms behind him as Sheriff Mullins threw another vicious punch into his face.

Stan shouted, "Stop it! Stop hitting him! Turn him loose, damn it! He's not guilty of anything!" He came scurrying from behind Sheriff Mullins' desk, trying to restrain the sheriff. Nick was near unconsciousness. The stream of blood from his nose dripped onto the floor when his head fell forward. With his head lowered, he was looking directly at Stan's boots. On the toe of each boot was the imprint of a gold star.

Stan pulled the sheriff away from Nick. "Stop it! Have you lost your mind? What are you trying to do, kill him?"

Nick began to regain his senses. He continued to stare at Stan's boots. "It was you!" Nick pointed to Stan.

"What?" Stan displayed a bewildered look. "What are you talking about?"

Sheriff Mullins and the deputies stared in curiosity.

"It was you at the river that night when Rufus and the preacher were murdered!" Nick angrily glared at him.

Stan's face paled. "No, Nicky—no, Nicky—you're wrong, Nicky—you're wrong!" He shook his head in denial.

"I saw those boots that night—those stars on the toes! It was you! I saw those boots below that sheet that covered you! You helped kill Rufus—who was like a father to you!"

The sheriff warned, "Keep your mouth shut, Stan!"

Stan sobbed and burst into tears. "Oh, God forgive me! Oh God, Nicky—please don't look at me like that! I loved Rufus! Oh, God...I loved him! I'm sorry, Nicky! I'm sorry, Rufus!"

Nick looked at him with contempt. "How could you have gone there with those cowardly bastards and help kill Rufus?"

The sheriff again cautioned, "Damn it Stan, shut up!"

Stan continued to cry. "I didn't know it was going to be Rufus—I swear to God I didn't, Nicky! They just called me and said they were going to whip a nigger for molesting a little white girl. If I'd known it was Rufus..."

"Why didn't you do something to stop it?" asked Nick.

"Oh God, Nicky—when it goes that far, there's no way to stop it! I just had to go along with it! I had no choice! And I didn't know that Bronson would shoot Rufus!"

"Then it wasn't Lauren who told the sheriff that I was hiding at the preacher's house a couple of nights ago! It was you!"

"Yes, Nicky—I'm sorry! The sheriff told me to find you. I wanted you to get away! I even told you to go! He said he wanted me to bring you back for questioning! He didn't want you spreading the story around! I hope you don't hate me!"

"Stan, I thought I could trust you! Damn it, man—I only feel pity for you!" Nick's expression was one of contempt.

In anger, Sheriff Mullins glared at Stan. "You're nothing but a weakling! You couldn't keep your mouth shut, could you?" Speaking to the deputies, he said, "You guys take Parilli out of here! Put him in my car and wait for me!"

"What are you going to do with him?" asked Cowboy.

"Don't ask questions, just do as I say!" said the sheriff.

Stan stepped forward. "Surely you don't plan to kill him! Can't you just lock him up in jail?"

"Hell, even in jail he'd shoot off his mouth! This whole episode could get blown out of proportion! If this thing gets to be public knowledge, our goose is cooked! Only a few of us know anything about this! Let's keep it that way!"

Nick struggled to free himself when the deputies began to hustle him toward the front door. At that moment, the door swung open and Lauren walked into the room. She carried a small bundle under her right arm. At her first glimpse at the spectacle before her, she gasped and instantly froze in her tracks. She stared at the deputies holding Nick—and then at Nick, who stood before her in his blood-soaked shirt.

"What's going on here?" she demanded. "What have you done to him?"

"Now, wait a minute, Lauren," pleaded the sheriff. "You've got this all wrong…"

"Tell me what's going on! Why is he bleeding like that?" She glared at the deputies. "Turn him loose! Right this instant!"

The deputies looked at Sheriff Mullins. After a nod of his head they released him. Nick immediately sat in a nearby chair.

"Now Lauren, you've got to listen to me!" said the sheriff. "He came in here telling a bunch of lies! He insulted me! And that crazy story he told about Rufus and the preacher getting killed—that was all just a lie! Rufus probably just ran off somewhere after they whipped him! We've got no proof he was murdered! He even made a bunch of accusations against Stan. Lauren, I think he's crazy!"

"What kind of accusations did he make against Stan?" Turning her eyes to Stan, she noticed that he had been crying.

"Why, he accused Stan of being a member of the Klan! Have you ever heard such a lie?"

"It's not a lie, Lauren," said Stan.

Lauren calmly walked to her father's desk. She raised the bundle and emptied the contents on the top of the desk. After tossing the container aside, she lifted the white sheet and hood, displaying them to the group. "Is this also a lie, Daddy?"

Her father's jaw fell open in disbelief. He stared at the items in horror. "Where did you get that stuff? Those are not mine!"

"I made a special trip to come here and show you this. I found these items in that little 'forbidden closet' in the hall by Willie Mae's room. Now I know why the closet was forbidden! It was the only place you could hide this hellish costume without anybody discovering it! This stuff is yours, all right!"

Awestruck by the drama that was playing out before them, the others in the room silently watched. The sheriff became angry. "Well, supposing it does belong to me! The Klan is a good thing, at least most of the time! We do a lot of good. I'm not going to apologize about it!"

"In other words, you helped kill Rufus! And the preacher!" In contempt, she glared at him.

"Now wait a minute, honey." His tone had again become conciliatory, "I wasn't there that night, and I can prove it! I've got at least a dozen witnesses! I was at a political meeting in Knoxville!"

"Whether or not you were there makes no difference, Daddy! You're just as guilty as the rest of them!"

"No, darling—I'm not guilty of such a thing! Please don't think that of me!" He was now pleading.

"Nicky was right when he warned me that it was a mistake to report the murders to you! But I wouldn't listen to him! I want you to turn Nicky loose! I'm taking him out of here!"

"Now, honey, I can't do that...I've got to put him in jail. He's got a bunch of charges against him. I can't just let him go."

"You'll let him go, all right! You don't have any choice! I know enough about your deceptive lies and corruption to put you *under* the jail!"

"Can't we just forget all this? Haven't I always been good to you? You don't know anything *bad* about me except that I belong to the Klan. You can't even prove that. And even if you did, nobody would care!"

Lauren cast a contemptuous look at him. "I know about the payoffs from the bootleggers, and about you helping Uncle Lester bring liquor into the county, and the way you keep the jail is so filthy that it's not fit for human beings! But most of all, I know about you and Willie Mae! I saw you with her in her bedroom yesterday! It would break my heart to tell Mother about it—but so help me, if you don't let Nicky go, I'll tell her. And I won't stop there! I'll tell everybody in town and every police agency in the state about your crimes!"

"Now, honey—you wouldn't do that to your Daddy..."

"The hell I wouldn't! And furthermore, I want your guarantee that nobody will bother Nick or me until we get out of town together! If anything should happen to either of us, even if it's not your fault, I'll spill the beans on you!"

"Lauren, Lauren! Please tell me you're not leaving with him! What about our plans for you becoming a doctor?"

"*Your* plans, Daddy—not mine! Yes, I'm leaving here with him right now—that is if he'll still have me!"

"Please don't do it, honey!"

"We're leaving now, Daddy. Come on Nicky." She walked to him. He slowly stood as she helped steady him. Everyone in the room only stared when she helped Nick toward the door. She turned to her father. "Do I have your guarantee that we won't be bothered?"

"Lauren, please don't do it!"

"Give me your guarantee!" she demanded.

Her father wearily hung his head. "I guarantee that you won't be bothered."

"And guarantee that we won't be followed!" she insisted.

"I guarantee that you won't be followed," he answered, grudgingly.

When they started for the door, Cowboy Galyon moved toward them. His face displayed anger when he grasped Nick's arm. "Now just a damned minute, Parilli! I ain't gonna let you just walk outta here!"

"Turn him loose, Galyon. Let them go!" said the sheriff.

"Are you gonna just let him leave?" asked Galyon.

"Listen to me, you damned idiot!" shouted the sheriff, "Don't bother them again, do you hear me?"

Unmoving and speechless, everyone in the room watched as Lauren led Nick through the door and slammed it behind her.

She helped Nick into her car and drove away. From habit, she drove toward her home. For a long while neither of them spoke.

"Where are we going?" asked Nick.

"I don't know," she answered, "I just know that we're going—somewhere!"

"Pull in here at that service station and park for a minute," suggested Nick. "We need to discuss what we're going to do."

She drove the car to the side of the station and parked.

"I've got to go somewhere and get out of these bloody clothes," Nick said. "Also, this time I *do* need to see a doctor. My nose is broken."

"Oh, Nicky!" She moved closer to him. When she hugged him, he gently pushed her away.

"Lauren, I'll get blood all over you!"

"I don't care. It just breaks my heart to see what they've done to you. I'll be glad to get you out of here."

"Where are we going?"

"Where would you like to go?" she asked.

"We can figure out our ultimate destination later. We need to figure out where we're going *right now*. I need a doctor, a bath, and a change of clothes."

"Let me take you to our clinic," she suggested.

"No, it's not safe. Also, I'd have to do too much explaining there. First, I need to clean up and then you can take me to a doctor."

"Well, we can't go to my house. Do you want to go to the preacher's house?" she asked.

"No, I'm afraid for us to go back there. It's too risky. I'm too screwed up to think clearly. I don't know. You make the decision. Just make sure it's a safe place where nobody can find us. I don't think you realize the danger we're in! Just by being with you, I've placed you in danger, too!"

"But Daddy promised that he wouldn't let anybody bother us. I don't believe he'd go back on his word to me! He wouldn't dare risk anybody hurting me."

"Lauren, I don't trust the cops. But even if I did, some of those Klan members don't give a damn what your father promised! They'll come after me, and probably you too, now that you're with me!"

"Do you really think they'd kill you? Or us?"

"Well … I think they would kill *me*. Look, honey, it's not your fault, but you've always lived such a protected life you don't realize the evil that men are capable of. Trust me! If they find us, I'm as good as dead!"

"My God, Nicky! I didn't realize that we are in that kind of danger!" She started the car and slowly pulled out of the station.

"Where did you decide to go?" he asked.

"Just leave it to me. Lie back in the seat and get some rest. I notice that the bleeding has almost stopped. It will help to hold your head further back. Here, take my handkerchief and hold it against your nose."

He reclined in the seat, pressing the handkerchief to his nose. She drove several miles out of the city, finally pulling the vehicle into *The Cozy Comfort Inn,* an obscure, secluded motel located at an intersection in a small community about ten miles west of Cedar Valley.

Lauren looked at Nick. "This motel is the place I stayed in last night … after I caught Daddy in bed with Willie Mae. I couldn't stand to stay in the same house with him anymore."

The small motel was almost empty, for only a couple of cars were parked in front of occupied rooms. She drove to the office and parked. He removed the handkerchief from his face and peered out the window. "If I'd known it was this easy to take you to a motel, I'd have done it weeks ago."

"But you didn't take me. I took you!" She laughed.

"Lauren, you'll have to get the room. If anybody sees my bloody face the whole town will know about it. Get this corner room—I can see that it's unoccupied." He pointed to the room.

"Why do you want a corner room?"

"Lauren, please! Just do it! I want to be able to see traffic coming from both directions." He hung his head and held his hands to his swollen face.

"But what about our car? Wouldn't it be easily seen parked in front of that corner room?"

"No, you can park the car in back of the motel. You won't be taking anyone's space because the place is almost empty."

Lauren left the car and paid the motel clerk. She obtained the room that Nick had requested, drove to the back of the motel, and parked her car.

Soon they were inside the room. While Lauren toured the entire quarters, fussily inspecting every aspect of the interior, Nick walked to the front window. He pulled the curtains slightly apart and peered at the highway intersection. Traffic was sparse. He could see down Lakeside Road for three blocks. The other window offered a view of at least a mile down Highway 70. He walked to the bed and reclined on his back.

"Nicky, I've got an idea. Why don't you take a shower and I'll get you some medical help."

"Do you mean you'll bring a doctor here? Doctors don't make house calls, Lauren."

"This doctor will." She smiled and picked up the phone. After a brief conversation, she hung up the phone. "Bobbie Sue, the nurse at the clinic is coming here to fix you up."

Nick leisurely showered, but because he had left his shaving kit and all of his clothing at the preacher's house, he was unable to either shave or change into clean clothing. Also, throwing his bloody shirt away meant that he would remain shirtless during his stay in the motel room.

Responding to the knock at the door, Lauren ushered Bobbie Sue into the room and introduced her to Nick. She was an attractive, middle-aged blond woman who carried a perpetual smile on her face. Upon entering the room she vigorously hugged Lauren. She then placed her medical bag on the bed beside Nick. He lay on his back as the nurse pulled a chair beside the bed and began her work. She asked for no explanation in regard to the cause of the broken nose. She only smiled and kept her focus on the job at hand.

"I'm not a doctor, you know," she informed Nick, "I'm just a nurse. I guess Lauren told you that."

Nick laughed. "I don't care what you are, as long as you can fix my nose. While you're at it, fix that cut over my eye."

"Well, I can't *fix it.* I can only clean it, give you something for pain, and apply some medication to help reduce the swelling. I'll have to put a new bandage on that cut over your eye. Actually, you'll need to see a doctor soon. If you don't, your nose may end up being crooked."

"It serves me right for sticking it into other people's business," Nick answered.

When Bobbie Sue finished, Nick thanked her and left for the bathroom to examine her handiwork in the mirror. Lauren also thanked the nurse for filling in for her while she took the day off. Since Lauren hadn't yet made plans in regard to leaving Cedar Valley, she decided to postpone any decision about quitting her job until after talking with Nick. She would discuss it with Bobbie Sue tomorrow. Nick and Lauren thanked her for coming to the motel. They said their goodbyes, and Lauren hugged her as she left.

For the first couple of hours, Nick worried that the Klan was searching for him. He repeatedly walked to the window and peered between the curtains at passing traffic. With the sudden realization that he was exhausted, he finally relaxed on the bed, almost falling asleep. Lauren switched off the lamp, kicked off her shoes and cuddled beside him. Soon they drifted off to sleep.

Nick awoke to the smell of food. Before opening his eyes, he felt her moist lips gently touching his own in a gentle kiss. As she knelt over him, her scented tresses of raven hair brushed his face. He looked up into the blue eyes of Lauren.

"I went out and got us something to eat." Her eyes came to life when she smiled. "I didn't want to wake you. I hope you like hamburgers and fries. I brought us a Coke, too."

"Damn it, Lauren! You shouldn't be leaving the room! What would we do if somebody saw you? Please don't do it again."

"I'm sorry, honey. I didn't even take the car. I walked. There's a drive-in restaurant and some stores just a block away from here. Nobody saw me. Besides, only a few cars were on the road. I was really careful."

"Well, I don't mean to be hateful with you, but you just need to start realizing the kind of danger we're in. Anyway, thank you for the food, honey. I'm hungry. What time is it?"

"It's after eight. You slept all day."

"I'm not surprised. I haven't slept much in a couple of nights. Lauren, my nose is really sore. In fact, my whole face is sore. I'll bet I look awful to you."

"It doesn't look that bad, honey. It will heal."

"God, I hope so. It feels like it will never heal!"

Taking a seat on the bed beside him, she opened the bag of food. He sat up and moved close to her so that their bodies touched. She then placed pillows against the headboard behind them. They sat together on the bed and leisurely ate their meal. She seemed to be lost in thought.

"Nicky, I just feel terrible about my father. I almost hate him, but I still have a soft spot in my heart for him. Does that make sense?"

"Well, your father *does* love you, Lauren. I don't want you to ever stop loving him. I'm beginning to realize that there's a lot about life that doesn't make sense. Your father, Stan, Rufus, the preacher…the war."

"What do you want for us, Honey? I guess I just took you for granted. You may not even want me anymore…Do you still want me, Nicky?"

He turned and kissed her. Looking into her eyes, he smiled and said, "I love you, Lauren. Of course I want you."

Lying close together on the bed, they clung to each other, talking softly, sometimes passionately kissing. Nick was becoming aroused. The room gradually grew dark from the approaching twilight. She playfully kissed him and suddenly sat up in bed. "Nicky, I can't believe that we're finally together! No restrictions, nobody to tell us we can't be together, and nobody to tell us we can't be in love with each other! I'm so excited! Just think! We can do anything we want to do!"

"Yeah, that's true—but don't start celebrating yet. There are still some men out there that would like to see me dead. We've gotta be careful and figure out what we're gonna do."

"Honey, we'll figure it out. We're safe while we're here in the motel. Let's just enjoy our time together, just for tonight. We'll make some plans in the morning. It'll turn out okay."

She got up and left the bed. "Nicky, I'm going to take a quick shower. While I'm in the bathroom do you want to watch some television?"

"No, I'm content just lying here. Hurry back. Being in a motel room with you is beginning to drive me crazy." He leisurely lit a cigarette and relaxed on the bed.

She turned on the lamp by the bed and left for the bathroom. He immediately got up and again peered out the window, inspecting the highway, looking for any suspicious vehicle traveling the road. He returned to the bed and sprawled on his back, recalling the unusual events of the day. He knew that he and Lauren should talk about their future plans. But that could wait, for tonight he only wanted to be with Lauren—to pretend that they were all alone—the only people in the world.

She hurriedly returned from the bathroom trotting, giggling, and shivering with chill. He caught a brief glimpse of her in her panties and bra before she switched off the lamp. Muted light from the partially open bathroom door provided the only lighting to the room. She pulled back the covers and quickly disappeared beneath them, tucking a pillow under her head. "Hurry up, Nicky—I'm cold! Get under the covers and keep me warm!"

Nick extinguished his cigarette and crawled under the covers. He hugged her shivering body. "Your skin feels cold," he said. The scent of her excited him. He pulled her to him and kissed her passionately. She responded with enthusiasm.

"You're so warm, honey," she said. She passionately kissed him and squeezed him tightly, slightly aggravating the soreness of his face and his swollen knee.

"Ouch!" he complained.

"What's wrong, honey?"

"I'm just sore, that's all."

"I'm sorry—I didn't mean to hurt you."

She threw her leg over him and ravenously kissed him. Breathing passionately, she crawled on top of him. Apparently, her newly found freedom had awakened passions within her that she had long ago repressed. Nick's face began to sting, and his knee started to throb.

"Lauren, I may not be up to this. I may have to take a rain-check until tomorrow night!"

Her voice trembled with passion. "Don't worry, honey. I'll be gentle."

Chapter 21

From between the curtains, a slim band of gloomy morning light filtered through the semi-darkness of the motel room. With Lauren beside him, Nick lay on his back soaking in half-sleep, waiting for her to awaken.

For the entire night he had been absorbed in peaceful, dreamless sleep, but the soreness of his injured face gradually brought reality back to him. His mind was plagued with ambivalence. On the positive side, he felt a renewed sense of freedom. He knew that after he and Lauren left town, her father's domination and Mike Bronson would be forever removed from their lives; however, a nagging anxiety remained: the possibility of being discovered by a Klan member before he had a chance to leave Cedar Valley. Also, he was saddened by the fact that he had placed Lauren's life in danger.

He began to have second thoughts about taking her with him when he left town. Maybe she belonged here with her parents, where she would be safe. He also wondered if she would change her mind about leaving her home, and if she had truly broken the chains that bound her to her father.

As his contented sleepiness faded, his anxiety returned. He feared that the exhilaration he felt from the renewal of his relationship with Lauren could easily lull him into complacency. He also realized that she wasn't capable of fully grasping the danger of their situation.

He got up and walked to the window, again surveying the traffic on the highway. The few cars that passed pulled a trail of mist behind them from the steady rain that permeated the gloomy morning. He realized that one small slipup could spell disaster for both of them. *We can do this!* he thought. *Things will turn out just fine! We just have to be careful!* He walked back to the bed and crawled under the covers beside Lauren.

When he thought of Stan, he felt a deep sadness. Like Lauren, who retained a love-hate feeling for her father, Nick had mixed feelings about Stan. In his desire to be a part of something that he considered to be worthwhile, he had foolishly become a member of the Klan. It was more an error in judgment than an act of evil. In spite of his betrayal, Nick still held affection for him.

Lauren stirred and rolled over onto her back. He watched her as she slept. Strands of disheveled hair half-covered her forehead and her open mouth expelled a gentle snore. He had never seen this side of her, this human side; for he had only known the ravishing Lauren, the Lauren of resplendent beauty. He was strangely captivated by the revelation of the *real* Lauren.

With an abrupt snort, she awakened. In an attempt to identify her surroundings, her sleepy blue eyes explored the room. A gradual recognition dawned in her expressive eyes. She brushed the stray strands of hair from her face and turned to face Nick. When she smiled, Nick felt that she was more beautiful than he had ever seen her.

"Good morning, sweetheart," she greeted. She vigorously stretched her arms and expelled an elaborate yawn.

Nick laughed. "Well, now I know how you really look."

"Oh, Nick! Don't look at me. My hair is a mess and I haven't even put on any makeup." She made a feeble attempt to straighten her hair.

Ignoring her self-consciousness, he pulled her close to him, embracing her warm body beneath the blankets of the soft bed. Tresses of her hair fell across his face, and with his head pressed against her breasts he could feel the beating of her heart. Together, they basked in the warmth of their entwined bodies as they nestled in the comfortable bed.

He suddenly felt a pressing urge to get moving. He whispered into her ear. "Honey, if we don't get up and get started, I'll be tempted to stay in bed with you all day."

"Yeah, I guess you're right, darn it." Her tone expressed reluctance. "How does your nose feel this morning?" She suddenly sat up. "Let me look at it."

She examined his face and seemed reasonably satisfied. She frowned. "Nicky, don't you think you should see a doctor this morning?"

"No, not yet. We don't have time for that. I can do it later. We need to make some plans. We haven't really talked about what you and I are going to do. If you'll remember, before you rescued me at your father's office, I had planned to leave this town—leave *you.* And now, here we are together. What do you plan to do?"

"What do you mean, *'what do I plan to do?'* I plan to go with you! Don't you know that?"

"Lauren, I love you. Since we met, I've always wanted us to spend our lives together. But now, I'm afraid for you! Maybe you ought to go back home with your mother and father, where you'll be safe. I could always come back for you someday, when all this crazy stuff dies down."

"Are you really that concerned about my safety, or are you just having doubts about whether or not you love me?"

"Honey, I swear I love you! That's why I'm so concerned for your safety! I couldn't leave you for any other reason! I don't want anything to happen to you!"

"Unless you tell me right now that you don't love me, then I'm going with you! Stop trying to protect me! I'm a big girl now! Where are we going? Do you still plan to go to Louisiana?" Her eyes searched his face.

"Yes. I'm going to Buras, Louisiana, at least for now. My uncle will give me a job. Then after I get on my feet I may settle somewhere else. If you're determined to go with me, I won't try to make your decisions for you. But I just want you to realize the danger we're in until we get out of this town."

"Honey, I realize the danger! I've only known you for a short time, but I feel like I've known you forever. It seems like I've waited for you all of my life. I want to stay with you. I thought you already knew that. I want to go wherever you go. But I don't want us to wander around like Gypsies or escaped fugitives for the rest of our lives. We had to do that when we first started dating. But now we're *free!* We don't have to live that way anymore. If we're going to have a life together, I want to settle down somewhere. I've always dreamed of becoming a teacher. When I get my certification, I have enough credits from college to start teaching. I never wanted to be a doctor. That was Daddy's dream—and someday…I hope that you would want to marry me…"

Nick grinned. He stood and walked to the side of the bed and knelt beside her reclining body. "Lauren, will you marry me?"

Laughing, she suddenly sprang from the bed and knelt beside him, hugging him. "Yes, Nicky! Yes! What a romantic proposal! When will you marry me, Nicky? Today?"

He echoed her laugh. "How could we possibly get married today? We might have to dodge bullets between our marriage vows! Why don't we wait until we get to Louisiana? That way, my uncle can give us a proper wedding."

"Okay, I guess I can wait a few more days. Do you still plan to go back to college after we're married?"

"And have you support me with your teacher's salary? What kind of a man would let his wife support him?"

"Don't look at it that way! Yes, I'll support you! And after we get on our feet financially, let's settle in a place where I can teach and you can go to school! I promise I'll support us while you finish college!"

He laughed. "We can't plan our whole life together this morning! Let's wait until we're married and settled. Then we'll make some definite plans."

"Honey, I'll go wherever you go, but I'd sure like for us to live somewhere in the South. After the way you've been treated here, I'm afraid you'll never want to live in this part of the country."

"Lauren, I realize that some of my experiences were bad, but I found that most of the people are good. *Where* we live is not as important as *how* we live. When I first got here I thought I'd found the ideal place; but it's like a soldier once told me—people are pretty much the same everywhere you go."

She smiled. "I'll go with you no matter where you choose to live. But I sure hope it's somewhere in the South."

Nick changed the subject. "We need to get moving. Are we taking your car to Louisiana?"

"Yes, it's a lot better than yours." She chuckled. "What are you going to do about your car?"

"I'm just going to leave it. It would be too dangerous to hang around here and sell it. It's not worth much anyway. What do you have to do before we leave?"

"I need to stop by the clinic and quit my job. I sure hate to leave them like this with no notice, but I really have no choice. I was supposed to quit in a couple of weeks, anyway, to return to college. I also need to draw my money out of the bank. Then I have to go by the house and pack some clothes and tell Mother 'goodbye.' That's about it."

"Listen, Lauren. You still don't get it! That's one reason I considered leaving you here. We can't casually drive around town telling people goodbye. We've gotta get out of here! I know you hate to leave your mother, but you'll just have to call her and tell her goodbye. Also, you can call the clinic to

334

tell them you've quit. Anyway, what if your mother tried to talk you out of leaving with me? And what if your father is at home? You mentioned drawing your money out of the bank. Do you have a checkbook on you?"

"Yes, I always keep it with me."

"Can you cash a check somewhere on our way out of town? We'll be heading toward Chattanooga."

"Yes, I know a couple of places."

"Well, we're going to need enough money to get to my uncle's place. How much cash do you have on you?"

"About a hundred and fifty dollars, I think."

"Well, I don't have a whole lot of cash. We'll just have to pool our money and leave here with what we have. My uncle will let me have all the money I need when we get to Louisiana. You can buy some clothes then. We can pick up any personal items we need on our way. Now do you see how I've complicated your life? Because of your connection to me you can't even stop by your house and tell your parents goodbye! Are you still determined to go with me?"

"Nicky, I've made up my mind. I'm going with you. I'm glad that we're getting out of this town. I criticized you when you told me that you were intending to leave Cedar Valley without reporting the murders to my father. You said it was too dangerous. And now I can see that you were right! I'm so sorry, Nicky! If I hadn't rescued you from my father and his deputies when I did, they might have even killed you! I was so naïve and blind!"

"I tried to tell you, Lauren. It was a bad mistake for me to report the murders to your father."

"Nicky, I know that my father did some terrible things, but I still love him. And after all, he didn't take part in the killings. Do you still plan to go to the federal authorities and report the murders? If you do, there will be an investigation and my father could go to prison. That would kill my mother! If he were sent to prison, who would take care of her? Also, I'm afraid it would come between us in our marriage. And remember—Daddy was merciful enough to let us escape from

335

Cedar Valley. I realize that your walking away from these murders would violate everything you believe in, but for the sake of my family—and for *my* sake, maybe you ought to let it go. Maybe you shouldn't report it." Her eyes searched his face for an answer.

"Lauren, I was so naïve when I first came to the South. I used to believe that justice was simple; however, I can now see that it's extremely complex. Don't worry. I have already decided not to report the murders to the authorities. When I found out your father is in the Klan I realized that I'd have to back off. If I were responsible for sending him to prison— what would happen to us? To you and me?"

She seemed relieved. "But can you live with that decision?"

"I'll have to *learn* to live with it. If I report the killings, both your father and Stan could be charged as accessories to murder. They might even go to prison! Even if they were acquitted, their names would be dragged through the mud for years."

"But, Nicky, I know that letting the Klan go scot-free must be a bitter pill for you to swallow."

"Not as bitter as seeing your heart broken over your dad being sent to prison. Also, I can't bear the thought of Stan going to jail. He was just a pawn in their hellish game. All he's guilty of is being gullible and stupid! But it makes me sad, because it's almost like Rufus and the preacher never existed."

Lauren looked into his eyes. "I know that you must feel that you're doing a terrible wrong by not reporting everything. I even told you that one time—remember?"

"Right or wrong, there are just some things a man can't do and live with his conscience. If I report the murders, it will destroy Stan as well as you and your family. In addition, our lives would be in danger throughout the trial."

"If you reported it and the Klan members were sent to prison—how much time do you think they'd get?"

"That's really a moot point, Lauren. I don't think a Southern jury would ever convict them. First of all, since they'll probably never find the bodies, the jury wouldn't believe my story anyway. After all, Southern people resent a Yankee meddling in Southern affairs. Another reason they'd never be convicted is because Bronson is probably gone from Cedar Valley for good. I don't think anybody will ever find him."

"But what if the police find the bodies? And Bronson? Would the Klan be convicted then?"

"Lauren, the Cedar Valley police *don't want* the bodies found! Some of them were involved in the crime! They *buried* the bodies! Also, the only reason they'd want to find Bronson is to kill him in order to silence him! And even if the Feds came in here and dug up the bodies, the Klan would probably never be convicted. The Klansmen are close friends, neighbors, and fellow church members of the people who would be on the jury!"

"So you don't believe that you can find justice in a Southern court room?"

"The only kind of justice you can find in a small town in the South is *Southern Justice.* Stan once told me that in the South, 'justice comes in different packages.' In the case of Stan and your father, maybe they've already experienced *the iron hand of justice.* Just look at what your father's sins have cost him! And Stan...his betrayal of me and the murder of Rufus will haunt him for the rest of his life! Maybe they've been punished enough. Maybe they've received their justice."

"But what about the other Klan members? Our not reporting it will mean that they'll all go free—with no punishment!"

"Well, even if we help send these guys to prison, they'll just be replaced by a new group of Klansmen. And after all, they didn't really take part in the actual murders. So what would we really accomplish? A guy without any clout trying to fight the Klan is as futile as attempting to get rid of all the flies in the South with a fly swatter."

"Nicky, I just hope you can live with your decision and not regret it."

"My main regret in not reporting the crime is that Bronson will get away with murder. He's the real culprit! If only he could get what's coming to him I believe I could accept letting the others get away with it. You know, it's kinda ironic, but Bronson is the biggest threat to your father's future. Your dad would be better off if I had killed Bronson with that tire-tool."

"How do you figure that?" Lauren eyed him with curiosity.

"Think about it, Lauren. Bronson is really the only person who could send your father to prison. Since Rufus and the preacher are both dead, I'm really the only witness—and I'm not going to report it, or testify, so I'm no longer a threat to him. If Bronson were to be caught and charged with murder, in order to receive a lighter sentence he'll rat on all the other Klan members, including your dad. If Bronson's gone from here, your dad had better hope he stays away from Cedar Valley and never gets caught."

"But what about the other Klan members? Couldn't they also rat on their fellow members?"

"Lauren, they have no reason to ever tell what happened. They wouldn't want to incriminate themselves. They'll go to their graves without talking. They also would be better off if Bronson were dead. Only Bronson has the motive to send your dad and the other Klan members to prison. Your father would be off the hook if Bronson could somehow just disappear from the face of the earth."

"I'm so sorry that you got caught up in all of this evil mess."

Nick paused and lit a cigarette. "A very wise Negro soldier once told me that I shouldn't try to 'fix' things in the South. 'Just let the South be what it is,' he told me. But I had to poke my nose into something that I couldn't really do anything about."

"Nicky, I hope this experience hasn't caused you to give up on your quest for fairness and justice. I hope that you continue to fight for what you believe is right."

"I intend to continue to fight injustice, but I've learned that it doesn't pay to wage a one-man battle in the midst of the enemy's camp! After all, you can't fight City Hall! Some evil is so deeply rooted in society that it's just too big for one man to handle. My puny testimony about the murders would never bring about a conviction. Not in the Deep South. It goes against everything I believe in to walk away from my moral duty of reporting the crime. But this time I feel that it is the lesser of two evils. Ever since I came to the South I've had to face some moral dilemma."

Lauren hugged him. "Try to not blame yourself, Nicky. At least you and I will be away from here...and we'll be together."

Nick snuffed out his cigarette. "You know Lauren, you and I both say that we want justice. But we change our minds when it begins to cost us something! The price of your father and Stan going to prison is more than either of us is willing to pay. I guess most people feel the same way. Justice is always for somebody else—not for us, or our families and friends. Justice is really not so simple after all!"

"You're right, Nicky. I can't pay the price." She hung her head. "Thank you, honey, for deciding not to report anything. I just couldn't bear to see my father go to prison."

"I'm not doing it for your dad, Lauren. I'm doing it for you...and Stan."

Nick changed the subject. "Well, I guess we'd better get dressed and get ready to get out of here. What time do we have to check out of the motel?"

"Noon, I think. We'll be out long before then," she said.

"Well, let's get ready to hit the road."

In preparation to leave, they both got dressed.

"Oh, Nicky! I'm so excited! I need to go to the store down the street before we leave. I'll be right back."

"No, Lauren! It's too dangerous! We can buy whatever we need when we get out of town. What if one of the Klan sees you?"

"But I need to buy you some kind of shirt. You can't leave town without a shirt! I also want to call the clinic and quit my job. I also need to call my mother and tell her goodbye. I'll pick us up a sandwich at that little drive-in. Why are you so worried? It's just a block down the street."

Nick walked to the window and peered between the curtains. He looked in both directions, noticing that traffic was light. He could see the drive-in restaurant and the couple of stores that Lauren had mentioned. The rain now fell heavily. The distant rumble of thunder and the darkening sky promised a stormy day. It was not an ideal time to set out on a long trip.

"Lauren, I guess it's safe for you to go to the store, but it's really pouring rain. You're sure to get soaked. And we didn't bring an umbrella inside with us."

"I can get one out of my car. I won't get very wet. The sidewalk beside the motel has an overhang."

Nick removed a towel from the bathroom. "Here, put this over your head when you dash for the car. And hurry back!"

The intensity of the rain increased and the wind picked up. She covered her head with the towel as she made her way to the car and got the umbrella. As she ran the short distance toward the small shopping center the rain fell in torrents and crisp gusts of wind almost inverted her umbrella. Lightning flashed, and the repeated rolls of thunder became closer.

She trotted to the window of the drive-in restaurant, which was just opening. She placed an order for a sandwich and coffee for each of them that she promised to pick up in five minutes. She then hurried next door and dashed into the *Valley Variety Store*, closing her umbrella as she entered. She removed the towel from her head and shook the wetness from her hair.

The elderly store manager was seated by the cash register reading a newspaper. Lauren noticed that he was the only person in the store. She smiled at him, closed the umbrella and tucked it under her arm. "Sir, may I use your telephone?"

"Sure, ma'am. Help yourself," he answered. He pointed to the phone on top of his counter. First, she called the clinic and resigned from her job. She also called her mother, informing her that she would soon write her a letter with a full explanation of her quick departure. She then bade her a tearful farewell.

Lauren wiped the tears from her eyes and looked up at the store manager. "Sir, where do you keep your men's shirts?"

He put aside his paper. "What kind of shirts, ma'am? Tee-shirts or shirts with a collar?"

"Tee-shirts."

"We've got some on that aisle right behind you, ma'am, just on the other side of that counter display." He pointed, picked up his newspaper and resumed his reading. The telephone rang and the store manager lazily picked it up. "Hello...Hello? That's odd. Whoever it was just hung up," he mumbled to himself.

She walked around the display and began sorting through the stack of shirts, looking for a medium size. She located a couple of suitable shirts and tucked them under her arm. Between the headers at the top of the display, she looked toward the window at the darkening atmosphere, noticing that the storm was now raging. Repeated flashes of lightning were accompanied by peals of thunder that shook the earth, and the heavy downpour of rain began to flood the street.

A pair of headlights pierced the wall of rain as a police car pulled into a parking space in front. Two deputies stepped out of the car into the drenching rain and dashed into the store. Cowboy Galyon removed his ten-gallon hat and slung the water from it onto the floor. Bird Dog swabbed his hair with a handkerchief.

Lauren squatted down behind the counter display. She began to tremble as she now realized that Nick had been accurate in his assessment of the danger they faced.

341

The store manager at the cash register suspiciously eyed the deputies. Cowboy Galyon replaced the hat on his head and the deputies walked up to the man.

"I've got a couple of questions for you, mister," said Galyon. "We're lookin' for a man, an' we'd like to know if you've seen him. He might have a woman with him, and they might be drivin' a black 1951 Buick."

"Well, I haven't noticed that kind of car pullin' in here. And I ain't seen a man and a woman together. What does this feller look like?"

Lauren continued to hide behind the counter. She began to fear that it was all over for Nick and her.

Galyon continued. "He's about six-feet tall...maybe about my size an' build. You'd know 'im if you seen 'im. Kinda has his face all beat up from tryin' to fight th' law. He's probably armed, because he took the weapon from a deputy that he was fightin' with. He may have blood on his shirt, but hell, I doubt it. He's prob'ly bought himself another shirt by now. He might even send his girlfriend out to buy him a shirt. She's a real pretty thing—black hair, dark complexion—man, you'd sure remember *her* if you saw her!" Cowboy pulled off his hat and again slung the moisture from it onto the floor.

The store manager glared at him. "Officer, I don't want to offend you but I just waxed this floor. What's this man done that would make you look for him? What's he guilty of?"

"That's police business, mister! I'm askin' the questions here! And don't worry about your damned floor! We're here on an important police investigation!" Galyon was angry.

"Well, I've had some dealings in the past with the police in this county. The man may or may not be guilty of anything! But even if he is, I ain't seen either him or that pretty girl you described. I can't help you mister. Now if you'll excuse me, I've got some business to 'tend to in the back of the store." He walked away.

"Now wait a minute, mister!" said Bird Dog. "We ain't through askin' questions yet!" The store manager continued to walk toward the rear of the store.

Galyon glared in his direction. "He's kind of a smart-ass, ain't he? Hell, let him go, Bird Dog. He don't want to help us. I don't think Parilli is in this part of the county anyhow. He's probably in another state by now."

"But what if he ain't? What if he's still here, an' goes aroun' spreadin' th' story about that night at th' river? What do we do then?"

"Damn it, he's already spread th' story! Can't you tell by th' way that store manager's actin'? I'm afraid he's already gone from here, an' will go to the federal government with the story. If he does that, there'll be Feds swarmin' this place! If he is still aroun' here, we need to find him before he gets out of here to tell that story! Damn! We need to go, but look at that rain come down! Let's wait 'til it slacks up a little bit!"

"That's okay with me. Listen, Cowboy, Sheriff Mullins gave us strict orders not to bother either his daughter or Parilli. I don't mind goin' after *him*, but I draw th' line when it comes to goin' after her!"

"To hell with her! I don't give a damn what the sheriff said! I don't want to go to prison over this. If only Bronson hadn't lost his head and killed that nigger!" Galyon seemed to be disgusted.

"Well, we might get away with killin' th' nigger. It's killin' that white preacher that's got me worried!"

Galyon said, "I just had an idea. Parilli's probably already gone. But if he ain't, I know how to flush 'im out. That nigger Bronson killed...*Rufus*...He has a daughter that Parilli is friendly with. Th' sheriff said that Parilli had stayed there some of the time. If he's still aroun' here, she'll know where he is."

"Yeah, that's true," said Bird Dog. "But what if she won't talk? What do we do then?"

"Damn it, Bird Dog! I can get her to talk! I'll do whatever it takes!"

"But ain't she got a son? What about him?"

343

"Hell, he ain't a threat. Besides, he's just a snotty-nosed brat. I think he's retarded. Somebody told me he can't even talk! He's harmless." said Galyon.

In her crouched position, Lauren was becoming tired. Realizing that Nick would be worried about her, she desperately wished that the deputies would leave.

The elderly store manager walked back toward the front of the store. "Are you policemen still here? Is there something else I can do for you?"

"No, you don't have enough sense to recognize either one of th' suspects even if they walked in here an' confessed to you. Let's get outta here, Bird Dog!" As the deputies walked out, Deputy Galyon turned and spat onto the floor.

The manager watched as they drove away. He returned to his seat and picked up his newspaper. The lightning flashed and thunder rumbled as the violent wind drenched the windows with sheets of rain.

"You can come out now, young lady," he drawled. "They're gone."

She came out from behind the display. The owner noticed her tremble. "Take the shirt, lady...It's on the house. Goodbye, and good luck to you and your young man!"

"Thank you, sir! And God bless you!"

Lauren opened her umbrella as she hurried out into the violent storm. Ignoring her order of food at the drive-in restaurant, she ran toward the motel. When she was nearing the building, a violent gust of wind blew her umbrella inside out and ripped it from her grasp. She continued to run until she arrived at their room. Just before she reached for the door, Nick flung it open. She quickly dashed inside into his waiting arms.

Her hair was wringing wet, and her sodden dress clung to her body. She began to sob, uncontrollably. Nick took her into his arms and pulled her wet, trembling body against him. For a long while he held her. Her emotions began to calm and her crying dwindled to sniffles as she spoke. "We've got to get out

344

of here!" she said, "Two deputies came into the store while I was there! They're looking for us!"

He led her to the bed and sat her down beside him. She placed her head on his shoulder and again began to cry. He hugged her tightly. "I know, honey," he said. "Right after you left here, I saw the police car drive by here and pull in at the store soon after you went inside. I could see the store from the window. I looked up the number of the *Valley Variety Store* in the phone book and called to warn you. But when the store clerk answered, I didn't know how to warn you because by that time the deputies were already in the store. So I just hung up!"

"Nicky, we've got to get out of here! *Right now!* They're going after Mary Rose! I was hiding in the store and overheard the deputies talking about it! We've got to get to her house and tell her and Caleb to get outta there as quick as they can! They think she knows where you are! They're going to try to make her tell them how to find you! They might even harm her!"

"Damn! Let's get moving! I warned Mary Rose to get out of there! Maybe she's already gone! God, I hope so!"

He stood and scooped up his personal items from the dresser top and stuffed them into his pocket. She handed him the shirt that she had brought to him, which was now wet from the storm. He slipped on the shirt and ran a comb through his hair. "I'll get the car and pick you up at the door!" he said.

"Nicky, you're gonna get soaked! My umbrella blew away!"

"That doesn't matter. I'll make a run for the car! When you leave just put the room key on the dresser by the door!"

He dashed out into the violent storm and sprinted for the car. The atmosphere was as dark as night, and the cloudburst of rain drenched his body. The violent bursts of wind caused him to stagger until he finally reached the car.

He pulled the car close to the door and she quickly slid into the front seat beside him. He switched on the headlights and sped toward Cedar Valley.

"Nicky, we're both soaking wet! I'm cold! We need some dry clothes!"

"Lauren, right now, dry clothes are the least of our worries!"

The relentless downpour of rain cascaded down on the car roof in a deafening roar. Although his vision was limited, he drove even faster. "Do you have any regrets, Lauren?"

"About what?" Her eyes reflected anxiety.

"About us."

"No, Nicky. I don't have the slightest regret. Why would you think that I'd have regrets?"

"Just look what I got you into! Look at how things are with you and your father! And you're leaving town without telling your mother goodbye, and we're desperately trying to save somebody's life as well as our own!"

"But that's not your fault. You didn't ask for this. Ever since you came into our town you've only tried to help people. You've opened my eyes to some bitter truths! But I hope my mother never learns the truth!"

Nick increased his speed as the storm became even more violent. The sudden bursts of wind rocked the car and the wipers flapped frantically in a futile effort to swab away the drenching rain from the windshield.

"Nicky! It's raining so hard I can't see the road! Slow down!"

The car suddenly fishtailed and hydroplaned into the opposite lane. "Hold on, Lauren! The roads are flooding! God, I hope Mary Rose and Caleb are already gone!"

"What are we gonna do when we get there, Nicky? Suppose she's not gone? What if the deputies are there? Or maybe the deputies haven't arrived there yet, but Mary Rose is not prepared to leave? Do we take her and the boy with us to Louisiana? We can't just drive away and leave them!"

"Lauren, I don't know! You're asking me so many questions I can't answer them all! Not everything in life is planned! All I know is that we have to go there and do something! Sometimes we just have to do what we know is right. We'll have to figure out what we're gonna do when we get there! We may do more harm than good. If you remember, the last time I tried to come to someone's rescue, two people died! If Mary Rose and the boy are already gone we'll just keep on driving to Louisiana."

Driving recklessly through the drenching rain, Nick again bypassed the downtown area of Cedar Valley. To steer clear of the Klan members, he avoided the main road to the preacher's house. He knew a more isolated route. Instead of approaching the house in the usual way, he decided to access it from the rear. Preacher Temple had once mentioned a small, narrow road, barely wider than a trail that passed directly behind the houses of both Rufus and the preacher. Nick swung the car off the main road onto the unpaved country road.

"I may be screwing up by taking this route. We have to pass through a valley and across a little bridge. The storm may have flooded out the bridge or maybe even washed it away! But I'm afraid to take the main road. That route will be swarming with deputies!"

The violent wind whipped the car as the deluge of rain became mixed with hail. The car fishtailed through the rivulets of water in the rutted road, causing Nick to fear that the car would become mired in the mud. The blinding bolts of lightning and ear-splitting cracks of thunder began to terrify Lauren. She held her hands over her ears and trembled. Nick placed his hand on her knee and gently patted her. "It's going to be okay, Lauren. Don't worry…it's just a little storm… it will soon pass…"

The muddy road was curvy and narrow, and sprinkled with scattered patches of wet weeds. They topped a hill where the road was straight, and puddles of water stood in the meadows on either side; then they drove through a thicket, where the wetness saturated the air and accentuated the spicy scent of pine.

They could sense the moldy dampness of the gloomy forest when the car dipped toward the nadir of the valley, just below the preacher's house. In the darkness of the heavily wooded valley, the base of the road became a cushion of pine needles and leaves, and the air became dank and smelled of mildew—a moist, snaky sanctuary for moss, toadstools and saw-briars. Fifty yards ahead on the hill above them he could see the houses of both the preacher and Rufus, where Mary Rose and Caleb had been living. He saw Mary Rose's car parked beside the house. *Damn! She hasn't gone yet!* he noticed.

At the base of the valley they rounded a gradual curve. As the headlights cut through the darkness of the heavy downpour, Nick could barely make out some kind of barrier blocking the road. He slowed the vehicle and came to a stop.

He visually examined the scattered branches that blocked the narrow lane. The organized arrangement of the limbs suggested that someone had deliberately placed them across the road. About twenty yards directly ahead of him he could see the thick growth of willow trees and the small bridge spanning the usually narrow creek, which had now swollen to twice its normal size and threatened to wash away the bridge. Nick backed up the car, and then slowly drove around the barrier and headed toward the narrow bridge that would deliver them to Mary Rose's house.

Peering through the heavy downpour of rain, Nick almost failed to see the stocky man who stepped out of the woods and stood in the road directly in front of their car. He took a stance in the center of the narrow road with his raised pistol pointed directly at the windshield of Lauren's car. The man pointing the gun was Deputy Mike Bronson.

A few feet away from him, Nick braked the car, easing slowly forward, worrying about his course of action. He hadn't enough space to turn the car around, and it would be foolish to attempt to back the vehicle all the way to the main road. They were only a few yards from Mary Rose's house, but in the most godforsaken spot in the entire county. They were trapped.

"Oh, Nicky! It's Mike Bronson! What are we going to do? Do you think he'll try to harm us?" She was terrified.

Although Nick knew that Bronson meant to kill him, and possibly even Lauren, he didn't want to terrify her even more.

"I don't know what he's planning to do, honey. I'll talk to him. Maybe he won't harm us. At least, I don't think he would harm *you*."

He stopped the vehicle and killed the engine. Bronson cautiously approached the car. Nick looked to the right and saw the deputy's car about twenty yards off the lane almost hidden among the sycamore and willow trees. Nick could hear the roar of the swollen creek directly behind the deputy.

Bronson spoke. "Okay, get out of the car, both of you! And no tire-tools, this time! The last time we met, you stole my gun. Git your hands up and keep 'em where I can see 'em, Parilli! I'm watchin' you like a hawk. If I see the slightest sign that you're packin' a gun, I'll shoot both of you!" His broken jaw hindered his speech and the left side of his head was swathed in a thick bandage.

They stepped out of the car into the drenching storm. Nick immediately raised his hands above his head. Ignoring the rain, Lauren walked around the vehicle and stood beside him.

"What do you want, Bronson? Do you want to kill me? Don't be a fool! You're in over your head!" He hoped to stall for time, or possibly get close enough to tackle him and hold him until Lauren could escape.

"Please, Mike," pleaded Lauren. "Don't get yourself into more trouble than you're already in. Please let us go!"

"Hell, I'm getting' wet," said Bronson. He moved a few feet to his right and took a position beneath the protective umbrella of a large oak tree beside the roaring creek. He sneered at Lauren when he spoke. "Lauren, you chose your fate when you took up with this Yankee. Everything was fine 'til he showed up. He's stirred up this valley 'til it'll never be the same. I could never let him go, now! I'd have to hide out for the rest of my life! Get over here where I can see you better, Parilli! And you stay away from him, Lauren! I don't want you to get in the way when I kill him!"

She began to cry. "Mike, you used to care for me. You told me so. If you still care just a little bit for me, please don't kill him! Please!"

Bronson laughed. "You better be worried about your own skin, Lauren!"

Nick said, "It's me you want, Bronson. You need to let Lauren go!" He turned toward her. "Get in the car, Lauren, and drive out of here! *Now!*"

"Whoa! Not so fast! Lauren, you ain't goin' nowhere! I ain't sure what I want to do with you yet. I may kill you, and then again, I may not. I think I'll just let Parilli ponder on that for a while. Yankee, I'm gonna kill you first, so you'll never know what I did with her." He laughed. "I'll bet you two lovebirds are getting' plenty wet, standin' out there in the rain. It ain't half bad underneath this tree."

The intensity of the storm had diminished. The rain was steady but the wind had subsided, and the thunder rumbled from a great distance away. Most of the low-lying area around them had flooded. The roaring current of the bloated creek carried trash and broken limbs on its brief journey to the Tennessee River.

"Bronson, before you kill me, can I ask you something? Did a Klan member recognize me at the river that night when you killed Rufus and the preacher? How did you find out I was there?"

"I don't mind answerin' your questions since I'm gonna kill you anyway. The guy you slugged with some kind of weapon didn't recognize you. After you told Stan Mullins you witnessed the killings, Stan told Sheriff Mullins about it. Then the sheriff told me. I told all th' Klan members you were there, so even if I wasn't goin' to kill you, you're as good as dead, for th' Klan is lookin' for you. But I'll just save 'em th' trouble by killing you myself. Sheriff Mullins said I oughta lay low for a while 'til this thing blows over. He kinda toyed with the idea of lettin' you go, but I told him that would be stupid. I knew that you'd carry this thing in your craw and keep reporting it 'til you got somebody to believe you, and screw up this town for the next fifty years!'"

"Bronson, was the sheriff there that night?"

"No, he wasn't there. He was at some kind of meeting."

"How did you know where to find me today—that I'd be driving this road?" asked Nick.

"I drove to that nigger woman's house to see if she knew where I could find you. It looked like she was packin' some things in a car, gettin' ready to leave. I figured you'd know when she was leavin' and you'd be comin' back by here to see her before she left. And I knew you wouldn't risk takin' the main road. This is the only other way to their house. I know all of these back roads. So I just drove on down here and waited for you. It looks like my hunch paid off! You played right into my hands!"

There remained but one more question to which Nick wanted an answer, but he dared not ask it in the presence of Lauren: *Did the sheriff send you here today to kill me so that you could return Lauren to him?* Whether he died today in this dismal hollow or fifty years from now, he knew that he would go to his grave without knowing the answer.

Lauren pleaded with him. "Please Mike! Nicky and I have already talked about this! He has decided to never breathe a word of this to anybody!"

"Are you kiddin'? He'll never be able to keep his mouth shut! He's one of them do-gooders that tries to reform the world. Git over there by that creek, Parilli! Our conversation is over."

"No! No! Please don't kill him, Mike! Please…"

In the stillness of the forest, the terrible explosion from behind the oak tree was almost as loud as an exploding mortar shell, and echoed through the surrounding trees. The load of buckshot caught Bronson in the center of his belly, propelling him backward into the roaring creek behind him. Looking to his left, Nick saw Caleb stepping from behind the oak tree holding his shotgun. Lauren screamed and buried her face in her hands. Nick stood in awe, with his mouth agape.

351

Then, with the shotgun in his hand, Caleb calmly walked to the creek and peered down directly into the deputy's fearful eyes. Bronson was not dead, only mortally wounded. Caleb again raised the shotgun to his shoulder and aimed it directly at Bronson's face.

"No, Caleb! No!" Nick screamed. But his plea was too late. The two-second span of time before he fired seemed like an eternity. The blast from the second barrel took away Bronson's face.

A piercing scream resonated from the pine thicket to the left. Mary Rose came running out of the woods toward them. Moving almost mechanically, Caleb dropped the shotgun. Then, as if awakening from a dream, he ran to his mother and hugged her.

Nick and Lauren stood motionless, in total disbelief of the event that had unfolded before them. Lauren cried and turned her head away from the roaring creek that enveloped Bronson. Nick walked to her and tenderly took her into his arms. "Don't look at him, honey! Just don't look!"

He gently led her to Mary Rose and Caleb, who were still sobbing. Lauren and Mary Rose stooped down and hugged the small boy. For a long while they cried.

While the two women cuddled Caleb, Nick walked to the rampaging creek that cradled the body of Bronson. Almost completely submerged, his body was barely visible. Only the tangle of vines that ensnared his right foot prevented the raging body of water from floating the deputy's body to the Tennessee River, which was only a stone's throw away. Glancing to his right, Nick could scarcely see Bronson's car, for it was almost totally obscured by the low-hanging branches. The lonely, wooded hollow was likely the most isolated place in the area, traveled in the past only by the preacher.

The rain had completely stopped and the sun reappeared. The silence of the gloomy forest returned, broken only by the gushing roar of the violent creek that now carried the red stain of blood. Glancing at Bronson, Nick felt that it was a lonely place to die.

Kneeling down, he casually untangled the vine that bound the deputy's ankle to the creek bank, freeing his foot. The raging water quickly claimed him. Nick stood and watched the swift current carry the body downstream and disappear as it was swept around a bend in the creek on its short journey to the river.

Nick strolled back to the shotgun and picked it up. He then opened the trunk of the car and tossed the weapon inside.

Lauren told Mary Rose and Caleb goodbye and walked back to Nick. He opened the car door for her and helped her inside. He watched her through the open window as she again hung her head and began to cry. Her voice trembled when she spoke. "Poor Mary Rose…and poor Caleb. It's so sad. I know he did an awful thing, but he's just a little boy! What do you think they'll do to him? Will they send him to prison? It really scares me to imagine what an all-white southern jury might do to a Negro who killed a white man—especially a white *policeman!*"

"I wouldn't worry too much if I were you, Lauren. Our fate is not always predictable. Wait here in the car for a minute. I want to talk to Mary Rose and the boy. I'll be right back."

Nick once again joined Mary Rose and her son. With the small boy still clinging to her, she looked directly into Nick's eyes. "I'm sorry Nick. After the mechanic fixed the car, we went back to the house for only a few minutes. We had everything packed in the car and just about to leave when Caleb saw the deputy stop at our house. Caleb recognized him from his red hair. When the deputy drove down here and parked, Caleb got his shotgun and followed him. By the time I realized what was going on, it was too late…Just too late. I'm so sorry. We were so close to getting out of here! I know that Caleb will have to be punished for this…Nick, do whatever you have to do. I realize you'll have to report it to some kind of authority."

"How did you and Caleb get down here, Mary Rose? Neither of you crossed the bridge over the creek. Caleb just seemed to appear out of nowhere!"

"Caleb crossed the creek over a little foot bridge just a little way up the creek. I ran after him over the same route."

"Why did it take so long for you to leave here?" asked Nick.

"It took the mechanic a long time to fix the car," she said.

"Mary Rose, there are some evil men who are coming after you and Caleb. They think you can tell them where to find me. They're on their way here at this very moment! Take the boy and go!! Do it *now!*" He could see her car atop the hill on the other side of the creek.

She hesitated. "But I want to do the right thing," she said.

"Get the hell out of here, Mary Rose!" yelled Nick. He bent down and hugged Caleb. "Thanks, son, for saving our lives. Goodbye Caleb."

Mary Rose said, "But Nick, I…"

"Get in your car and go! Goodbye, Mary Rose!" said Nick.

She sighed with relief. "Goodbye, Nick. I'll never forget you. God bless you!" She took Caleb by the hand and ran across the bridge and up the hill to her car. Nick felt that a weight had been lifted from his shoulders when he saw her drive away.

He returned to the car, sat down beside Lauren and took her in his arms. She again began to cry. For a long time he held her until her sobbing subsided.

"Lauren, are you alright?"

"Yes, I'm okay now. But that was just so horrible! I can't believe this terrible thing happened! I'll never forget it!"

"Things will get better, Lauren. I saw things like that in the war. You'll be fine. It just takes time." He continued to hug her.

"Nicky, I guess this will change our plans. We just witnessed a murder! I thought we were just beginning our journey together, but first I guess we really should go somewhere and report it to the authorities. I know that you always try to do the right thing."

"You're right, honey. It's just my nature. I always try to do the right thing."

Nick started the car.

"Where are we going?" Lauren asked.

"To Louisiana, of course. Isn't that where we were planning to go? If we leave right now we can be there by tomorrow night."

She appeared to be puzzled. "But aren't we going first to some police agency and report what we just saw?"

Nick continued to hug Lauren as he peered across the lonely meadow. "I didn't see a thing," he said.

ABOUT THE AUTHOR

Don Pardue grew up in a small town in East Tennessee. After completing a tour of duty in the U.S. Air Force during the Korean War, he received his education at Tennessee Wesleyan College, Atlanta Art Institute, and the University of Tennessee, where he earned a BFA degree and later taught courses in graphic design.

During his career he worked as creative director for a Knoxville design studio. He is now retired and spends his free time painting and writing in Lenoir City, Tennessee, where he and his wife, Barbara reside.

He is the author of five novels: *Blossoms of Winter, Tom, Dick, and Harriet, Maiden Harvest, Random Reflections, and Southern Sanctuary.*

All are available on ***www.Amazon.com***

Made in the USA
Columbia, SC
11 July 2017